Halfway down the walk, G_____ stopping, _____ her under a tree only a few feet taller than he was. "I have wanted to be alone with you all evening."

She peeped up at him from beneath her dusky lashes. "Have you?"

Her voice was breathy, and the pulse in her neck throbbed again. Was she nervous or excited? "Do you want to be alone with me, Elizabeth?" Her eyes widened at the use of her name. He stroked her cheek as he had earlier in the day. "May I use your name?"

"Yes, and yes." Her voice was breathy as she leaned into his touch. "What do you want me to call you?"

"Geoffrey. Very few people call me by my first name." In fact, no one did. "I would be honored if you did so."

"Geoffrey." She pronounced his name as if she was savoring the sound and how it felt as she said it. "I like it. It's a strong name."

"I want to kiss you." Desperate to kiss her was more accurate. "I've wanted to kiss you since this afternoon." And before.

He waited as she studied him. After a moment or two she rose on the tips of her toes and reached her hands around his neck. "I want to kiss you, too."

He clasped her waist. If he didn't have his hands firmly anchored, who knew where they would wander? Most likely all over her body, and it was too soon for that.

He brushed his lips against hers as he'd done after tea. She let out a soft breath and touched her mouth more firmly against his. He pressed light kisses on her lips and jaw before returning to her mouth and gently claiming her. . . .

## Books by Ella Quinn

**Published by Kensington Publishing Corporation**

# You Never Forget YOUR FIRST EARL

## ELLA QUINN

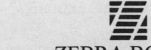

ZEBRA BOOKS
KENSINGTON PUBLISHING CORP.
http://www.kensingtonbooks.com

ZEBRA BOOKS are published by

Kensington Publishing Corp.
119 West 40th Street
New York, NY 10018

All Kensington titles, imprints, and distributed lines are available at special quantity discounts for bulk purchases for sales promotion, premiums, fund-raising, educational, or institutional use.

Special book excerpts or customized printings can also be created to fit specific needs. For details, write or phone the office of the Kensington Sales Manager: Attn.: Sales Department. Kensington Publishing Corp., 119 West 40th Street, New York, NY 10018. Phone: 1-800-221-2647.

Zebra and the Z logo Reg. U.S. Pat. & TM Off.

First Printing: June 2018
ISBN-13: 978-1-4201-4518-2
ISBN-10: 1-4201-4518-5

eISBN-13: 978-1-4201-4519-9
eISBN-10: 1-4201-4519-3

10 9 8 7 6 5 4 3 2 1

Printed in the United States of America

# Chapter One

Geoffrey, Earl of Harrington, first son and heir to Marquis of Markham, set out from his rooms. He was excited that his task to find a wife was finally finished.

Today was the day he would ask for Lady Charlotte Carpenter's hand in marriage. He had written to her guardian and brother-in-law, Lord Worthington, requesting the appointment. Soon he would wed the most sought after lady on the marriage mart and begin his journey to the Continent where he would take up his position on Sir Charles Stuart's staff.

He rounded the corner into Berkeley Square. There were a damn lot of people out at this hour of the morning. He entered the Park and shock halted him. It looked like some sort of catastrophe in the making. Lady Charlotte's family's two Great Danes were with several footmen.

A rough-looking man was being led away, and Lady Charlotte stood with her hands on her hips, her face flushed, saying something to the Marquis of Kenilworth. The last gentleman Geoff wished to see. The man had been a thorn in his side since he'd returned to Town. Still, he was certain Kenilworth had not yet requested to marry her.

But what the devil could be going on at this time of the morning?

"I'm coming with you. She won't trust a man by himself," Lady Charlotte proclaimed.

Geoff's attention was drawn to a weeping female servant. The two youngest girls, Charlotte's sisters, were trying to comfort the woman. Lord Merton, Worthington's cousin, had joined the fray.

"Charlotte, you cannot," Lord Merton said, glancing from her to Kenilworth. The man shrugged as if to say he did not care and was not going to become involved. "Worthington will not allow it."

It took a few seconds more for Geoff to understand exactly what Worthington, Charlotte's brother-in-law and guardian, would not allow. Then he saw that Kenilworth had his carriage a short distance away. Hell and damnation! There was no way Geoff would allow her to go off with that licentious bounder!

"I completely agree." Geoff strode forward to add his voice to the side of reason. "Lady Charlotte, you may not accompany Lord Kenilworth. I forbid it."

"*You.* You have no business telling me what to do." Her voice shook with growing anger. "Nothing will keep me from going. If need be—"

Geoff had never seen her in such a taking. He was about to attempt to calm her when her brother-in-law appeared.

"Go where?" Worthington asked as he reached them. Lady Worthington was beside him but almost running to keep up.

"Miss Betsy abducted another young woman." Charlotte narrowed her eyes at Geoff before she turned her back on him. "Kenilworth is going to the inn where they are taking her. I am going with him."

"Kenilworth?" her brother asked.

"I'll keep her safe," the man said.

"I object." Geoff started after Charlotte as she moved away toward Stanwood House.

Kenilworth grabbed Geoff's shoulder. "You have no business disagreeing. It is her guardian's decision to make and he has done so."

He jerked out of the other man's grasp. "I see what's going on," he said to Worthington. "You are encouraging Kenilworth's suit over mine."

Worthington turned and stared at Geoff as if he was mad. "This man"—Worthington pointed at Kenilworth—"has actually asked to marry my sister, which is more than I can say for you. I suggest you leave, before you are forced to do so."

This could not be happening. Geoff couldn't believe what he was hearing or seeing. Lady Charlotte, the woman he had decided was his perfect wife, was driving off with that bounder Kenilworth. And not only had her guardian refused to stop her, he was aiding and abetting Kenilworth.

Snapping his mouth shut, Geoff wrenched his gaze from the carriage. All his planning, all the time and effort he had put into courting Lady Charlotte . . . all for naught. What the devil was he supposed to do?

Drat it all! He needed a wife and soon. Still, there must be a chance that all was not lost. There must be a way to get her back. "My lord—"

"If you'd wanted to marry Lady Charlotte"—the Earl of Worthington cut Geoff off as he began striding away, as if there was nothing further to discuss—"you should not have disappeared in the middle of the Season."

He had not *disappeared*. He had specifically informed Lady Charlotte that he must attend his father. "But I wrote you expressly stating that I wished to speak with you about Lady Charlotte," Geoff said, following Worthington out of the square. That, after all, was what was properly expected from a gentleman wishing to marry a lady.

Worthington halted and turned so quickly, Geoff almost ran into the man. "Be that as it may, I fully expect my sister to wed Kenilworth." They had reached the front door and Worthington stood aside as Lady Merton was issuing orders to a footman placing a trunk on her coach. He pressed his lips together before saying, "Accept the facts as they are and focus on finding another lady."

Geoff's breath rushed out as if he'd been punched in the stomach. That was untenable. How the devil was he to find a wife of whom his father would approve and wed her in the short period of time he had?

His mouth opened but nothing came out. Finally he croaked, "This late in the Season? That will be almost impossible."

"You should have thought of that before you left Town." Worthington inclined his head. "I suggest you get started. Lady Holland's ball is this evening. The eligible ladies still here should be present."

But none of them was Lady Charlotte. Then again, if he wished to take the position with Sir Charles—whom Geoff had been told was now in Brussels to try to manage the Prince of Orange—he must wed. Worthington was right. Geoff had no more time to waste on Lady Charlotte. He had to find a lady who wanted to marry him and not drive off with another man. But whom? No other lady had attracted his attention. And he'd not paid attention to any other female all Season.

He jerked his mind back to the ball this evening. Had he even been sent a card to the entertainment? Not that it mattered. Even if Lady Holland had not invited him, he could attend. She was a friend of his mother's and would not turn him away. No hostess would bar an eligible gentleman. She would also be able to introduce him to the ladies he hadn't yet met.

He barely stopped himself from raking his fingers

through his hair. How could this be happening to him? He had always been lucky before. Nothing he had ever wished to accomplish had been difficult. Yet now, less than a month before he was due to take up his position with Sir Charles Stuart, Britain's ambassador to France and the Hague, a position that required him to have a wife, he must find a suitable lady. For some reason, the Fates must be out to get him.

Geoff started down the street and out of the square toward his rooms on Jermyn Street. He had been so certain of his future with Lady Charlotte.

Granted, he had been at his family's main estate for the past three weeks attending his father and waiting for news of his acceptance to a post in the Foreign Office as an aide to Sir Charles Stuart. Geoff's father, the Marquis of Markham, did not believe in young men engaging in dissipation while waiting for their sires to die. He himself had spent time in the Foreign Office as a young man, and had determined his eldest son should do the same.

Not that Geoff had in any way objected. The idea of living in Europe and learning more about the cultures and how diplomacy affected the world fascinated him.

Confirmation of his posting came three days ago. The only hurdle he had yet to bring about was his marriage. He had thought that would be easily accomplished. His father had given him permission to wed the prize of the Season, Lady Charlotte Carpenter. Lady Charlotte was everything a hopeful diplomat could wish for in a wife, possessing a perfect bearing and manners. She was never too loud. She was never out of temper—although she had seemed a bit crabbed of late. She was, in fact, moderate in all aspects of life. And beautiful, with golden curls and sky blue eyes. She, her sister, the former Lady Louisa Vivers, and their friend, the former Miss Stern, had been dubbed the Three Graces.

An hour after the messenger had arrived at his father's

estate with the news of his appointment, Geoff had left Fulbert Hall determined to meet with Lady Charlotte's guardian and finalize the wedding plans. Now he would have to begin all over again. How had it all gone so wrong?

"My lord?" His groom held his pair of Blue Roans as he followed Geoff.

He had completely forgotten about his horses and carriage. "Take them to the stables. I shall walk back."

"Very good, my lord."

Geoff did not wish to return to his rooms, but couldn't think of where else to go. Obviously, he needed advice if he was to find a wife quickly. His elder sister was in Town. She might assist him, but his pride would, no doubt, take a beating. And he'd rather not go through that.

Grandmamma was, however, also in the metropolis. She would be more than happy to find him a bride. It shouldn't be that hard. He was extremely eligible and all he required was a lady of good birth, amiability, the ability to hold a conversation—she would, after all, be discussing world events with other diplomats and their wives—a graceful dancer—he could not imagine having a wife whose abilities might disgrace him—intelligence, and a certain elegance. Yes, that was all he required. He would like a lady who was not hard on his eyes, but a great beauty was not required. In fact, it might be better that she was merely pretty.

Love was not important. Not to him. The dilemma was that many young ladies appeared to want a love match these days. In his opinion, it was a messy way to start a marriage. Neither his parents nor grandparents had had love matches.

He was certain his grandmother would be able to think of someone. And who better to know exactly what was expected of the future Marchioness of Markham than the Dowager Marchioness of Markham.

Feeling more the thing, Geoff began strolling toward Grosvenor Square before he realized that the day was still young, and if he wanted Grandmamma's help, he should not descend on her before eleven o'clock at the earliest.

The only other choice was one of his clubs. He stood for a moment debating whether to go to Boodle's or White's. At this time of day, Boodle's was likely to be filled with provincials. Listening to talk of crops and the like did not appeal to him. He shrugged. White's it was then. He made his way in the opposite direction toward St. James Street.

All the way from Berkeley Square Geoff's feelings of ill usage grew. How could Lady Charlotte have gone off with Kenilworth when she must have known—indeed, Geoff had told her—that he'd planned to speak with her brother? On the other hand, she did appear to be exceedingly reluctant to reside overseas. And Kenilworth had done his best to monopolize her attention. Geoff grimaced. The man had done a good job of it as well.

Fully expecting to be the only gentleman present at this hour of the day, he entered White's and saw that he was mistaken. When he strolled into the morning room on his left several gentlemen were reading newssheets, and the aroma of coffee scented the air. He glanced around looking for anyone with whom he was acquainted. Seeing no one, he crossed the hall to the other morning room.

"Harrington." Mr. Gavin Turley, the eldest son of Viscount Turley, hailed Geoff as he stepped through the door. "Haven't seen you in weeks. What have you been up to?"

"I've been with my father." He sat in the large leather chair on the other side of a low table. A footman brought him a cup of tea, and he took a sip. It was comfortable being known in a club well enough that they knew what a fellow drank. Coffee might smell good, but he couldn't stand the taste. He thought of not mentioning his most pressing dilemma, but he was desperate. "If you must know, I'm in the market for a wife."

Turley stared at Geoff for a few moments, then turned his

attention to the teacup that he twisted around before looking up again. "Are you indeed?"

"Yes." Geoff nodded. "And quickly. You might have heard . . . Well, it is no matter." There was no need for the whole world to hear from him how shoddily he had been treated by Lady Charlotte. Making sure that others knew he wished to marry, however, was prudent. After all, he was an eligible match for any lady.

"Tell you what," Turley said, leaning forward. "Come around to my father's house this afternoon on Green Street and join us for tea." Turley raised a dark blond brow. "If you don't have other plans, that is."

An image of a lady with the same light flaxen hair came to Geoff's mind. Lady Charlotte had introduced him to Miss Turley. The sister of Mr. Turley and the daughter of Viscount Turley. "Do I recall correctly that you have a sister who is out?"

"You do." He leaned back in the dark brown leather chair. "She is enjoying her first Season. She is very pretty—at least I think so—and amiable as well. Even when I try her temper, she manages not to give me a bear garden jaw."

He debated telling the man that he had already been introduced, but decided not to. Joining Miss Turley for tea was as good a place as any to begin, Geoff supposed. "I have no other obligations. In fact, I would be delighted."

"Excellent." The other man set his cup down and rose. "We shall see you at three o'clock this afternoon."

He rose as well and held out his hand. "I look forward to it."

Once Turley was gone, Geoff tried to remember everything he could about the man's sister. She was pretty. Although, he could not remember much about her features. Her brother had blue eyes. He assumed she would as well. There could be no objection to her breeding. The title was quite old. They had come over with the Normans if he remembered correctly. To his knowledge, there had never been a scandal in the family. His grandmother would know more about that. After Lady Charlotte had introduced him to Miss Turley he had stood up with her for one country dance. As best he could recall, she was a graceful dancer and had kept up the conversation with him. Whether or not she was suitable to be his wife was yet to be determined. He shrugged. With any luck, he would know more later today.

# Chapter Two

Geoff went into the dining room and ordered breakfast. Therefore it was more than an hour later before he hired a hackney to take him to Markham House in Grosvenor Square where his grandmother resided during the Season.

Her elderly butler opened the door. He half expected the old servant to creak like an ill-oiled hinge when the man bowed. "My lord, welcome. Her ladyship is in her parlor."

"Thank you, Gibson. Can you tell me if that blasted parrot is with her?"

"The admiral is taking his exercise, my lord. I shall announce you."

Geoff gave thanks to the deity. After the animal had bloodied his fingers when he was a child, he had not been able to stand his grandmother's damn bird. "That is quite all right. I can find my way."

Before the butler could protest, Geoff gave the servant his hat, ignored the faint look of censure on the man's face, and swiftly ascended the stairs. He turned right at the landing, then left down the corridor toward the back of the house.

When he reached his grandmother's apartments, he knocked. Several moments later, a cousin, almost the same age as Grandmamma, opened the door.

"Harrington, how nice of you to visit us. I see you did not wish to wait for Gibson." One might expect an indigent relation to curtsey and scrape, but not Cousin Apollonia. Although, that was to the good when it came to his grandmother. "You probably hurt his feelings."

"Better hurt feelings than an injury." It wouldn't have surprised Geoff if the servant had fallen down the stairs. "He's not very steady on his pins. How is it he has not been made to retire?" He gave his cousin an affectionate peck on the cheek she offered.

"I must say I agree that he has become quite wobbly. Yet, for all that, her ladyship does not wish for a younger butler. She says it would unsettle her. One cannot really blame her. You know how set in her ways she is. Having to train someone new *would* try her nerves." Apollonia placed her hand on Geoff's arm. "Not only that, but having never married and possessing no family, it would be cruel to make poor Gibson leave his home and friends."

Well, that put Geoff in his place. "When you put it that way, it makes me feel unkind to have wished him in retirement. I suppose I shall just have to continue to help him from falling down the stairs." They were strolling from the antechamber decorated in cream, a green color that looked like the sage in his mother's garden, and gilt, to his grandmother's parlor that always reminded him of being in a garden. "How is Grandmamma doing?"

"She has not slowed down at all." His cousin smiled fondly. "I think she believes all her gadding around keeps her young. Although"—Apollonia slanted him a look—"we no longer dance until the small hours of the morning. Midnight is our preferred time to return home." She tapped a finger on his arm. "If you attend Lady Holland's ball this evening, I shall expect you to stand up with her. She prefers dancing with younger men. She claims they are more spritely."

Geoff bit back a laugh. "Of course I'll dance with her."

Yet, if this evening was like any other, his grandmother would not lack for suitable dance partners.

"And not only her ladyship," Apollonia continued. "There should be at least a few marriageable young ladies with whom you may stand up. If their dance cards are not full. Still, it is the end of the Season and many in the *ton* have traveled to Brussels."

Trust his cousin to be awake on all suits. Still, the incident with Charlotte had only just occurred. "How do you know about Lady Charlotte?"

"My dear boy"—Cousin Apollonia raised one red brow—"the news that Lady Charlotte would wed Kenilworth was all over Town before you returned. You played your hand very badly when it came to her."

Had he truly been so blind concerning Charlotte? He thought he'd done all that was necessary to secure her hand. But wait. "*Before* I returned?"

"Surely you noticed all the attention he paid her?"

"I did, yet I did *not* know they were betrothed." And she had never said a word about being betrothed, which was strange.

"You cannot imagine that people would simply come up to you and tell you?"

"No." Though he wished someone would have stopped him from making a fool of himself.

Apollonia drew him through the double doors leading to Grandmamma's parlor. "Look who has come to see us."

Grandmamma turned to face him, and Geoff quickly stepped forward and went down on one knee in front of her chair, taking her hands in his. She would not see seventy again, but she looked and acted a decade or so younger. "Grandmamma, you are even lovelier than ever."

"Palaverer." Her tone was stern but her warm gray eyes danced. "You should be ashamed to offer an old lady a Spanish coin."

"Not I. I am not so untruthful." He stood and bowed. "I am here to beg a dance from you and to solicit your help in finding a wife."

Her lips curved into a smile. "I shall be glad to help with both."

He pulled a footstool over and sat at her knee. "That is what I hoped you would say."


"Well, young lady." Miss Elizabeth Turley's aunt, Lady Bristow, sailed into the Turley House morning room and took a seat. "Lord Harrington has returned, and he is in desperate need of a bride."

Elizabeth set down her embroidery hoop and took a breath. She had known her good friend, Charlotte, had decided not to accept Harrington. If he ever got around to proposing, which he had not. She had even introduced Harrington to Elizabeth.

Still . . . *desperate for a wife?* That did not sound good. "How do you know?"

A footman came in with a fresh pot of tea, set it down, and left. Elizabeth began to pour. Fixing her aunt's cup as she liked it.

"I had it from Lady Collingwood. He has been accepted for a posting with Sir Charles Stuart, but he must be married. And, as you are aware, Lady Charlotte will have none of him. In fact, Lady St. John saw her riding in Kenilworth's carriage this morning, followed by Lady Merton's coach a few minutes later. So, Harrington has clearly been rejected." Aunt Bristow accepted the cup of tea from Elizabeth. "He must leave for the Continent shortly if he is to take the position, and he must have a wife." Taking a sip she raised a brow. "The question you must answer is what you are prepared to accept."

She had been wondering where Charlotte had gone

when what Aunt said caught Elizabeth's attention. "Accept?" She tasted her tea and added more sugar. Aunt had clearly decided to add more Assam to the blend than Elizabeth preferred. "I do not understand."

"Two or three weeks is hardly time enough for a love match," her aunt scoffed. "Will you accept compatibility with a chance for love to grow later?"

Absolutely not. That was exactly what her cousin Lavvie had done, and the marriage had been a disaster. Only her husband's death had saved her. Not only that, but from what Elizabeth had seen this Season, two weeks time was more than sufficient to fall in love. Lady Louisa Vivers, now the Duchess of Rothwell, had done it in a few days if not sooner. Dotty and Merton had not taken long either. In fact their gentlemen had fallen in love as well. As for Charlotte, she had taken longer to fall in love with Lord Kenilworth, but she must have for she would not have agreed to marry him unless she was in love, and he was in love with her.

Elizabeth was perfectly aware that did not mean she and Lord Harrington would fall in love in that short of a period. Yet, a few weeks would be plenty of time to know if they could have a love match. She had to ensure there was a chance of love before she could agree to marry a man.

"I do not know," she said slowly, setting her cup down. Elizabeth selected a piece of seed cake. "It will depend how I feel about him." At first Lord Harrington had reminded her of Lord Merton with his tall, blond looks. Lord Harrington, though, didn't have the same somber disposition Merton had had until he married Dotty. That most likely came from still having a father and mother. Lord Harrington's blue eyes seemed to smile more often than not. The problem was that his orbs had been trained almost exclusively on Lady Charlotte all Season.

Taking a bite of the cake, Elizabeth savored the blend of spices, considering her aunt's question. "Firstly, I must get him to notice me. It would be extremely helpful if Gavin was friends with him."

"Friends with whom?" Her brother strolled into the room and snatched up three pieces of cake and began to gollop them down as if he had not eaten a substantial breakfast just two hours ago.

"Lord Harrington." Elizabeth poured him a cup of tea, adding extra sugar and milk.

One side of his mouth tipped up. A definite sign that he was up to something. "I was at Eton and Oxford with him. Why?" Finishing the cake, Gavin lowered his long frame down onto a chair across the table from her and took the teacup.

"I believe Harrington would be an excellent match for your sister," their aunt said as she appeared to study Gavin for several moments. "We need to find a way to bring her to his attention."

"Were you?" Elizabeth asked her brother. "You never mentioned it before." Ideas began flying through her mind until one stuck. "You," she said to Gavin, "could invite him to dinner this week."

Her brother's eyes widened innocently as he swallowed the rest of his tea. "Could I, indeed?"

"Yes, and I think you should," Elizabeth said decisively.

Setting his cup down, he began to rise when the tip of Aunt's cane hit him in the stomach. He made a slight "oofing" sound. "Not so fast, young man. We have some plans to make."

Gavin looked ready to bolt, and if Elizabeth didn't do something quickly, she would lose her chance. "You have been after me all Season to marry. You have even held up Lady Louisa's and Lady Charlotte's matches to me. Their brother helped them. It is your turn to assist me."

"Aside from that," their aunt said, not moving the cane from Gavin's flat stomach, "Harrington is searching for a bride. He must marry or lose the position his father managed to talk Castlereagh into giving to him. Elizabeth is correct. You should invite him to join us for dinner."

Gavin leaned back against the chair, and Elizabeth quickly handed him more tea and the last piece of cake. "There is nothing wrong with inviting him to dinner, but I have an even better idea. I shall invite him to tea."

Aunt's sharp gaze focused on Gavin, and her cane resumed its place next to her chair. "Why tea?"

"It is more informal. If they like each other, you or Lizzy could suggest they take a stroll in the garden or some such thing." Absently, her brother devoured the cake. "And if that goes well, we can ask if he'd like to accompany us to the ball one evening or dine with us another evening." Gavin raised a lazy brow and focused on her. "Will that do?"

Tea? She considered her brother's offer. That would give her an opportunity to get to know Harrington a little more. Elizabeth graced her brother with a wide smile. "It will, indeed. Thank you. Let me know once you have spoken to his lordship, and he has agreed to join us for tea."

"As it happens"—Gavin smirked—"I saw him earlier today at White's, and I have already invited him for today."

"Gavin, you wretch!" Elizabeth wished there was something hard at hand to throw at him, but settled for a pillow. "Why did you not tell us straightaway?"

Catching the pillow, he grinned at her before placing it on the sofa. "It was much more fun to see you and Aunt try to wheedle me in to doing something for you."

He swallowed the rest of his tea. "I'll see you later."

"Where are you going?" Aunt asked.

Gavin's eyes widened. "To Tattersalls and my clubs. I'll wager Harrington is not the only gentleman seeking a wife this Season."

"Indeed he is not." Their aunt nodded. "I am delighted to

see you are finally taking your sister's desire to find a husband seriously. Please be back for tea."

"To be sure, I will." He grinned. "Never let it be said that I did not support my sister's marital ambitions."

"Well, that was not what you said about Merton!" Elizabeth reminded her brother.

"Merton wouldn't have done for you, Lizzy." Gavin bent down and kissed her cheek.

"Gavin," Elizabeth said, suddenly worried over her lack of knowledge. "I do not know Lord Harrington well. What is he like?"

Her brother's brows drew together slightly. "Nice chap. Gets on well with almost everyone. Devilish clever. Took a first at Oxford. One can't call him bookish because he's interested in sports as well. Not much in the petticoat line, which should make you happy."

"Gavin Turley," Aunt said in a derisive tone. "You know better than to mention a subject like that to your sister."

"Better she knows now than find out later. Look at what happened to Lavinia. If anyone had bothered to tell her what Manners was, I doubt she would have married him."

"I cannot deny that." Aunt's lips pressed together as if she'd eaten a lemon.

"Can we get back to discussing Lord Harrington?" Not that Elizabeth didn't agree that her cousin's marriage was the worst imaginable, but she needed to know as much as she could about Lord Harrington before his visit this afternoon. And now was her only opportunity to do so. "What else can you tell me?"

Gavin sat back down. "He can be a bit stuffy. Nothing like Merton, of course. But he, or rather his father, is concerned about breeding, scandals, and alike."

"There is nothing wrong with the Turleys," Aunt opined. "If there had been, your mother would not have been allowed to wed your father. And neither side of your family has had any scandals whatsoever. Not even an elopement."

"We're a dull set," Gavin said as he grinned at Elizabeth.

"There is nothing dull about it at all." Their aunt glared at him. "It simply means that we have more sense than many others."

It occurred to Elizabeth that she was missing a crucial piece of information. "Gavin, what made you invite Lord Harrington to tea? You have never done anything like that before, even when I suggested it previously."

"Ah." He rubbed the back of his neck. "Well, I was at White's this morning trying to get some news on what the Corsican was doing, when he came in the morning room. We started talking and he mentioned he was in the market for a wife. I thought about it for a few moments, and decided that you and he might rub along well together. You have always wanted to travel, and, as everyone and their dog knows, he is going to work for Sir Charles Stuart."

She almost groaned. This had the potential to be extremely awkward. "What you are saying is that we will both be attempting to see if we would like to come to know one another better."

"Precisely." Her brother looked relieved. "Look, Lizzy, you don't have to decide to marry him today."

"Well, that's true," she mumbled to herself. "If he comes."

"Don't worry." He grinned. "I'll bring him up to scratch."

# Chapter Three

After visiting his grandmother, Geoff strode into his rooms where his valet, Nettle, awaited him.

"Welcome back, my lord." Nettle held the door open as Geoff entered. "Were you able to decide on a date for the wedding?"

Suddenly feeling weary, he handed the servant his hat and gloves. "There will be no wedding to Lady Charlotte. I'd like a brandy, bath, and luncheon in that order."

The news appeared to stun his usually imperturbable valet as it was a moment before Nettle responded. "Very good, my lord."

Not good at all. Several minutes later, Geoff had donned his banyan, and was sitting in his small, but well-appointed, parlor with a glass of madeira in his hand. Starting over again did not appeal to him in the least. Still, there was nothing he could do about it. Worthington evidently favored Kenilworth's suit over Geoff's own. If only he had not left Town, he was sure he could have either been wed to Lady Charlotte by now or had a date to marry. How could he have been so wrong about what he had thought was their understanding?

He took a large drink of wine, savoring the warmth as

the liquid slid down his throat. He detested having to go through all the work of courting a lady again. Yet, whichever lady he decided to marry, he must press for an early wedding date and leave for the Continent directly after the ceremony.

The Austrians and Prussians had already fought and won their battles against Napoleon's brother-in-law, Joachim Murat, King of Naples, and restored Ferdinand IV to the throne. But since then the Corsican remained ensconced in Paris raising an army, and Wellington was gathering his army in Brussels.

The duke wanted as many of his Peninsular army as possible. Unfortunately, many of them were still in America fighting a war England could not possibly win. Half of the *ton,* including the Duchess of Richmond, had decided to remove to Brussels when Napoleon escaped from Elbe. Although to be fair to the duchess, her husband had been posted to Brussels. She was not there, as many of his other countrymen and women were, to frolic in Europe.

And then there was the drama surrounding the Prince of Orange who had been placed in charge of the allied military until Wellington arrived. Rumor had it that even Sir Charles had had a devil of a time reining in his majesty. Even with all that going on the great man himself did not arrive until the fifth of April.

Geoff could not imagine anything more exciting than to be in the middle of all the preparations for the battle and the subsequent reinstatement of King Louis XVIII to the throne.

Having been advised how difficult it was becoming to find suitable quarters, his father had already arranged houses for Geoff and his wife in The Hague, Ghent, and Brussels. It was expected that they would entertain foreign and British officers and their wives as well as the Prince of Orange, and other dignitaries.

Charlotte, he knew, would have been the shining star of the government's delegation. He just prayed the lady he ended up marrying could do half as well.

His valet appeared at the door. "My lord, your bath is ready."

"Thank you, Nettle."

A few minutes later, Geoff sank into the hot water and tried to relax. But thinking what his father would have to say about his failure to wed Charlotte made his muscles tighten despite the warm water. He must write to Father before he found out about Geoff's failure from some other source.

Abandoning his bath, he quickly dried himself, pulled on a pair of breeches and a shirt, and sat at his desk.

Yet, before he had finished mending his pen, Nettle appeared with a letter. "From his lordship your father, my lord."

"Perdition." This could not bode well for him.

Geoff braced himself for the scathing commentary on his being such a gudgeon as to not have been able to secure Lady Charlotte he was sure the missive held. He poured another glass of madeira, took a swallow, and pried open the seal.

*My dear Harrington,*

That was unexpected.

*It has come to my attention that Lady Charlotte Carpenter is betrothed to the Marquis of Kenilworth. According to your mother, who was the bearer of this unfortunate piece of information—* Geoff was sincerely thankful he had not had to give his father the bad news—*the fault is entirely mine. If (again according to your mother) I had not insisted*

*on you attending me, you would most likely be
celebrating your nuptials to the lady.*

That was most likely the truth. If he'd been in Town, he
would have made absolutely sure Charlotte had not gotten
to know Kenilworth.

*Your mother has also informed me (As you might
be able to ascertain this is becoming wearing. I
have never known myself to be so mistaken in so
many things at one time) that you have shown
yourself to be capable of selecting your own bride
and, in the event you require advice, your
grandmother and Cousin Apollonia are in Town to
provide you any guidance you might require.*

*Your mother has also included a short list of
ladies you might consider, but are not to feel
constrained to offer for. (I honestly do not know why
she did not write to you herself.)*

*Aside from that, you no longer have the leisure to
wait on me again. I am reminded that you did not
have time to come here in the first place. Therefore,
I must accept your decision concerning a bride.*

*As you already have a copy of the settlement
agreements I had drawn up, feel free to contact
Fielding & Connors, our London solicitors, to tailor
the agreements to the lady you select.*

> *Yr. father,*
> *Markham*

Geoff read the letter twice more to make certain that the
missive was indeed from his father. The words were as close

as the old man had ever come to apologizing for anything. No doubt he had his mother to thank for that. Mama had been visiting her mother in Bath when Geoff had been home. Otherwise he was certain he would have known about Lady Charlotte's betrothal to Kenilworth before arriving back in Town.

That she had become engaged so quickly made little sense to him. In fact, she seemed to welcome him at first. He gave himself a shake. It didn't matter now. What was done was done, and he had taken steps to move on.

He took another swallow of madeira.

Nevertheless, he was damn sure he would not have wanted to be present for what must have been an extremely unpleasant conversation between his parents. Although, he very much wished he had been listening at a keyhole. His normally complacent mother must have been in rare form for his father to write such a contrite letter to him.

Geoff took a breath, and his shoulders felt as if a great weight had been lifted off them. Not having to worry about his father's approval would make his search for a wife a great deal easier.

He glanced at the second sheet of paper written in his mother's neat hand and read the short list.

*Lady Mary Linley*
*Lady Emily Oakwood*
*Lady Jane Summers*
*Miss Judith Farnham*
*Miss Elizabeth Turley*

During the course of the Season, he had been introduced to all of the ladies, except for Lady Jane, at one point or another, and had danced with most of them. Beyond that, he had no idea which of them would fit all his qualifications.

He picked up his pen, dipped it in the inkwell, and crossed

Miss Farnham's name off the list. She was a wretched dancer, and, therefore, did not meet one of his more important requirements. His feet ached just thinking about the time he'd stood up with her. She was perfectly amiable, but the poor lady had no sense of the music. And he could not have a wife who would cause a foreign dignitary pain or embarrassment.

Lady Mary was known for her reserve, but she was graceful and seemed intelligent. A few gentlemen had likened her to an icicle. Geoff would have to become better acquainted with her to know if that was true. He did not want a wife who was cold. No man would.

Lady Emily appeared to be an agreeable young woman. Yet she was only seventeen and occasionally suffered from bouts of giggles. Something she would outgrow, eventually. One hoped. Yet not soon enough for his needs.

He knew nothing about Lady Jane Summers, but she should be at the ball this evening.

And then there was Miss Turley. It was interesting that her name had come up twice today. Geoff had danced with her only once. As best as he could recall she was a graceful dancer and had kept up the conversation with him. He should remember more about her than that. Geoff took another drink of wine. Flaxen curls. Yes, he had thought her quite pretty in a quiet sort of way. And her eyes *were* blue.

He glanced at the clock. In only two hours, he would know her much better. The other ladies would have to wait until this evening.

Geoff smiled to himself. It was a good thing he'd run into her brother this morning. Tea would give him an opportunity to discover if she would be a good choice of wife. And, if so, he could secure a dance for this evening's ball—he assumed she would attend.

He leaned back in his chair and drained the glass. The

start of today had been nothing short of a disaster, but it was gradually improving. He was sure he would soon find a lady he would like to wed.

Elizabeth and her aunt returned from shopping and morning visits with less than an hour until tea. After finding Elizabeth pacing, her aunt said it was better for her to be busy than have too much time to think about Lord Harrington joining them. At the time, she had protested, but in the end, her aunt was right. Instead of being nervous, she was simply rushing to be on time.

She strode into her bedroom as Vickers, her maid, was taking out Elizabeth's brush and comb, placing them on her toilet-table.

"The verditer blue glazed cotton, I think, Vickers." The color reminded her of the turquoise ring her mother loved. "We are having a guest to tea."

"That's the one I thought you'd pick." She shook out the gown before holding it over Elizabeth's head. "Mr. Broadwell mentioned a gentleman was coming. Not that he would gossip about you."

"Or not to the junior staff." She was well aware that the senior staff knew of her father's hopes she marry this Season.

"That's what I meant." Vickers fastened the small buttons on the back of Elizabeth's gown. "Not everyone needs to know everything."

Elizabeth sat at her dressing table as her maid took the pins out of her hair and rearranged it into a knot high on her head. She had recently had her hair cut to take advantage of the curls around her face that previously defied all attempts to be tamed. They now framed her face nicely.

After threading a ribbon through the curls, Vickers

clasped a single strand of pearls around Elizabeth's neck. She added the matching earrings.

"The Norwich shawl, miss?"

The shawl had been a present from her aunt, and accented a number of her gowns, including this one. "Yes."

A few minutes later, the shawl had been draped over her shoulders and she had her reticule in her hand. "Well? Will I do?"

"You're as pretty as a picture." Her maid's lips tilted up slightly. "Best be going. You don't want to keep them waiting too long."

Now that she was dressed and about to go down, Elizabeth's stomach started to behave as if there were butterflies flapping around inside it. Her hands became damp and she had to run them down her skirts. To make it even worse, Lord Harrington had arrived more than five minutes ago.

Normally, she would have already been in the drawing room, but Aunt had decided Elizabeth should enter the parlor after Lord Harrington arrived instead of being there first.

"Will it not be rude of me to be tardy?" she had asked, not understanding why she should be late when the gentleman had been invited to her house.

"Better a little late," her aunt said tartly. "It will give him something to look forward to. Now remember what I told you. Men like the hunt."

Not only Aunt, but Charlotte, as well, had warned Elizabeth not to allow Lord Harrington to be too sure of her. It was no good at all to allow a gentleman to think a lady was not worth chasing after. "Have no fear on that account. I will not allow him to treat me as he did Lady Charlotte."

Aunt had given her a nod of approval.

Now, as she was about to step into the drawing room,

Broadwell, her father's butler, stopped her. "Miss, her ladyship said tea will be served on the terrace."

"Thank you." That was actually a wonderful idea, though it made her no less nervous. She was not used to being the center of attention. That distinction had always gone to her friends. Yet, with her brother, aunt, and Lord Harrington already present, she could not help but to stand out.

The day was not too warm and the garden was in full bloom. She made her way to the back of the house as male voices drifted from the direction of the morning room and garden.

Two sofas, two chairs, and three tables had been set on the terrace, replicating the seating arrangement in the drawing room. Her brother lounged in a chair to the right of one sofa, her aunt was in her usual place to the left, and Lord Harrington sat on the small sofa opposite where Elizabeth usually sat.

At that moment, her brother saw her and stood. Lord Harrington followed closely behind.

Stepping forward to her, Gavin took Elizabeth's hand. "My dear, in the event Lord Harrington has not been presented to you, please allow me to do the honors."

She squeezed her brother's fingers gratefully. "Thank you, but I met his lordship at a ball a few days ago." Raising her gaze to Lord Harrington, she smiled. "Welcome. I am glad you were able to join us. Please have a seat. Tea will arrive shortly."

Lord Harrington lowered his tall frame onto the sofa across from her. He really was a fine, handsome man. Although he was not as broad as some gentlemen, he filled out the shoulders of his coat well. His cravat was elegantly tied and a sapphire nestled in its folds. She was pleased to see that he had eschewed the new trousers for pantaloons and highly shined Hessian boots. This was not a man who would need the extra padding in his calves that some did. Her brother did say he liked sports and it showed.

Elizabeth supposed she should not think about such things, but she couldn't help herself. Now she would see if handsome did as handsome was. She sent a little prayer to the deity that Lord Harrington did not disappoint her. Particularly as she was already disposed to like him.

# Chapter Four

Broadwell entered carrying the tea tray, followed by a footman with a second tray holding a plate with small sandwiches.

Once the trays had been placed on the low table between the two sofas, Elizabeth poured a cup for her aunt before addressing Lord Harrington. "How do you like your tea, my lord?"

"A splash of milk and two sugars, please." He watched her carefully as she poured, which Elizabeth found to be a little odd. It was something all ladies learned to do.

She placed two biscuits on a plate. "Cook's ginger biscuits are excellent. Would you like a sandwich as well?"

"Please." He smiled, but it was a tight polite one that made his well-shaped lips appear rigid.

Good Lord. Was he always this stilted or could it be that he was a bit nervous? Well, whatever it was, she would have to try to put him at ease. She handed her brother his tea. Not waiting for her, he selected several sandwiches and biscuits. To ensure Lord Harrington had an equal chance at sustenance, she quickly placed more sandwiches, biscuits, and a lemon curd tart on his plate. There, at least he wouldn't starve.

"I hear that you will be traveling to the Continent soon." Hopefully, that would draw the man out.

He set his cup down. "Excellent tea, Miss Turley."

Elizabeth could not help but preen a little. "Thank you. It is my own blend."

"To answer your question"—his eyes lit up and he leaned forward slightly—"yes, I shall travel shortly to the Continent where I will join Sir Charles Stuart's delegation." Harrington frowned slightly. "There are just a few matters to which I must attend before departing."

Matters such as acquiring a wife, she assumed. "How excited you must be. I have longed to travel."

"Have you, indeed?" His lovely blue eyes lit up, and she nodded, encouraging him to continue. "I know some ladies do not wish to be so far from home."

Ah, he must mean Charlotte. Now that Elizabeth thought about it, she was surprised Lord Harrington had expected her friend to be happy so far away from family. "I am sure there are some ladies and gentlemen, as well, who do not wish to leave England. I, however, am not one of them." She gave him a cheering smile. "I grew up hearing about my father's and grandfather's grand tours. And my grandmother had cousins in France she visited on occasion. I have always wanted to see the places they talked about."

"I too heard the same stories." He leaned forward eagerly, as if he had found a kindred soul. Elizabeth hoped it was so. "Although I shall most likely never take a grand tour, I expect I will be able to visit many of the countries and cities they did."

They continued to talk about the grand cities of Europe, but her aunt and brother, surprisingly, only contributed to the conversation when addressed.

Before she knew it, all the tea had been drunk, and the food eaten. Lord Harrington would soon leave, and he had yet to mention Lady Holland's ball this evening.

"You are lucky indeed to have been offered the position. I envy you the opportunity." Elizabeth rose.

Harrington sprang to his feet. "I have my father to thank for that." He held her gaze for a moment, then said, "I am escorting my grandmother to Lady Holland's ball this evening. Would you do me the honor of standing up with me?"

"I would be delighted." Elizabeth pursed her lips as if in thought. "The supper dance is still open."

Ever since Dotty, Louisa, and Charlotte had found husbands, Elizabeth had been much in demand. Not that any of the gentlemen other than Lord Harrington had piqued her interest. Since Charlotte had indicated she was not interested in the man, Elizabeth had begun saving a dance for Harrington, just in the event he asked. Her idea had finally borne fruit.

"Excellent." He inclined his head. "I look forward to this evening."

"As shall I, my lord." She curtseyed and he bowed over her hand but did not try to take it in his or even kiss the air above it as almost every gentleman did, leaving her unsure what to make of him. Was he interested in her or not?

Once Gavin had accompanied Lord Harrington into the house, her aunt looked at Elizabeth. "Well, what did you think?"

"After his initial stiffness, he was quite charming." Even if he didn't kiss her fingers.

"He's a handsome man," her aunt mused.

She had studied him as he'd strolled off with Gavin. She had been right. It was clear his tall frame and broad shoulders had no need of padding anywhere. "Yes. His eyes in particular are a beautiful color blue. They almost match the sapphire he wore." His hair was blond but slightly darker than hers. "I like the way his hair curls."

"But he is not pretty," Aunt said. "Not like Byron."

"No. He is very manly looking. His jaw is firm." Not able to get the vision of his shoulders and shapely legs out of her mind, Elizabeth fought the urge to sigh. She might be a little too interested in his physical attributes.

"And he was attentive to you," her aunt prodded.

"Yes, he was very attentive." Especially when he talked about going abroad. In fact, that was almost the only thing he discussed. He had not asked anything about her likes and dislikes.

"Very well." Her aunt's tone was a bit impatient. "He is tall, blond, and handsome. He appears, from his conversation, to be intelligent and well read. He comes from a good family. He will be a marquis someday, and he wishes to be wed." Aunt Bristow arched a brow. "Tell me. What is it about him that you do not like?"

Her aunt was right. Something about Lord Harrington had struck Elizabeth as . . . off. She pushed his physical looks aside and focused on what was bothering her. Lord knows it wasn't his appearance. It was not his demeanor as such. It was . . . was he really interested in *her*? "He wants this position so badly that I believe he will marry any suitable lady just to have it." She scrunched up her face. "Do you know what I mean?" Her aunt stared at her, clearly not understanding. She'd have to find a different way to put it. "It strikes me that in a way he is like a fortune hunter. He does not care who he weds, so long as he can have what he wants. In the case of a fortune hunter it is the money. In Lord Harrington's case, it is the position with Sir Charles." She rubbed the space between her eyes, trying to ease the tension she felt. "I do not wish to be the means to an end."

Aunt rang the bell on the table next to her. "You do not think he cares if his affections are engaged."

A footman appeared carrying two glasses and a decanter of claret. After setting it down, he returned to the house.

"I am not even sure if he cares about compatibility."

Aunt handed Elizabeth a goblet of wine. "If he told Gavin he was looking for a wife, he certainly seems to have got over Lady Charlotte rather quickly." Elizabeth should have noticed that earlier, but she had been too excited Lord Harrington was joining them for tea. "He did not appear to be interested in anything about me other than my wish to travel overseas."

"We shall take it one step at a time then," her aunt said after a few moments. "I know you are interested in him, but marrying the wrong man is worse than not marrying at all. Not that many would agree with me."

Especially her father. "I suppose that is the only course I can take."

Who would have thought that a gentleman who was so easily pleased could be such a problem?

If they never discussed anything personal, how would she discern if Harrington could come to love her? Or if she could love him for that matter?

He was so focused on his goals, Elizabeth could not be certain he even presented his true self. Except that she was positive he wanted that position and needed a wife to go with it.

Geoff's phaeton was waiting when he reached the pavement. He turned to Turley and offered his hand. "Thank you for inviting me to tea. I greatly enjoyed speaking with Miss Turley."

Gavin grasped Geoff's hand, shaking it. "I'm glad you came. You seemed to have a great deal in common."

"Yes. We do." He'd thought so as well. At least he now knew she would enjoy living and traveling overseas. Unlike Lady Charlotte, who was appalled at the idea of being so far away from her family. He had been surprised at how lovely Miss Turley was. Her gown was the same sky blue as her eyes. When she talked of traveling, they sparkled like the sun on the sea. And even though her gown was modestly cut, the swells of her breasts beckoned him to explore. This evening he would further his conversation and knowledge of Miss Turley. "I shall see you at the ball."

"Until then." Her brother stepped back as Geoff climbed into his carriage.

Once his groom had scrambled onto the back, he started his horses and headed for his rooms. How had he missed how vivacious Miss Turley was when he'd met her previously? Then again, he could not recall what they had discussed the only time they had danced together. Merely that she made easy conversation.

Naturally, he would give due consideration to Lady Mary, Lady Jane, and Lady Emily, as his mother had suggested, but the thought that in Miss Turley he had found the right woman to fill the position as his wife persisted.

She was conversant in politics, both domestic and foreign. She wished to travel. She knew how to draw a person in to conversation and put them at their ease. Geoff felt a little guilty that he had acted so awkwardly with her, but he had to know what her abilities were. Still, she had passed his little test, and she need never discover what he had done. He must remember to ask if she spoke French and Italian. German would be helpful as well. Although French was essential, he supposed he could hire a tutor for the other two languages if necessary.

He did not particularly care how musical she was. As a married woman, she would not be called upon to play or sing. Still, he could not imagine she had not been trained in music and art. His mother had filled many hours playing both for her own pleasure and her family's. Now that he thought about it, he would like a wife who was musical.

Mentally, he reviewed the list he and his father had

discussed, trying to remember if there were any other important requirements his wife must have and decided he had recalled each of them.

All in all it had been a very productive afternoon. As soon as he was sure Miss Turley was the lady for him, he would ask her father for an interview.

The streets were busy with fashionable carriages and other more plebian vehicles. But not so crowded that he had to focus his whole mind on his horses, and he found his thoughts straying to Miss Turley's more obvious physical attractions. Her nose was straight but not sharp. Her lips were well shaped and seemed to naturally tilt up at the corners. How would they taste? Would she respond eagerly to his kisses? And her hair. Her curls seemed to have a life of their own. All during tea he had wanted to wrap one of her curls around his fingers and discover if they were as silky as they looked.

Geoff might not look for love in a marriage, but he would like to have passion. That would require obtaining a wife who enjoyed conjugal relations. Strange that he hadn't considered that aspect until spending time with Miss Turley today. Although he'd thought Lady Charlotte would be perfect for the position as his spouse, kissing her had never occupied his mind like kissing Miss Turley was doing. And not only kissing her mouth, but the swell of her breasts as well as other parts of her nicely rounded body. His staff stiffened as he tried to imagine what she would look like naked.

"My lord, you passed your building."

His groom's voice made Geoff look around. He was at the end of the street. How the devil had that happened? He felt like the variest coxcomb letting a lady take up so much of his mind. "I'll get down here."

"As you wish, my lord."

"Bring the town coach around at nine-thirty this evening. I'll be attending the Holland ball."

"Yes, my lord."

Geoff climbed down from his phaeton and began strolling back to his rooms. He'd have to make a decision as to which lady he'd focus on soon. Perhaps as early as this evening after he spoke with the other three ladies.

He entered his rooms and glanced at the clock. It was not quite five. He should have asked Miss Turley if she would like to go driving during the fashionable hour. He would have enjoyed spending more time speaking with her. Geoff began to hope one of the other three ladies was not a more appropriate choice of wife.

A letter was on a silver salver in the middle of the entry table. He took it to his desk and popped off the seal, shook it open, and read. Tom Cotton, a friend from his home neighborhood and who had joined the army, was in Town for a few days and asked if he was available for dinner that evening. He dashed off his acceptance. It would be good to meet up with Cotton again.

A little more than two hours later Geoff entered Boodle's and found his friend drinking a glass of wine. "Well met."

"Harrington." Cotton clasped Geoff's hand and slapped his back. "It's good to see old friends. How have you been doing?"

"Well. I hope to take a position with Sir Charles in Brussels." Geoff sat in one of the leather chairs next to his friend. A servant brought him a glass of wine.

"I'll wager you won't be there long. As soon as Wellington wins this war, you'll be on your way to Paris. The government will want Louis back on the throne as soon as they can get him there."

"I can't fault that thinking. There's no point in allowing

time for someone else to create mischief." He took a swallow of wine. "How have you been doing?"

Cotton grinned. "Just made major. I doubt if it would have happened if it hadn't been for Napoleon escaping. I shall most likely see you in Brussels."

It would be good having friends already present. Geoff wondered how many of his old school chums were going to fight. He'd known several younger sons who had joined the army. How should I contact you?"

"I'll be with the Second Regiment of the Life Guards under Fitzgerald. If you go to wherever the army's head-quarters is set up, it won't be too hard to find me."

He pulled out a pocketbook and made note of his friend's unit. "I should be there by the middle of June if not sooner."

"Well"—Cotton smiled—"I hear there is no end of en-tertainment in Brussels. If you're lucky, you'll get there before all the parties end."

Geoff hoped he did as well. Whomever he married would enjoy a bit of frivolity. "Have you heard anything of what Napoleon is doing?"

"Raising an army, one supposes. I know more about our troops. Although, I imagine you've already heard about the petty conflicts that are going on. One of the German generals is upset over not getting the command he wanted and asked to resign from his position. The King of the Netherlands is constantly complaining about one thing or the other."

Geoff took another sip of wine. "My father's complain-ing that The Peace Party is causing problems in parliament, accusing Wellington of being a murderer. His brother wrote to m'father about it requesting his help, which, of course, he'll get. Even if Father has to come to Town. Which he doesn't like above a half."

"I don't envy the duke having to deal with all the fighting

among the foreign commanders." Cotton set his wineglass down. "Let's eat. I have a hankering for a rare beefsteak."

Rising, Geoff said, "That sounds good."

As they strolled into the dining room, he wondered what would happen this evening at the ball. Would he be able to choose the lady he would wed from his mother's list? He sent a prayer to the deity it was so. The more he heard about Brussels, the more he wanted to be off.

# Chapter Five

Several hours later, Geoff escorted his grandmother and Cousin Apollonia into Lady Holland's overfilled ballroom. What a crush. "I do not know how we will move in here, nevertheless dance."

"Never fear." Grandmamma patted his hand. "Sufficient room is always made for dancing. Remember that many of the guests will simply move into position and others will clear the way."

"Have you seen any sign that Lady Mary, Lady Jane, or Lady Emily are present?"

"I have not seen Lady Jane or her mother in some time, however, her father is to your right against the wall at the far end," Cousin Apollonia informed him. "I do not see either Lady Mary, or Lady Emily, but Miss Turley is behind us."

He turned suddenly and saw her party being greeted. "Do you have eyes in the back of your head?"

"Indeed I do." Cousin Apollonia smiled smugly. "I am astonished you have not noticed them before. Shall we linger for her party?"

"If Grandmamma doesn't mind." He glanced down at her.

"Not at all." His grandmother looked at him, a curious

expression on her face. "I am looking forward to speaking with her aunt."

More likely, she wished to study Miss Turley. Geoff was not at all sure how he felt about that. His grandmother was a formidable old lady, and he didn't want her scaring Miss Turley off.

A few moments later, Turley hailed Geoff. "Harrington, well met."

"Good evening, Turley." Geoff turned and inclined his head to the man. "Miss Turley"—she offered her hand, and he bowed over it—"how fortunate that we arrived at the same time."

She was even more beautiful than she had been this afternoon. Her flaxen hair was a riot of curls. A Prussian blue ribbon studded with pearls peeped out from between them. Once again, he wished he could touch one. Pull it down just a little to see if it would pop back up. If they were betrothed, he could take such a liberty. "It really is a squeeze."

Just then, Lord Fitchley approached Miss Turley. "Miss Turley, my dance, I believe."

"It is, my lord." And just like that she went off with the other man.

Geoff didn't know what he'd expected, but it was not that. He had wished to talk with her.

"My sister is much admired," Mr. Turley mused. "If you wish to stand up with her at the next ball, you had better request a set this evening."

It probably behooved Geoff to be much more attentive to Miss Turley than he'd been to Lady Charlotte. He did not have time to waste.

He followed Cousin Apollonia and Grandmamma through the crowd to the back of the ballroom where Lady Mary's father, the Duke of Groton, stood. She was off to his side, her head together with another lady's, and didn't seem to notice Geoff's approach.

"Harrington." The duke, a friend of his father's, inclined his head. "Congratulations on your position with Sir Charles. I wish you well."

"Thank you, Your Grace." Geoff glanced at Lady Mary. "I came to ask your daughter to dance."

"Allow me to introduce you, Mary." She hurried to her father. "May I make you known to Lord Harrington? Markham's heir, you know."

Lady Mary turned her cold, pale blue eyes on him, and Geoff repressed a shiver. "How do you do, my lord?"

He bowed, and when she did not even offer her hand, he tried to think of a way to remove himself as quickly as possible. Yet, her father was there and he must still ask her to stand up with him. "I am well, thank you." For some reason, he felt an urgent desire to run a finger between his collar and his neck. "I would like to ask you to stand up with me."

Lady Mary's chilly blue eyes rested on him for several moments as if she could not believe he'd had the temerity to request a set. "My card is full."

"Perhaps at the next ball," he said only to be polite.

One pale brow lifted. "Allow me to make clear to you, my lord, that I have no desire to live abroad."

Geoff had never been spoken to so dismissively. On the other hand, he could cross her off his list. Not only was she not interested in the life he offered, she was not at all suitable for the position. "In that case, I shall bid you good evening."

"Good evening, my lord, and good luck."

Before he could respond, she turned and smiled at a gentleman approaching her, and her countenance no longer appeared as if she belonged encased in ice. So that was the way of it. He would simply have to concentrate on the other ladies.

Keeping to the sides of the ballroom, Geoff circled looking for Lady Emily. In fairness, he ought to give the girl another opportunity. Finally, he gave up and focused on locating Lady Holland. She would know if Lady Jane was present and be able to introduce him.

"Lord Harrington." The very woman he was looking for came up beside him. "I require your assistance to dance with a young lady who has no partner."

"I would be happy to stand up with her." Her ladyship placed her hand on his arm. "By the by, I am seeking an introduction to Lady Jane Summers."

"She is Lady Jane Garvey now," her ladyship said archly. "They married a few weeks ago. I dare say you are not the only one unaware of it. The wedding took place quietly in the country. I was told only because I am a good friend of her mother's."

Perhaps that was the reason neither his mother nor his grandmother and cousin had been informed of the marriage. It seemed his list had narrowed down to two, Miss Elizabeth Turley and Lady Emily. "Can you tell me if Lady Emily Oakwood is present this evening?"

"Indeed she is." Lady Holland glanced toward the far end of the ballroom. "Her mother is not far from the orchestra balcony. The woman with the gold turban and white feathers."

Geoff glanced in the direction she indicated. "I shall find Lady Emily after this set."

"Thank you." Lady Holland gave him a grateful smile.

She led him to a painfully shy young lady and he immediately set about trying to put her at ease. Yet, it was not until a quarter of the way through the country dance that the girl—she was clearly still too young to have had a Season—started enjoying herself. When he returned her to her mother, he was glad to see other young men gathering around to stand up with her.

After the set, he found Lady Emily and her mother. It took only a few moments of gushing conversation about balls and other entertainments before he was thankful her card was full.

Geoff would have liked to have had more choices, but at least he could now focus all of his attention on Miss Turley. This time he would not let the lady slip through his fingers.

There were still a few more sets until he could dance with her, and he allowed his hostess to pair him with young ladies needing partners until—finally—it was time for the supper dance.

It had dawned on him as he watched Miss Turley dance every set of the evening, he was damned lucky she'd not already been partnered for the supper dance. Her brother was correct. She was popular. It would serve Geoff well to follow the man's advice and discover which entertainments she would attend and reserve sets before other gentlemen could be there before him.

"Miss Turley." He bowed over her hand. "My dance, I believe."

She smiled politely, but not with the warmth he had seen Lady Mary give the unknown gentleman, and he felt the lack of it. Could he make her smile at him that way? What would he have to do to achieve his goal? "It is, indeed, my lord."

Geoff led her to the dance floor and they took their positions. When he placed his palm on her waist, he wanted to draw her closer to him. Then she placed her hand on his waist, and her light pressure warmed him through his clothing. His hand practically engulfed her much smaller one. He wished he could touch her hand bare skin to bare skin. "I have been looking forward to this dance all evening."

Yet, instead of her smiling adoringly at him, she answered coolly with a polite smile. "Thank you for saying so. You are very kind."

Somehow he would have to discover the way to make her passion flare.

Elizabeth had looked forward to this dance with him all night as well. For reasons she could not explain, and despite her misgivings, she found herself drawn to him. She longed to find out how it felt to be in his arms. Still, she was not about to tell Lord Harrington that. With great difficulty, she managed to keep her response to him polite and nothing more.

Her waist warmed when his hand held her firmly, and even through their gloves, she felt a connection. He would be a kind, if not the most attentive, husband, and she wished to marry and have children. How easy it would be to simply encourage him to propose. But was that not exactly what she did not like about him? His willingness to wed without love.

Dotty's whispered advice rang in Elizabeth's ears.

*Make him fight for you. If he is worthy of your regard, he must prove it. You deserve a man who will love you.*

Her friend was right, and Elizabeth knew in her heart she could never be happy without the chance of a love match.

At the beginning of the Season, she had been willing to please her father and had done all she could to attach Lord Merton. Now though, she decided it was much better to please herself than anyone else. After all, she was the one who had to live with the man, and getting rid of a husband was next to impossible.

The music began and they twirled around the room. Unlike some gentlemen she knew, Lord Harrington did not attempt to hold her closer during the turns. Did that mean he was not attracted to her, or was he merely being proper?

"You dance extremely well," he said.

"It is easy when one's partner is skilled." Elizabeth knew she was prevaricating. Still, she could not let him think he had won her over before he showed in some way that he cared for her beyond mere compatibility.

In fact, he danced exceedingly well. She felt as light as a feather being steered around the floor. His hand was firm and sure on her waist, and she found herself wanting to draw him closer, lean into him. No other man, not even Lord Merton, made her feel so . . . warm.

Lord Harrington smiled down at her, and she wondered if he felt the same something between them that she did. She would see. Despite knowing that he was in a hurry to find a wife, Elizabeth would not be rushed. This was for the rest of her life, and she had to get it right.

Once again their conversation revolved around the events in Brussels. He told her of a conversation he'd had early this evening with a friend who was in the Life Guards. Actually, she was fascinated by the personalities and the squabbles that seemed to abound.

When he told her a story he'd heard about a Prussian delegate, he used several German phrases. He did not appear astonished when she responded in the same language, but smiled as if he had been proven correct in something.

"How many languages do you speak?" he asked.

"Four, including English." His smile at her answer reminded Elizabeth of the one her governess used to give her when she had done particularly well in her lessons.

Despite that, she enjoyed dancing with him, and she was not prepared for the set to end. When his hand left her waist, all the warmth left as well.

All too soon, he was escorting her back to her aunt.

"Which balls do you plan to attend this week?"

"To be honest, I do not know. My aunt receives and accepts the invitations."

He seemed perturbed as his deep blue gaze focused on her. "I would like to request a set at each of the balls or other entertainments that will have dancing."

Only one dance? Surely if he was interested in courting her he would ask for two. That brought her back to the way he had *courted* her friend. It was as if he did not care enough to request more dances if only to spend more time with the lady he professed to be courting. Any man Elizabeth married would have to enjoy spending time with her in whatever form it took. Nevertheless, perhaps it was more than he had requested before. "Very well. I do not know which ones are available."

He stopped their amble to her family. "I would like the supper dances, if you have them."

She gave him a small smile. "If they are available, they are yours, my lord."

They joined her brother and aunt. Once in the supper room, Gavin quickly found a table for them. He held a chair for her aunt, and Lord Harrington held Elizabeth's chair.

Ever since the evening her cousin, Lavinia, had attempted to arrange for Lord Merton to compromise Elizabeth, her brother had insisted he escort Aunt and Elizabeth to their entertainments. Not that their aunt had anything to do with what her cousin had done. Aunt would have been appalled. Elizabeth did not think Gavin could be having much fun, but she was thankful all the same. She felt more secure when he was around. Papa would never think it was his duty, even though it was.

When her brother and Lord Harrington went to obtain food and drink, her aunt leaned toward her. "How is it going with Harrington?"

"I am not sure." She faced her aunt and spoke in a low tone so as not to be overheard. "I have never had a gentleman be so happy that I was able to speak other languages or discuss politics. Although, considering he will be a diplomat, that might not be surprising. He made a point of asking me for one set at every ball and dance, but no more." Elizabeth was sure he had felt the same connection she had, but he did not appear to wish to spend more time with her. She had never been so confused by a gentleman's behavior. "I do not know what that means, what he means."

"That he's a slow top," her aunt said with disgust. "It is

exactly this type of wishy-washy conduct that caused him to lose Lady Charlotte."

"I think you might be right," Elizabeth said slowly as she thought how differently Lord Kenilworth treated her friend. He hardly left her side, and when Charlotte danced with other men, his entire focus was on her and no other. Merton and Rothwell had—and still did—behave in the same fashion with Dotty and Louisa.

Lord Harrington appeared interested in Elizabeth. Yet he did not act like a man who needed the woman he would marry for herself. She was certain more time in her company would allow them to grow closer. Would that change his behavior, or would she have to find a way to bring him around, or was he not interested in *her?* And if it was up to her, what should she do? She did not know how to suggest they spend more time together. Elizabeth felt like throwing up her hands.

Gavin and Lord Harrington returned to the table followed by a footman carrying a tray, bringing an end to her musing.

"Your brother was kind enough to show me the foods you liked best." Harrington smiled at her as he took the seat next to hers. "I hope you agree."

She glanced at the plates filled with her favorite fare and selected a macaroon. "I do indeed. Thank you."

"It was my pleasure entirely." He smiled again before applying himself to a lobster patty.

The conversation—for the third time today—revolved around the coming conflict with Napoleon and the difficulty Wellington was having assembling his old staff and other officers.

"I heard that they are bringing regiments back from America as quickly as can be," Elizabeth said.

"They are indeed." Lord Harrington gave her another

approving look. "But whether they'll arrive in time is anyone's guess. Not only that, but there are too many raw recruits."

She had heard from one of Gavin's friends at the Horse Guards that Wellington wanted his old Peninsular army back. "At least the peace treaty with the Americans has been signed, and the longer Napoleon remains in Paris, the more likely it is that Wellington will be able to gather the army he wants."

Lord Harrington turned to her. "How come you to be so well versed?"

"I believe it is important to be informed," Elizabeth said. Not to mention that her friends, Louisa and Charlotte, were also adamant about knowing all there was to know about politics and the situation in France, and they had spent a great deal of time discussing the state of affairs and what it meant for England.

When Harrington smiled at Elizabeth this time, it almost reminded her of the look her dancing master gave her when she had done particularly well. Wonderful. First her governess, now her dancing master. That was not the type of response she wished to see in a potential husband.

Aunt Bristow rose and Gavin and Lord Harrington scrambled to their feet. "This is all very well, but it is time we took our leave." She inclined her head. "My lord, perhaps we shall see you later."

"I look forward to it, my lady." He bowed to Aunt before taking Elizabeth's hand. She sucked in a breath as her fingers began to tingle under his touch. "Until tomorrow evening."

She dipped a shallow curtsey. At least he had touched her hand this time. Yet her response was entirely inappropriate considering she did not even know if he liked her. Perhaps her aunt was right and he was just a slow top, and did not know how to express himself. "Until then, my lord."

Gavin escorted her and their aunt to the hall. "It looks like things are going well."

Aunt snorted. "Trust a man to think that."

"I don't understand." His brows lowered as he speared her with a look. "They danced together and he joined us for supper. What more do you want?"

"Two dances, my boy." Aunt rapped his arm with her fan. "And an invitation to drive out with your sister." When Gavin didn't appear to understand her meaning, she heaved a sigh. "Any gentleman seriously pursuing a lady in hopes of marrying her should be spending much more time with the object of his desire."

After a few seconds, a light appeared in his blue eyes. "I hadn't thought about it, but you are absolutely correct." He helped them into their coach. "I won't be back until late this evening, and tomorrow I am going out of Town for a day or two. I will see you when I return."

Aunt Bristow's already massive chest puffed out with indignation. "You promised to assist Elizabeth."

"And so I shall." Gavin's eyes twinkled wickedly. "Trust me."

"I suppose we must." Elizabeth waved as the coach left. She hoped he would return soon. What could he be up to?

# Chapter Six

Geoff said farewell to Miss Turley before making his way back to his grandmother and Cousin Apollonia.

He had been quite pleased with the progress he'd made with Miss Turley this evening. He was certain that if he'd held her closer during their waltz, she would have allowed it. Perhaps the next time they danced a waltz he would test his theory. The idea of her body closer to his made his cock harden. Still, even if he did not choose to skirt propriety, in a few days he should be able to speak with her father and arrange their marriage.

His two older relatives were in close conversation when he arrived at the sofa they occupied.

He waited until Apollonia had paused for a breath before saying, "Shall I escort you home now?"

Grandmamma's thin, silver brows drew together as she gazed up at him. "The question is are you ready to leave? The night is still young and you have danced with only one of the ladies on your list and that just the once."

"It turns out that Miss Turley is the lady I wish to wed." He wasn't about to tell his grandmother about the snub Lady Mary gave him. Aside from that, he was happy with his choice. "She has granted me a set for each of this week's entertainments."

"Only one?" Cousin Apollonia's brows now resembled Grandmamma's. "That does not sound promising. If the lady was interested in you, she would have granted you two sets."

"I only requested one," he said, trying to keep the indignation from his voice. Both his cousin and his grandmother cast glances to the ceiling. What the devil was the matter with them? And how irritating it was that they reacted in the exact manner. "What else would you have me do?"

Grandmamma rose, and Apollonia followed less than a second behind her. "We are ready to depart."

Geoff escorted them to the hall and they waited while their carriage was brought around. His two relatives shared the gossip they had heard until he helped them into his grandmother's coach. "I shall walk from here."

"You will accompany us," Grandmamma commanded as if she was speaking to a recalcitrant child.

For a moment he thought of denying her, but that would accomplish nothing. He climbed into the carriage, taking the backward-facing seat. The inner lights had been lit, enabling him to see their expressions clearly. "I take it you wish to speak with me?"

"Indeed I do." She sighed and shook her head. "However, I require a glass of sherry for this discussion."

Perdition! Geoff detested waiting. Whatever he'd done to upset her, he wanted to have it out sooner rather than later. But by the look on their countenances, he was not going to get his way.

Several minutes later, his grandmother was sitting on a small sofa next to the drawing room fireplace that had been lit. Cousin Apollonia sank onto a chair next to the sofa, farther away from the heat.

Geoff had poured both ladies glasses of sherry. He stood,

his elbow braced along one edge of the mantel. "Apparently, I have done something to upset you."

"Apollonia, dear, please pour Harrington a brandy, unless you would prefer wine?"

"Brandy is fine, but—"

"And take a seat," Grandmother said acerbically. "I don't like to have to look up at you. It makes my neck hurt."

He moved from the fireplace to the sofa across from her as his cousin handed him a goblet of brandy. "I very much wish you will tell me what all this is about. Quite frankly, I'm all at sea."

"I imagine you are." Grandmamma's tone had dried considerably. "Have you or have you not decided to court Miss Turley?"

"I have. Indeed, I am in the process of doing so." Hadn't he already told them that? Why else would he have made a point of making sure his name was on her dance cards for the next week?

"Are you, indeed?" One of Grandmother's brows rose, and she speared him with her dark gaze for a few moments before saying, "You do not behave as if you are courting her."

He glanced at his cousin, but there was no help there. She took a swallow of wine and said, "Have you made arrangements to take her riding, or walking?"

Geoff felt like squirming, but did not know why. "No. I have not."

"And you are standing up with the lady only once at each ball, and dancing with other ladies as well?" Apollonia asked as if she couldn't believe what she was hearing.

"Naturally." He wanted to tug on his cravat. It had not felt this tight all evening. "I am a gentleman. It would not do to ignore other ladies. I do not understand what the two of you are getting at."

"You were right." Grandmother glanced at Apollonia and shook her head. "He is not in love."

"I am sorry to say that was clear when he did not remain by her side, ma'am." His cousin's lips formed a moue. "He wasn't in love with the other one either."

"I do believe you are correct. If he is going to marry, he clearly needs our help."

Geoff's jaw began to ache, and he was becoming more than a little tired of hearing them discuss him as if he was not present. Finally, he bit out, "Help. With. What?"

His cousin's eyes widened. "Your courtship, of course. What else would we be discussing?" She slid a look to Grandmamma before continuing. "It's become clear to us that you have no idea how to conduct a successful campaign for a wife."

His grandmother nodded. "Indeed. You are making a complete shambles of it."

He couldn't believe what he was hearing. "Excuse me?"

"Do you even like the girl?" Cousin Apollonia shot at him.

Geoff should have known even the tone he used to depress pretentions wouldn't work on her. "Of course, I do." He would never consider marrying a lady for whom he had no affection at all. He had even struck Miss whatshername from his list because he would not like to wed her. And he had been glad—relieved was more like it—when Lady Mary refused him. "One must have amiable relations with one's wife."

"But you do not love her." His cousin's tone was one of complete disgust.

"I fail to see what love has to do with marriage." Geoff could name any number of couples who had wed for love and were miserable. He would choose not to be unhappy in his marriage.

"You would know what you were about if you were in love. Be that as it may"—his grandmother's fingers fluttered—"you require help, and we have decided to assist you."

"As long as"—his cousin's eyes narrowed ominously—"you like the lady."

"Well, I do." He gave a decisive nod. "We are extremely compatible. She speaks all the required languages of a diplomat's wife, she has an excellent seat"—that was according to her brother—"she is able to drive her own carriage, and she is well versed on English and European events. She also wishes to travel."

"Oh, good Lord." He'd swear Apollonia rolled her eyes. "But do you *feel* anything for Miss Turley?"

Geoff thought about it for a moment. He must like her. After all, he enjoyed being in Miss Turley's company even more than he liked being with Lady Charlotte. He even wanted to kiss her. Well, more than merely kiss her. He had a strong desire to see her naked in his bed with her long blond curls around her. He had never felt such an intense desire to have a lady before. "Yes. Yes, I do."

His grandmother and cousin exchanged looks. Finally, Grandmamma said, "Give him the list."

Rising, Cousin Apollonia went to a small cherry writing desk with a tooled brown leather and gilt inset, drew out a sheet of paper, and handed it to him. "You must follow these instructions unreservedly."

"If you do not," Grandmamma added in a portentous tone, "you will not succeed in gaining Miss Turley's hand."

Geoff read the paper his cousin had handed him. Both sides were filled with lists of things his relatives thought he must do. Surely, courting a lady was not this time consuming.

*Remain by her side all evening even if she dances with others.*

Or ridiculous.

*Glare at other gentlemen so that they will know you have chosen her.*

It took him several seconds before he could find a polite way of telling his grandmother what he thought about her suggestions. "In other words, you want me to make a complete cake out of myself?"

"No." Grandmamma took a large drink of her sherry. "We want you to win your lady."

"If you were *in love*," Cousin Apollonia said in a tone one would use to speak to a slow-witted child, "you would do everything on that list without question. You would not even have to be told what to do."

Geoff snapped his mouth shut. This was incredulous. What could they be thinking? "You want me to pretend to be in love?"

"No, we want you to court Miss Turley properly." Grandmamma rose from her seat. "Come, Apollonia, we've done all we can. It is up to Harrington now. If he loses Miss Turley like he lost Lady Charlotte, it will be on him. How much time do you have to convince the lady to wed you?"

"Two or three weeks. However, I do not understand what is so difficult about that."

His cousin mumbled something about leading a horse to water as the ladies departed the drawing room.

Geoff glanced at the list again.

*Send a note asking the lady to drive out with you.*

*Always ask for two dances.*

That wasn't too bad. Taking a lady driving didn't make a man look ridiculous. Many gentlemen drove with ladies in the Park. Ladies liked appearing during the Grand Strut. And he did need to try out his new rig.

He could request a second dance in the same missive. He would send her a note first thing in the morning. But he'd be dammed if he was going to follow the rest of his grandmother's and cousin's advice. He'd look like a regular popinjay.

The butler handed him his hat and cane, then opened the door. "A good evening to you, my lord."

"Thank you, Gibson."

It wasn't until he was halfway to his rooms that he began to speculate as to why his grandmother and cousin were so insistent that he love Miss Turley, or could possibly love her. Was compatibility not more important than love? From what he knew of love matches, they were messy and unreliable, causing heartache more often than not. The pair involved was either in alt or in despair. There seemed to be no middle ground. No room for compromise.

He knew for a fact that his grandparents' match had been arranged. They seemed quite happy together. Until his grandfather had died, that was. Ergo, it made no sense that Grandmamma would badger him about being in love. He refused to hazard a guess what Apollonia was about. Most likely merely supporting his grandmother.

Still and all, Miss Turley struck him as a calm, intelligent woman. Surely she would agree with him that love matches were not at all to be desired. For some reason, that idea sat awkwardly in his mind. Would she, he wondered, agree with his grandmother instead of him? Did she want or expect a love match?

He gave himself a shake. There was no way he'd ask her. That would be tempting fate, and he did not need anything or anybody standing in his way.

Once he had returned to his rooms, Geoff threw the list on his desk and poured a glass of wine and drained it. He eyed the piece of paper his grandmother had given him and would have thrown it in the fireplace, but it was a warm evening and the fire hadn't been laid.

Tomorrow he would start his campaign for Miss Turley's hand, again. He had not a doubt in the world that by the end of the week, he would be betrothed.

Geoff woke early the next morning still sure of his success. Rather than rushing off to write to Miss Turley, he consumed a leisurely breakfast and two cups of tea. Only then did he stroll into his parlor and sit at his writing table to compose his missive to Miss Turley.

It was important that his request not appear as an afterthought. After all, he had never actually *thought* of asking for a second waltz until his grandmother and cousin pointed out to him that he should do so. That she would expect him to stand up with her twice if he was courting her. Still, he must be careful to strike the right tone. He did not wish to appear to be desperate—even though he was.

Blast it all, he hoped she still had a set available.

# Chapter Seven

The following morning Elizabeth lay in bed contemplating the previous evening. Actually, Lord Harrington's behavior. Was he truly caper-witted as her aunt had said, or did he simply not know how to court a lady? And what did that mean? It appeared to her that every gentleman she had met during the Season had known exactly what to do once his affections were engaged.

Unless his affections were not engaged. That brought her back to the thought she'd had when he came to tea. He would wed any lady.

She listened to her maid busying herself in the dressing room. Her door opened and one of the maids was stoking the fire. Soon it would be time for her to rise. Aunt did not adhere to the idea of breaking one's fast until ten.

Elizabeth blocked out the sounds of the house rising and went back to her cognitions.

No, not *any* lady. The woman he married must meet certain qualifications beyond the normal ones of birth, family, and character. The blasted man had practically interviewed her. But that did not mean he would come to love the lady he married. Only that whatever female he decided to wed had a role to fill that he required for his position with Sir Charles.

The all-important position with Sir Charles.

If that was all Lord Harrington wanted, Elizabeth could not live with that, merely being a player in his life. She wanted and deserved for her husband to love her. Even if she had to refuse to marry the only gentleman who had captured her interest, love was more important.

Throwing back the bed curtains, she swung her legs over the side. Her father would be furious with Elizabeth for refusing Lord Harrington, but, perhaps, Aunt would take her in. Surely she would do that for her twin's daughter.

There was little Papa could do to force Elizabeth to wed a man who did not love her. Not if her aunt was on her side. Gavin might even help her.

An hour later she and her aunt were finishing up their tea when Broadwell entered the breakfast room carrying a silver salver. "A messenger brought a letter for Miss Elizabeth."

Aunt Bristow held out her hand. "Give it to me."

Elizabeth waited, feigning patience until her aunt opened the missive and read it. Aunt passed it to Elizabeth. "Harrington wishes you to accompany him on a carriage ride this afternoon, and he has requested a second set for this evening's entertainment. Very proper"—her aunt smiled—"and unexpected."

She scanned the note.

*My dear Miss Turley,*

   *It is my greatest desire that you ride with me this afternoon at five o'clock. It is also my wish that I be allowed to stand up with you for two sets this evening. I was remiss in not previously requesting the second dance.*

> *Yr. devoted servant,*
> *Harrington*

Well. What was she to think of his invitations? She glanced at her aunt. "*This* is a surprise."

"I am only amazed that he did not think of it before." Aunt Bristow's acerbic tone made Elizabeth grin. Her aunt looked at Broadwell. "Is his lordship waiting for a response?"

"Yes, my lady. I sent the lad to the kitchen for tea while Miss Elizabeth prepared one. Shall I send for him now?"

"Absolutely not," Aunt said. "Miss Elizabeth shall finish breaking her fast. Then, and only then, will she pen her answer."

"Yes, my lady." The butler bowed.

Before he left the room Elizabeth said, "Please give the messenger some toast or biscuits as well."

"I'm sure Cook is taking care of him, miss. Shall I bring you another pot of tea?"

The butler's face remained impassive, but she thought she caught the corner of one lip twitch. "Yes, please."

"It has occurred to me," her aunt said, "that Harrington had been given to expect he shall always receive what he wishes. He will require proper handling if you are to marry and be happy."

"I had come to much the same conclusion this morning." She placed her fingers on her aunt's hand. "Thank you."

"I should have taken you in when your mother died. I regret that I did not." Folding her lips, Aunt stared at the opposite wall. "Elizabeth, no matter what happens, you will always have a home with me."

"Thank you," Elizabeth said, thanking God that her wishes had come true. "You cannot know how much that means to me."

Aunt gave a wry smile. "Oh, I think I might."

It wasn't until another half hour had passed that Elizabeth went to the morning room to write her acceptance. Even though Lord Harrington had exhibited good sense in asking her to drive with him, there was no point in appearing too eager.

She took her time mending her pen and formulating what she would say. Finally, she decided to be brief and to the point.

*Dear Lord Harrington,*

   *I shall be delighted to ride with you this afternoon. You may fetch me at five minutes to the hour.*

           *Regards,*
           *E. Turley*

She read the letter over, sprinkled sand on the paper, sealed it, and rang for Broadwell. Her answer to his request for a second set could wait until this afternoon while they were on their drive.

A few moments later the butler entered the room. "Yes, miss?"

She held out the missive. "You may take this to Lord Harrington's messenger."

He bowed as Elizabeth looked at the clock. It had been not quite an hour since the invitation had arrived. "There is no hurry."

Broadwell's step immediately slowed to a turtle's pace. "As you wish, miss."

That afternoon, Elizabeth dressed in a new carriage gown

that was almost the same color as her eyes. Lord Harrington arrived at precisely five minutes to the hour. As she descended the stairs, she took time to admire the way his Prussian blue jacket of superfine showed off his broad shoulders. His waistcoat was of blue and white stripes with thin strands of gold thread accenting the stripes matching the gold in his hair. His pantaloons were molded to his well-formed legs, and, even at this distance, she could see herself in his highly polished boots. Other than a gold pin, his only ornaments were a quizzing glass and a pocket watch. In short, there was everything to admire about his person.

It was his interest in her she was not at all sure of. With luck, after this afternoon she would know more.

"Miss Turley." He bowed as she curtseyed and held out his hand. "I am delighted you accepted my invitation."

"I am pleased that you asked." She smiled just enough to show him she was content but not enough to allow him to think he had won her over. *He* might be in a rush to wed, but she was determined to ensure he loved her or could love her before she took such a permanent step.

"Come." He placed her hand on his arm. "I wish to show you my new phaeton. It was specially designed for the rougher roads on the Continent."

Happily and in an almost boyish fashion, he pointed out all the ways in which the carriage had been modified. "As you can see, it is much more stable than the usual phaeton."

"Your carriage maker did a fine job." Elizabeth, however, was more interested in the matched pair of Belgian horses with coats that were almost blue. She stroked their noses as they snorted into her hands. "Aren't you handsome," she murmured to the horse. To Lord Harrington she said, "I have never seen a Belgian with this color before. What is it called?"

"Roan Blue." His grin widened. "They are not at all in the common way."

"I should say not." The wheeler lipped at her bonnet and she leaned back a bit to remove the hat from his notice, then stroked his nose. "Will you take these lovely fellows as well?"

Reaching out, he scratched the space between one of the horse's ears. "Indeed I shall. I'll require horses that don't tire easily."

From all the accounts Elizabeth had heard, one did not leave one's cattle at posting houses on the Continent. Not if one wished to keep the horses. And, because of the war, the roads were in sad repair, making travel uncomfortable. "From what I have heard of the state of the roads, they will work well."

"That is the conclusion I came to." Still grinning, he assisted her into the carriage.

Once he was settled on the other side of the carriage, he started the horses toward the Park.

Their conversation soon fell into the normal pattern of discussing politics. When she tried to guide the conversation into other venues, such as the latest plays at the theaters or opera, he turned the subject back to Europe. Even when they reached the carriage way in the Park, he barely stopped to greet friends and acquaintances. Never once, except to verify some bit of information about her, did he ask about her likes or dislikes. He did not even mention his request for a second set. At that point, Elizabeth decided that if he did not bring it up, neither would she.

By the time Lord Harrington headed back to her house, Elizabeth understood exactly what Charlotte had meant about him being too sure of himself. Lord Harrington might be one of the handsomest gentlemen she had ever met, but, despite the physical awareness she experienced when she was near him, he had a long way to go before Elizabeth felt she could accept a proposal of marriage from the man.

She danced once with him that evening, and once each

during the next two evenings. The waltzes were all that a lady could hope for. Her waist warmed, lighting little fires where he touched her. She felt as light as down as he led her around the floor. Elizabeth was a little disappointed that he did not attempt to draw her closer during the turns, but that she could have forgiven if he at least attempted to come to know *her*. Yet he had not, and she was really making very little progress knowing him as a man, rather than a soon-to-be diplomat.

If he did not change his tune soon, she might as well leave for the country and wait for the Little Season to commence.

A few mornings later, Aunt Bristow entered the Turley House breakfast room with a card in her hand. "You will never believe what we have been invited to."

Elizabeth tried to see who the card was from, but her aunt was waving it around too much. "I cannot even guess."

"An End of Season breakfast at Stanwood House," her aunt said, excitement infusing her tone.

"An End of Season breakfast?" she echoed. "I have never heard of such a thing."

"Nor have I. I think it's a hum, but for what reason I have no idea. Still, I have it on good authority"—meaning Aunt's lady's maid had been gossiping again—"that Lady Charlotte and Kenilworth will soon wed. And as Lady Merton and the Duchess of Rothwell have arrived back in Town, I believe the rumor to be true." Aunt accepted the cup of tea Elizabeth handed her. "I absolutely do not understand why no one in that family seems to be able to wait to marry."

*Because they are in love and care more about beginning their lives together than a grand affair.*

She was certain her aunt was correct and her friend's wedding would take place soon. If not for a fitting at her modiste's shop, she would have gone to Stanwood House straightaway. As it was, she was not able to visit Charlotte until that afternoon when she found her friend with Dotty and Louisa.

"Elizabeth," Charlotte greeted Elizabeth, bussing her on the cheek. "How are you?"

"I am well enough." She took in her friend's glowing cheeks and the way her eyes twinkled. "I would ask you how you are faring, but you look as if you are walking on clouds."

"That is one way to put it." Charlotte grinned. Elizabeth was thrilled. Her friend had never looked happier.

Once Dotty and Louisa had embraced Elizabeth as well, they passed around the glasses of champagne and arranged themselves on the sofas.

Elizabeth smiled broadly as she glanced at Charlotte. "I did wonder if your original plan to wait until summer to marry would last."

A bright pink glow infused her cheeks. "I discovered I was as unable to wait as the rest of my family. There are still a few weeks left in the Season. Do you have any prospects?"

"I have had my eye on one gentleman," Elizabeth said slowly, knowing that Lord Harrington was not a favorite in this circle. "And, as you are no longer on the market, he is looking in my direction."

"Harrington." Charlotte's lips pressed together and the corners turned down. Elizabeth nodded, not sure she wished to hear what her friend would say. "You must put him through his paces before you agree to wed him. He is entirely too sure of himself."

Indeed he was. It was as Elizabeth had thought. He had treated Charlotte in the same manner. Or had he? After all, he had been away for several weeks and had only just returned. "I tend to agree. At least, he used to be very sure of himself. He had a bit of a shock when he realized that you were betrothed to another gentleman."

"I hope you're right." Charlotte gave her a dubious look. "How is he behaving toward you?"

How to explain it? "He has been attentive in a strangely cool fashion." Elizabeth told her about the one dance per event and single carriage ride. "I often feel as if I am being interviewed for a position, as he never asks about what I enjoy. If I touch on anything personal or even the theater, or something like that, he changes the subject to the position with Sir Charles. I simply do not know what to make of him."

"Make him show you he cares," Louisa said in her forthright manner. "And do not allow him to break your heart."

That had been exactly what Elizabeth had been concerned about. She was so very attracted to him that she was afraid—despite doing her best to look at him objectively—she might fall in love with Lord Harrington. If he did not return her regard, she would end up being miserable. "The infuriating thing is that I would adore living the life he has to offer, but I cannot marry a man I do not, or could not, love."

"Nor should you," Charlotte said. "Trust me when I tell you that there is nothing better than loving a gentleman and having him love you in return. I cannot imagine having relations with a man I did not love."

"Relations?" Elizabeth was not at all sure what her friend meant.

"Oh, dear." Dotty sighed. "Has no one ever told you what goes on between a man and a woman?"

Elizabeth's cousin, Lavvie, had made some subtle hints, yet from what Elizabeth could gather from what her cousin had said, it was horrible and painful. Since her cousin had left Town and might not ever return, she was still in a state of ignorance about what went on between a man and a woman. Asking Aunt was out of the question. "Not precisely."

"I was afraid that might be the case. I discovered it quite

inadvertently, but once Dominic and I . . ." A blush infused Dotty's cheeks. "I will just say I was glad to have the information." Dotty glanced at Louisa.

"Yes, well." Louisa also blushed. "Grace told me, and it was very helpful."

"If no one objects"—Dotty looked at Charlotte and Louisa who shook their heads—"we shall tell you what you can expect."

The next several minutes proved to be more illuminating than Elizabeth would have thought possible. Who would have thought that men and women became so—so intimate? "The man actually enters the woman's body?"

"Have you been to Lord Elgin's museum?" Dotty asked.

Elizabeth did not understand what the marbles had to do with anything. "Yes, my cousin took me there earlier in the Season."

Louisa scrunched her lips and her brows drew together. "Did you notice that the male statues have a dangling bit between their legs?"

Thinking back, Elizabeth had noticed and had asked her cousin, but Lavvie rushed her through without ever answering. "Yes."

"That grows much larger," Dotty said. "And that is what he will enter you with." Elizabeth opened her mouth to ask where, when her friend continued. "Where you bleed from during your courses."

She must have look appalled because Louisa said, "It only hurts once, and after that it is really very enjoyable."

Dotty eased Elizabeth's mind by adding a few other things she could expect to experience with her potential husband. Some of which she had trouble believing. "He will really put his tongue *there?*"

The two married ladies nodded, while Charlotte turned bright red.

When they had finished, a faint line creased Dotty's brow. "Do you have any questions?"

"Not at the moment." As far as Elizabeth could tell, her friends had been extremely forthright in explaining things. "Thank you. I now know how I must proceed."

If nothing else, the discussion made her determined to ensure Lord Harrington—or whomever she married—loved her before the marriage.

# Chapter Eight

Elizabeth arrived home just as Gavin drove up accompanied by a gentleman she had never seen before. An extremely good-looking gentleman at that. His hair was a sable color and curled quite as much as Elizabeth's did. His bright green eyes twinkled at something her brother said. His nose was aquiline, his lips well molded, and his chin was strong, but neither was it square. He did have the most delightful dimple on his right cheek when he smiled, which he seemed to do a great deal.

Yet, despite his undeniable good looks, she was not drawn to him in the same manner she was to Lord Harrington. Which, as it happened, turned out to be fortunate.

"Gavin, it has been days!" She hovered between hugging her brother or taking him to task. "Where have you been?"

"All will be made clear in a moment." Once they were in the hall, Gavin said, "Elizabeth, may I make you known to Lord Littleton. Littleton, my sister, Miss Turley."

"Miss Turley." Lord Littleton smiled as he bowed, and she could name several young ladies who would have swooned the instant he had touched her hand. His address was excellent.

"My lord, a pleasure to meet you." She inclined her head then gave her brother a questioning look.

Obviously quite pleased with himself, Gavin said, "Lord Littleton has agreed to pretend to be interested in you." For no apparent reason whatsoever, her brother frowned. "The only proviso is that you must not fall in love with him."

They must be out of their minds or joking. Why in Heaven's name would she fall in love with Lord Littleton? "You must be—" The earnest looks on both their countenances made her swiftly understand they were entirely serious about carrying out this farce. "But why?"

"From what I heard," Gavin said as he led them back to the morning room, "Harrington only began to behave as if he wanted Lady Charlotte after Kenilworth had snapped her up. I saw Littleton at the fi—er sporting event I attended. He drew women like flies." Gavin pulled a face. "No offence, Littleton."

"None taken." The man grinned good-naturedly. "Women of all sorts seem to find me interesting."

"So," her brother said, "I thought that anyone could get the idea you might be interested in Littleton—even a dunderhead like Harrington—and he would finally realize what's what." Gavin nodded his head decisively as if this all made sense.

They were mad. Completely out of their minds. Bedlamites, the two of them. Gavin for even coming up with such an idea and Lord Littleton for going along with it. Elizabeth rubbed her forehead. "I do not understand why we must engage in this playacting."

"It would not be only you pretending you might be interested in me," Lord Littleton explained. "I would be seen to be interested in you as well."

This still seemed unnecessary. Either Lord Harrington

would want her for herself or not. She did not like to engage in deceptions. "To what purpose?"

"My dear lady." Lord Littleton possessed himself of her hands, his gaze capturing hers.

Good Lord, the man was dangerous. She sent a prayer of thanks to the deity that she was not affected by him. "Do you do that on purpose?"

He shook his head and stared at her. "Do what?"

Elizabeth narrowed her eyes at him. "Look into a woman's eyes as if she were the only lady on earth you wished to be with."

"Ah, no," he said a little sheepishly. "It just happens. I can't seem to stop myself."

"It's like this, Lizzy"—her brother cut in—"any gentleman who's interested in a lady doesn't wish to see another man making up to her." He gave his friend a disgusted look. "Littleton agreed to help, but you can see how dangerous it is for him to be in Town. He truly can't help himself from flirting, and he'll soon find himself in a bumble-bath if he remains too long. He's not ready for a leg-shackle yet, but he'd be bound to raise some lady's expectations and that won't do."

"That's it exactly." Lord Littleton must have realized he was still holding Elizabeth's hands and released them. "But that's not the only reason Turley and I thought I'd be the best one. You see, Harrington and I never got on well together. That will give him the extra incentive to court you properly."

"And," Gavin added, "Littleton is so full of juice that he is just as eligible as Harrington. Other than the title that is."

Her brother and Lord Littleton focused their gazes on her, and she glanced from one man to the other. "I understand." Or she thought she did. Men were such strange creatures. She wondered why Lord Harrington did not like

Lord Littleton. He seemed amiable enough. "Very well, then. How do we begin?"

"First you have to promise not to fall in love with Littleton," her brother said. "That would make this dashed inconvenient."

For all his lordship's good looks and charming manner—not to mention those eyes—he did not make her heart flutter as Lord Harrington did. Nor had his touch made her want to sink into him when he had held her hands. "I promise."

"Good." Gavin nodded. "Which set did you promise Harrington?"

"He requested the supper dance." She recalled that he had asked for another set, but she had been so out of sorts with him that she hadn't answered. "That is the only set he will get this evening."

"Do you have another waltz on your card?" her brother asked.

There were only to be three this evening. One was the opening set, and she did not have a partner for that dance as yet. "Yes. The first set is a waltz."

Her brother's eyes danced with mirth as Lord Littleton bowed over her hand again. "Miss Turley, would you do me the great honor of allowing me to partner you for the first set?"

Elizabeth fought to keep her laughter in as she inclined her head. "Why, yes, my lord. I would be delighted to dance with you."

"Perfect." Her brother preened. "This will work out just as we want."

Although Lord Littleton dined with them that evening, it was decided he should arrive at the ball after her party solely because she did not want anyone to think that she favored him. Especially when she was to stand up with the man for the first dance.

Lord Harrington arrived as she and Lord Littleton were taking their places for the waltz. As they twirled around the floor, she caught a glance at Lord Harrington. The scowl on his handsome face was all she could have asked for. Apparently, her brother had been correct. Lord Harrington appeared to be much more interested in her when she danced with Lord Littleton.

"Miss Turley." Lord Harrington came up to her as soon as she had been escorted to her aunt. "Did you save me a second dance this evening?"

She gave him a look that she hoped was both sad but thoughtful by pursing her lips, and raising her brows as if saddened. "I did not, my lord. After I sent the note to you accepting your invitation for the carriage ride, I realized that I had not answered your question about the dance." Not entirely the truth, but close enough. "As you did not remind me during our drive I forgot about it and gave the set to Lord Littleton."

Lord Harrington's rigid lips barely tilted up, and Elizabeth thought she had lost him for good. Then he said, "I would like to request a second set for tomorrow."

Not for the first time, she wished that her aunt would agree to attend more than one event an evening, or remain after supper, but she would not, and Elizabeth's card was full. "I am sorry to say that I have no more dances available, my lord."

When it came time for her waltz with him, she wondered if he would bring the subject up again and was not disappointed. As before, she felt the heat of being in his arms as he twirled her around the floor. They had been, again, discussing his future position, when he abruptly said, "Forgive me for not obtaining a promise from you for a second set. It was foolish to have not realized and asked you again for the dance during our drive."

He sounded so contrite Elizabeth's heart began to yearn

to apologize to him as well, yet she kept in mind what her friends had said, and merely replied, "I wish you would have remembered as well."

Her brother's scheme was working even better than she could have imagined it would.

Leaning against a pillar in the ballroom, Geoff couldn't stop himself from scowling at the sight of another gentleman leading Miss Turley out to dance—for the second time this evening. Not only that, but Lord Littleton, the man who currently held her in his arms, had led her out for the opening set last evening and secured the supper dance this night as well.

Littleton had to be the reason Miss Turley didn't have another set to give Geoff.

Damn it all to perdition. He hadn't liked the man at Eton or university, and he damn sure didn't like him now that the blasted fellow was trying to steal his bride. Everything came too easily to Littleton, and Geoff was bound and determined that Miss Turley would not be one of them. She was his.

He just had to find a way to make her—and everyone else in the *ton*—understand that simple fact.

There must be something he could do. If things progressed as they had with Lady Charlotte, he'd lose Miss Turley as well. That meant losing his position with Sir Charles. An untenable proposition.

Turning to walk out of the ballroom, Geoff ran into one of the people he least wished to see. He bowed. "Cousin Apollonia, how are you this evening?"

"Better than you, I dare say." She'd raised one brow, and her tone was as dry as the desert. "I can only assume you did not take her ladyship's advice."

He was not going to have this conversation. Not now

when his temper was already frayed to a fine thread. There was only one thing to do. Geoff inclined his head. "Please excuse me," he said in his haughtiest tone. "I was just leaving."

"I do not doubt it." His cousin's remark was like a knife twisting in his gut. "Mayhap next time you will listen to older and wiser heads." She glanced to where Miss Turley danced with Lord Littleton. "Two in one Season. I wish you better luck next time, but I doubt you will have it."

As Geoff strode off with as much dignity as he could muster, his cousin's light laughter followed him. He was not going to be made a fool of. Somehow he would get back into Miss Turley's good graces.

Twenty minutes later he strode into his rooms and began searching his desk. "Nettle!"

"I did not expect to see you so early, my lord."

"The ball was a dead bore." Papers spilled off the desk scattering on the floor. "I need that list."

"List, my lord?" Geoff's valet stood just out of arm's reach or he might have grabbed the man. He had always prided himself on his calm temperament. Now he wanted to strangle someone.

"Yes. I threw it on the desk a few days ago after I got back from my grandmother's house."

"And would the list have been in her ladyship's hand, my lord?"

"More likely Cousin Apollonia's."

He raked his fingers through his hair. "Blast it all. Where could it be?"

Nettle stepped forward, opened a drawer, pulled out a piece of paper, and held it between his thumb and forefinger. "Would this be what you are searching for, my lord?"

Geoff snatched it from his valet's hands. "Yes." He read down the items. "First thing tomorrow I want you to go find roses."

"Roses?" His valet's brows rose briefly. "What kind of roses, my lord?"

He read the list again. "Pink. Have them put some greenery with them as well."

"And after I have procured the blooms?" Nettle appeared perplexed as he well might. With one major exception, that had made him look like a popinjay, Geoff had never given flowers to anyone.

"I'll have a note ready to go with them to Miss Turley."

"Ah, very good, my lord. I will endeavor to arrive at the market when it opens. I believe this will require my personal interest."

"Good man." He poured himself a large glass of brandy. "Have the messenger wait for an answer." Geoff just hoped she didn't take an hour to respond like she had the last time. Although then, he had not been on pins and needles wondering if she would accompany him instead of already having an engagement with Littleton.

Geoff sat down at the desk. He had to strike the right tone with her. Not desperate, but clearly exhibiting his desire to spend time with her. Why the devil was Littleton in Town this late in the Season in the first place? Or at all? Usually, he was mired in his estates.

Geoff blew a breath. Worrying about the man wouldn't help him. He had to focus on his quarry.

*My dear Miss Turley,*

*I apologize again for not seeking a second set from you before your card was full.*

That he had not made sure to secure that second set from her still enraged him. Come to think of it, that was the evening Littleton showed up.

*Please allow me to stand up with you twice at the
Somerville ball for the second set—they were both
waltzes—and the supper dance, and two dances at
the subsequent events.*

*It would also be my honor to take you driving
this afternoon at five o'clock.*

*My servant will await your answer.*

> *Yr. humble and devoted servant,*
> *G. Harrington*

Damn, Littleton. It looked like Geoff was going to have
to make a cake of himself after all.

He glanced at the corner of his desk where Nettle placed
important correspondence and there was a letter from his
father.

*Dear Harrington,*

*As I have not heard from you regarding your
courtship of Miss Turley, I trust you have it well in
hand. Events are moving rapidly on the Continent.
You should be ready to depart as soon as possible.*

> *Markham*

Hell and the Devil confound it! What else was on that
blasted list?

*Send flowers, bonbons, ices at Gunter's, or whatever she
enjoys most.*

How was Geoff supposed to know what Miss Turley
liked? They had never discussed it.

*Always offer an invitation in person. It is less likely she will refuse.*

Blast it all! He crumpled the note and threw it in the fireplace. "Nettle," Geoff called. "Wake me when you return from the market in the morning. I'll take the flowers to her myself."

"Very good, my lord."

Was that laughter he heard in his valet's voice? Drat it all. Nettle might be the first, but he wouldn't be the last one to find Geoff's situation ludicrous.

His life would have been much easier if his father had simply arranged a marriage for him. But Geoff hadn't wanted that. He'd wanted to select his own wife—and look where it had gotten him. In a pickle, that's where.

# Chapter Nine

Geoff paced his small parlor. There must be a better, more secure way to gain Miss Turley as his wife.

He stopped. Even though his father would not arrange a match . . . that did not mean Miss Turley's father could not arrange a match for her. That would make courting her unnecessary and the whole process much quicker.

He tried to remember what he knew of the viscount. Unfortunately, not much, except that rumor had it he wanted his daughter to wed and wed well. There was nothing unusual about that. What man did not wish for a good match for his children? Geoff didn't even know if Lord Turley was in Town. He certainly had not been at tea that day or at any of the entertainments.

It appeared that her brother was more in evidence than her father. Did that mean he would have to apply to Gavin Turley? Then again, he had encouraged Geoff's interest in Miss Turley. On the other hand, her brother was a good friend of Littleton's and seemed to be promoting a match there as well. Perhaps Turley did not care who she married as long as she did. Even Geoff could not deny that Littleton was extremely eligible. Geoff just wished the man would be eligible with some other lady. Then again, perhaps Miss

Turley favored him. He had noticed how her eyes sparkled when he had first discussed the overseas posting with her. Yet, lately, she had not seemed quite as interested.

He could not lose her.

The best way forward was to approach Lord Turley immediately, before she decided that she would rather remain in England. The problem was how the devil was he to find the man?

White's or Boodle's. His lordship was bound to frequent one or the other. Unless he was a Whig. Unthinkable. If Gavin Turley was a member of White's, so must his father be.

Grabbing his hat and cane, Geoff left his rooms and headed for his club. Even if Lord Turley wasn't there, Geoff could discover if he frequented White's and, if so, how often. Or if he'd have to visit Boodle's as well.

Several minutes later he ascended the steps to that most venerable of gentlemen's clubs—according to his father—and said to the master, "Good evening, can you tell me if Lord Turley is here at present?"

The man bowed. "No, my lord. He usually comes in the morning for the news from the Continent."

Geoff peered past the master, and not seeing anyone else he knew said, "Thank you. I'll return tomorrow."

On the way home, he revised his plans. He would send the flowers to Miss Turley—much less awkward than handing them to her personally—with some sort of extravagant message. An homage to her luminous skin or some such thing. Come to think of it, her skin was extremely fine. It reminded him of silk or a rose petal. Would it feel as soft? Once again, he found himself wanting to touch her. Knead her plump breasts, and take her nipples into his mouth. She always smelled of lavender and lemons. What would she taste like? With any luck, soon he'd discover for himself how soft she was.

He wanted to explore her mouth and make her writhe

with desire for him alone. His cock hardened as he thought of plunging into her wet silk. He groaned. He had to stop thinking about her before lust for Miss Turley had him doing something stupid.

But her hair. Tonight the way her curls had been arranged, her tresses reminded him of pale gold glinting in moonlight. Her laugh had been light and airy.

*Good Lord!* He was becoming poetical. That would never do. The last time he'd attempted to write poetry, his sister had gone into whoops and asked if he was really planning to send it to a lady.

He would have to write a nice note to go with the flowers though. Geoff would have them delivered early. Then he'd go to White's early in the morning and remain there until Lord Turley arrived. Once they'd spoken, and Geoff made his intentions clear, he and Miss Turley would become betrothed, and he'd have her in his bed. Once that happened, she would be his.

"Where is he?" Elizabeth had forced herself not to look for Lord Harrington when he was not by her side.

"Left in a huff," Aunt Bristow said, her eyes sparkling wickedly. "Gavin, I was not at all happy with you when you didn't return as quickly as I wanted you to, but I think you concocted exactly what was needed to bring Harrington up to scratch."

"I wish I could take all the credit," her brother said. "But it was Littleton here that first had the idea."

The very handsome, but completely rakish Lord Littleton inclined his head.

Elizabeth still had trouble believing that his lordship had agreed to help her, and now to find out it was his idea . . . "How? I mean, what made you think of it? And why?"

He turned a pair of warm green eyes on her, and, once

again, she knew why the gentleman was so dangerous. Gavin had warned her not to fall in love with his friend. Fortunately, her taste ran to blue eyes and blond hair.

One particular pair of blue eyes at that.

"My grandmother used to tell the story," Lord Littleton began, "of how she and my grandfather married. Apparently, Littleton men are famous for attempting to avoid the parson's trap. Yet it turned out that he liked her a great deal, but couldn't bring himself to do anything about it. One of her cousins visited with a friend and they hatched a plot to make my grandfather jealous, and it worked. Once Grandfather saw that another gentleman might be interested in my grandmother, he made it his objective to marry her."

"How very devious." No wonder her brother and his lordship were so certain this scheme would work. "Was he happy that he wed her?"

"He said he was the happiest man on earth." Lord Littleton smiled at Elizabeth. "Turley said you like Harrington, and we all know he must marry." Lord Littleton shrugged. "I thought I would do you a good turn."

"I hope it works." She pulled her bottom lip between her lips. "I hope it is me he likes and not just the position."

"I don't think you have to worry about that." Lord Littleton grinned. "From the look on Lord Harrington's face, I predict it will not be long before he calls on your father."

"He certainly looked as if he'd like to murder you," Gavin said to Lord Littleton.

"As long as he doesn't put thoughts to action," his lordship responded drily. "Would you like to give Harrington more incentive by riding out with me tomorrow, Miss Turley?"

"Thank you, I would." Elizabeth responded to his grin with one of her own. "Even if he begins to behave as he should, I do not wish to give in too easily."

"Lord, no, my dear," her aunt said. "There is nothing wrong with letting a man chase you."

That was what her friends had said as well. She wished Charlotte, Louisa, and Dotty were here, but they were all getting ready for Charlotte's wedding in the morning. When she was told, Elizabeth had been sworn to secrecy and had not even confided in her aunt.

Elizabeth prayed Lord Littleton was wrong about Lord Harrington approaching Father. He could and would give his permission far too soon. That could ruin everything. "Gavin, what if he does ask to see Papa right away?"

Her brother rubbed his jaw as he thought. "I'll keep Father away from his usual haunts for a day or two. That should do it."

"I hope you are right," Elizabeth said, unconvinced. "I wish he would leave Town for a while. However, if Lord Harrington does come I will not be at home tomorrow morning. Aunt and I are attending the Worthington End of Season Breakfast."

"Dear me," Aunt said. "I'd almost forgotten about that. Harrington surely will not attend."

"Trust me, my lady, when I say he will be in a bad way by the end of tomorrow," Lord Littleton laughingly assured them. "I agree that keeping him away from your father is a good idea. I've always thought Harrington was a bit of a cold fish when it came to the ladies. Hooking him is what you want."

Hooking him? If other gentlemen thought Lord Harrington was cold, did Elizabeth really want him?

Early the next morning, Elizabeth and her aunt were among the first guests to arrive at Stanwood House in Berkeley Square.

Charlotte, standing next to Lord Kenilworth, was radiant, and his lordship appeared besotted. That was exactly the look Elizabeth wanted to see on Lord Harrington's face when he gazed down at her. Hopefully, her brother's scheme would work to bring him around.

"Congratulations." She curtseyed to Lord and Lady Kenilworth. "I hope you will be extremely happy."

Charlotte glanced at her new husband. "We already are. And you? How is it going?"

"Well, I think." Under the guise of bussing Charlotte's cheek, Elizabeth said, "I'll tell you about it if you have time."

"Find Dotty and Louisa, and we'll meet at the table on the terrace," Charlotte whispered.

The same place they had gathered at Dotty's wedding breakfast. "In an hour?"

Charlotte nodded. "That should be sufficient time for me to finish here."

"Hatching plots already, my love?" Lord Kenilworth murmured in what even Elizabeth thought was a sensuous tone.

"Only helping a friend." Charlotte smiled.

An hour later, Charlotte, Louisa, Dotty, and Elizabeth were sitting at the round table on one corner of the terrace. A footman served champagne, small sandwiches, and ginger biscuits.

Once Elizabeth and the others toasted the bride, Charlotte asked, "How can we help you?"

"I'm not sure I require your help," Elizabeth said. "I do want your opinion. You see, my brother's friend, Lord Littleton—"

"Never tell me Littleton has taken an interest in you!" Louisa exclaimed.

"No, no." Elizabeth couldn't stop a giggle. "He has decided to help me with Lord Harrington."

"This should be interesting." Louisa took a sip of wine.

"It is rather. He is trying to make Harrington jealous." Elizabeth looked at her friends. Louisa placed her fingers over her mouth as if to stifle a laugh, Charlotte tilted her head in a considering manner, and Dotty's brows came together in a look of concern.

"Is it working?" they all said at one time.

"Well, he only started a few days ago, so it may be too early to tell. But I think it might be." Elizabeth started to fidget with the fringe of her shawl, but took a drink of champagne instead. "At the ball last night, my aunt said that Harrington was extremely upset and glared at Lord Littleton and me when we were dancing."

"That certainly sounds promising," Charlotte commented. "I never had the impression he was jealous of Kenilworth. He only seemed inconvenienced that I preferred Kenilworth over him." She tapped her fingers on the table. "Matt said that he complained that he would have to find another lady to wed."

That was what Elizabeth had thought. In spite of her resolve, she began twisting the fringe on her shawl. If she had another drink of wine, she would drain the glass. Glancing at her friends, she asked, "Do you think that means he cares about me?"

Charlotte, Dotty, and Louisa exchanged looks. Finally, Dotty said, "I am not sure. Are you certain you want Harrington? I mean, must you marry this Season?"

"I could wait, but I have been drawn to Lord Harrington." She glanced at Charlotte. "I was very glad when you decided you didn't want him. Other than his inability to discuss anything personal, I like him a great deal and think I could easily fall in love with him. Yet, I want him to fall in love with me as well." It would break her heart if he didn't love her in return.

"Of course you do." Charlotte leaned over and hugged Elizabeth. "I think it is a good plan. Still, if this does not make him see that he wants you, then you must give him up."

"I agree," Louisa said.

"I do as well," Dotty added.

Elizabeth took a large breath and blew it out. Giving him up was the last thing she wanted to do. Still, they were right. Even if he offered her the life she wanted, without love it would be worthless. Not marrying him was the only course she could take. "Thank you."

Just over an hour later, she arrived home to find a bouquet of the most beautiful pale pink *Thigh of Nymph* roses she had ever seen. "These are lovely."

Broadwell handed her a card. "They are for you, miss."

For a moment she wondered if they were from Lord Littleton, but the familiar strong, slashing handwriting told her they were from Lord Harrington. Perhaps this would give her some indication if the scheme was working.

*My dear Miss Turley,*

*These roses reminded me of you. Please accept them as token of my admiration for you.*

*If you have the second set and the supper dance left on your card for Lady Somerville's ball this evening, it would be my honor to claim them.*

*Are you free to drive out with me at five o'clock this afternoon? If you are already engaged, I would like to ask you to accompany me tomorrow at the same time.*

*Yr. devoted servant,*
*Harrington*

"Oh, my." He was definitely not giving up on her. She handed the card to her aunt. "What do you think of that?"

Aunt Bristow quickly read the note. "Very nice. Now if

Gavin can keep Harrington away from your father, we may bring this to a successful conclusion."

Elizabeth turned to Broadwell. "Have you seen Mr. Turley this morning?"

"Yes, my lady. He is in the breakfast room."

She and her aunt scurried down the corridor and came upon her brother as he was leaving the room. "Gavin, your plan is working, but someone must keep Lord Harrington away from Papa. Will you be able to do it?"

"I've done better than that." Her brother gave them one of his insufferable smirks. "I convinced him he needed to visit Grandmamma. A letter arrived from her this morning complaining of something on the estate she was unable to resolve."

What on earth could it be? Grandmamma had always been able to deal with any of the estate problems. Gavin had to have done something to cause their grandmother to write Father.

Elizabeth gave him a smile. "Well, I do not know how you brought it about, but thank you very much." She almost hugged him, then remembered how he hated having his clothing mussed. "I did not expect you to go so far out of your way."

"Listen, puss." He chucked her under her chin like he had when she was a child. "It was no trouble at all for me, and it will save our scheme. Father had heard Harrington was looking for him, and I can tell you you are correct. He would have spoilt the whole thing. He had every intention of giving Harrington the go-ahead. With him gone, he's given me the job of speaking with Harrington. Not only that, but he has given me the power of attorney to consult with our solicitor about your settlement agreement, if it comes to that."

"Of all the sapskulls." Aunt cast her eyes to the ceiling. "All I can say is well done, Gavin."

"Well done indeed." Elizabeth heaved a relieved breath. If Papa had given Harrington permission to wed her, which was exactly what everyone thought her father would have done, there would be no reason for him to court her properly, and for her to make sure he could love her.

"What have you got there?" Gavin asked.

She had almost forgotten about Harrington's letter. And when had she begun to think of him in such a familiar manner? "A note from Lord Harrington. He sent it with the flowers. He has asked for two dances this evening, if I have them free, and would like to take me driving this afternoon." She read over the missive again. "I have already promised Lord Littleton I would drive with him. I shall tell Harrington"—she had done it again—"that I have a prior engagement, but shall be happy to join him tomorrow." Elizabeth considered denying him the second set, but decided not to. "I shall accept his request for two dances."

"That will take the sting out of discovering you went driving with Littleton." Her aunt nodded approvingly.

"I may go on the strut this afternoon." Her brother grinned wickedly. "I'd like to see Harrington's face when he finds you with Littleton."

"Do you truly think he will be in the Park?" Elizabeth asked. She did not know why Harrington would be.

"He'll be there if only to see who you are with." With that, her brother sauntered off.

# Chapter Ten

Geoff ripped open the answer from Miss Turley and growled.

Damn it to hell. He'd wager Miss Turley was riding with Littleton this afternoon. Geoff couldn't believe he'd let the man get the better of him. But what if it wasn't Littleton? What if some other gentleman had seen her, and admired her beauty, and asked her to ride with him? There was only one way to find out.

Geoff considered taking his phaeton, but decided to ride his gelding instead. The phaeton would be more impressive, but it couldn't maneuver the way a horse could. And he did not wish to draw attention to himself. All he wished to do was ascertain with whom Miss Turley was with.

If it was Littleton, Geoff was sure he could still win the lady's hand. But if it was another man, he must know what he was up against.

He sent a message to the stables that at five to five his gray, Hercules, was to be brought around.

He was halfway around his second circuit when he saw them. Littleton and Miss Turley. Her head leaned toward his and she laughed. Even though they were at a distance from Geoff, he could hear her light laughter on the air. Laughter that he should be causing.

Cursing, he rode back to his rooms. She was dancing two sets with him this evening, and he'd make damn sure she would rather be with him than Littleton.

Once again, Geoff escorted his grandmother and cousin to the ball. As soon as they arrived, he found them a pair of seats and began searching for Miss Turley. Her aunt, he knew, always arrived at the beginning of a ball. By this point, they would be deep into the ballroom.

He moved along the edges of the room, thus avoiding ladies with daughters to marry off. Finally, he saw her standing with her aunt and brother. She was easily the most beautiful lady in the room. Tonight, she wore a white gown with silver netting that caught the candlelight and twinkled when she moved. Pearls hung from her shell-like ears. Around her graceful neck she wore a double strand of matching pearls.

Littleton escorted her out for the first set. Still, Geoff had the first waltz and the supper dance. Keeping out of sight, he leaned against a pillar, waiting for his opportunity to stand up with her.

Two sets later, he bowed to Miss Turley, taking her hand. "My dance, I believe."

"It is, my lord." A small smile graced her lips. He wanted more from her.

"Thank you for agreeing to two sets." He placed his palm on her waist and wanted to draw her closer.

She shrugged lightly. "I had a set open. Why should you not have it?"

Why indeed. The music began, but he waited until the

turn before closing the space between them. Geoff was pleased she did not complain or attempt to move back. Gazing down at her, for the first time he could think of nothing to say.

Miss Turley's head tilted slightly to one side as she gazed back at him. "Lady Somerville has done a wonderful job decorating."

The ballroom was filled with gold and pink silk. Large bunches of lilies had been set in each corner and potted plants lined the sides of the room. The French windows, as well as the long windows lining the wall, were open, allowing a slight breeze into the ballroom. How would Miss Turley decorate for their first ball? "Yes, she has."

When he said nothing more, he could swear he heard her sigh. "I read that some elements are creating a problem with funding for Wellington."

"I have heard the same. Why can they not understand that he and the army is all that stands between us and Napoleon? We dare not allow him to win."

"We must pray cooler heads will prevail. When do you depart for the Continent?"

"I don't know yet." He would not say that it depended on her.

"My brother knows a number of gentlemen who are in the army and traveling to Brussels and the surrounding areas. I suppose you do as well."

"We most likely know a number of the same fellows." He did not wish to discuss the coming war with her, but he didn't know what else to say.

The second set was just as frustrating as the first, and he left the ball not knowing if he had managed to secure her or not. Geoff only knew that he had to do something to ensure Miss Turley was his.

* * *

The next morning, fate was against him again, and Geoff couldn't figure out what he'd done to deserve such Turkish treatment. He had finally decided to visit Lord Turley and ask for Miss Turley's hand in marriage, but when he arrived at their town house the butler had said Lord Turley left early that morning for his estate, and only Mr. Turley knew when his lordship would return. Yet, he was not expected back until later that afternoon. Geoff didn't bother asking if Miss Turley was at home. She would be at Lady Worthington's End of Season Breakfast.

He reached the pavement in front of Turley House and turned toward his rooms.

He could go to one of his clubs, but chances were all he'd hear about was the last entertainments of the Season, if there was anyone about at all with the breakfast going on this morning. Although he had received an invitation to the event, after the way he had left things with Lady Charlotte, he had sent his regrets.

"Ho, Harrington." Lord Endicott quickened his step as Geoff turned and waited. "I didn't see you at Lady Worthington's breakfast."

"No, I got caught up with something else." Such as trying to find the father of the lady Geoff now wished to wed.

"You missed the surprise of the Season." Endicott fell in beside Geoff.

He turned with the other gentleman toward Jermyn Street. "What surprise is that?"

"Lady Charlotte Carpenter and Kenilworth married this morning. The End of Season Breakfast was actually their wedding breakfast."

"What's so strange about that?" Geoff knew she'd marry Kenilworth. Everyone knew they would wed. Oddly enough, for all that Geoff had wanted her as his wife, he didn't feel bad about it. He had Miss Turley now. Or he would have her soon. "Other than Lady Worthington not announcing it was a wedding breakfast, that is?" Which was rather odd, now that he thought about it.

"Seems Kenilworth didn't know he was getting leg-shackled today." Endicott chuckled. "That's the reason for the subterfuge about the wedding breakfast."

How could it even occur that a gentleman wouldn't know he was getting married? "That doesn't make sense. You must have heard the story wrongly."

"Not at all. I was there and heard the man himself. Kenilworth was laughing about how he'd been after Worthington for days to set a date, and the lengths Lady Charlotte had gone to keep him in the dark." Endicott laughed again. "Never seen a man so happy to be humbugged."

Geoff wasn't sure he'd want to be the groom at a surprise wedding. In fact, he did not like to be caught unawares at all. And for the first time, he was actually glad he had not wed Lady Charlotte if she went around doing foolish things like that.

He couldn't see Miss Turley behaving in such an impudent manner. Perhaps he was luckier than he had known to have *lost* Lady Charlotte. Of course, that made him even more resolved to get Miss Turley to the altar. Despite what his cousin had said, he was not going to lose her. One way or the other, he was going to get the lady to the altar.

Endicott continued to talk about the wedding breakfast while they made their way to Jermyn Street. Eventually, he asked, "How goes your quest for a wife?"

"Between you and me, I had hoped to make an offer for Miss Turley today." Geoff grimaced. "But her father is out of Town for a few days."

"Turley, hmm? Bad luck, that," Endicott said sympathetically. "Seems like a nice chit. Pretty enough, but too quiet for me."

Geoff had no intention of telling Endicott that Miss Turley was not nearly as quiet as she appeared next to Lady Charlotte or Lady Louisa—mayhap because Miss Turley did not put herself forward. He didn't need Endicott to become interested in her. Geoff also found he did not like her being referred to as a "chit." She might be in her first Season, but she was extremely mature. "She suits me."

"M'mother's been after me to marry, but it looks like I'll have to wait until next Season," Endicott confided. "Can't say I'm interested in any of the ladies left."

"I have been told," Geoff said, "that many families are taking their daughters to Brussels, now that the English are no longer welcome in Paris."

"Can't see that's such a good decision with Boney on the move." As Endicott's sentiments were the same as Geoff's, there was nothing more to say on the subject.

Once they reached their respective buildings, Geoff said, "I shall see you at Lady Somerset's ball, I expect."

"Of course." Endicott waved a salute. "Good luck with your lady."

"Thank you." Geoff only wished he was confident enough to call Miss Turley *his* lady to anyone but himself.

He entered his rooms to find several letters on the small mahogany table against one wall. Selecting the one addressed from the foreign office he opened it.

*Dear Lord Harrington,*

*I am writing to inform you that Sir Charles sends you his compliments and requests you be available prior to the middle of June. You are to travel to Brussels where Sir Charles is currently advising the Prince of Orange.*

*Yr servant, etc.*

The middle of June! Damnation. That only gave Geoff just over two weeks to marry and make the journey to

Belgium. He'd have to track down Miss Turley's brother today and hope that he didn't have to travel to Suffolk to meet with her father.

The last time he'd left Town it had not gone well for him.

Shortly after luncheon, Geoff once again climbed the shallow steps to Turley House and knocked on the door.

"My lord." The butler bowed. "Mr. Turley will see you in the library."

Unlike with Worthington, at least this time when Geoff had left a message stating he wanted to see a gentleman about a lady, the gentleman was present.

He followed the butler down the corridor on the left side of the hall to the back of the house. The door opened to a room filled with bookshelves and windows. A massive desk with chairs in front of it stood in the center of the room between two windows. Gavin Turley sat in a large leather chair behind the desk.

"Sir." The servant bowed. "The Earl of Harrington to see you."

Turley stood. "Harrington, well met." He waved Geoff to a small sofa in front of an unlit fireplace. "Please have a seat. Broadwell will bring tea unless you'd like brandy or wine."

"Tea, if you please." He didn't need to drink spirits during this interview. Too much depended on receiving the answer he wanted.

Turley took the chair opposite Geoff. He and Turley discussed the happenings on the Continent until tea was brought in and set on the table between them.

Once they each had a cup, Turley said, "I take it you wish to discuss my sister."

Geoff took a sip then set down the cup. "I had hoped to speak with your father about my intentions toward her."

"Unfortunately, he was called away. Estate business, you understand. I have no idea when he will return." Turley's tone was genial, but there was an undercurrent of something that Geoff couldn't place beneath the man's bonhomie.

Geoff inclined his head, and wondered if he had wasted his time coming here. He took another sip of tea. "Of course."

"He did, however, charge me with seeing to Elizabeth." Turley's smile seemed to have a few too many teeth, and Geoff started to feel slightly off balance. "What exactly did you wish to discuss?"

Thank the Fates that he would not have to wait any longer. This was finally his chance to become betrothed to Miss Turley.

His opportunity to procure a wife and arrive in Brussels in a timely fashion. "As you are aware, I have taken an interest in your sister." The man raised a brow as if he did not quite believe Geoff. "I would like to marry Miss Turley. The time I have spent with her has convinced me that we would deal well together."

"I see." Leaning back against the plump cushions of the chair, Turley formed a steeple with his fingers. "Does my sister know you are interested in marrying her?"

Drat. The man had to know Geoff had not spoken with her about it. "Naturally, I wished to speak with her father first."

"Very proper." Turley agreed too easily for Geoff's peace of mind. "As to the amount of time you have spent with her, I do not accept that it is sufficient to form an opinion as to whether or not my sister would agree to marry you. Lord Littleton has, I dare say, been in her company as much as you have. That said, I can and shall give you permission to court her. It is, nevertheless, up to Elizabeth if she wishes to accept your proposal."

"Lord Turley—"

"Will tell you the same thing," Turley said, cutting Geoff off.

This was not at all what he had expected. It was, in fact, quite the opposite. Since the beginning of the Season, rumor had it that Lord Turley wanted to get his daughter off his hands and was prepared to accept any reasonable offer.

Had gossip been wrong or was Mr. Turley lying? Geoff had half a mind to seek out his lordship, but that would mean wasting several days traveling and, with Littleton sniffing around her skirts, Geoff did not have the time to spare. He would just have to deal with the brother's answer.

"Thank you." He hid his growing anger at being denied an immediate acceptance. "Do you know if Miss Turley is at home?"

"Not at the moment." Gavin Turley grinned as if he'd won a hard-fought match. "Join us for tea. She will be here then."

Standing, Geoff held out his hand as the other man came around the table between the two chairs. "Thank you. I shall do as you suggest."

"We shall see you then." Turley escorted Geoff to the front door. "I wish you the best of luck in your quest. If it makes you feel any better, I think you and my sister would suit as well. She is, however, the one you'll need to convince."

"Thank you again." The door closed behind him as he walked down the steps.

Devil take it. His grandmother and cousin were right. He would have to go beyond dancing twice in an evening with her, sending flowers, and taking her for rides in the Park. There was no way around making a fool of himself. He'd have to find that dratted list again.

No matter what he had to do, one way or another, he would convince Miss Turley to be his bride. If only he could find a way to get Littleton out of Town, Geoff would have no competition for her hand.

# Chapter Eleven

Elizabeth peeped around the corner at the top of the stairs just in time to see Lord Harrington walk out the front door. Her dances with him left her feeling more confused than ever. Lately, he seemed to have lost all his conversation.

She waited until he would have had time to reach the pavement before glancing at her brother. "What did he say?"

"I'll tell you in the library. If our aunt is here, you'd better bring her, too. I don't want to have to tell the story twice."

"She has gone to visit a friend." Elizabeth hurried down the stairs, catching up with Gavin as he held open the library door. Sinking onto the smaller of the chairs facing the desk, she folded her hands in her lap. "Tell me everything."

"I suspect you know he asked to marry you." She nodded. That was the only reason Lord Harrington would wish to speak with her brother. "I told him only you could make that decision." She opened her mouth, and he held up a hand. "He was not happy, but I went on to say that I would give him permission to court you."

Oh, that was perfect! "And what did he say to that?"

"He didn't look any happier than he had before, but thanked me and asked if you were at home."

"We were all correct. He is interested in marrying me, but without the effort of fixing my attentions."

"You are probably right." Her brother nodded. "On the other hand, he might simply want to make sure he'd cut Littleton out. I told him he could join us for tea."

"Tea again?" The last time he had come for tea, it had accomplished nothing.

"I'll make sure you have some time alone with him." Her brother's easy manner suddenly became sober. "Lizzy, is this . . . he is what you want, isn't he?"

"I am almost positive," she tried to assure him. "We do have a great deal in common." Even if Lord Harrington did not realize it yet. "And I would dearly love the life of a diplomat's wife. I have always had an interest in foreign travel."

Gavin came around the desk and took her hands. "Lizzy, I want you to have a good life. The life you want. If you think Harrington is the one, I shall continue to help you."

"Thank you." Blinking back tears, Elizabeth recalled how angry she was when he had interfered with her cousin's plan to force Lord Merton into marrying her. Yet, Gavin had been right. Dotty and Merton belonged together. Papa, on the other hand, wanted Elizabeth to marry well and this Season. He had been furious with Gavin for interfering, but her brother remained firm, and now he was helping her again. "You are the best brother I could have. But Papa—"

"I'll take care of him." Gavin scowled for a moment. "Mind though, if you find you don't want Harrington, I'll send him to the right about before Papa returns." Her brother lightly squeezed her fingers. "I don't want to rush you, but you'll need to make a decision soon. I doubt Grandmamma can keep our father in the country the rest of the Season. Not since he knows Harrington is looking for him."

She was surprised her father had agreed to leave at all. "Yes." Elizabeth nodded. "Yes, of course." Not only was Papa a problem, but Aunt said that Lord Harrington had only a short time to wed and leave for the Continent. Even if she wished to wait, she could not. "If he begins to seriously court me"—because after all no one would say that one dance an evening, although he had begun asking for two even though it had not yet happened, and the occasional ride *could* be considered serious—"I should be able to soon know my mind."

"That's all I ask." The corner of Gavin's lips tilted up and the sparkle came back into his eyes. "Do something to take your mind off Harrington for a few hours. Take your maid and a footman."

"That is a wonderful idea." Elizabeth took out her handkerchief, dabbed the tears gathering in her eyes, and blew her nose. "I believe I shall go shopping."

"Tell you what, have the bills sent here, and I'll pay them. No point in you ending up at *point non plus* before quarter day."

Not that she ever was short on funds. She'd discovered early on to manage her pin money. "Thank you again." She reached up to hug him and he stepped back. "I almost forgot you don't like your cravat mussed."

"No, I don't." He smoothed one of the folds in his neckcloth. "If you knew how long it took me, or how many cravats I went through to achieve the Mathematical, you'd never try to embrace me again."

Even though she loved seeing a gentleman in a well-tied neckcloth, she did not understand the necessity of them tying their cravats themselves. "It would probably not take half as long if you had your valet tie it."

Gavin's jaw dropped in astonishment. "I'm not such a coxcomb that I'd have my valet tie my cravat." He reached up as if to grip his neckcloth, then dropped his hand. "I'd never be able to hold my head up again."

"I shall on no account mention it again," she said, trying

to mollify him. After all, he was doing her a great service with Lord Harrington. "I just thought it would be easier."

"Easier is not the point, my girl. It's developing the skill. Why, Beau Brummell is said to go through up to twenty cravats a day before he is satisfied."

Even after breaking with the Prince Regency, there was no one with as much influence over gentlemen's fashion as Brummell. Going as high up on her toes as she could, she leaned forward and bussed his cheek. "I shall see you this afternoon."

After informing Cook that they would have company at tea, Elizabeth found her aunt had returned. She told Aunt about Harrington's—would she call him by his title in private if they married?—visit with Gavin. Naturally, she approved of Gavin's response to his lordship.

Several minutes later they set out in the town coach to Bond and Bruton Streets. Yet, even though Elizabeth and her aunt visited Hatchards and found several books that looked as if they would keep her attention, in addition to glove makers, several milliners, and Phaeton's Bazaar, she could still not keep her mind off Harrington's visit this afternoon.

Was there anything she could do to make him wish to spend more time with her? She had already tried getting him to talk about himself, and the conversation always came back to his assignment with Sir Charles. Perhaps she should be more forward. Then again, she did not wish to make Harrington think she was a sad romp. If only he would take more of an interest in what she liked, they could discuss their differences and similarities.

In short, all she knew about him was that he was extremely handsome, loved to travel, was an excellent dancer, excited about his future position. . . . Now that she considered it, she knew a great deal more about him than she had thought. Except how he actually felt about her.

Yet, short of asking him directly—which she could never do—how was she to discover that?

Then her aunt's words came back to Elizabeth.

*"There is nothing wrong with letting a man chase you."*

She heaved a sigh. It might be better to focus on how she would *know* if Lord Harrington cared about her. There had to be signs, behaviors that he should exhibit.

Again, she thought about the way her friends' husbands had behaved, and they all had one thing in common. Possessiveness.

The men's gazes followed their chosen lady if she ventured away from them, and they attached themselves to her side when their lady was near. Elizabeth had also noticed distinct glares from the gentlemen when another man was too affable to the lady. At one point Lord Merton had actually told a gentleman wishing to dance with Dotty to go away.

Would Harrington ever want her by his side all the time? If he did, then was that the key to knowing if he cared for her? If he loved her?

If it was, he had a long way to go.

"What has put you in a brown study?" her aunt asked.

"I simply do not know if I will be able to discern by Lord Harrington's behavior if he cares about me."

"My dear Elizabeth." Her aunt chuckled. "Believe me when I tell you that his behavior will make it perfectly clear how he feels about you."

Recalling what her friends had told her about marital relations, she found herself fighting the heat rising in her cheeks. "I certainly hope so."

Geoff held out his hand to Nettle and waited while he carefully placed another length of starched linen into Geoff's hand. He took a breath before wrapping the cravat around his neck and began to tie it. Several minutes later, he had finally achieved the perfect Waterfall.

His valet beamed. "Excellent, if I may say so, my lord."

"You may, and after only four attempts." Ever since he'd seen Lord Alvanley wearing it, Geoff had been determined to accomplish the same result.

He had heard often enough that ladies liked a well-tied cravat. He only hoped that Miss Turley was pleased. "Where is that list?"

"In your desk, my lord."

After learning that he must indeed court Miss Turley, he had decided to apply at least three of his grandmother's and cousin's suggestions each time he met with her.

Geoff opened the drawer and found the paper on top. Taking it out, he read down their recommendations until he came to one he thought had merit.

*Ask her questions about what she likes. By the end of the conversation you should know her favorite color, which flowers she prefers, and her favorite piece of music.*

More flowers were clearly in order. While he was drinking tea with her he would request a second set for the ball tomorrow evening and ask her to ride with him in the Park the following day as well. That would make two evenings in succession where he danced with her twice and two days in a row that they would drive out together. Maybe then he would be able to make some progress with her.

He turned his attention back to the list.

*Take her someplace she would like to go. Gunter's for an ice is always pleasant. A picnic in Richmond is nice as well, as is the theater, but you would have to get up a party.*

Gunter's it was. He had neither the time nor the inclination to ride out to Richmond with a group of other people. Getting up a party for the theater was easy enough. He had only to invite her brother and aunt. Geoff would have to discover what types of plays she enjoyed. He had a fondness for comedies, but this was about what Miss Turley wanted. He hoped their tastes were similar.

He arrived at her house just as Lady Bristow had been assisted from their coach.

"Good afternoon, my lady."

"Lord Harrington, we are glad you could join us."

"As am I." Geoff hurried over, edging the footman out, to take Miss Turley's hand. "Miss Turley, I hope you had an enjoyable day."

"Good afternoon, my lord." She smiled up at him as she placed her fingers on his arm. "We did indeed. And you?"

He gazed down into smiling blue eyes. Courting her would not be nearly as onerous as he had originally thought. "Much better now."

A light blush colored her cheeks. "Let us have tea. I think Cook may have made some of her special biscuits."

"My lady, Miss Turley." Littleton strode toward them.

Damn the man. Why couldn't he stay away from Miss Turley?

Had Geoff truly not made his interest in her clear? He'd thought . . . but perhaps his grandmother was right, and he was the only one who was certain he wished to wed Miss Turley.

Fortunately, Littleton had had to greet Lady Bristow before he could acknowledge Miss Turley. Geoff whispered to her, "Thank you for agreeing to the dances and to drive with me tomorrow. You have made me an extremely happy man."

She smiled at him again, and he found he enjoyed having her regard a great deal. Now all he had to do was keep Littleton from making any progress with her.

"You may join us for tea if you wish, Lord Littleton," Lady Bristow said.

Geoff cursed to himself. That was not what he'd hoped for.

"Thank you, ma'am"—he bowed—"I would indeed."

Now that Geoff had been given permission to court Miss Turley, perhaps he should hint Littleton away.

Geoff placed his other hand over Elizabeth's hand on his arm, but as they turned to go into the house, Littleton said, "Miss Turley. You are looking especially delightful today. I could not wait until our ride to see you again."

Hell and damnation! Geoff had been right. She was riding with the bounder today. He'd have to ensure that never happened again.

"Thank you, my lord." The corners of her lips tilted up and he was glad to see that the smile she gave the man didn't seem as bright as the one she'd given him.

Drat it all. What the devil was happening to him that he was now studying her so closely as to notice, or hope, he had noticed the difference in her smiles?

Obviously, being told he could court her didn't mean other gentlemen had to stay away. Or perhaps Turley hadn't spoken to Littleton yet. Yes. That must be the case. Apparently, it fell upon Geoff to inform his lordship that Elizabeth was taken. Although, showing him might be better. He'd simply have to monopolize her time during tea.

When she sank onto the sofa, he ignored her aunt's hand motioning him to a chair next to the sofa and sat next to her. He thought he saw Littleton's lips twitch and wondered what the man planned to do, and what Geoff could do to limit his lordship's attentions to Elizabeth.

The tea tray was brought in followed by her brother. While his soon-to-be-betrothed wife poured—a duty, he was pleased to see, she performed with as much grace as his mother—Turley strolled with Littleton to a door leading out to the terrace. The men spoke in voices too low to hear, but Geoff trusted Turley would inform Littleton that Geoff planned to marry Elizabeth. That she was off the Marriage Mart.

Yet, what if Littleton wished to wed her as well? He had

already stood up with her twice on two different occasions. And Turley had said it was up to his sister to decide.

Damnation, that's what Geoff had forgotten to do. There was another ball this week. He was not going to miss his opportunity to dance twice with her again. "Miss Turley, would you do me the honor of dancing the first waltz as well as the supper dance with me at Lady Jersey's ball?"

A faint line formed between her well-arched brows. "How I wish you would have asked me earlier. The first waltz is taken." She tilted her head a little and smiled. "I still have the second waltz available if that would do."

"Yes." It was not as important as the first dance, but it would do. "And the supper dance?" he prompted, reminding her that she had already promised it to him. "I believe that is a waltz as well."

"Yes. Your name is already on my dance card." She nodded. "I believe you are correct that it is a waltz."

Setting his teacup down, he glanced at her. "Your garden looks lovely."

"Thank you. My mother planted it." Her voice was soft with longing, as if she remembered her mother fondly. After a long moment, she said, "Would you care to take a stroll?"

"Thank you. I would enjoy that." Standing, he offered her his hand and she took it. As long as no one else decided to join them, this would give him a chance to discover her favorite flower, color, and music.

Littleton started toward them and Geoff bit off a curse. "Miss Turley"—his lordship bowed—"tea was lovely. Unfortunately, I must depart. I shall see you at five."

Geoff held fast to her fingers on his arm, holding her up so that she was unable to curtsey. "I look forward to it."

"And I look forward to our drive." Littleton inclined his head to Geoff. "Harrington."

"Littleton." Geoff inclined his head as well, trying not to

clench his jaw. He hoped the dratted man went back to the country soon. Littleton was much too interested in Miss Turley. "I wish you a pleasant day."

"Do you, indeed?" The man lifted a brow. "I rather thought you just wished me gone."

# Chapter Twelve

Elizabeth stifled a laugh. Harrington's jaw began to tick, and she rather thought that he wished Lord Littleton would fall into the Thames and drown or have some equally unfortunate accident.

"Shall we?" She led him outside before either man could make another comment. "My aunt received a letter from one of her friends who is in Brussels. It appears they are doing nothing but attending myriad entertainments."

"I've heard that as well." He grinned, then sobered. "Although it is no laughing matter, you might already know that Lord Fitzroy Somerset, our chargé d'affaires in Paris, was forced to gather the rest of the embassy people and flee to Dieppe."

"I had not heard. That is no way for a country to treat diplomats." She was relieved that Lord Fitzroy had had the foresight to take his people and leave instead of staying in hopes that they received the passes they required.

She had led him to the arbor at one end of the garden where they were out of sight of the house.

"I have to agree." Lord Harrington raised her bare hand to his lips, causing her to suck in a breath as he pressed a kiss on to her knuckles. "I would rather talk about you. It seems that we are always discussing other things, and it occurred to me that I don't even know your favorite color."

Her heart began to beat faster. This was what she had been waiting for. His interest in the person she was as opposed to how suitable a wife she would be. "Pink."

"Any color pink?" he asked. "There seem to be a great many different shades."

"The same pink as the roses you sent. My mother planted dozens of different colored pink rose bushes." They had stopped strolling, and she gazed into his eyes. "They make me think of spring and the earth renewing itself. What is your favorite color?"

Harrington seemed taken aback. "No one has ever asked me before." He paused for a moment. "I think it must be green like the ash tree leaves when they first appear."

"Shall I assume we both enjoy spring?" She was glad she hadn't sounded arch or too coy.

"I believe you can say that. I love the feel and smell of the air as it turns mild." Somehow she found herself a little closer to him. Her skirts almost brushed his legs. "What about flowers?"

"I think you have already discovered my favorite blooms." Warmth rose in her cheeks as his gaze captured hers.

"Have I?" He stood even closer as he twined his fingers through hers.

Elizabeth's heart was pounding so hard, she was sure he must be able to hear it. "The pink roses you sent were exquisite." She was breathless, and he was becoming perfect. Was it all due to Lord Littleton's supposed interest? "They are my favorites."

"What music do you like best?" Lord Harrington's voice was low, and a shiver ran through her as he bent his head as if he might kiss her.

"You have not yet told me your favorite flower." She raised her face to his, their lips only inches apart.

"The same roses I sent you." With one finger, he lightly stroked her cheek and it was all she could do not to lean into his caress. "The petals remind me of your cheeks. Soft and silky."

"Oh." Inane as it was, that was all she could think of to say.

*Please let him kiss me.*

He took a curl and wrapped it around his finger, then let it go. His palm cradled the nape of her neck. If he didn't kiss her, she would go mad. "What about music?"

Music? Why were they talking about music when they should be kissing? "I am very fond of Mr. Pleyel."

One hand held her waist, and the other played gently with her curls. "I prefer Storace and Beethoven."

His breath tickled her ear. They were close, so close. If she moved an inch, her skirts would touch his boots. If he then moved, their bodies would touch. She tried to keep herself from sinking into him. A little voice urged caution, but a moment later she couldn't hear it over the racing of her blood.

With one finger he lifted her chin. And his lips were close, so close to hers.

*Yes, yes, yes!* She closed her eyes, knowing it was finally going to happen.

"Miss," a footman called from the other side of the hedge. "Her ladyship says you must dress if you're not to be late for your ride."

"I'll be along in a moment." Elizabeth was going to murder her aunt. She searched Harrington's eyes. They held a heat she had never seen in them before. "I am sorry."

"As am I." Instead of stepping back, he brushed his lips lightly across hers. Not a kiss, but the promise of one. It was as if he had lit a spark in her, and she wanted what would come next. "I shall see you this evening."

"I look forward to it." Perhaps then she could experience her first kiss.

Harrington's smile—sweet and sad at the same time—touched her very soul. "We should go before your brother comes looking for you."

"Of course," she answered by rote. She had, apparently, forgotten how to think. No one had told her about that part. Her friends should have told her about thinking of nothing but kisses. Or not being able to think when kisses might be on offer.

Placing her hand on his arm, he led them out of the garden and into the parlor. Gavin was there to walk Harrington to the front door. They would have no more private time together until later. She sighed as they left the room.

"I take it that means all went well?" her aunt asked.

"Better than I could have hoped." Elizabeth raised her fingers to her lips. "Much better than I had hoped."

From his behavior last evening, she had never dreamed he wanted to kiss her. And for the first time he had asked about her, and they had actually talked. Elizabeth felt as if she was walking on air, or clouds. Had she fallen in love so easily?

She glanced at the clock. She had fifteen minutes to change for her ride with Lord Littleton, an airing she now had no wish to make.

"Lizzy." Her brother's voice brought her out of her reverie. "What did you do to Harrington? He was almost jaunty when he left."

The question was not what she'd done to him, but what he had done to her. She shook her head. "I don't know.

Geoff left Turley House and could not resist strutting a bit. He had accomplished more with Miss Turley—Elizabeth. He was certain he could now think of her by her first name—

in the past two hours than he had in the last two weeks. Not only did he know her favorite color—pink—which flowers she preferred—pink roses—and her favorite composer—Pleyel, but he had almost kissed her, and she had allowed it. Indeed, Elizabeth responded as if she'd wanted him to kiss her. If it hadn't been for her damn appointment with Littleton, Geoff would have kissed her, and kept kissing her until she agreed to marry him. Then she'd be his.

Still, he could not afford to be generous to Littleton. Today would be the last time he took Elizabeth riding. Geoff would make sure of that by occupying her afternoons from this day forward.

Guiltily, he remembered his reaction to what Grandmamma had said. Now that he was on his way to securing Elizabeth as his wife, he supposed he should thank her and his cousin for their advice. He would also make his intentions known to the rest of the *ton*.

He'd seen several gentlemen remaining by their ladies' sides at balls and other entertainments. He would stay by Elizabeth's side this evening and every evening thereafter. At least until they were wed. No one was going to take her away from him.

A large roan, Endicott's beast, stood held by a groom in front of the building just beyond Geoff's.

He recognized the young servant holding the horse, and said, "Once Lord Endicott has come out, run back to the stables and fetch my horse as well."

The lad pulled his forelock. "I'll be quick about it, my lord."

Geoff might not be able to take his lady riding, but he could accompany her and her escort. He grinned to himself. Littleton was not going to be a happy man.

"You look to be in much better spirits than I've seen you in lately," Endicott said as he took the reins from the groom and tossed him a coin.

"I am, indeed." The boy ran off, presumably to ready Geoff's Hercules, a large gray gelding he'd had for three years now. "I have ordered my horse to be brought around and must change. Will I see you in the Park?"

"You will. Not that I expect to find more than a bit of exercise there."

Not long afterward, Geoff guided his horse out of St. James Square and toward Hyde Park where he joined Polite Society at its finest. He was halfway around the carriage drive when he saw Elizabeth. It pleased him to note that she spent more time greeting friends than speaking to his lordship.

Threading his way through the crowd, he finally came up beside Littleton's carriage, and doffed his hat. "Good afternoon, Miss Turley, Littleton."

"Good afternoon." Elizabeth's smile grew brighter. "I did not expect to see you here."

"No?" Geoff glanced at Littleton but the man ignored him, so Geoff focused his efforts on Elizabeth. "How could I not come when all the most beautiful sights are here?"

By the way she blushed, he was sure she knew he referred to her. "Are they truly, my lord?"

He captured her gaze with his. "I am absolutely firm in my belief." For several minutes he kept pace with the curricle, chatting with Elizabeth and greeting friends and acquaintances. Once he was sure news of his interest in her would be on the tongues of all the gossips, he took his leave. "Until this evening."

She held out her hand, and he took it. "I shall look forward to our dances."

"No more than I shall." Geoff pressed his lips to her gloved fingers, wishing they were bare, wishing he was kissing her rosy lips, wishing he had her alone and to himself. Wishing—he tamped down his nascent lust. Riding a horse with a stiff cock was not comfortable.

Littleton's back was straight as a poker, and he continued to ignore Elizabeth and Geoff's conversation. With any luck, his lordship now understood that Miss Elizabeth Turley was taken.

"That went well." Elizabeth had been shocked to see Harrington in the Park today.

Not even in her dreams had she thought he would make a figure of himself by remaining by the carriage, speaking with her but not Lord Littleton. On the other hand, his lordship had not spoken with Harrington either. *He* might not have seen the raised brows and speculative glances, but she had. Everyone would be watching them tonight.

She glanced at Lord Littleton. "Do you not think Lord Harrington is coming around?"

"Sooner than I'd thought." Lord Littleton mumbled something else she did not catch.

"I beg your pardon, but I could not hear the last part."

"I'm not sure I meant for you to hear it." They had reached one of the gates. Once he drove through it, he sighed. "Your brother and I made you promise not to fall in love with me. Apparently, I should have made a promise not to fall in love with you."

"You cannot be serious." She scrambled for something to say that would ease the sudden tension between them and her blurted words. "You are not ready to marry."

"Apparently, with the right woman I am." He pulled up in front of her father's house. "I should not have told you. It has made things difficult between us. Harrington was always the gentleman you wanted, and it now appears that you shall have him." Lord Littleton took her hands in his. "However, if it goes wrong, if you discover he is not the gentleman you want, I'd ask you to consider me. I will never be more than a baron, but I'm wealthy. I have several estates, and I would do my best to make you happy."

He looked so earnest and sad. For several moments she couldn't speak. "You are a wonderful man—"

He held up one hand as he released her fingers. "You do not need to say more. I know where your heart lies."

A footman came out and helped Elizabeth down from the curricle. "Thank you. For everything."

Lord Littleton nodded then drove down the street.

"Goodness, who would have guessed?" she said more to herself than anyone else.

"Did you say something, miss?" her father's butler said.

She looked up to the top of the steps where Broadwell held the door open. "Nothing, Broadwell. Nothing at all."

Well, this had been an interesting day. Gentlemen had paid her very little attention during the Season, now two men wished to marry her. Yet, only one made her breath shorten and her heart race. Her lips still tingled where Harrington had touched them with his.

Elizabeth felt sorry for Lord Littleton. There was little worse than wanting someone who did not want you. The chances were that she would not be in London next Season, but her friends would be. She'd write to them, asking for their help finding Lord Littleton a wife worthy of the man.

The rest of the afternoon and into evening, Elizabeth couldn't settle. She tried resting, reading, and embroidery, but was too nervous to concentrate. No, that wasn't the right word. *Excited* suited her mood much better. She wanted nothing more than to spend time with Harrington. If only this evening would come sooner. Yet, it seemed as if the clock never moved, and that she had been glancing at it every few minutes instead of every hour as she thought.

"Elizabeth," her aunt said, walking into the morning room. "You are going to fag yourself to death before this evening if you do not stop pacing."

"I do not seem to be able to stop myself." Elizabeth glanced at the clock again and her aunt heaved a sigh.

"It is late notice, but, if you'd like, I shall write Harrington and ask if he wishes to take potluck with us then accompany us to the ball this evening."

"Oh, would you?" That would be wonderful. It was only just over two hours until dinner. "Do you think he will accept?"

"All I can do is send the invitation." She opened her mouth to ask when the card would be sent, but before she could say a word, Aunt continued. "Which I shall do immediately. I suggest you call for Vickers and take a bath. That should calm you down."

"Thank you." Elizabeth bussed her aunt's cheek, and repaired to her room.

Sooner than she had expected, her bath was set up and filled with warm water. She forced herself to remain in the tub until the water cooled. She tried to forget her aunt had sent Harrington an invitation to dinner, yet it didn't work.

Was he coming to care for her? Did he wish to kiss her as much as she wanted to kiss him? She had so many questions and precious few answers.

If only someone would tell her if he was joining them for dinner!

"Miss, it's time to dry off and dress." Vickers's pragmatic tone helped to soothe Elizabeth's still-frayed nerves.

Her aunt was right. All this speculating and worrying was doing her no good at all. She stepped out of the bath and took the towel her maid handed to her. After donning her chemise, stockings, stays, and petticoats, she sat while Vickers combed her hair and rearranged it.

Elizabeth paid no attention to her hair or the gown her maid chose. It was clear that Harrington was not coming. She would see him at the ball, but, clearly, despite almost kissing her today and spending time with her at the Park, he did not care enough to dine with her.

"I've never seen you so out of sorts," Vickers said. "One minute in alt and the next cast down in despair."

Elizabeth had never felt like this before. And she did not like it at all. She would tell her brother she wished to go home. Or if Papa would not have her, she'd speak to her aunt.

Several minutes later, her mind made up to leave Town, she strolled into the drawing room, and her heart stopped. Harrington was there, splendid in a dark blue jacket and breeches. His neckcloth was so artfully arranged, it must have taken ages and many cravats. How long had it taken to achieve such a masterpiece? Good Lord, she was acting like a feather-brained ninny.

Then he was with her. "Good evening."

"You came." She could have bitten her tongue off. What a stupid thing to say. "I mean—"

"I could not stay away." He kissed the palms of her hands, closing her fingers around them. "Please tell me you are delighted to see me."

"I am. Very pleased to see you." Her heart felt like it would burst out of her breast, and she had trouble forming sentences. "You look fine."

"It was kind of your aunt to invite me." He continued to hold her hands as he gazed down at her.

"I am glad she did." She would have been even happier if *anyone* had told her he would be here. For the love of Heaven. She did not even know what she was wearing. One of her pink gowns, but which one? Not that it mattered. It was too late now to change. Still, she did wish to look well to him.

# Chapter Thirteen

"You are a vision." From the moment Elizabeth had seemed to float into the room, Geoff couldn't take his eyes off her. Her pale pink gown sparkled in the candlelight, the skirt hinting at the curves beneath it. Aquamarine-tipped pins peeped out from her curls. The same stones dangled from her ears, and a large tear-shaped aquamarine hovered between her lush breasts.

The very ones he wished to touch. He would dress her in sapphires, rubies, diamonds, and pearls.

Kissing her palms was not enough; he had to touch her. He did not think he had ever wanted a woman as much as he wanted her. Best of all, she seemed to want him as well.

The pulse at the base of her neck had quickened when he'd touched her hands. Her scent mixed with her usual lavender and lemon intoxicated him. Would she taste sweet or tart? He could imagine her lips softening under his and her body heating as he kissed first her neck, then her breasts. God! He was obsessed with her breasts.

Drat it all. If he kept this up, he'd spill before he even kissed her.

"I would like to arrange a party for the theater. What plays do you like the best?"

She gazed up at him, her lips slightly parted. Her eyes had grown darker. "I prefer comedies."

"Shall I organize it?" Geoff wished he could take her alone without chaperones. "Your aunt, brother, you, and I."

Elizabeth's lips tipped up at the ends. "I should enjoy that immensely. I have not attended the theater."

"In that case, we must go. One cannot visit Town and not see a play."

The sounds of her aunt and brother talking reached them and they sprang apart. Elizabeth went to a side table where a crystal decanter set. "Would you like a glass of claret?"

"Yes, please." What he needed was a cold dip in a lake. He took the glass of wine from her. "*Everyman in His Humour* is playing at the Theater Royal. Perhaps we could attend to-morrow evening."

"We must ask my aunt. We are supposed to attend a ball, but perhaps we can send our regrets."

He had not been focused on tomorrow's ball, but the one this evening. This was the ball where she would dance twice with him—not for the first time, but for the first time after he had almost kissed her—and he would do his best to keep her by his side. "I did not forget. I merely thought you would enjoy the theater instead of another ball."

"I *would* take pleasure in attending the theater." She slid a look at the door as Lady Bristow and Gavin Turley entered the drawing room. "There you are. I thought you had for-gotten us."

"Thank you for inviting me." Geoff stepped forward and bowed to Lady Bristow. "I apologize for arriving a bit early."

"No matter, my lord." She inclined her head. "You had my niece to keep you company."

Elizabeth's cheeks grew rosy. "We have been discussing the theater. Lord Harrington invited us to accompany him to a comedy playing tomorrow evening." She poured glasses of wine for her aunt and brother, then one for herself. "Would you like to attend?"

"Indeed, I would. I had meant to take you, but we never seem to have a free evening." Her aunt took the wine and sipped. "Gavin, have you plans for tomorrow?"

"I do, but that should not stop you from attending." He shook Geoff's hand. "No need to have even numbers for the theater in this case."

"Very well." Geoff took a drink of the excellent claret. "I shall notify the manager we will attend."

No sooner had they finished their wine when dinner was announced. He had hoped that the seating would be informal, but he was disappointed. Although the table was reduced to seat four, he sat on her ladyship's right, across the table from Elizabeth who sat at her brother's right.

He soon discovered he was indeed taking potluck. The first course consisted of le potage printanier, with two removes, followed by a loin of pork, jugged hare, and baked cod in cream sauce, and three removes including French beans with almonds, and a green salad. The last course consisted of various creams and jellies. Very much what one would expect for a family dining alone. Yet, the food was superb. He could easily imagine her presiding over a much larger table of dignitaries, politicians, and foreign aristocrats.

"I must tell you, my lord," Lady Bristow said, her pride clear as she spoke. "Since her mother's death two years ago, my niece has managed not only the town house, but the country households as well."

That would explain her maturity. Elizabeth was indeed the perfect wife for him. Not only did she meet all the qualifications on his list, but there was passion between them. That was an unlooked-for boon.

He smiled at her. "It is clear you are doing exceptionally well."

"Thank you." She colored again. "I was fortunate that my mother taught me what I needed to know."

Geoff would not allow Elizabeth to make light of her talents. "I will tell you frankly that my mother taught my eldest sister, but she had a deuce of a time putting instruction to action."

She chuckled lightly and said, "In that case, I shall take credit for my labors, and thank you again, my lord."

"We will leave you gentlemen to your port," Lady Bristow said, rising.

As he watched Elizabeth follow her aunt out of the dining room, Geoff resolved to find time to be private with her at the ball. It was time to gain her agreement to wed.

The door closed behind the ladies, leaving Geoff and Turley to their port. Once the wine was poured and the decanter placed on the table, the servants withdrew.

"Have you any idea when your father will return?" Geoff planned to propose soon, and, as a minor, she would require her father's permission to marry. Her brother had said he'd been left in charge of Elizabeth, but did that mean Lord Turley had given his son a power of attorney to do all that was necessary for her to marry?

"Sometime this week, I believe." Turley twirled his glass, watching the dark wine coat the glass. "You and my sister appear to be getting on well." He held the glass up as if to inspect the ruby color. "You do know that your attentions to her this afternoon in the Park have caused talk. It is all around the clubs."

"I suspected as much." Geoff took a swallow of the port. It was a fine vintage. "I plan to ask your sister to marry me." He looked at the lady's brother. "I have reason to believe she will accept my proposal."

Turley leaned back in his chair. "If the looks she was giving you this evening are any indication, I think you may be correct. I won't stand in your way if she wants you, but I take leave to tell you that I expect her to be treated well."

"I would never mistreat a woman, especially my wife." The very idea was repulsive to Geoff. Not only that, but his family would disown him.

"That is all I ask." Turley took a swallow of wine.

Geoff had the feeling her brother would like to have said more, but he was glad Turley did not. What was between Geoff and Elizabeth would remain between them.

"We should join the ladies." Turley rose and Geoff did as well. "My aunt will want tea before we leave for the ball."

Elizabeth was persuaded by her aunt to play and sing a ballad on the pianoforte. Her playing was more technically correct than passionate, as it should be, but her voice reminded him of a lark. Clear and sweet, and just what he liked. He looked forward to evenings where she would entertain him and, later, their children.

After tea was served, their little party left for the ball. As they entered, note was taken of his arrival with her family. Although he wasn't happy to have to give her up to Littleton, who led her out for the first set, that was the man's only dance with her.

This evening, rather than bow to the wishes of his hostess, Geoff stayed with Turley and Lady Bristow while Elizabeth danced, making sure she returned to him and was by his side. When she danced with other gentlemen, he resolved not to allow his attention to wander. By the time this ball was over, the *ton* would know he was serious about making her his wife. All he had to do was convince her she wanted to wed him.

"Are you having a good time?" The supper set had ended, and Geoff glanced around for her brother or aunt. For once, neither of them was in sight.

"This has been a delightful evening." Her sky blue eyes seemed to sparkle. "Do you think we have time to visit the conservatory before we go down to supper? Lady Deauville is quite proud of it."

"I don't see why we should not." It would give him time alone with her. Time he badly wanted. "Do you know where it is?"

She pointed to the other side of the ballroom. "Through the arch near the French doors."

They made their way to the opposite side of the room, strolling through the arches that led into the conservatory. Other guests were present, but most of them were leaving. The glasshouse was rectangular, covering almost one entire side of the town house. A path looped down one side and up the other so that when Geoff and Elizabeth began their exploration, they were alone. The sound of water trickling came from one end of the room.

"It is beautiful." She glanced around, delight clear on her mien. "The lanterns are like fairy lights."

Dozens, perhaps hundreds of tiny glass lanterns hung from the trees and had been strung above. "And stars."

They greeted other guests that had come up from the second path.

"Start on the right side and you will end up here," one of the ladies said.

"Thank you." Elizabeth smiled, and they started down the path.

Halfway down the walk, Geoff stopped, facing her under a tree only a few feet taller than he was. "I have wanted to be alone with you all evening."

She peeped up at him from beneath her dusky lashes. "Have you?"

Her voice was breathy, and the pulse in her neck throbbed again. Was she nervous or excited? "Do you want to be alone with me, Elizabeth?" Her eyes widened at the use of her name. He stroked her cheek as he had earlier in the day. "May I use your name?"

"Yes, and yes." Her voice was breathy as she leaned into his touch. "What do you want me to call you?"

"Geoffrey. Very few people call me by my first name." In fact, no one did. "I would be honored if you did so."

"Geoffrey." She pronounced his name as if she was savoring the sound and how it felt as she said it. "I like it. It's a strong name."

"I want to kiss you." Desperate to kiss her was more accurate. "I've wanted to kiss you since this afternoon." And before.

He waited as she studied him. After a moment or two she rose on the tips of her toes, and reached her hands around his neck. "I want to kiss you, too."

God, she was going to be the death of him.

He clasped her waist. If he didn't have his hands firmly anchored, who knew where they would wander? Most likely all over her body, and it was too soon for that. As much as he wanted to feel her breasts, they would have to wait.

He brushed his lips against hers as he'd done after tea. She let out a soft breath and touched her mouth more firmly against his. He pressed light kisses on her lips and jaw before returning to her mouth and gently claiming her.

Her puckered lips moved under his innocently, and he knew she had never kissed another man. He was the first. He'd be the first for everything. The long dormant primitive part of him urged Geoff to find a room and take her now.

Before he lost what sense he had, he lifted his head, breaking the kiss. "Perfect."

"Are you sure?" She searched his eyes. "It was my first time."

"Absolutely." He feathered his thumb along her swollen lips. "I could not have imagined a better first kiss."

He couldn't believe he had wasted the Season chasing after Lady Charlotte when Elizabeth Turley was the lady he truly wanted. Now that he had her, he would not let her go.

Elizabeth sighed as Geoffrey's lips touched hers again. His kiss was soft, and firm, and wonderful. Her friends had been right. The way a gentleman kissed changed everything. She could not imagine kissing any other gentleman.

It was all she had ever dreamed about in a kiss. She touched his soft curls, pulling his head down to her again. His hands were on her waist, but his thumbs swept up almost touching her breasts. She wanted more. And she never wanted what they were doing to stop.

Still, they *were* at a ball, and people *were* viewing the conservatory. Someday they would be in a place where they could go on as long as they wished. Unfortunately, it was not this evening.

"We should go down to supper." Although, no matter what delicacies were offered, none of them could match his kiss.

"I suppose we should." Geoffrey—she loved saying his name—appeared to be as reluctant as she was to leave the confines of the conservatory. "Although, I would much rather remain here with you."

Frissons of pleasure swept over her. Slowly, she placed her hand on his arm, and they ambled to the far end of the glasshouse back up the other path. He opened the door to the corridor, the cooler air washing over her as they left the hotter air keeping the plants safe.

# Chapter Fourteen

"There you are, Harrington." Two older ladies that Elizabeth had seen before but had not been introduced to approached. They were both dressed in the height of fashion, but the lady in a coquelico red gown, a color few women could wear, had something about her that commanded one's attention. "I was told you were viewing the conservatory." The lady in the red gown raised a pair of jewel-studded spectacles on a stick. "You may also introduce me to the young lady."

Next to her, Geoffrey had stiffened slightly. Elizabeth tightened her fingers on her arm in an attempt to comfort him.

"Grandmamma." He bowed. "May I have the pleasure of introducing you to Miss Turley. Miss Turley, my grandmother, the Dowager Marchioness of Markham."

His grandmother! Elizabeth was not prepared to meet Geoffrey's family. She had assumed they were all in the country. Before her nerves overcame her good sense, she schooled her countenance, remembered her training, and sank into a deep curtsey. "My lady, it is a pleasure to meet you. I was unaware that Lord Harrington had relations in Town."

"Very pretty." Her ladyship nodded approvingly. "Har-

rington probably wishes we weren't always underfoot."
Without waiting for Geoffrey to respond, Lady Markham
glanced at the woman next to her. "Miss Turley, this is my
cousin and companion, Miss Covenington."

Elizabeth's curtsey was respectful but shallow. "It is a
pleasure to meet you as well, Miss Covenington."

"Have you had supper yet?" Geoffrey asked as they all
turned and began to stroll back into the ballroom.

"No," his grandmother responded. "We decided to find
you and join you for supper. I assume you have not been
down either."

"No. Miss Turley and I wanted to view the conservatory
while most of the guests were elsewhere."

Elizabeth admired how quickly he came up with an
answer to her ladyship's question. He hadn't even flushed.

"And how did you enjoy the glasshouse, Miss Turley?"
His cousin strolled with her as Geoffrey took his grandmother's arm.

"It was lovely." After the kiss, Elizabeth had barely noticed anything about the conservatory at all. "The plantings
are interesting and there are hundreds of small lanterns that
make it almost magical." There. That was a better answer
than she had thought to give. "Have you seen it?"

"Only during the day, I am sad to say. Your description of
it sounds charming. I must make a point of viewing it before
we leave this evening."

Fortunately, as she could not think of anything more to
say at the moment, they had reached the supper room.
Geoffrey found a table near the entrance, and once she and
his family were seated, he went off to the refreshment table.

"Miss Turley." The dowager focused her sharp gray eyes
on her. "What a pleasant surprise. I am very pleased to be
able to get to know you."

It was all Elizabeth could do to keep her jaw from drop-
ping. What had he told his grandmother about her? Or had

she simply noticed or heard about the attention Geoffrey was paying to her? She fought the heat rising in her neck. She would not lose her countenance, not with a woman she hoped to have as a family member and who might have a good deal of influence over Geoffrey.

"Indeed, my lady. I am happy to meet members of Lord Harrington's family." Elizabeth didn't know why it was so difficult to find a topic about which to speak. She had been trained for years in making small talk. "Do you reside in Town all year?"

"For a great deal of it. I have a house in Bath, and the Dower House in the country." Lady Markham folded her hands on the table. "This is your first Season, is it not?"

"It is. My aunt, Lady Bristow, is sponsoring me."

"I remember when both she and your mother came out," her ladyship said, fondly. "You are very like your mother. She would have been proud of you."

Mama had been an accredited beauty, which Elizabeth was not. Although she was well enough. "I wish she could have been here."

Miss Covenington reached over and patted Elizabeth's hand. "It is difficult to lose one's mother. I am not sure one ever completely recovers from the loss."

Her throat began to close painfully at the other lady's thoughtful touch. Mama's death could still bring tears to her eyes, and she did not wish that to happen this evening. "Yes, it is. I did not have enough time with her, yet she prepared me well."

"I am sure she did," Lady Markham said. "Did you know that a duke offered for her?"

Elizabeth shook her head. Her mother had told her many stories of her come out, but never that one. "I had no idea."

"Her father was not happy about it when she refused him, but she insisted on Turley. I hope they were happy."

"They were. My father has still not gotten over her death." Elizabeth did not think he ever would. Her aunt said that she reminded him too much of Mama. Then again, so did Aunt even though she and Mama were not identical twins. That was probably the reason he was always so short with her. Elizabeth straightened her shoulders. "I too shall marry for love."

"As we all should." Her ladyship nodded and exchanged a look with Miss Covenington.

Did that mean Lady Markham had married for love or that she missed not having a love match? Yet, before Elizabeth could ask, Geoffrey came back followed by a footman.

Expertly, he guided the placement of the various delicacies on the table. Once the plates had been set on the table and the champagne poured, he took the seat between her and his grandmother. "I told your aunt we were having supper with my grandmother and cousin."

"That was kind of you." Aunt and Gavin had most likely wondered where Elizabeth had got to. "Does she still plan to depart directly after supper?"

"She does. I shall escort my grandmother and cousin to their carriage at the same time." Geoffrey took a bite of an ice. "This is quite good. It is lavender."

Elizabeth tasted the one he'd brought her. "It is excellent. I wonder if Gunter's provided it."

Lady Markham and Miss Covenington opined that the ice had to have come from Gunter's. After that the conversation roamed through a variety of topics, but never once on Geoffrey's future position. It was the first Elizabeth had been in his company that he had not mentioned it at some point.

"Miss Turley," the dowager said. "I would be delighted if you would join us for tea in two days' time."

Elizabeth almost choked on the sip of wine she had just

taken, but quickly brought herself under control, and gave the only response she could. "What a wonderful idea, my lady. I am happy to join you for tea."

"Excellent." Her ladyship glanced at Geoffrey. "Harrington shall escort you."

Well, that answered the question of whether her aunt was invited as well. Obviously not.

"And I am delighted to accompany you," he said, quickly dispelling any notion that he was being imposed upon, by asking, "Shall we go driving in the Park after tea?"

Then it occurred to her that his grandmother might think that a betrothal was imminent. For some reason she could not explain, Elizabeth felt as if she were being rushed to make a commitment to him.

Not that she did not wish to wed Geoffrey. She was fairly certain she did. One could not experience the feelings she had when he had kissed her and not wish to wed a gentleman. As to that, one should not be kissing a gentleman she did not wish to wed. She merely wanted a bit more time.

On the other hand, time was not something he had. Even though he had not mentioned a date he must arrive on the Continent, she was certain it was in the very near future. Not only that, but she would have to make a decision before her father returned within the next week.

She curved her lips into a smile as Geoffrey squeezed her hand.

Three older ladies stopped to speak with his grandmother when he whispered, "I only hope the admiral is not present."

"The admiral?" Did Lady Markham have an admirer?

"Her parrot," Geoff replied in an undervoice. "To say he is embarrassing is an understatement."

"I have never seen a parrot." And Elizabeth would very much like to.

Geoffrey groaned. "At a later date, then."

Lady Markham turned her head and stared at him. "Are you disparaging Nelson again? You used to be fond of him when you were a child."

"No, my lady," Miss Covenington said. "That was Edwin. Harrington and Nelson have never got on."

Lady Markham frowned. "Was it indeed Edwin? Now that I think on it, I believe you are correct."

Who was Edwin? Apparently, Elizabeth was not to discover the answer this evening. The ladies rising took Geoffrey's attention. Elizabeth would have to remember to ask him about whom they were speaking.

Geoff signaled a footman and ordered the carriages. By the time the ladies found their wraps, and Elizabeth's family had joined them, the coaches were waiting at the bottom of the steps.

Turley had decided to attend another event, so Geoff helped Lady Bristow into the coach before turning to Elizabeth and appropriating her hand. He raised it to his lips and whispered, "I wish I could kiss you again."

Her eyes searched his for a moment. "As do I."

He kissed her fingers on by one. "I shall dream of you tonight. May I hope you will dream of me?"

He knew he was taking a risk. Mayhap pushing her too fast. Yet, she *had* kissed him.

After a few moments a small smile tugged the corners of her lips. "I do not see how I can help but to dream of you."

"That is all I can ask at the moment." He handed her into her carriage and closed the door.

"Lord Harrington," Lady Bristow said. "I am sorry to say that we will not be able to go to the theater tomorrow night. I was reminded that Lady Jersey's ball is tomorrow. It would not be wise to send our regrets after already accepting. One does not snub one of Almack's patronesses."

"I understand, my lady." He wasn't happy about it, but needs must.

He gave the coachman the order to start the carriage before striding to Grandmamma's coach to attend to her and Cousin.

The evening could not have gone better. He had been proud of Elizabeth's grace and poise when she met his grandmother and cousin. If she had been nervous—and considering his grandmother's reputation, no one could blame her if she was—it had not shown. She appeared to get on well with both his relatives. Even Grandmamma's command that Elizabeth join her for tea had not put her out of countenance in the least.

His courtship of her and the way his family was taking to her could not be going better. He knew she would find favor with his mother. She had been on the list Mama had sent. And he assumed that his father would welcome Elizabeth as well. There was nothing about her not to like.

Now that his life was back on course, it was time for more changes. "Grandmamma, I have decided to give up my rooms. I shall move back into my apartment in Markham House the day I bring Miss Turley to tea."

"We cannot discuss that in the street. Get in and we shall talk about it on the way home. I'll have my coach take you back to Jermyn Street afterward."

"As you wish." He climbed into the carriage, taking the backward-facing seat, as usual when he rode with them.

"From what I witnessed just now, I take it things are progressing well with Miss Turley." Grandmamma kept her steady gaze on him.

"I would say my courtship of her is going very well." He wondered if his grandmother had a point to make and, if so, when she would get to it.

"By the by, I like her a great deal." Grandmamma smoothed her skirts. "She will make you a splendid wife."

"She is very well informed," Cousin Apollonia added.

"I agree. I am fortunate to have found her." He was now certain she would agree to marry him. "Within the next few days, I shall ask her to marry me."

His grandmother nodded. "I shall order the rooms your father and mother had when they were first wed made ready. They are larger than your old apartment, and they are sufficient for a family when you are in Town."

Geoff was surprised that neither his grandmother nor cousin had asked if he liked Elizabeth. "Thank you for thinking of them."

He hadn't considered that his parents had had rooms in Markham House when his grandfather was still alive. Yet it made sense. His father had been with the diplomatic corps when they married and Mama had gone with him. There would have been no need for them to have their own town house for the short times they were back in England.

He wondered how long it had been since they had been redecorated. Not that it mattered. He would give Elizabeth a free hand in refurbishing them as she saw fit.

"I'll write Father as soon as she has accepted me," Geoff said, more to himself than the ladies.

"He will be pleased." Grandmamma lapsed into silence, but he could hear her thinking.

Another few minutes brought them to the town house. He jumped down, then assisted the ladies from the coach. "I'll see you in two days if not before."

"Harrington." Grandmamma took his hand. "I hope Miss Turley is the lady you truly want to marry."

"Of course she is." He bussed her cheek. "There is no reason for you to be concerned."

Moments later he was on his way to his rooms. There

was no reason to wait. He would propose tomorrow at Lady Jersey's ball. He would rather have done the deed at the theater, but Lady Bristow had recalled the ball, so, the ball it was. He might as well make it memorable by announcing their betrothal. Lady Jersey would appreciate that. As soon as possible after Elizabeth's acceptance, she would be his wife.

As usual, Nettle was waiting for Geoff when he arrived back in his rooms. "We are going to move to Markham House in the next few days."

"Very good, my lord." His valet took his coat, hat, and gloves. "Shall I resume making preparations for our departure?"

"Yes." He wondered how quickly he and Elizabeth could hold the ceremony. "Arrange our journey for ten days hence. Make arrangements for us at the Three Cups." A friend from Eton who was an officer with the 95th Rifles had recently written to say that transport from Harwich to either Ostend or the Hook of Holland was becoming increasingly difficult to find. He and his soldiers had waited over a week for a ship and a second week for the wind to be in the right quarter.

Not only did Geoff not have the time to waste, but he didn't like the idea of Elizabeth being on a ship filled with soldiers, horses, and who knew what else. It was a shame his father didn't have a yacht. "Find a captain with a ship who is willing to sail up to the River Stour and anchor up the river from Harwich until he hears from me."

"Yes, my lord." Nettle had taken out a pocket book and pencil and was making notes.

"I want the ship far enough away so that she cannot be commandeered." Geoff prayed they would not have to wait long for the right winds to make the passage to Holland.

"I'll write my father as well. He might know someone with a sailing vessel."

"Very good, my lord. I shall start on this first thing tomorrow."

And he would send more flowers—pink roses—to Elizabeth with a note telling her how much he was looking forward to their ride that afternoon and dancing with her that evening.

Tomorrow night couldn't come soon enough.

# Chapter Fifteen

Despite Geoff having arrived at the ball with Elizabeth and her family again, it seemed as if the Fates were once again against him. Every time he had tried to get Elizabeth alone, someone claimed her attention. To make it worse, the miscreant was usually a gentleman wishing to dance with her. He found himself almost growling at the last one. Unfortunately, until he had a commitment from her, he could not insist she stand up only with him.

Finally, at the end of the first waltz, which had been much too late in the evening as far as he was concerned, Geoff took Elizabeth's hand and pulled her behind the potted plants—fortunately, there were a row of them lining the wall of the ballroom near the French windows leading out to the terrace. "I need to speak with you."

Not the most romantic words, but he must remove her from the room without anyone seeing them. Once they'd made it out the doors, he hurried her to the end of the terrace where the only light came from wall sconces several feet away.

Ivy climbed the brick wall, and an ornamental tree provided a distraction for anyone glancing in their direction. He drew her deeper into the shadows. Thank God no one else had decided to make an assignation here.

Before she could catch her breath, he kissed her. Not the slow, seductive kisses he'd given her before, but one of possession. She gasped in surprise, and he swept his tongue into her mouth. Tentatively, she touched her tongue to his, and he groaned, holding her tightly against him. Slanting his head, he deepened the kiss, and a little sigh of what he prayed was delight escaped from her.

Elizabeth's hands played with the hair at the back of his neck, and he moved his hands from her waist to her breasts, easing the tempting mounds out of her stays, feathering each of her nipples with his thumbs until they were furled buds.

Geoff wanted her out of her clothing, naked and writhing beneath him. But he could only have that if she agreed to marry him.

Moving one hand down to the top of her buttocks, he caressed her, thanking God for short stays. "Do you have any idea what you do to me?"

"The same thing you do to me? Touch me again." She moaned as he rubbed her breast.

He'd removed his other hand from her breast to bring her closer, wanting her to feel how much he desired her. Yet, she probably didn't know what the hard rod she had to be feeling meant.

Geoff moaned as his cock pressed against his breeches, wanting to be released. If only to save his sanity, he had to get this proposal over with. But as he eased back, she held him tighter.

"Do not let me go." As he'd done to her, Elizabeth pressed light kisses along his jaw.

"I need to ask you something."

"Then you should not have started kissing me." She swept her hand over his buttocks—mimicking what he had done to her—and he wanted nothing more than to hold her against the wall and make her his in the most fundamental way he could.

He'd planned to go down on one knee and ask her to marry him, but if he was on his knees now, he'd be under her skirts savoring her taste. Soon, he promised himself. "Elizabeth"—he kissed her neck and down over her chest to the tempting hollow between her breasts, and licked— "will you do me the honor of being my wife?"

She stilled as if she had not expected the question. He held his breath as he waited for her to respond. Finally, she reached up, placing her hands on his cheeks, and whispered, "Yes."

Thank God, thank the Fates, and any other being that held his destiny in its hands. "You have made me the happiest of men."

Geoff breathed a sigh of relief that Elizabeth had accepted his proposal. He'd never before worked so hard for a lady's attention, and it would have devastated him if she had said no. Not only because he wanted her, but now his position with Sir Charles was secure. He was grateful he could make definite plans to leave for the Continent. They would need to marry and begin their journey to Belgium as soon as possible. Yet, to his surprise, overriding even his position was his increasing desire to make her his. He had never wanted another woman as much as he did her. His compulsion to touch Elizabeth was almost overwhelming.

Geoff had to fight his desire to throw her over his shoulder and carry her out of the ball. It was all he could do not to take her up against the wall. He needed to bed her and soon. "The music has ceased. We should go back and tell your aunt and brother."

"I suppose we should." She kissed him softly. "Before someone finds us."

Stepping back, he took a critical look at her and adjusted her bodice, fondling her breasts as he returned them to her stays and enjoying her sharp intake of breath and the look of desire in her eyes his attentions provoked. If only he could stroke her mons, he was sure she would be wet for him.

"Do I look mussed?" Geoffrey asked as if he hadn't done anything at all.

Elizabeth's breasts were heavy and swollen. Her nipples still tingled where Geoffrey had rolled them between his fingers when he covered them again. The throbbing between her legs was almost unbearable and her knees had turned to blancmange. She struggled to bring herself back under control while he caressed down her back and over her derrière. When had he become such a devil? She wished she was brave enough to caress him.

"Elizabeth, sweetheart?" Geoffrey prodded, a wicked smile on his lips. He knew exactly what he was doing to her.

Taking a breath, she straightened his cravat and ran her hand through his hair. "Not anymore."

Elizabeth placed her hand on Geoffrey's arm. Her legs were still a bit unsteady. She did not know if it was from his caresses or the fact that she was finally sure that he loved her.

He could not have said the things he did and kissed her that way unless he loved her. He had still not *told* her he loved her. That was what had made her hesitate before she had agreed to be his wife. Some men, her aunt had said, had trouble saying the words, but showed their love with deeds. Geoffrey could not be more considerate of her, and the way he kissed and touched her . . . There could not be anything better.

She was glad her friends had told her what to expect, especially the kissing with tongues part, otherwise Elizabeth would have been shocked. As it was, she reveled in Geoffrey's taste and the flames that coursed through her veins from her lips to the place between her legs. She had felt his hard length against her and was excited that he wanted her. And he had asked her to dream about him as he would dream about her. He must love her.

"Are you ready to go in?" he asked, continuing to touch her in small ways, as if now that he had started he could not stop.

Elizabeth did not wish to rejoin the ball. She would much rather have remained out here all night. "I suppose we should tell my family that we will marry."

"And my grandmother and cousin." In a matter of minutes, everyone at the ball would know.

"Will they be happy about our betrothal?" She began to worry her bottom lip. Elizabeth supposed they might be expecting Geoffrey to offer for her. Yet, that did not mean they wouldn't have liked another lady more.

"I can promise you they will be delighted." He caressed her cheek, running his thumb across her lips. "My grandmother was very taken with you."

That made her feel better. Elizabeth had never before considered how nerve-racking it was to be joining a new family.

He tucked her hand in the crook of his arm and they strolled into the ballroom. After being in the dark, the candles glowing from the chandeliers and wall sconces made the room seem brighter than before. A few people turned their heads when she and Geoff entered the room. Two middle-aged ladies both wearing turbans adorned with feathers whispered to one another. And she fought the blush rising in her cheeks.

They found Aunt and Gavin not far from the French windows. Had one or the other or both of them known what was going on?

"Have you been strolling?" Aunt asked, looking closely at Elizabeth. Nothing though, not gossiping ladies or her aunt's scrutiny, could dim her mood.

"I have been proposing," Geoffrey responded, a grin on his face.

Just like that, their betrothal was suddenly real. Elizabeth smiled at him. She had never been so happy! "And I have been accepting."

Gavin raised his glass of champagne, and said in a loud voice, "Congratulations. May I be the first to wish you happy?"

Any remaining doubts she felt left her as her brother called for more champagne and others gathered around to hear the news. Geoffrey was slapped on the back by some of the gentlemen, and a few of the ladies embraced Elizabeth.

"When is the wedding?" Lord Endicott asked.

She glanced at Geoffrey. It had to be soon. He looked at her, but did not answer. Right then, it was up to her. "As soon as a special license can be procured and an appointment with the vicar made."

There would be no time to have new gowns made. Fortunately, the pale colors of a lady just making her come out suited her. Other garments could be procured once she was on the Continent.

Elizabeth had every faith Wellington would be successful and before long Napoleon would be in a prison of some sort. And she and Geoffrey would be living the life they wanted.

"Harrington," she heard her brother say in a low voice, "we must discuss the settlement agreement soon. If you will have your information sent to my solicitor, I am certain he can have the initial contract completed by tomorrow or the next day."

"My father must approve any contract," Geoffrey said. "It would be better if you could send me your lawyer's information. He knew I wished to marry, and I believe that he has sent his requirements to his solicitor. As soon as I have your lawyer's information, I'll attend to the matter."

"Certainly," her brother agreed.

Geoffrey turned his focus back to her. "We must find my grandmother and tell her before someone else does."

"I did not expect my brother to be so loud." She winced. "That was not well done of him."

"I can't blame him." He squeezed her hand in a reassuring manner.

As they were about to excuse themselves to tell his family of their impending marriage, she heard Miss Covenington's dry voice. "I can only think of one reason there is such a crowd gathered around you."

"Are we to congratulate you?" his grandmother asked.

"If you please, ma'am," Elizabeth said, hoping Geoffrey was right.

"In that case, I wish you the best," Lady Markham said. "We will be able to discuss this at length when you visit me."

Elizabeth curtseyed and lied. "I shall look forward to it."

She did not know what it was about the Dowager Marchioness of Markham, but she scared Elizabeth to death.

The next day, Elizabeth changed her gown three times before deciding to wear the first one she had tried on. "I do not know why I am so nervous." She pressed her palms to her flushed cheeks. "It is not as if I haven't met Lady Markham before."

"There's no accounting for nerves," her maid said prosaically. "Like as not, it's that you'll be part of her family soon."

"Yes, that must be it." Or perhaps it was that she had made her decision, and her life was about to change dramatically and in very short order. "The pearls, I think."

Earlier her brother had written to their father informing him that Elizabeth and Geoffrey were to marry. Papa would be so happy that she had made a good match. She expected to find him back in Town no later than tomorrow afternoon.

Today, Geoffrey was to apply to the Archbishop's office at Doctors' Commons for the special license and speak to the vicar at Saint George's Church about the timing of the wedding. He had also planned to write to his father to instruct their family solicitor to contact Papa's solicitor regarding the settlement agreements.

She was busy as well. After writing to Lady Worthington—Elizabeth did not know exactly where her friends were at the moment—and asking her to inform Charlotte, Louisa, and Dotty of the wedding, Elizabeth had spent several hours with her aunt at the modiste. Unbeknownst to her, Aunt Bristow had arranged for the woman to begin making up a new wardrobe for her.

"Once you are married," she had said, "there is no reason for you to dress like a girl just out. A little faith and forethought was all that was needed."

"But I don't understand how she could have sewn this many gowns in such a short time," Elizabeth had replied after having her fifth dress fitted.

"As your father will not be put to the expense of another Season for you, I decided he could well afford new clothing for your married life." Aunt indicated that Elizabeth should turn around. "Aside from that, it is nearly the end of the Season, so not as many orders are coming in."

She briefly wondered if her father would agree that all these new garments were necessary, but he wasn't there to object, and by the time he received the bill, she and her aunt would be gone.

If last night had felt like she was living a dream, this morning Elizabeth felt as if she had been thrown onto the back of a runaway horse.

"If you don't stop fidgeting," her maid said, "I'll never get your hair properly done."

She wanted to say she wasn't fidgeting, but it wouldn't be true. "I'm trying." Albeit not very successfully. "Just put it in a knot and be done with it. I cannot sit any longer."

Vickers stuck a comb in Elizabeth's hair and clasped the pearls around her neck. "There."

She added a pair of earrings before her maid fitted a new bonnet on her head. A glance at the clock informed her that she still had several minutes before Geoffrey would arrive. "Have you ordered the trunks to be taken down from the attic?"

"First thing this morning. They are in the next room over. You will need more than the two you have. Do you want me to have Mr. Broadwell make arrangements for their purchase?"

"Yes, please." She quickly reconsidered. "If you wish, you may visit the shop and select the trunks and other luggage you think we shall require."

A smile appeared on her maid's face. "Yes, miss. I'd be happy to."

She hoped that the look meant Vickers planned to remain with Elizabeth. It would be nice to have one's own servants with her. "You will come with me, won't you?"

"If you want me to. There's nothing keeping me in England, and I think I'd like seeing something of Europe. Even if it's only a little bit of it."

"I do want you with me." It occurred to her that she was leaving everything she knew. She should discuss the possibility of being able to take her footman, Kenton, and her groom, Farley, with her as well. That way she would have three people she knew and trusted with her.

Somewhere a clock struck the hour. Geoffrey would be

here any moment. "I do not know when I shall return. It will be sometime before dinner."

"I'll look into the additional trunks while you're gone." Vickers handed Elizabeth her gloves.

There was so much to accomplish in such a short time. Elizabeth took a breath. She could do this.

# Chapter Sixteen

Elizabeth was standing at the top of the stairs when her father's butler opened the door to Geoffrey. As if he knew exactly where she would be, he gazed up at her and butterflies took up residence in her breast as his eyes met hers and he smiled.

He had to love her the way she loved him. If only he would say the words. On the other hand, she had not told him how she felt.

Geoffrey took her hand as she reached the bottom tread. "You are enchanting."

"Thank you." His look and his touch warmed her in a way no one or nothing had before. "You look very handsome."

"I'm glad I please you." He led her to the door. "I have a surprise for you after tea."

"Will you give me a hint?" He lifted her to the step of his phaeton, his large hands lingering on her waist.

"I shall tell you that it is a tradition in my family." He leaned forward, his lips close to her cheek. "I wish I could kiss you."

Tingles started from where he held her and spread through her body. "I would like to kiss you as well."

"Perhaps later." He helped her the rest of the way onto the seat before going around to the other side and climbing in.

Where did he think they would find a place to be alone to indulge in her new favorite pastime? They would be in his grandmother's house and after that the Park. Granted, some people made use of the paths into the woods, but she was not sure she would wish to do something that daring. "I must confess that I am a little anxious."

"You aren't alone." Geoffrey cut her a swift look. "My grandmother can be formidable when she chooses to be."

"In a way, she reminds me of Lady Bellamny." Although, actually very nice, Lady Bellamny, one of the leaders of the *ton*, had been terrorizing the younger set for years. Elizabeth always found herself being on her best behavior around the lady.

"I don't think Lady Bellamny is nearly as hard on ladies as she is gentlemen," Geoffrey retorted. "I live in dread of receiving one of her set-downs. Poor Bentley had the misfortune of receiving one, and he didn't attend a ball for a week."

"I shall simply mind my manners." Elizabeth prayed she would not do anything stupid around Lady Markham.

Geoff checked his pair for a second as two young ladies crossed the street followed by a maid. Elizabeth wasn't the only one who was nervous about what Grandmamma would do. He only prayed that she would not have that dratted bird with her and that she didn't ask him about his feelings toward Elizabeth.

He liked her a great deal, better than he had thought it possible to like a lady, but that was all he truly wanted. A wife with whom he could converse on a number of topics and with whom he could have an amiable marriage. Naturally, the passion he and Elizabeth seemed to share was important as well. He must produce an heir, and he looked forward to making their children. The sooner they could start the better.

He hadn't been able to get the taste and feel of her breasts out of his mind. He couldn't wait until she was naked and beneath him on his bed. Geoff had almost told her that earlier but thought kissing was a better thing to say. That she had been extremely receptive to his advances last evening gave him hope that she would enjoy their coupling as well as he would. Yet, he must take care not to frighten her. If he wanted her willingness to continue, he'd have to ensure that her first time was enjoyable.

While he drove his carriage through the streets, their conversation was confined to small talk about the weather and other unimportant things. That was just as well. More than half his mind was occupied with her. Whether she was with him or not, for some reason he could not seem to get Elizabeth out of his thoughts.

Every time Nettle mentioned something that needed doing or there was a decision to be made, Geoff thought of her and what she would like. There was a great deal to discuss with her and plans to be made, but before meeting with his grandmother was not the time. Afterward, they would be able to discuss their journey.

Several minutes later, he drew up in front of Markham House. All of his belongings had been carted to his family's town house earlier today. Nettle had taken care of that while Geoff had been busy writing to his father about his betrothal and to the solicitor about the settlement agreements. He did not want Turley to know that the same agreement Father had drawn up for Lady Charlotte would be used for Elizabeth. Therefore, the lawyer would have to have the contracts carefully rewritten.

By now, his valet would have made the rooms he and Elizabeth would share more habitable. After tea, Geoff planned to give Elizabeth a ring he'd selected for her from several his grandmother had at the house. Then he'd show her their apartment. And after that . . . he had hopes they would be much closer than they had already become.

Everything was proceeding as it should, and his life was in order again. As long as nothing happened to put a spoke in his wheel, he'd be fine.

"Here we are." He was pleased his voice didn't reflect how nervous he was. The worst of it was that he had no idea why he should be at all worried. It was not the first time Elizabeth and his grandmother had met. Geoff gave himself a shake. Nothing could possibly go wrong.

Elizabeth smiled at Geoffrey as he lifted her from the phaeton. When her feet touched the pavement, he held out his arm. Instead of simply placing her fingers on his arm, she tucked her hand in the crook. "I am ready." She lied. She was not at all prepared for this meeting. Praying she was making a mountain out of a molehill, she said, "Lead on. We would not wish to be late."

An elderly butler, whom Elizabeth was certain would fall over at any minute, bowed as he opened the door. "My lord, miss, her ladyship is waiting in the back drawing room for you."

"Thank you, Gibson. We do not need to be announced. Her ladyship has already met Miss Turley, and this is now my home as well."

"Yes, my lord. If you insist." Even though the older man had acquiesced, it was clear he was not happy about it. In what she was certain the butler thought was an inaudible voice, he muttered, "I shall never grow used to modern manners."

A burble of laughter rose and Elizabeth pressed her lips firmly together. If Geoffrey insisting they not be announced upset poor Gibson so much, her laugher would not help matters.

"I dare say no one is asking you to," Geoffrey said diplomatically.

He led her down the corridor on the left of the hall, and when they were out of hearing, said, "He is going to fall down dead one day."

"I suppose we all will," she replied. "What I do not understand is why he has not been retired."

"Yes, well, that is exactly what I said, and I was told it would lead to his early demise."

"Thank you for telling me." She would make a point of not mentioning her opinions on her ladyship's butler.

"If my father spent more time in Town, I daresay he would demand someone less . . . er, with more vigor. But he is not. Therefore, Grandmamma rules the roost here, and shall continue to do so for several years yet."

Elizabeth nodded. "I understand. It makes little sense to upset her for no reason."

"Precisely." He gave her a smile that had nothing to do with lessons and everything to do with touching. "Let us beard the beast."

"Geoffrey, you shall not speak of your grandmother like that."

He gave her a boyish grin. "Just don't peach on me."

"As if I ever would." She smiled back.

When had her life become so wonderful? She had been so concerned that he did not want *her,* and any lady would do, but his behavior had changed dramatically for the better after Gavin and Lord Littleton played their little game.

Poor Lord Littleton. She hoped he found another lady. He was really a very nice man.

They entered the back drawing room and the knot that had grown in her stomach unfurled when she saw Lady Markham smile.

She came forward to greet them. "How lovely to see you, my dear." She bussed Elizabeth's cheek. "Thank you for bringing her, Harrington. Please have a seat. Tea shall be here directly."

"Thank you for inviting me, ma'am. This room is beautiful." The walls were covered with a large floral print on a cream silk. Leaf green curtains softened the long windows, outside of which yellow roses grew. The furniture was in the neoclassical style, neither too fussy nor too delicate looking.

"You already know my cousin and companion, Apollonia," the dowager said.

"Yes, indeed." Elizabeth held out her hand. "How do you do?"

"Very well, thank you." Apollonia glanced at Geoffrey. "I can see the two of you are doing well, too."

For no reason at all, warmth rose up Elizabeth's neck and entered her cheeks.

"We are." Geoffrey bussed his cousin's cheek.

Apollonia sank onto a chair next to the sofa upon which the dowager had chosen to sit. Elizabeth and Geoffrey sat on a small chintz-covered sofa opposite the other ladies, making sure to keep at least a little distance between themselves.

Almost as soon as they had taken their places, the door opened and Gibson entered followed by a footman carrying a large tray. In addition to the teapot and cups, there were biscuits, tarts, and seed cake. The tray was placed on the low table between the sofas.

"Will you pour, my dear?" the dowager asked.

"Certainly." If this was a test, she was sure to pass it easily. She had been pouring tea for years. "Do you take sugar or milk, my lady?"

"One sugar and a dollop of milk."

"I would like two sugars and a good amount of milk," Apollonia said.

Elizabeth handed the cups to Geoffrey to give to the ladies as she fixed his tea.

He placed a piece of everything on a plate for her, then helped himself to several biscuits, a lemon tart, and a slice of seed cake.

Taking a sip of the tea, she tasted a smoky flavor. "Do you use lapsang souchong in your blend, ma'am?"

A small smile played around Lady Markham's lips. "How astute of you, my dear. I do indeed. I find it more interesting."

Elizabeth wondered if there would be more tests, but apparently her ladyship had discovered what she wished to know as the rest of the next hour passed in general conversation.

Finally, Lady Markham rose. "Harrington, I am sure you will wish to show Elizabeth where she will live when you visit us." The older lady held out her hands to her. "Welcome to the family, my dear. I am positive you will be an asset to us."

She thought that was a strange thing to say, but perhaps her ladyship referred to Geoffrey now being able to take the position with Sir Charles.

Elizabeth curtseyed. "Thank you, ma'am."

Once the ladies left, she turned to her betrothed. "What is this about our rooms?"

"We have been given the apartment my father and mother occupied when they first married. He also served as a diplomat overseas, so they were not often in residence." Geoffrey took her hands and kissed first one then the other. "That is the tradition I referred to. Would you like to see them?"

Elizabeth's heart skipped a beat. She had never before been in intimate quarters with a gentleman to whom she was not closely related. Still, she was betrothed. No one would think it was wrong for her to view her new home, such as it was. And his grandmother had suggested it. "Yes, I would like that very much."

He led her back to the hall, up the stairs, then down the corridor to the right. "My parents have the rooms at the back of the house. My grandmother has an apartment almost identical to ours on the other side."

They had only taken a few steps when he opened a door to what appeared to be a small hall with a round marble-topped table and a parquet floor. The walls were covered in a dark patterned silk. That would have to change. It made the room appear dingy.

Doors stood on the right and the left. Geoffrey opened the one on the left first. "This is your bedchamber."

She stepped into the room that was decorated in different shades of medium and dark green. "Oh, dear."

He grimaced. "It does not become you."

"No." Green was a color she could never wear and would not feel comfortable living in. "May I change it?"

"Of course." He held her hand. "One of the reasons I wanted you to see the . . . our apartment was so that you could order new decorations and hangings. I daresay, once you select the colors you wish, the redecoration could be done in very short order."

But probably not before they left. Toward the front of the chamber on the right were two doors. "Where do these lead?"

"The first one goes to your dressing room then into a shared parlor and small dining room. The second"—his eyes warmed and he got the same look he'd had when he'd kissed and fondled her—"is to a corridor leading to my chamber."

Heat rushed into her cheeks. Her hands flew to her face.

Of course he would have a bedchamber in their apartment. There was no reason for her to blush.

"Come." He drew her into his arms. "I didn't mean to shock you."

"You didn't . . . I mean, I should not have been. We will be married, after all."

Geoffrey pressed his lips to her neck and jaw. "An event to which I am looking forward."

His mouth claimed her, and she moaned, pressing into him. Yet, all too soon, he raised his head, breaking the kiss. "I'll show you the parlor. It is large enough for two sofas, some chairs, a chaise, if you'd like, and two desks."

He was right; the room was much larger than she could have imagined, and light. Long windows that opened to balconies flanked the fireplace. Even the colors—pale blue and cream—were perfect. "This is a beautiful room."

"I've always thought so." He had a wistful smile as if he was remembering being in the room with pleasure.

"Did you spend much time here as a child?"

"When I was home from school during the Season. My grandfather was still alive then."

"Were you very close to him?" She had scarcely known her paternal grandfather. Her parents had always had their own houses.

"I can't say we were close, but he always managed to slip me a bonbon or something I'd like, and my parents would pretend not to notice." He walked over to a cabinet and opened the middle section. "Ha! They are still here." He took out a set of spillikins. "I hoped I'd find them. Do you play?"

"Oh, yes. My whole family becomes very competitive over spillikins."

His family did as well. "We shall have to play sometime."

Elizabeth peeped into another room. "I like the dining room as well."

The walls were covered with yellow paper that had a white

pattern running down like stripes. "And the paper appears to be new. The only one we will have to change is my bedroom and the entry."

He glanced at the clock. "The last room to show you is my bedchamber."

She swallowed and her mouth dried at the thought of going into his bedroom. Elizabeth gave herself a shake. Goodness, it was not as if he was going to throw her onto the bed and have his way with her. At least she didn't think he would. Although, if the rest of it was anything like his kisses and caresses, it would not be bad at all. In fact, it would be quite enjoyable.

Geoffrey opened the door and she entered. The first thing she saw, indeed the only thing she saw, was a massive walnut bed covered with a bright red and gold paisley duvet.

She forced herself to glance around. Two large pillows were against the headboard, but smaller, decorative pillows were scattered around. A night table stood next to one side; she could not see the other side for the bed hangings in the same red and gold. It reminded her of a description of a harem.

Unwilling to be struck dumb, Elizabeth cleared her throat and said, "It is quite grand."

Geoffrey began to laugh. "I suppose I should be grateful you didn't run screaming out the door."

"No, I could not have disgraced myself so." She began to chuckle. "I do not think it could have always been this way. The hangings look much newer than the ones in my chamber."

"I honestly have no idea. This is the first time I've been in the room. Nettle brought everything over this morning while I was out." He wrapped his arms around her. "We shall change the duvet and hangings if you like."

She shook her head. "I shall become used to it."

There was something about it that made her feel warm and a little tingly.

After kissing her lightly, Geoffrey sighed. "I will have Gibson arrange for fabric samples to be sent over for your bedchamber, and not in green."

"Perhaps I should write down what I would prefer." They went back into the parlor and she sat at the lady's desk, unsurprised to find ink, pen, and paper ready for her use.

This was a very well-run house. That made her think of the house she and Geoffrey would have. What would a foreign house be like?

Elizabeth was excited to be starting her new life. She hoped they would have children soon. Dotty and Louisa were already expecting, and Charlotte would not be far behind them.

She finished the list and handed it to Geoffrey. It would be the first time she was able to decorate without anyone second-guessing her. "I would think the housekeeper might be the most proper person to have this."

"You may be right, but you can depend on Gibson to know."

It was almost five and they were to ride in the Park. She wished she had not been so missish about the bedcover and hangings. Perhaps she and Geoffrey could have kissed and touched some more. Elizabeth would have liked that.

Still, she could not forget that that bed was where she'd spend her wedding night.

# Chapter Seventeen

Well, that hadn't worked out as well as Geoff had thought it would. He had planned to forgo the carriage ride and introduce Elizabeth to one of the benefits of married life. Instead, that damn bedcover had had her acting like a spooked filly.

After the way she had responded to him last evening, he'd thought she was ready. Obviously, he was mistaken, and it was most likely his fault. He should have taken a look at the bedchamber first. As it was, at first glance, the room reminded him of a brothel, and he'd had to resist the urge to glance up at the wooden canopy and see if there was a mirror affixed. Who the devil had picked that fabric?

As for Elizabeth, Geoff would clearly have to spend more time alone with her. Fortunately, that should not be hard to arrange. From now until they reached the Continent, he would monopolize her time.

If she was in their rooms while she selected the new fabrics—the frequent thought of her naked, her light blond hair spread around her as she sprawled on that red bedcover made his cock swell—he'd be there too, helping her. It was a shame her bedchamber was such a dismal color. Who could have known color would play such a large part in how one felt? He couldn't imagine her spending any time at all there. It must be redecorated immediately.

Curse it. He could not understand how he could be so focused on her that she filled his thoughts to the exclusion of almost everything else. And Elizabeth would be his in a way no other female had been. She would be his wife, and helpmate.

Dread filled him at the thought of losing her. He'd have to act quickly to secure her. Until they married, there was still a possibility she could jilt him. Unless he took steps, enjoyable steps, to ensure she could not leave him.

"I should tell you that I received a letter from my father earlier today. He and my mother have decided to come to Town for our wedding. M'mother doesn't want to miss seeing me married."

"That does not surprise me." She glanced out one of the parlor windows. "When will they arrive?"

"I'm not precisely sure. He failed to tell me either when they were leaving or when they'd arrive." Their visit would likely put off Geoff's departure by a few days, days he did not have to waste—even with Elizabeth agreeing to a quick wedding—if he wished to join Sir Charles as soon as possible.

"Is your mother as daunting as your grandmother?" When Geoff looked at Elizabeth, she was staring at him.

"I have never thought so. Although I suppose she could be. I have always thought of her more as a mother hen."

"A mother hen?" She chuckled. "You have raised my curiosity. I look forward to meeting her."

A footman stood at the head of the staircase. "Have my carriage brought around."

"Yes, my lord."

Once the servant had gone, he placed his palm on Elizabeth's waist. "Would you like to look at fabrics tomorrow?

We can have luncheon together here and spend the afternoon deciding what you would like."

A crease formed between her blond brows. "Can it be arranged that quickly?"

"I shall ensure it is." He felt a tremor pass through her as he placed his lips next to her ear, and she sighed. "We have a ball this evening, do we not?"

"Lady Haverstock's." The pulse at the base of Elizabeth's throat beat faster as he stroked the back of her neck.

"I want all of your waltzes that have not already been claimed." He'd be damned if he'd agree to another man holding her in his arms.

She turned her head slightly, catching his eyes with hers and giving him a coy look. "Do you, indeed, my lord?"

*Minx*. Make that no other man would touch her. "As well as any other sets that have not been claimed."

Her eyes widened. "All of them? Whatever for?"

Touching his lips to hers, he said, "So that everyone will know you are mine."

Geoff backed her into the corridor, pulling her into his arms as he did. Elizabeth slid her hands up his jacket and around his neck. "Do you believe such drastic measures are necessary? Lord Littleton left Town, and no one else is interested in me."

Geoff didn't think Elizabeth would jilt him, but he wasn't taking any chances. "I wish to spend time with you." Her eyes searched his, but in this he was being completely honest. He ran his tongue along the seam of her lips. "Open for me and let me taste you."

Pressing against him, she sought his mouth with hers. Their tongues touched, and danced, and he wanted nothing more than to carry her back to his bed. He cupped her breast, and she sighed. "We could go back into the bedroom."

Before she could answer, Gibson's voice drifted up the stairs. "Find his lordship and tell him his carriage is waiting."

Geoff was about to curse himself for ordering his phaeton, but it was for the best. After her reaction to his bed, he needed to bring Elizabeth along slowly. Let her get used to the idea, and perhaps change the bedcover and hangings.

"We should go." He tucked her arm in his. "One does not like to upset the upper servants."

"Especially when they are not yours."

"Precisely." He had learned at an early age not to distress his parent's or his mother's servants.

By the time they got to the Park, it was clear the news of their betrothal had spread.

Tom Cotton, riding on a bay mare, came up to them. He glanced at Geoff, then at Elizabeth. "I see the news is true. Congratulations on your betrothal."

"Thank you." He took Elizabeth's hand. "My dear, may I present a good friend of mine, Major Cotton. He is on his way to Brussels. Cotton, my betrothed, Miss Turley."

"Major"—she smiled—"I am delighted to meet any of Harrington's friends. I hope we will see you when we arrive in Brussels."

"I shall look forward to it, Miss Turley." Cotton bowed. "I leave tomorrow and will be on the watch for you." He looked at Geoff. "Quarters are filling up. Have you already made arrangements? If not, I'll see what I can find."

"We have, thank you." He assured his friend.

"I'll look forward to seeing you there." Cotton inclined his head. "Miss Turley, Harrington. I'll let you continue your drive."

He started the horses again as his friend rode off to a group of military gentlemen a short way from them.

"He seemed nice," Elizabeth said.

"Yes, he is. If nothing else, we'll know one person there."

"Perhaps we shall invite him to dinner." Her eyes began

to twinkle, and for an instant he was jealous of his friend. Then he realized she was looking forward to having their own home.

"We will do that." What would living with her be like?

They continued and took a turn around the Park, accepting congratulatory remarks from their acquaintances that had not been at Lady Jersey's ball last night. When he pulled up to Elizabeth's house, he remembered that she had not accepted his invitation to have luncheon with him. "Shall I come for you just before one o'clock tomorrow?"

Her smile was as bright as the sun, and he knew she remembered the time he'd forgot to press her for a commitment. "Yes, please."

When he returned home he was informed that his grandmother was in her rooms and wished to see him.

That would give him an opportunity to ask about his bedchamber. "Thank you, Gibson. I shall go directly."

Moments later, Apollonia admitted Geoff to Grandmamma's apartments. "I had almost expected you to still be here when we returned." She motioned to the table. "Please join us for tea."

He bussed her cheek. "Elizabeth and I made plans to drive in the Park."

"Yes, my dear, I am well aware of that, but I had thought—" She pulled a face. That was odd. "Well, I've probably said too much."

Too much about what? What was she up to? "By the way, I assume Mama decorated the one bedchamber in green. It is her favorite color, but who used red and gold in my bedchamber?"

His grandmother gave him such an innocent look, he knew something was going on. "Did you not like it, my dear?"

"It is rather . . . rather . . ." How did one explain to

one's grandmother that the bedchamber reminded him of a brothel?

"Enticing?" A wicked look appeared in her eyes. "Did you know that in some ancient cultures, decorating the sleeping chambers to encourage marital relations, including erotic wall murals, was considered to be entirely appropriate, and even desired?"

What the devil? Geoff felt his face getting hot. He hadn't blushed in years. "I know nothing of the sort." He really did not want to have this conversation with his *grandmother!* "Who would have told you such a thing in the first place?"

She waved her fingers in an airy fashion, and said, "Your grandfather had a wide range of friends." As if that explained it. "Nevertheless, I know you and Miss Turley have not been acquainted with each other long." Grandmamma smiled benignly. "And I thought it would help."

"Well, it didn't. She was shocked by it." That ought to teach her not to interfere.

"I have to admit I had not thought of that." Grandmamma knitted her brows for a moment before smiling again. "I am sure you will be able to overcome any fears she may have."

*"Sounds like Henry."* Squawk, squawk. *"Sounds like Henry."*

"That is quite enough from you, Nelson." She turned her attention back to Geoff. "Now, as I was about to say, I regret that poor Miss Turley was taken aback, but I am greatly surprised you were not able to calm her."

Henry? His grandfather Henry? "What did that dratted bird mean by I sound like Henry?"

*"Sounds like Henry."*

"Apollonia, please cover the admiral's cage. I cannot have him interrupting when he's in one of his moods."

"I shall have to fetch it from the morning room," his cousin said, quitting the room.

*"Kiss me here, lovey. Kiss me here. That feels good."*

What the devil? He pulled his attention from the bird and focused on its owner. "Grandmother, please answer my question."

"Yes, well." Her lips formed a moue. "You have always reminded me of your dear grandfather."

There was more to it than that. "I am quite sure Elizabeth and I can figure out our relations."

"I merely wished to help you along." His grandmother shrugged. "It worked for your grandfather."

Worked for— "I thought you had an arranged match."

"And so we did." She set the cup down. "Or so he thought," she added in an undervoice.

He almost asked what Grandmamma had meant by that last bit, but decided he didn't want to know.

"Would you please sit down?" She glared up at him. "I do not like the way you stand over one, glowering."

"You had not asked me to sit before," he protested as he lowered himself onto the chair next to her.

"That is your fault for distracting me." Geoff waited patiently while she poured another cup of tea. "Now then, as I said. We did not know each other at all well when we married. Your grandfather was extremely susceptible to certain colors and our marriage changed for the better as a result."

Based on the bedcover, it wasn't hard to guess which colors brought the greatest results. They had affected him as well. "I see."

"I doubt it," Grandmama said, holding the cup in front of her mouth. "But you shall. Now leave me to my tea. I am sure you have something you ought to be doing."

Such as enticing Elizabeth back into his bedchamber. He rose, and bowed. "Will I see you at dinner?"

"No, I am dining with friends. If you plan to attend Lady Haverstock's ball, I shall see you there."

"Elizabeth likes pink. She made a list of fabrics that I

gave to Gibson when we left," he said, before leaving the room. "And she is having luncheon here tomorrow."

"All shall be ready for her." His grandmother made a shooing motion with her hands.

*"Must leave, must leave."* The bird flapped its wings as Apollonia re-entered the parlor and placed the cover over its cage.

He had never expected to have such an embarrassing conversation with his grandmother of all people. He should never have mentioned the bedcover and hangings. But who would have guessed that she had picked the colors?

Geoff needed to walk. He took his hat from Gibson and left the house. What the deuce did Grandmother mean by her marriage changing? Unless she simply meant that—no, he was not going to think about that.

Nothing had gone the way he'd expected it to today. Not to mention that dratted bird. He hoped Elizabeth never acquired one.

# Chapter Eighteen

Elizabeth had intended to go straight to her room when she returned home, but the sounds of movement in the next chamber stirred her curiosity. She peeked in to see three new black and tan leather-covered traveling trunks. "They look well made."

"I thought you'd like them," Vickers said, opening one of the trunks. "This one has a place for shoes so that they don't have to be wrapped separately."

"How clever." She opened the other trunk and found it lined in silk. "And elegant. I am surprised you found them already made." She thought her maid would come back with regular wooden chests.

"They were ordered by a lady who was going to Europe and decided at the last minute she'd stay in England instead. I can tell you, the merchant was happy for me to take them off his hands. I'll have Kenton paint your initials on the bottoms."

Something else that would change. Her name. Goodness, it seemed like her life was being turned upside down. Her name, her rank, and her status would all change, not to mention having a husband, a home of her own, and traveling to Brussels.

Thinking of all the new clothes her aunt ordered for her, Elizabeth asked, "Will five be enough?"

"It should be." Vickers pulled out the packing list they had drawn up, handing it to Elizabeth. "I think they'll do. If not, I'll go back to the shop."

"I see you have crossed off several items."

"That's what I've packed," her maid said.

"Very well. I shall rewrite it and give it back to you."

She took the list to her desk and ended up adding a few items. By the time she was done, it was time to dress for dinner and the subsequent ball.

Yet despite the distraction of the trunks, the news that her father was returning to Town, and the reports of the Corsican's movements, she could not get her mind off that bed— Geoffrey's bed. Her breasts grew heavy, almost as if he was touching her.

Thanks to her friends, she was aware of how intimate she would be with him. Yet, that didn't explain why her skin became so sensitive merely thinking about him and *that* bed. What would have happened if Gibson had not called for him?

After dinner, as she and her aunt drank tea, her thoughts wandered again to the bed, or rather, she and Geoffrey in the bed.

"Elizabeth, are you sure you wish to attend the ball?" her aunt asked. "You look flushed, and you would not want to take ill before your wedding."

"No, I'm fine." She applied her fan, hoping that would help. "It is a little warm in here."

Her aunt raised one brow but said nothing more. A few minutes later Geoffrey was announced.

Elizabeth rose immediately and went to him. "Good evening."

Taking her fingers in his hands he raised first one then the other, placing light kisses on them. "Are you all right?"

"It is just that the room is warm," she said loud enough for her aunt to hear. When Aunt began to draw on her gloves, Elizabeth whispered, "I cannot stop thinking about your bed."

He seemed surprised at first, but soon his eyes began to sparkle. "I think I know the reason. We can discuss it when we find some time to be alone. I believe Lady Bristow is ready to leave."

However, when they arrived at the ball, so many people stopped to congratulate them on their betrothal, they could barely make it into the ballroom before the dancing began.

Slowly, as if each knew what the other wanted, Geoffrey and Elizabeth began making their way toward the French windows. They lost her aunt somewhere between the potted plants and the orchestra. And when the second dance began, he whisked her out through the French windows and onto the stone terrace.

"I thought we would never be able to escape." She smiled up at him.

"I'm shocked there are so many people left in Town." He wrapped his arm around her waist. "This way."

Instead of going to the far side of the terrace, he led them down the steps and into the small garden. Tall posts with lanterns hanging from them marked the paths.

Geoffrey turned off the main path to another.

"Where are we going?"

"You'll see." He drew her closer to him, his arm tightening around her waist. The light grew dimmer, but the scent of night-blooming jasmine and night-blooming nicotiana filled the air. "There is a night garden, or at least that is what I think it's called. Back here."

A few moments later, they entered a small circular garden with a fountain in the middle and a bench to one side. Flowers of various sizes, all of them white, reached for the moon.

"I've never seen anything like this. How did you know about it?"

"Lady Haverstock is a friend of my mother's and described the garden when she visited earlier in the year. I hoped you would like it."

Elizabeth gazed up at him. Although the garden seemed alight, his face was still in the shadows. "And I do. Vastly. Thank you for bringing me here."

He placed his handkerchief on the bench. "It is the only place I could think of where we could be alone for a while."

She lowered herself onto the seat, being careful to sit on the handkerchief and not the stone. Geoffrey took the place next to her. They were so close one would not have been able to put a piece of paper between them.

He twined one of her curls around his index finger. "You were bothered about the cover and hangings on my bed. Shall I have them changed?"

Elizabeth leaned against him, reveling in the comfort of his large, strong body. "Not bothered, but . . . I do not know how to explain it. I could not stop thinking of it, and the more I thought of it the more my skin began to heat." She hid her face in her hands. "I know I sound silly."

"Not at all." As he stroked her back, he pressed his fingers along her spine, and she wanted to melt into a puddle. "Could it be that you were imagining what will happen in that bed? Or has no one told you?"

"Lady Merton"—suddenly Elizabeth's mouth went dry again—"told me some of what to expect."

He shifted so that he was facing her, and placed both hands on her waist. His voice hardened. "Did she upset you?"

"No, no, nothing like that. She said that it was very enjoyable with the right man." Elizabeth tried to search his eyes, but it was too dark.

"Never doubt that I am the right man, the only man for

you." Geoffrey claimed her lips, and she opened for him, tangling her tongue with his.

Tilting his head, he deepened the kiss, and she moaned. The sound came from somewhere deep inside her. Her bodice sagged; then his fingers eased her breasts from her stays. He cupped them, languidly caressing one while he took the other one into his mouth. Flames licked her skin. She held his head to her, wishing he could kiss her lips and her breasts at the same time.

Elizabeth felt as if she would combust if something did not ease the tension in that place between her legs. The throbbing grew worse, and no matter how much she wiggled, she couldn't get comfortable.

"What is it?" Geoffrey's voice was deep and seductive against her neck. "Don't be afraid or embarrassed. You can tell me, ask me anything. I am here for you."

Elizabeth's face was burning, but if she could not tell the man she would marry, then whom could she tell? "Between my legs. That place . . ."

"Ah, I understand. Allow me to make you more comfortable." He lifted her onto his lap. "There is no need to be embarrassed."

The fingers of one hand continued to stroke her breast, as his tongue stroked hers. If it hadn't been for the feel of cooler air, she wouldn't have known her skirts were rising. Suddenly, his hand cupped her mons, pressing against her, inviting her to press against him. Geoffrey found the nubbin Elizabeth had been told about, and began gently stroking it.

"You are so wet," he whispered. "Let go. Come for me."

He slipped his finger into her channel, and suddenly, the tension that had gripped her exploded and her body felt as if waves where crashing over it.

"Elizabeth? Sweetheart?" He held her tightly against his body. "Are you all right?"

"I'm fine. No. I'm better than fine. Much better. I am

excellent." She flung her arms around his neck and kissed him. "I think the bedcovers are exactly the right color."

Geoffrey barked a laugh and held her lightly as he pulled her skirts down. After lacing her gown up, they sat quietly while he held her in his lap. Eventually, he said, "We had better be getting back. Would you like to go home?"

"Yes." After experiencing such exquisite pleasure, she could not imagine staying at the ball. Perhaps he would show her more tomorrow.

Geoffrey wanted nothing more than to take Elizabeth to their apartment and make love to her. If he could have figured out a way to do it, he would have done exactly that. But he could not very well say, *My lady, I have decided to take your niece home with me but will promise to return her before dawn. Or perhaps never.*

Still, there was tomorrow, and he and Elizabeth would have all afternoon.

By the time they re-entered the ballroom and found Lady Bristow, she was ready to depart as well. Claiming a headache, she did not even invite him in for tea when they reached Turley House.

"I do apologize," her ladyship said. "I rarely have a sick head, but with all the planning for the wedding, I have not rested properly. I know you said as soon as all could be arranged, but have you settled on an actual date?"

"I shall procure the special license in the morning." Geoff had planned to do that today, but the settlement agreements took all his time. "My parents should arrive the day after that." He glanced at Elizabeth and mouthed three. She nodded. "In three days, we should be ready."

"Three days it is then," Lady Bristow said. "Come along, Elizabeth. You have looked flushed all evening."

Geoff thought he'd go into whoops at the saucy look his betrothed tossed him. But he assumed a suitably sober mien, and said, "Yes, my dear. You must rest."

"Yes, dear." Her words were appropriately docile, but this time the look she gave him was so sultry, he almost dragged her back into the coach. "If you insist."

"Minx," he whispered as he kissed her hand. "I have changed my mind. I'll come for you at eleven-thirty, if you have no objection." Geoff wanted Elizabeth alone with him for as long as possible.

"I'll be waiting." For some reason he could not let her go, and he slid his fingers along hers until there was nothing but air.


The next morning, Geoff arrived at the Archbishop of Canterbury's office in Doctors' Commons when the doors were unlocked at nine.

Earlier, he had found the newest copy of Debrett's to acquire the date of Elizabeth's birth and her full name. Elizabeth Catherine Amelia Turley. The name fit her. That her birthday was on the twenty-ninth of June he must remember. It wouldn't do to forget one's wife's birthday. He winced thinking about the time Father had forgotten Mama's birthday. He had spent months making it up to her.

"Good morning," he said to the clerk who looked as if he could use another cup of tea. "I would like to arrange a special license."

The young man pulled out a piece of paper. "May I have your full name and that of the lady?"

"Geoffrey Augustus Charles, Earl of Harrington. My betrothed is Elizabeth Catherine Amelia Turley . . ." He gave the clerk the names of their fathers as well.

"The lady is a minor," the clerk said. "Do you have the permission of her father or guardian?"

"Yes. Viscount Turley has given his permission and the settlement documents have been signed." Which was the only reason Geoff had not procured the license yesterday.

He'd been surprised and relieved at how generous his father had been. Turley had methodically reviewed the documents Geoff's father had sent, many times stopping and asking for clarification. In the end, he signed the settlements without asking for any changes.

"If you could return in an hour, I shall have the license prepared for you."

Geoff glanced around and found four chairs set against a wall. "I'll wait." The clerk sighed. He was about ready to give the young man a piece of his mind when he thought better of it. Becoming angry would not do him any good and might make getting the license take even longer. "I do not have any other business in this area, and the wedding is the day after tomorrow. I am taking a post with Sir Charles Stuart and must leave for the Continent immediately after." Geoff swallowed his gore. "I would appreciate any help you can give me."

The clerk studied him for a moment and said, "My brother is with the Life Guards. When you get to Belgium—"

"If you will write down his name," he said, interrupting the man, "I will make a point of looking him up and send you word." His younger brother, Rob, who was still at Eton, was bound for the army in another year. Geoff thanked the deity that his brother was not going on this campaign.

"Thank you. He does not write as often as he could." The clerk pulled out another piece of paper and began to write.

When the young man was finished, he disappeared through a door and Geoff could do nothing but wait. Yet, it was not long before the clerk returned.

"Here you are." Geoff took the papers the young man handed him. He perused the license, then read the second sheet. "Hawksworth. What the devil is the Duke of Somerset's heir doing in the army?"

The clerk sighed again. "You have obviously never met my

father." The young man held out his hand. "I'm Septimius Trevor."

"Lord Septimius, I promise I shall send you word." Even if he had to hunt down the man's commander.

"That is all any of us can ask. Thank you again." Lord Septimius had a ghost of a smile on his countenance.

Geoff arrived back at Markham House less than an hour later. "Nettle," Geoff called as he strolled into his apartments.

"I'll be right there, my lord." A few moments later his valet appeared, appearing somewhat put upon. "My apologies, my lord, there was some difficulty with the laundress, but that is none of your concern."

If they were staying here longer, Geoff thought it might be his concern. His valet had been with him for years and was never out of sorts. He took out the special license. "See that this is put where we can find it for the wedding."

Nettle glanced at the document. "I'll put it in your jewel box. And the wedding, my lord?"

"The day after tomorrow, God willing. I hope to depart the following morning."

"Very good. I shall have everything in readiness."

"I know you will." The clock chimed eleven. "I am going to fetch Miss Turley so that she can select fabrics after lunch. Please make sure they are in the countess's bedchamber. Tell Cook that I will have a guest for luncheon and wish to eat at noon instead of one. After that, you may have a free afternoon."

Nettle bowed and returned to the dressing room, and Geoff started off to Elizabeth's house. After today, they would have luncheon in their own dining room. He couldn't wait until she was with him permanently.

# Chapter Nineteen

Elizabeth glanced at the clock once again. In only a matter of minutes, Geoffrey would be here to collect her. Unfortunately, her father had arrived home two hours ago and was going on and on and on about how he had not yet met Lord Harrington. Good Lord! She did not recall that he had met Lord Merton, but her father had been ready to throw her into his arms.

Papa had given her brother his power of attorney to act with regard to her betrothal to Geoffrey, and Gavin had done exactly as he should, but Papa had—for reasons known only to him—taken umbrage. Her brother was calmly but firmly reminding their father of that fact.

Papa's back was to her and the door. She rose slowly and began to inch her way out of the room.

She was almost there when her father turned. "Elizabeth." Drat! If she did not leave, she would be late. "What arc you still doing here? This cannot concern you."

Her fist clenched, and she opened her mouth to argue that her settlement agreement and her marriage were most certainly of interest to her, then realized she had been excused.

Not that it mattered. Gavin had explained the contract to

her. And, at this point, there was nothing her father could do to ruin her wedding. "Of course, Papa."

She fled the drawing room. Vickers was ready with Elizabeth's bonnet, gloves, and shawl. A few moments later, she was in the hall. Fortunately, one of the footmen was there instead of the butler. "I am expecting Lord Harrington. Please open the door the moment he arrives. He will not need to be announced as we shall be departing immediately."

"Yes, miss, but I think his lordship is here now."

She glanced out the sidelight window. He was in the process of bringing his phaeton to a stop. If only she could run out to meet him. Glancing behind, she breathed a sigh of relief that the door to the morning room was still closed. With any luck at all, she should be able to leave before her father saw her. Elizabeth did not want Papa to meet Geoffrey when he was in one of his moods.

As she had instructed, when Geoffrey reached the door, the servant opened it. "My lord." She smiled at him. "Imagine us both being so timely. Shall we go?"

He held out his arm and, smiling brightly, Elizabeth took it. "I am so looking forward to the fabric samples."

Geoffrey lifted her onto the phaeton and went around to the other side. Once he had the ribbons in his hands, he slid her a look. "I think I know you well enough to ascertain when something is not right. What is it?"

She played with the fringe on her shawl for a moment, trying to decide what to say. "It is nothing that need concern you."

"Everything that upsets you matters to me." He glanced at his horses then turned his attention back to her. "I would not like us to begin our life together with secrets."

Elizabeth closed her eyes for a moment and tried to tell herself her father was not his concern, but he would have to meet Papa eventually. In two days time, as it happened. "My father returned early this morning and is in a temper. When I left, he was shouting at poor Gavin."

"Is he usually difficult to get along with?"

"Since my mother's death"—she blew out a breath— "almost anything can set him off. He has become irritable and morose. He will give my brother something to do, then complain that he did it. I no longer know what to expect from him and neither does poor Gavin."

Geoffrey placed one gloved hand on hers. "In that case, we shall hope he does not visit too often. If he insulted you in any way, I should be forced to tell him what I thought."

Other than her brother, she had never had anyone who would take her side without a reason. "Would you truly?"

"Of course. I'm your husband." His fingers tightened around hers. "Or I soon shall be."

His loyalty to her was a surprise. She had not expected it, but perhaps she should have. Tears of joy pricked her eyes and she blinked them away.

Turning her hand, she clasped his larger one. "As I shall be your wife."

A few moments later, he pulled the horses to a stop in front of his family's town house. As he had before, he lifted her down, but this time it was a slow slide along his body. Memories from the night before came rushing back. What would it be like to be in their apartments where no one would interrupt them? Would he show her what being his was like?

"I shall not need my carriage again until after tea," Geoffrey said to the butler. He led her down the corridor on the left to a small dining room. The table was set for two. "Is my grandmother joining us?" he asked the footman.

"No, my lord. Her ladyship and Miss Covenington are out and do not intend to return until late this afternoon."

That was good news. Even though Elizabeth liked the dowager and her companion, she was glad to have Geoffrey to herself.

The room had three long windows onto a side garden. The table had one place setting at the end and the other next to it on the side. He pulled out the chair next to the head of the table for her.

Once he had taken his place, and bowls of white soup had been served, she asked, "What did you do this morning?"

He grinned. "I went to the Archbishop's office and obtained our special license."

"I would love to see it." She was really going to marry him.

Well, that was a silly thought. She wouldn't be here eating luncheon alone with Geoffrey if they were not going to wed. Having the license merely made it more certain to her.

Elizabeth had heard of special licenses, of course. Her three closest friends had been married by them, yet she had never had reason to look at one, and she wanted to see hers.

"It's in my room. I'll show it to you when we go up to our apartment."

Immediately an image of the bed invaded her mind, and her body started to tingle. "Perfect."

Bread, cold meats, cheeses, and a green salad followed. He told her of the arrangements he had put in place for their travel to Harwich and then on to Ostend. "We can reach Harwich in one hard day, if you do not mind spending that much time in the coach."

"Not at all. I enjoy traveling." The two days she and Gavin had spent making the journey to Town had been wonderful. She'd loved every part of the trip. The inns, watching the mail coaches, even the sometimes bad roads.

"Excellent." Geoffrey spread mustard onto a piece of ham. "I shall instruct my valet to arrange for luncheon to be served in Chelmsford. That is our halfway point."

"If I may"—with both his mother and grandmother in residence, Elizabeth did not wish to overstep—"I shall ask your cook to pack a basket for us. I imagine we shall have to leave quite early."

"You may order things as you wish for our journey, our rooms, and for the houses in which we will reside." He finished the ham, glanced at her plate.

A sense of freedom infused her soul. Even though she was responsible for all her father's estate houses, and the tenants, she had never been given carte blanche as Geoffrey was offering.

Glancing at him, she caught him looking at her. She didn't know if he was done eating, or if he was simply interested in her repast. "Are you ready to go to our rooms?"

"Not unless you are. Would you like a piece of beef? It's excellent. In fact I shall have some more myself."

At first, she had felt nervous eating alone with him, but now it all seemed so normal. As if it was the most commonplace thing in the world. "Yes, I would love a slice." She tucked into the meat, and for a few moments they ate in silence. They had not spoken about their journey to Holland and Elizabeth wanted to know more about his plans. "Have you already booked our passage on a ship or will we have to wait?"

"I found a ship that arrived in England from the Caribbean not long ago. It is privately owned, and has, thus far, managed not to be conscripted to transport troops and equipment." Geoffrey flushed as if pleased with himself then grimaced. "She is on her way to Harwich with instructions to wait out of sight of the port for us to arrive."

She was glad that he had misgivings about holding a ship for their sole use. "I think that was very well done of you. After all, we can always take others along with us if necessary. And you do need to get to Sir Charles."

Geoffrey blew out a breath. "We do."

The "we" pleased her a great deal.

A few minutes later they climbed the stairs to their apartments. The minute she opened the door to her bedchamber she cringed. "I really must change the color of this room. I do, however, like the style of the furniture."

He glanced around then pointed to a low table set between a chaise on one side and two chairs on the other. "The sample books are there. Would you like to go through them alone, or shall I help?"

"Please stay. I would like your opinion." She sat on the chaise and he took the place next to her.

The swatches were arranged so that they could be removed from the books and draped or held up. After a few minutes, she had the fabric samples she liked placed on every piece of furniture in the room.

"I think I shall change these two." She swapped the small cream and pale pink stripe she had placed on the chaise with a large, airy print and placed the stripe on the chairs. "That's better. All that is left is the walls and hangings." Picking up two pieces of silk wall paper, she held them up, but they were too close for her to see how they'd look on the walls. "Will you hold these against the wall over there?" She pointed to the far wall. "Yes, I believe the cream and pink with the larger stripe is better."

Geoffrey lowered his arms, placing the swatch she had chosen on a table next to the wall. "That didn't take as long as I thought it would."

"No." She had been thinking about what she wanted since she first saw the bedchamber. Elizabeth scanned the room again. With the lighter colors it would appear much larger.

There was only one more space to decorate. She held up an elegant gold and cream stripe. "What do you think about this for the entry?"

"I like it." That had been easy.

She took the sample to the entry hall and placed it on the table. "Shall we call the housekeeper now?"

Sauntering toward her, he had a wicked glint in his blue

eyes. "I think we should discuss my bedchamber next." He drew her into his arms, kissing her thoroughly. "I thought we might see exactly how much the bedcover affects you."

"Hmm. A scientific experiment?" She slid her hands over his hard chest, and around his neck, pressing her breasts against him. Her body tingled wanting his attention.

He claimed her mouth again. "Very scientific. I can already note that your breathing has sped up."

"Are you not concerned that you will ruin your cravat? It is very nicely tied."

"I have more." He nibbled her neck and jaw. "Are you afraid?"

"No." She was too excited for words, but she was enjoying his seduction. When Elizabeth wiggled against the hard ridge hidden by his pantaloons, he groaned. She had been told it had many different names, and she wondered which one he liked best. He did say she could ask anything. "What do you call it?"

Taking her hand, he moved it over his member. "This?"

She nodded. It really was hard. Would it feel like wood or steel, perhaps?

"I call it a cock." His breathing quickened, and his voice became rougher. "What do you call it?"

"I have only heard it called a member." That seemed to be the most dignified name she had heard.

"I like your term better." Geoffrey claimed her mouth hard, as if he would perish if he could not possess her.

Elizabeth felt it swell even more under her hand, and had to ask, "May I stroke it?"

"Yes." He groaned as she slid her fingers down and back up again, keeping her touch light.

This was the part that would join them together. "It is very stiff."

"You are going to be the death of me." Geoffrey's hand cupped her breast, gently squeezing.

"I do hope not." She moved her other hand down over his derrière. "That would make for a very short marriage."

"Minx." Suddenly, he swept her up into his arms. "It's to bed with you, my dear."

Laughing, she hung on as he maneuvered through the doors and into his room where he tossed her onto the bed.

In no time at all, her shoes were off, and he pulled her to her feet. "I want to see you. All of you." Her gown sagged and a moment later fell to the floor. She raised her hands to lift her petticoats off. "Allow me. This is better than unwrapping a Christmas present."

Unable to stand still, she removed his tie pin, and then untied his cravat, pulling the long piece of linen off. Next, she unbuttoned his waistcoat, but she could not remove his jacket when he was unlacing her stays. Reaching behind her, she groped around until she found the buttons to his pantaloons, releasing them as her stays hit the floor.

He hissed sharply as his member sprang free into her hand.

"I never knew it was so soft." Like the finest satin.

"Come pull my jacket sleeves. I should have worn a looser one. At least I don't have to bother with my boots."

Elizabeth had wondered why he'd worn pumps. Now she knew. "You planned this?"

"I prayed for this." His voice was husky sounding as he stared at her. "Beautiful. I have never seen a woman as beautiful as you are."

She could not stop herself from blushing and feeling embarrassed. But she stayed still as Geoffrey explored her with his hands and eyes. Lifting her breasts and slowly running his fingers to her waist and over the swell of her hips.

She gasped as he buried his hand between her legs. "You are already wet for me."

Elizabeth had no doubt she was, but she wanted to touch him, too. "My turn." Unable to resist, she spread her fingers through the soft, curly hairs. Indulging herself in the feel of the taut skin spread over his hard muscles. "This feels wonderful. I had no idea you had hair on your chest."

"Many men do."

Spearing her fingers through his chest hair, she found the flat disks that were his nipples. She scraped one of them lightly with her teeth before licking them, then gave the other nipple the same treatment.

Geoffrey's muscles tightened as if he was having trouble holding himself still. Elizabeth moved her hands over his taut belly and reached his member, taking it into her hands. Again he groaned.

"You like this?"

"Yes. Just as you like when I stroke you between your legs." She'd had no idea it was that sensitive.

"I need you." He picked her up, kissing her as he placed her on the bed. "I wondered what color your nipples were. I have only seen them in the dark."

"The same color as yours." She grinned as she ran her nail over the one she could reach.

"I am trying to take this slowly," he ground out. "And you are making it very difficult."

"Should I apologize?" Even to herself, she sounded sultry.

"No. I adore that you want to touch me."

Geoffrey slid down her, his sleek well-muscled body lighting fires where he touched her. Elizabeth thought she would die of pleasure as he licked first one tightly furled nipple then the other before sucking. The ache started at the apex of her thighs, and she rubbed against him, like a cat.

"Do not stop." She tried to pull him back up and he chuckled when he released her breasts and moved his lips down over her stomach. Licking and nibbling as he went lower.

His broad shoulders spread her legs apart. Then he licked her *there*. The sensation was so exquisite, her body lifted off the bed, but Geoffrey held her down. The aching tension was stronger than it had been even last night. If she didn't come soon she was sure she would die of wanting.

He entered her with his finger. "Come for me, my sweet."

Waves crashed over her as she convulsed around him. Then she felt his member at her entrance, nudging, and tried not to tense. She knew this part would hurt, but not for long. She had to remember that.

"Please forgive me." Geoffrey kissed her. "There is no other way."

"I know." She was ready, Elizabeth told herself.

He deepened the kiss, and she tried to concentrate on tasting him until a sharp pain edged the pleasure aside. His hand moved between them and he rubbed the spot he'd rubbed last night. Soon desire spread through her and he moved thrusting inside her, and she wrapped her legs around him. This time when she came it was from even deeper inside, and she never wanted to let him go.

# Chapter Twenty

Elizabeth contracted around Geoffrey, bringing him to completion, and knew he had died and gone to Heaven. It must be because she would be his wife that he experienced so much satisfaction mating with her. Nay, happiness. He did not ever remember wanting a woman as much as he wanted her. Strangely, he desired her even more now than before.

He had given a great deal of thought to what he could do to lessen the pain she would experience, and he hoped he had succeeded.

Nuzzling her hair, he asked, "Are you all right?"

She turned her head, brushing her swollen lips against his. "I am better than I expected to be. It won't hurt the next time, will it?"

"No. It will be much better." He rolled off her, tucking her next to him before reaching for the cloth and bowl of water he had placed on his night table. He pressed the cloth gently to her nether parts before wiping himself and putting the linen back in the bowl.

Her hand lay on his chest, and Geoff tried to think of something to say, some conversation to start. He knew women liked to talk after copulation. But what would she wish to discuss? Then her breathing deepened.

*Damn. She is asleep.*

Geoff had never had a woman do that before. Now he would have to be the one to watch the time. They had hours yet. They would, however, be expected to join his grandmother for tea. And the housekeeper still had to come and take notes on which fabrics Elizabeth wanted and where.

They would have to dress soon. He could play lady's maid for her, but she, likely, had no idea how to help him. Although, it couldn't be that difficult. Still, he ought not to have let Nettle have the entire afternoon off.

One of her curls tickled his jaw. He'd wanted to take her hair down, but they had been so hot for each other, he'd forgotten. Carefully, he removed the ribbon that was threaded through her curls. Next he dropped the pearl-tipped pins on his night table. He found as many of the rest of the pins as he could before running his fingers through her hair, loosening it. Taking one lock, he pulled it down to her waist and let it go. Marveling at how it sprang to the middle of her back.

It became cooler in the room, but they were on top of the bedcover. Reaching over her slender shoulder, he pulled the fabric to him and flipped it over her. When she snuggled closer, Geoff tightened his hold. He'd never been this content with a woman. Generally, he wanted a short nap and couldn't wait to leave.

If only they could remain here the rest of the afternoon. Hell, the rest of the night and all day tomorrow.

Sometime later, a knock sounded at the bedroom door. Who the devil could that be? "I left instructions we were not to be disturbed."

"My lord." Nettle's voice filtered through the door. "Your parents will be here within the hour. His lordship's and her ladyship's valet and lady's maid have just arrived."

*Deuce take it!*

Geoff thought they would arrive just before the wedding. "That's devilish bad timing." Then he remembered he'd given his valet the afternoon off. "What are you doing here?"

"I had nothing else to do." Nettle sounded apologetic. "So I thought I would make the acquaintance of Miss Turley's dresser. She wished to view the dressing room. May I enter, my lord?"

The door opened a crack. "No! Give me a few moments." At least Nettle had knocked. Geoff shook Elizabeth's shoulder. "Sweetheart, you have to wake up."

Her eyes fluttered open. "Is something wrong?"

*You could say that.* "My parents are about to descend upon us."

She glanced around the room as if looking for someplace to hide. "What are we going to do? They cannot see me like this."

"Fortuitously, your maid is here." She opened her mouth, but he hurried on. "She can tell you how that happened." Jumping out of bed, he looked for her chemise and found it across the room on the floor. "Here." He handed it to her. "Put this on and I'll help you to your dressing room. We should have just enough time to dress and call the house-keeper."

Elizabeth nodded as Geoffrey assisted her with her stays and petticoats and gathered up the rest of her clothing. As promised, Vickers was waiting in the dressing room. Thankfully, without comment, she took one look at Elizabeth and began to help her with her gown.

It wasn't until her maid was rearranging her hair that Vickers finally spoke. "It's a fine dressing room. I'm glad Mr. Nettle took the time to introduce himself and agreed to let me come look at it." One giggle escaped Elizabeth and the others followed until she was laughing so hard, tears came to her eyes. "Sit still, miss. I'll never get your hair right if you keep moving."

She struggled to get herself back under control. "I cannot tell you how happy *I* am that you are here."

"We don't need to discuss that. You're betrothed, after all, and will be wed soon enough."

Just as Elizabeth rose from the table, Geoffrey ambled into the room, coming straight to her and kissing her on her cheek. "The housekeeper will be here any moment. Please do not ask me her name, because I don't know it. She has only been here a few years."

"In that case, we shall meet her at the same time."

Vickers harrumphed as she picked up the comb she had got from somewhere. "I'll be in the dressing room for the next few minutes, but I expect Mr. Nettle will want to introduce me to the rest of the staff."

Elizabeth's cheeks flooded with heat. Did the whole house know what she and Geoffrey had been doing?

"If you can stop blushing, no one will take any interest in what you and his lordship were up to." With that piece of advice, her maid strode out of the bedchamber.

"Thank you," she managed to choke out.

Geoffrey turned her around and into his arms, his face full of concern. "Are you unhappy that we—"

"No." She placed her fingers over his lips. "Never. I was simply shocked to hear your parents would arrive so soon."

"As was I." Bending his head, he kissed her. "Thank God, our servants are here. I don't know that we could have been fully dressed and ready to greet them if they were not." A knock came on the door. "That will be the housekeeper."

A few minutes later, Mrs. Droughty, the housekeeper, was taking notes and exclaiming over the changes Elizabeth was making. "I only wish you could see the changes before you leave, miss. If there is any way to make that happen, I'll do it. You have my word."

No sooner had the housekeeper left, than the house seemed to come alive with servants bustling about.

"Shall we go downstairs?" Geoff held out his arm. "I believe my parents have arrived."

She smoothed her skirts before placing her fingers on his arm. "I hope they like me."

"How could they not like you?" He gave her a smile meant to reassure. Still, Elizabeth was nervous.

They could very easily not like her. She was well aware that he'd had to travel to his family's estate to receive permission to marry Charlotte who was an earl's daughter with a large dowry. Elizabeth's father was a viscount, and her dowry was modest in comparison.

It was not as if Lord Markham could stop the wedding. No gentleman would cry off absent malfeasance on the part of the lady. And she had done nothing wrong. Not only that, but the settlement agreements had been signed, and Geoffrey had the special license. The one she'd wanted to see and hadn't had the chance to look at.

Still, if his parents did not like her, they could cause problems. No one was more aware than she of the misery an unhappy parent could and did cause. Still, they would be overseas for several years. And if she could give him an heir his parents might like her better.

Elizabeth gnawed on her lower lip. Trunks of all sorts were being carried out of the hall. She and Geoffrey had just reached the bottom step when a fashionable lady with blond hair stepped through the door, followed by an equally fashionable gentleman with light brown hair. Geoffrey had his mother's coloring, but looked almost exactly like his father.

Lady Markham glanced up. "Harrington, and this must be Miss Turley." Her ladyship held out her hands to Elizabeth. "I am delighted you are here. Do let me welcome you to the family, my dear."

For a moment she was so shocked, she could do nothing,

but Geoffrey led her forward, slipping an arm around her as they approached his mother. "Elizabeth has spent the last several minutes convincing herself you would be disappointed in her."

Really, she could have hit him. "How—"

"You're biting your lip raw," he whispered.

"Oh, my dear child!" Suddenly, she was smothered in a warm lavender-scented embrace. "You need not have worried. We are thrilled with Harrington's choice of bride." Lady Markham stepped back. "How could we not be? My mother-in-law writes that you are everything we would wish for in a daughter. She was extremely impressed with you." Her ladyship hugged Elizabeth again. "I hope I may call you Elizabeth." Not waiting for a reply, she narrowed her eyes at Geoffrey. "That was not well done of you to expose Elizabeth so. Do not do it again."

Elizabeth bit off a laugh as he took on a suitably humble mien. "Yes, Mother."

"At least I am not the only male to incur your mother's wrath," Lord Markham drawled as he strolled toward them. "Welcome to the family, my dear. We are indeed pleased you agreed to wed our feckless son."

Allowed out of Lady Markham's embrace, Elizabeth curtseyed to her future father-in-law. "Thank you, sir. I am happy to finally meet you."

"Now then," her ladyship said, "I know it is early for tea, but I am parched and hungry. We shall meet you in the morning room as soon as we have had a chance to wash and change. Elizabeth, I wish to hear about the changes you plan to make to that dreadful dark green room. I do not know what I was thinking when I had it done in such dismal colors. I am sure you will make it much prettier."

Her ladyship was still talking as she ascended the stairs, this time to her lady's maid who had come out on the landing.

Elizabeth felt as if she had just been in the middle of a whirlwind.

"She is very energetical."

"You have no idea. She was the one who would tramp around the home wood with us and never tired. We visited the Lake District one year and she wore us all out." Geoffrey held her hand as he led her toward the back of the house. "You see why I said you had nothing to worry about."

"I suppose not, but I agree with your mother. I wanted to hit you when you told her how nervous I was."

"Did she wish to strike me?" He tilted his head as if he was thinking about the idea, then said, "I believe you may be right. Fortunately, she would never do so." He smiled ruefully. "She decided years ago I was too old for spankings. Although, she found other ways to make me regret some of the things I got into."

This was a side of Geoffrey she had never seen before and Elizabeth liked it. "I will have your word, my lord."

"Yes, of course. I shall never embarrass you again. At least not around others." He pulled her to him. "When we are alone, that might be another matter."

She leaned back and raised her brows. "I beg your pardon?"

"I meant something you have not experienced before in our bed." His voice caressed her like velvet, and his mouth claimed hers.

It wasn't until she heard footsteps that they broke apart. This time she wasn't the only one who was flushed. Her wedding day, or rather night, could not come soon enough.

His parents entered the parlor followed by two footmen carrying trays. Lady Markham patted the space on one of the small sofas. "Elizabeth, please sit with me. I want to hear all about your plans to change your bedchamber and for the wedding."

After receiving their cups of tea and plates of cake and

tarts, Geoffrey and his father took chairs at a small round burled walnut table.

After she described the fabrics to her ladyship and confessed that, other than the date of the wedding, she knew nothing at all, Lady Markham raised her voice, "Harrington, I understand you have the license, but did you remember to speak to a clergyman?"

His eyes widened, and his jaw dropped. "I knew there was something I forgot to do. I am an idiot."

"Yes, well, we can discuss that later. However, I am quite certain both Elizabeth and I will have no trouble agreeing with you." Elizabeth pressed her lips firmly together to keep a burble of laughter from escaping. She had laughed more today than she had since her mother had died. "My brother Richard," her ladyship continued, "is in Town for a few days. I'll send a note round to him asking if he will perform the service." Lady Markham turned back to Elizabeth. "Please tell me that you will not object to having the service here. If it is nice we can have the service in the garden. One of the benefits of marrying by special license is that one can do what one wishes to do. It is a shame we will not have time to plan a large wedding breakfast, but I do understand the time constraints involved."

She had been admiring the view of the garden. The flowers were all in bloom and the small fountain was perfectly placed. Like a jewel in a box. A garden wedding sounded lovely.

She wondered what her aunt would say. "Not at all."

"Wonderful." Her ladyship smiled broadly. "I shall write to my brother now."

Putting her words into action, she immediately went to a cherry writing table, took out a piece of pressed paper, dipped a quill into the standish, and began to write.

Once she had finished the missive, she glanced at Elizabeth. "I would like to invite you and your aunt, whom I have not seen in years, to dinner, but I am afraid it is too late in the day." Lady Markham pulled a face. "I learned never to upset one's cook. Would she be willing to join us for tea this evening? Naturally, if your brother or father would like to come, they are welcome as well."

"You're right." Elizabeth chuckled. "Our cook would not be happy. I do think my aunt would be delighted to join you for tea."

"Excellent. I shall write to her as well."

A few minutes later the letters were set off by a running footman and she and her ladyship settled in for a comfortable coze. Eventually, as all conversations seemed to do these days, the situation on the Continent arose. "Did you hear that our embassy people were denied passports to cross the frontier and had to flee?"

"I heard about it not long ago. I gather they all made it to safety," Elizabeth replied. "I cannot imagine how dangerous that must have been."

"I am immensely relieved that *I* never had to sneak out of a country," her ladyship commented.

An hour and a half later, Geoffrey drove Elizabeth home. "I truly like your parents."

"It's clear they feel the same about you." He pressed his lips together and his brow furrowed. "My father wants us to remain in Town for two more days after the ceremony. He also made arrangements for us to pause our journey overnight." He let out a breath. "I do not know how to tell him we would prefer to leave immediately."

"I do not believe you can." She would actually like to spend more time with his mother, but he needed her comfort and support, so she placed her hand on his arm. "You said we have until the middle of June. Naturally, I would like to arrive before then as well, but we have time."

"Yes, we do." Glancing at her he grinned. "And we will be able to enjoy the bed again."

Fortunately, before he could continue with a conversation that was bound to embarrass her—something he had promised not to do except when they were alone and only about one subject—they arrived at her house.

When they reached the door, instead of being told that her father wished to see her immediately upon her return, she was greeted with the news that he was out and would not be back before dinner. However, her aunt was waiting for her in the morning room.

"I shall see you this evening," Geoffrey said, before placing a kiss in her palm and wrapping her fingers around it.

"I am looking forward to it." She waited just inside the door as he drove away, then hurried up the stairs to remove her bonnet and gloves before attending to her aunt. Her marriage to Geoffrey would be perfect. How could it not be?

# Chapter Twenty-One

A few minutes later, Elizabeth entered the morning room where she found her aunt reading a book. "Good afternoon. How was your day?"

"Good afternoon to you." Her aunt glanced up from a book. "As soon as I heard your father and brother arguing, I found there were several things I had to do that took me out of the house. I understand you managed to escape as well and had a busy day. From Lady Markham's letter, it sounds as if all went well. How do you feel about it?"

"Wonderful. Choosing the fabrics and paper for my room and the entry room was easy. Harrington has given me free rein to do as I wish." Elizabeth perched on the chair closest to her aunt. "His parents arrived and I was made to feel very welcome. Lady Markham is a woman of great physical and mental energy. She said she knows you."

"She is a few years older than I. Your mother and I were introduced to her when we came out. She was very kind to all the younger ladies. I do remember her as never tiring."

It surprised Elizabeth that her ladyship was older than her aunt. Lady Markham seemed younger somehow. "Did you accept her invitation to tea?"

"Yes. As I have not seen either your brother or your father

since their contretemps this morning, I did not include them in my response."

"If Papa is in one of his moods, it is just as well that he not join us." Elizabeth would have liked her brother to come.

"That is exactly my opinion as well." Her aunt nodded her head once. "He seems to be getting worse."

She worried about who would look after her father's house and him when she was gone, but there was nothing she could do about it. Papa didn't even want her at home anymore. It was in Gavin's hands now. "I believe you're right. He did not even greet me."

Aunt handed Elizabeth a cup of tea. "I suppose I should discuss what goes on between a man and a woman with you."

She considered telling her aunt that she'd had that conversation with Dotty and Louisa, but decided not to. Aside from that, Elizabeth wanted to know what her aunt would say, and if it was different from what she had heard and experienced with Geoffrey. "What do I need to know?"

"I gather you and Harrington have at least kissed." Aunt's brows came together slightly and Elizabeth nodded. "Has he been gentle?"

"I would say gentle and passionate." Not that she would tell her aunt how passionate.

Her aunt gave her a considering look. "Has he scared you at all?"

"No. Quite the opposite." Elizabeth's cheeks became warmer.

"In that case, I am sure I can leave the rest of it to him." Rising, Aunt said, "We must dress for dinner."

Elizabeth stared at her aunt as she left the room. It was a very good thing her friends had explained what happened between men and women, and much sooner than a few days before her wedding.

* * *

Later that evening, after tea had been drunk, and the wedding discussed—Lord Richard had written a charming note to his sister claiming to be delighted to perform the wedding ceremony—Elizabeth, Aunt, and Lady Markham climbed the stairs to Elizabeth and Geoffrey's apartments.

She opened the door to her future apartment, and stopped. The wallpaper had been removed from both rooms. In her bedchamber, the bed hangings and curtains had been taken down. In fact, only the furniture had not been touched. "How on earth did you manage this?"

Lady Markham fluttered her fingers. "It was not difficult. Our footmen assisted the decorator's assistants. The new paper will be finished tomorrow, as will the hangings and curtains." Her brows lifted slightly. "I trust the furniture will be recovered as well."

"But why?" Elizabeth couldn't imagine the amount of effort that had been expended.

"Why?" her ladyship asked. "We want you to feel at home while you are here. It may not be for long, but this will be your home whenever you are in Town."

She blinked in a vain attempt to keep tears of joy from overflowing. Blotting her eyes with her handkerchief, Elizabeth vowed not to turn into a watering pot. Yet, not since her mother had died had anyone done anything half as wonderful for her. Well, aside from her aunt sponsoring her come out. "T-thank you."

When they left to rejoin the gentlemen, Aunt whispered, "I could not be more pleased for you. Harrington is behaving just as he ought. He has hardly taken his eyes off you, and her ladyship is already treating you like a daughter. Your mother would have been extremely happy."

"I hope so. I am so happy." Never in her wildest dreams could Elizabeth have imagined such a welcome from Geoffrey's parents.

Not to mention the lovemaking she experienced with

Geoffrey this afternoon. It was everything she had been told it would be. There was no doubt in her mind that they would have a wonderful life together.

When Geoffrey entered the breakfast room the next morning, he was informed that he would be spending the day with his father. Much to his displeasure, Mama had decided that she was taking Elizabeth around to her group of friends, which included the wives of current and former diplomats as well as other influential ladies, because, "You know, dear, that it is always better to know people that can assist you if needed. I fully intend that Elizabeth be well armed, as it were. Your grandmother did as much for me."

It had not occurred to him before then how frightening ladies could be. Naturally, Lady Bellamny, one of the gorgons of the *ton,* scared him to death. As she did every other right-thinking male. But his mother? A shiver ran down his spine. How had he not recognized how powerful she was?

Even though he knew he would not be able to be alone with Elizabeth, he had thought they could spend time together today. He had developed a sensory need to see her, touch her soft skin, sink into her, and hold her while she slept.

"After you break your fast," Father said, "we will go to Whitehall. There are several gentlemen I wish you to meet." Geoff felt his father's eyes on him. "Have you selected a wedding present for your bride?"

Damn. Another thing he hadn't done. It was as if being with Elizabeth made him unable to think of anything other than being with her. "No. We can stop by Rundell and Bridge. I'm sure I'll find something she will like."

He knew the ladies would likely eat luncheon at home, but before he could mention returning to join them, his father said, "We shall have luncheon at White's."

"Am I not to see my betrothed until tomorrow?" He hated that he sounded like a peevish child.

Father's lips twitched. "No. Your mother informed me that Miss Turley has a great deal to accomplish and very little time to do it. Your uncle will meet us for luncheon to discuss the ceremony. I suggest you bring the special license."

That was yet another thing he hadn't done. Elizabeth had wanted to look at the license, and he wanted to please her. If he knew Uncle Richard, and Geoff did, the man would take it with him. Nothing was turning out as Geoff had planned. His life was scampering off away from him, and he had no idea when he would be able to get it back under his control.

He spent the day meeting gentlemen he would be glad someday that he had met, and thinking about his betrothed.

Later that afternoon, when he and his father finally returned home, a letter from Captain Higgins, the skipper of the ship Geoff had hired, was waiting for him.

*Lord Harrington,*

   *I am at anchor in a bay just north of Harwich. Please send word when you depart London in care of the Ship in Felixstowe. I will arrange to meet with you.*

                    *Yr. Servant*
                    *J. Higgins*

Thank God something Geoff had put in motion was working as he'd wanted.

When Nettle had made the arrangements, he'd assured Geoff that the ship was more than large enough to carry the horses, both his and his wife's—well, she would be by then—hacks, two carriages, Elizabeth's and his servants, and all their baggage in comfort. Still, he now wished he had toured the schooner himself. If only to satisfy himself the vessel was suitable for his soon-to-be wife.

Well, there was nothing he could do about it now. And, to be fair, Nettle had never given Geoff reason to question the man's competence. Apparently, being denied Elizabeth's company had put him in a contrary mood.

With nothing else to do, he looked in on her bedchamber. Even with the knowledge that his mother and grandmother had taken a hand, his jaw almost hit the floor.

The pale pink and white wallpaper had been hung. Several of the maids were at work hemming the curtains and bed hangings, and two men were re-covering the furniture.

"Oh, my lord." The senior maid got to her feet. "It's goin' to be so pretty."

"Yes, it is." And light, and so like Elizabeth. Geoff strolled over to the bed. "You are doing fine work here."

"Thank you, my lord." The woman flushed with pleasure as did the four younger women. "We've been up since dawn working on it. We all want to welcome the new Lady Harrington to her home right and proper."

The new Lady Harrington. His chest swelled like a bantam cock's. The last Lady Harrington had been his mother. Now it was Elizabeth. "I am sure my bride will be pleased. I'll leave you to it."

"My lord," his father's under butler, Preston, said. "Mr. Turley would like to know if you are at home."

Turley here? For what? They had already signed the settlement agreements. Geoff's muscles contracted. Had something happened to Elizabeth? Surely his mother would have sent word. "I'll be down directly."

A few moments later, he entered the front parlor where Gavin Turley sat reading a newssheet. "As long as you aren't here to tell me Elizabeth has cried off, I'm glad to see you. It's been a devil of a day."

"Cry off?" Turley barked a laugh. "Not likely. Your

mother and my aunt have her firmly in hand. But you're not going to see her until tomorrow morning. I've been sent to make sure that you don't get into trouble."

It was the night before his wedding, but Geoff had no desire to be with anyone but Elizabeth, nor did he wish to be cup-shot in the morning. When he said his vows, he would be sober. "As long as it doesn't involve getting top-heavy, whoring, or excessive gambling. What do you suggest?"

Turley chuckled. "I'd be in grave danger if I tempted you to do anything more than dine at Boodle's. As long as we stay away from the tables, we should come off all right."

Before they had a chance to leave, Gibson stood at the door and announced, "The Marquis of Bentley, and Earl Endicott."

What the devil? Had everyone thought about going out except Geoff?

"Met Bentley at the door," Endicott drawled as he sauntered into the room. "Are we having a party?" Both Geoff and Turley must have appeared confused. "You know. Night before the wedding and all that."

Bentley's face lit up. "I didn't know this was a party. Harrington, you're getting married? I'm getting married, too. In Town with m'father and thought I'd come by. I wish Miss Blackacre was here. I'd introduce you. She is the lady I'm going to wed. Wonderful lady. Didn't like to leave her. Have you met her?"

Geoff shook his friends' hands, welcoming them. To Bentley, Geoff said, "I have not had the honor to meet your betrothed."

The man was one of Geoff's closest friends, but no one dithered more than Bentley. When Geoff had left Town to attend his father, Bentley had been in love with Lady Louisa Vivers—now the Duchess of Rothwell—since he'd first set his eyes on her. Yet, at some point after Geoff left, his friend became engaged to another lady. "I did hear about your betrothal. I wish you happy."

"Yes, yes." Bentley's chest puffed out. "You must meet her sometime. Miss Oriana Blackacre"—he said her name as if it was a prayer—"and I shall marry next month. Excellent lady, and she won't change the portrait gallery. Mama wouldn't like that."

What had the portrait gallery to do with anything, Geoff didn't know, and he stifled any thoughts of asking for clarification. Bentley's attempts to explain anything were often long, drawn-out affairs, with a fellow being no better informed at the end than at the beginning.

Instead, Geoff said, "I thought you were in the country until your wedding."

"Father needed to take a bolt to Town because of something in the Lords, and I came along."

Most likely the war funding.

"Are you marrying Lady Charlotte?" Bentley's cheeks puffed out and he frowned. "Can't be. Didn't she just marry some fellow by the name of Kenilworth? I'm certain Oriana told me that."

"She did." Geoff's tone was terser than he would have it. He did not like being reminded of his failure. Even though it all worked out for the best. He could not imagine anyone more perfect for him than Elizabeth. "I have the honor to be betrothed to Miss Turley."

"Friend of the 'Graces,'" Endicott said by way of elucidation.

"They were duchesses?" Bentley asked, completely confused.

Endicott rolled his eyes. "Lady Charlotte, Lady Louisa, and Miss Stern were the Three Graces. You were here all Season, Bentley. How did you miss that?"

Suddenly his countenance cleared. "Oh, right. I remember

now. Well, she wasn't a grace, but I'm going to wed Miss Blackacre. Perfect for me."

"Turley and I were getting ready to go to Boodle's," Geoff said. "Would you two like to accompany us?"

"Don't mind if I do," Endicott said.

"Yes, of course." Bentley nodded. "Must support a friend."

A few minutes later, the four of them were off to Boodle's. Endicott bemoaned not having had the foresight to court any of the ladies before they were snapped up this Season.

Whereupon Bentley astonished them all by saying, "You haven't met the right lady. Once you do, you'll court her properly." Then he promptly fell into his usual way of things. "Good to make notes and have one's valet remind one."

Geoff was about to join Endicott's and Turley's laughter, but remembered the list his grandmother and cousin gave him. He would not be marrying Elizabeth without their help.

After dinner, they formed a set for cards, playing for penny stakes. None of them were heavy gamblers. They were all, except Endicott, reliant upon their sires for their incomes, nor did they have fathers who would happily pay their gambling debts. Geoff had learned his lesson his first week on the Town, which had been his last week until the next quarter day.

He returned home before midnight still relatively sober. The next morning he woke at dawn. In a matter of hours, he'd be a married man, and he looked forward to it more than he thought was possible.

# Chapter Twenty-Two

The day before her wedding, Gavin called to Elizabeth from the drawing room. "Lizzy, come in and meet Captain Sutton. He was with General Ross's forces going to the Americas and is on his way to Belgium."

Her brother had been receiving visits from some of his former school chums who passed through Town on their way to Holland to join the Duke of Wellington's army. To a man, they were excited to be fighting with the Old Hooky again, as they called him, referring to the duke's prominent proboscis. Even though there was concern about other seasoned officers and soldiers who would not make it in time. She'd listened closely to everything Gavin related about their conversation.

The captain, who had risen, bowed. "A pleasure, Miss Turley. I understand felicitations are in order."

He took the hand she offered but did not attempt to kiss it. "I am glad to meet you as well, and thank you." She lowered herself onto the sofa opposite the men. "What unit will you join?"

"Second battalion of the 95th Rifles, my old unit." His exhilaration at going was clear and for several minutes the discussion revolved around who would be taking what commands, and the gossip about the Earl of Uxbridge being sent to command the cavalry instead of Cotton. "Well, he's Lord Combermere now, but that was a change no one expected on account of Uxbridge running off with the duke's sister-in-law."

"I hope it doesn't cause problems," Elizabeth remarked, wondering who would have made such a decision.

"Not from what I've heard." The captain glanced at her brother. "Gavin tells me we may see you over in Belgium as well."

"Yes, indeed. We will depart soon after our wedding." She rose. "Speaking of which, I still have much to do, and I am going out with Lady Markham soon. Please remain seated. Captain, I hope to see you again."

By the time she'd had the final consultation with her maid about the packing for the journey, approved the final list of her items from the town house that would be taken to her new home, as well as sending for some pieces of furniture her mother had given to her that were still in the country, it was time to change for her outing with Lady Markham.

Elizabeth and her aunt were in the hall when her ladyship arrived.

"How lovely you look." Lady Markham beamed at Elizabeth. "I am so looking forward to our day together."

"I am, too." She returned her smile.


It wasn't long before the outing with her soon-to-be mother-in-law and aunt could be deemed a complete success. Elizabeth hadn't had so much fun in ages.

They shopped until packages filled the inside of the coach and the boot, had ices at Gunter's, and tea with several of the ladies Lady Markham knew in the diplomatic corps who imparted several pieces of advice to Elizabeth.

"At all times be discreet. There will always be someone

who will attempt to acquire information by listening to conversations. Therefore, you should never say anything you do not wish the whole world to know," one of the ladies said as she selected a lemon biscuit from the plate. "I have every confidence that the duke will prevail over his opponent. Still, the situation in Paris will be difficult for a time."

"Excellent advice," Lady Markham said. "I shall add that you must not be too ambitious for Harrington. This posting is by way of an experience for him. It is not his vocation."

"I had that impression." Elizabeth wondered just how long she and Geoffrey would be overseas.

Aunt Bristow invited Lady Markham to dine at Turley House that evening. "It will be pot luck I'm afraid, and we shall sit down early. My brother-in-law plans to close the house and return to the country after the wedding."

"I would be delighted." Her ladyship smiled. "I only wish I had more time to spend with Elizabeth before she and Harrington depart."

"Can you tell me, my lady, how long Harrington and I will be abroad?"

"Until you give birth to a son." Lady Markham pulled a face. "I was fortunate to have two girls before Harrington was born. When you become *enceinte* you must pray for a boy. That will ensure you have daughters."

"He has never mentioned his sisters." In fact, the only other family member he talked about was a younger brother.

"I should not wonder at that. They are both several years older than he is. One married a diplomat and is in Russia, and the other prefers the country." She heaved a sigh. "I do not expect to see either of them in Town until their daughters come out, and then only if they cannot persuade someone else to sponsor the girls. He and his younger brother, Edmond, are much closer."

After tea that evening, several minutes after her ladyship

took her leave, Elizabeth's father joined her and her aunt in the drawing room.

"I haven't seen much of you," he said in a morose tone. "And it occurred to me that after today I might not see you for a long time." Awkwardly, he patted her shoulder. "I'm proud of you for marrying so well. Harrington might not be a marquis yet, but he will be in time."

What a thing to say! Elizabeth hoped it would be years before he became a marquis. She was coming to care about her future in-laws a great deal. "Thank you, Papa."

"That's all I have to say. I'll see you in the morning."

She glanced at her aunt after he'd left the room. "That was rather odd."

"As we all know, he has not been the same since your mother died." Aunt shrugged. "There is nothing any of us can do about it."

"I suppose so." At least Elizabeth had not been able to do anything to help him. She stifled a yawn. "I'm going to bed. I'll see you in the morning."

"Sleep well. You have another busy day tomorrow."

Her whole life would change tomorrow, and for the better. She was marrying a gentleman she loved and who loved her as well.


When Elizabeth woke the next morning a sliver of weak sun slipped through a crack in the curtains, making a line across the Turkey rug. She glanced around her bedchamber. It would be the last morning she would ever awaken here, but she could feel no sense of loss or regret.

Knowing she might not return to her father's estate, she had brought almost everything of importance to Town. Her books and a few small paintings were now packed, and would remain that way until she and Geoffrey had their own home.

In a few hours, she would be married to the man she loved, and whom she was sure loved her, even if he hadn't said it yet. Then again, neither had she proclaimed her feelings and that did not make them less true.

Vickers entered the room carrying tea, toast, and a baked egg. "I thought you'd want to break your fast up here this morning. When you've finished, I'll wash your hair."

A few hours later, Elizabeth sat before her mirror as Vickers placed pearl-studded pins in her hair.

A knock came on the door. But before Vickers could answer it, Charlotte, Louisa, and Dotty entered the room. What a wonderful surprise!

"I do hope we are not disturbing you." Dotty bussed Elizabeth's cheek.

"Not at all." She began to rise, but her maid pushed her back down.

"You're not ready yet."

She met her friends' laughing eyes in the mirror. "I thought you would all be in the country. I'm sure the knocker at Stanwood House was off."

"Grace has taken the children and the dogs to Stanwood," Charlotte explained. "Worthington is here for some last-minute business at the Lords. There is some quibbling about paying for the coming war that must be halted. That is the reason we are here as well. We have discovered how effective ladies can be at swaying the political tone."

"We are staying at Merton House," Louisa said. "There was no point opening Rothwell House again for such a short time."

"As soon as your dresser has finished"—Dotty's eyes twinkled with joy—"we have some things we would like to give you."

A few moments later, Elizabeth was allowed to stand.

Charlotte scrunched up her nose. "I thought you might

wear pink, but you need something blue, so I brought you a pearl bracelet with aquamarines."

"Oh, dear." Louisa pulled a face. "I should have given this to you when you were sitting. This is old. My mother-in-law found it, and I immediately thought of you." She handed Elizabeth a heavy silver comb decorated with pearls and diamonds.

"Thank you. It is perfect! Vickers?"

"Leave it to me. It won't take much to replace the one I have in your hair."

Once that was done, Dotty grinned. "And this is borrowed." She pinned a small pink cameo broach onto Elizabeth's bodice.

"I cannot thank you enough." Her vision blurred as she hugged her friends.

"No crying." Louisa handed Elizabeth a handkerchief. "You will set us all off. And I for one am not a pretty crier."

"She said the exact same thing to us." Dotty and Charlotte laughed.

The door opened again, and her aunt strolled in. "I was told you had company. My ladies." Aunt inclined her head. "Your grace." Aunt curtseyed. "Elizabeth, your mother gave these to me for you to wear on your wedding day."

Her aunt held out a leather box. Elizabeth set it on the table and opened it. Nestled in velvet was a double strand, pale pink pearl necklace with a diamond clasp. "They are beautiful! I've never seen anything like them before."

Her friends, leaning over Elizabeth's shoulder, nodded their agreement.

"They are from the Far East, and were your great-grandfather's wedding gift to your great-grandmother."

"Vickers?" Elizabeth said again.

The maid removed Elizabeth's pearl necklace, replacing it with the pink pearls. "There are earrings here as well, but I think they are better for evening wear."

She looked at the elaborate pearl and ruby earrings, and nodded. "I'll put them away."

"I know it is late," Dotty said. "But who is attending you?"

"My aunt—"

"Elizabeth, my dear," Aunt protested, "I only agreed because all of your friends had retired to the country, or so we thought. I am perfectly happy to sit and watch the ceremony."

"In that case, I would dearly love it if one of you could stand up with me."

"Oh"—Charlotte's eyes twinkled merrily—"I am sure we can do better for you than we three married ladies. Oriana Blackacre arrived in Town this morning. She and her grandmother are staying at the Pultney. I know she is not as close to you as we are, but you do know her, and it is tradition to have an unmarried lady attend you."

"And," Louisa said, "at some point it is inevitable you will become better acquainted with her. Harrington and Bentley, her betrothed, are best of friends. He is in Town as well, and I will wager anything that he will attend Harrington."

"But will she agree?" Particularly at this late date.

"I am quite sure she will." Charlotte said. "I shall write her a note."

For the first time Elizabeth was happy the wedding would take place at eleven and not at an earlier hour. Geoffrey had argued for eight o'clock, but Lord Richard and his grandmother had objected to being ready before eleven. Naturally, they won. Elizabeth and Geoffrey could not have the wedding without his uncle.

Oriana was ushered into Elizabeth's bedchamber an hour after the note had been sent by a running footman. "What a surprise this is!" Oriana hugged everyone including Elizabeth. "And such an honor. Bentley visited this morning, and told me about the wedding, but I never expected to be asked to attend you."

"I do not know how you could have expected it when you'd left Town before Harrington even started courting Elizabeth," Louisa retorted.

"Very true," Oriana said, ruefully. "I was not in Town at all long."

"Everything has happened so quickly." Once Geoffrey had started to actually court her, it had not taken long at all for her to decide to marry him. "This has become a bit harum-scarum. Although, I do think we shall have a decent number for the wedding breakfast. Lady Markham took my aunt and me to visit all of her friends currently in Town yesterday and asked them to attend."

The other ladies began to talk, and Dotty pulled Elizabeth aside. "Do you love him and does he love you?"

"I do love him, and I believe he loves me as well. He"— Elizabeth searched for the words—"he has done everything we discussed. At the last ball he glared at every other gentleman, and"—she certainly wasn't going to tell even Dotty *everything*. That was between Geoffrey and Elizabeth— "remained with me throughout the evening. He has not said the words, but he wants to be with me all the time. And he talks to me as if he respects my opinions. Doesn't that sound like love to you?"

Dotty was silent for several moments before saying, "It does sound like he loves you."

Elizabeth breathed a sigh of relief. It was too late to change anything now, but having her friend's reassurance relieved the small part of her heart that was as yet unsure.

# Chapter Twenty-Three

Geoff glanced at the clock for the twentieth time in the past five minutes and continued to pace the morning room. Father's lips, indeed his whole face, were set in grim lines.

"What the devil can be keeping her?" Geoff had done everything he could to ensure this marriage took place. Had something gone wrong? "She should have been here a half hour ago."

"She certainly does not appear to be a particularly timely lady," his father grumbled.

"Piffle." Mama swept into the parlor, her silk skirts swishing with her movement. "Heaven forfend a lady wants to look her best on her wedding day." She glanced at the burl and gilt mantel clock. "It is only twenty-five minutes to the hour. Richard has not even arrived yet, and your grandmother has not come down." Mama fisted her hands on her hips. "You absolutely cannot expect your bride to be here a minute before five of the hour."

That was another twenty minutes, if Elizabeth was not later than that. Refusing to comment, Geoff hunched his shoulders and resumed his circuit around the room.

"I do not recall you being so late," his father mumbled.

"In that case, you have a very poor memory." Mama

lifted one regal brow. "I kept you waiting for a good fifteen minutes after the appointed time."

"Fifteen minutes!" Geoff was sure he would never have survived it. He'd have been at her door tossing her over his shoulder and carrying her to the altar.

"I am positive that cannot be correct," his father said.

"Merciful Heavens." His grandmother walked into the room followed by his cousin. "Have a glass of wine, but stop making such a fuss. Markham, I remember exactly how disgruntled you were waiting for Catherine. You had called for your horse as if you'd go to her father's house and fetch her to the church."

Geoff grinned to himself. At least he wasn't the only one who would have carried off his lady.

"Harrington, pour me a glass of claret and have one yourself. You are going to wear yourself out at this rate."

He handed his grandmother a goblet of wine, and said as loftily as he could manage, "I don't wish to be in my altitudes when I wed."

"If one glass of wine is going to make you cup-shot you've got more problems than you think," his grandmother said acerbically.

Geoff groaned, poured a glass of wine, and took a sip.

At five to the hour, his uncle, Bentley, and Gavin Turley arrived.

Had Turley come to tell Geoff the wedding was off? Good God! Despite everything they had done, and how happy Elizabeth seemed, he had become obsessed by the fear she would jilt him. "Where is Elizabeth?"

"She was coming down the stairs as I was leaving." Her brother pointed to Geoff's glass. "Is that claret?"

"Yes." He poured glasses for everyone.

The under butler his father brought with him appeared at the door and bowed. "The Duke and Duchess of Rothwell, the Marquis and Marchioness of Kenilworth, and the Marquis and Marchioness of Merton."

"Elizabeth invited us to the wedding ceremony," Lady Merton said as the party strolled into the room. "She is on her way." She turned her attention to Bentley. "Your betrothed will be her witness."

"Oriana here?" The man beamed. "Had breakfast with her but she didn't mention it. At least I don't think she did." The next second he was frowning. "Should I have escorted her?"

"Not at all." Lady Merton smiled reassuringly. "She is supposed to come with the bride."

"Well," Uncle Richard said. "It is time for us to take our places in the garden."

Several footmen carried more chairs out to the area to set up for the wedding. As soon as they were put in place, the housekeeper tied ribbons on them. Tables dotted the terrace and garden, all decorated with flowers and ribbons. The ballroom was full of tables as well. How many people had his mother invited?

Soon everyone was seated. Uncle Richard stood in front, and Geoff and Bentley took their places in front of Uncle Richard.

"Ah, just in time." He smiled with satisfaction. "Harrington, your bride has arrived. Perfect timing on her part, I would say."

Geoff swiveled his head so quickly, he thought he'd cracked his neck. Elizabeth was a vision in a pale pink gown that seemed to float around her. Her neck was adorned with a long necklace of pink pearls the likes of which he had never seen before. Her blond hair sparkled as the sun shined on it. "She is exquisite."

"Yes, she is," Bentley said, but he was gazing at the small dark-haired lady following Elizabeth.

It was only then that Geoff noticed her father as well.

The elusive Lord Turley. The man seemed shrunken.

Although tall and broad shouldered, his jacket was loose as if he had not been eating properly. Geoff gave himself a shake. Now was not the time to attend to anything but his wedding, and his uncle was already speaking.

Elizabeth's father stood next to Geoff, Elizabeth on his other side. Uncle Richard asked, "Who giveth this woman to be married to this man?"

"I do," Lord Turley said.

After taking her hand from her father's, his uncle gave it to Geoff. He tightened his fingers around hers, trying not to clutch them like a man drowning.

When he gazed into her upturned face and searched her eyes, he saw no hesitation or doubt. Instead her gaze held a warmth he had never seen before in any woman. It was very like the way his friend looked at his betrothed and his mother looked at his father, and—

"Repeat after me," his uncle prompted.

". . . to love and to cherish 'til death do us part." Geoff struggled not to let his jaw drop.

He knew he cherished Elizabeth. Yet, for some reason he had never realized that he was supposed to promise to love her.

If he'd thought about it at all, he would have supposed there were vows for arranged matches and different vows for love matches. He and Elizabeth didn't have an arranged marriage, but it was not a love match either. Perhaps he should have spoken to Uncle Richard about using the correct ceremony. Geoff would have if he'd had any idea it was necessary.

Yet, it was too late now. He had given his word to her and, as a gentleman, he must find a way to keep it. If only he knew where to begin.

Could he love her? What was love for a woman? He had never experienced the emotion. He'd never wanted to fall in love, and did not know if he would recognize it if he did.

Elizabeth's fingers tightened around his as she said her vows. She had promised to love him as well. Did she already love him or did she find it a strange requirement?

Soon he slipped the ring on her finger, promising to worship her body—Geoff was sure he already had done that, and would be more than pleased to continue to do so. A few moments later his uncle pronounced them man and wife.

There were several prayers afterward. But he hardly heard them. For some reason the scent of the roses mingling with Elizabeth's lavender and lemon aroma captured his whole attention. He found himself stroking the palm of her hand, and she leaned against him.

Geoff wanted nothing more than to carry her up to his room and sink into her. That is what should occur after a wedding. Not standing at doors and greeting people, then waiting for a cake to be cut. His cock strained against his breeches. Damn, if he didn't start thinking about something else, he would embarrass himself.

Elizabeth nudged him, pointing her chin at the neighbor's black and white cat who had found a place in the sun amongst the roses.

Would she like a pet? If so, what kind? A dog or a cat? Not one of those pug dogs. He'd rather she had a proper dog. Perhaps he, or better she, could ask for one of the Worthington puppies. After they arrived in Paris, there would be time to properly train the animal.

Uncle Richard stopped talking at the same time that Geoff glanced down and met Elizabeth's gaze. They were married. He finally had his wife. And that was all that mattered.

Elizabeth had never seen Geoffrey look so handsome. When he took her hand from her father's, he had smiled. Was he as happy about marrying *her*—as opposed to any other lady—as she was about marrying him?

She was pleased at how firm her voice sounded as she repeated her vows. When he promised to worship her body, his tone deepened, and her knees threatened to buckle. How embarrassing that would have been, to fall over at one's own wedding.

Soon it was over and the vicar instructed them to sign the register. Geoffrey wrapped his arm around her waist. "Wife."

"Husband," she shot back, giddy with happiness. "Although, I think we must sign our names before it is legal."

As soon as the formalities were over, glasses of champagne were pressed into their hands. Toasts were made to them for a happy and fruitful life together.

"I cannot tell you how happy I am to have you as my daughter." Lady Markham bussed Elizabeth's cheek.

"Congratulations, Harrington." Lord Elliott shook Geoffrey's hand. "And to you, Lady Harrington."

Elizabeth blinked at his use of her new name. She had been so busy preparing for the wedding, she had only thought about her name a time or two. "Thank you, my lord."

Footmen started dashing around with trays of food, and she and Geoff shared a glance. "We could go up to our parlor while the staff finishes setting up for the wedding breakfast."

"We could," he agreed. "You would be able to look at your new bedchamber."

"Do you mean to tell me it is finished?" She had never had a chamber made especially for her. Not even when she had moved from the nursery to another bedroom, had she got to decide on the decorations. Then again, her father's house was never her real home. That would be with her husband.

"They finished this morning." He stroked her back, causing pleasurable frissons to spread through her. She wished they could just repair to his bedchamber alone. "I cannot wait to hear what you think of it."

Elizabeth rose on her toes, and whispered in what she hoped was a sultry tone, "I think most of my enjoyment shall be experienced in your room, my lord."

"I shall make sure of that, my lady." He took her hand. "Let's go to our apartment before the wedding breakfast begins. We *are* married."

Yet, before they could leave the drawing room, they heard his mother's voice.

"Elizabeth and Harrington." Lady Markham walked in from the garden. "Our guests will begin arriving soon. You must take your places." She glanced over her shoulder at her husband. "Markham, you as well."

"The garden is not yet ready," Geoffrey objected.

"The wedding breakfast will be held in the ballroom. The other areas will be finished soon enough."

"I had hoped we would have time alone," Geoffrey murmured, holding out his arm to Elizabeth.

Placing her fingers on the soft superfine of his jacket, she murmured, "I had the same hope."

An hour later her mother-in-law released them to mingle with the guests with the admonishment not to disappear yet.

After slowly making their way around the ballroom, Elizabeth spotted Dotty, Charlotte, and Louisa. "If you do not mind, I wish to speak with my friends for a few minutes."

Geoffrey glanced in the direction Elizabeth indicated. "Of course not." He raised her hand and kissed each of her fingers. "I'll find you in a bit."

As if by silent assent, the ladies rose when she approached. "The terrace?"

They nodded and began to meander out the French windows. She signaled to a footman. "Please bring champagne and refreshments for four to me on the terrace."

"Yes, my lady."

Elizabeth smiled to herself. Even though it had only been an hour, she had been addressed as "my lady" and "Lady Harrington" so many times, her new title was no longer foreign to her.

She hurried out to join her friends. "Where is Oriana?"

"With Bentley," Charlotte said. "They have not seen each other in a week."

"Do you know"—Dotty looked at the other three—"I do not believe any of us were parted from our husbands for more than a day or two while we were betrothed."

"I think you are correct." Louisa's brow wrinkled. "I know Gideon and I were not."

"Neither were Constantine and I," Charlotte added.

"We were not either." Elizabeth signaled for her friends to sit where two footmen were setting up a table for them. "I cannot imagine having to wait two months to marry."

Her friends murmured their concurrence.

She raised her glass. "To us and our futures."

"Here, here," Louisa, Dotty, and Charlotte said as one.

"When do you depart for Holland?" Louisa asked after they had taken sips of champagne and filled their plates.

"In three days," Elizabeth responded. "Geoffrey and I wanted to leave at first light, but his parents asked us to remain for a while longer and we agreed. It is not as if we are simply going on a wedding trip and will return in a few months."

Charlotte finished swallowing a bite of food. "Do you know how long you will be away?"

"From what my mother-in-law said"—Elizabeth cast her eyes to the sky—"until I give birth to a son. She suggested I wish for girls."

Dotty hastily covered her mouth with her serviette and started to laugh. It took her a few moments before she could speak. "What did Harrington say to that?"

"I haven't had time to tell him." Elizabeth finished her glass of wine and poured another glass. "I was told only yesterday, and we have not been alone for more than a minute today."

"Harrington appears to dote on you," Charlotte ventured. "I was looking."

"As was I," Louisa said. "I am so happy you found love."

He had still not told her he loved her, but . . . "I am, too."

"Speaking of Harrington," Dotty said. "It seems he is missing you."

"He has our husbands in tow as well." Louisa smiled as Rothwell approached.

Geoffrey leaned forward, his hands on Elizabeth's chair, his fingers languidly stroking the back of her neck causing pleasurable thrills. "It is time to cut the cake."

"After which," Kenilworth said, "we shall provide cover while the two of you slip away. I remember how hard it was for Charlotte and me."

Elizabeth casually glanced up at Geoffrey to see if he showed any signs at all of being jealous of his lordship, but he merely grinned down at her. "We shall thank you for it. What do you say, sweetheart?"

"Yes, indeed." She covered one of his hands with her much smaller fingers. "I had hoped we would not even have a wedding breakfast." She rose as did the rest of the ladies. "I suppose we should go in."

One by one her friends embraced her.

Charlotte bussed Elizabeth on her cheek. "I wish you and Harrington the best of everything."

"I wish that for you, too." She kissed Charlotte's cheek and whispered, "Thank you for not wanting him."

"I know you will be happy." Louisa hugged Elizabeth.

"I believe we shall." She returned the embrace.

"Have a wonderful journey, and please remain safe," Dotty said, taking Elizabeth's hands.

"I—We shall. Thank you for everything." She stepped back and tucked her hand in Geoffrey's arm. "You must all join us in Paris sometime next spring."

They strolled into the ballroom, Elizabeth and Harrington in the lead.

# Chapter Twenty-Four

Less than forty minutes later, Geoffrey took her hand in his. "Through the door the footman just came out of. We'll go the back way."

That was when she noticed that her friends and their husbands had formed a barrier so that no one could see who came in or out of the door. "Lead on."

They slipped behind two large potted plants, then through the door. The corridor was narrow, but well lit. They walked to the end. He opened another door that led to a plain wooden set of stairs. She held up her skirts as they made their way up to the next level. A few moments later, they were in his bedchamber, and she was in his arms.

"I thought we'd never be alone." He brushed his lips across hers.

She wrapped her arms around him, encouraging him to kiss her deeply. "I have decided that the idea of the wedding breakfast is to keep the bride and groom away from each other as long as possible."

"At least they have done away with the bedding ceremony." His lips roamed along her jaw and down her neck. "Although, then you would already be naked. Shall I act as your maid?"

"Yes, please. And I shall act as your valet."

It did not take long before her gown slipped to the floor and she had tossed his cravat over a chair. He placed her gown carefully over the same chair, but threw his jacket on the floor. Sweeping her into his arms, he climbed onto the bed.

His hands slid over her body, lighting fires wherever he touched. Elizabeth wiggled, trying to encourage him to go straight to the place where all her needs coalesced, aching for him to enter her.

"Patience, sweetheart." He cupped her breasts, licking and sucking first one then the other until she wanted to scream with frustration.

As he did before, he licked and kissed his way down to the place between her legs, and sucked. She arched her back trying to push herself closer to his mouth.

"Is that what you wanted?" His voice was low and tight.

"More." She gasped, struggling for air as her body tensed. "I want you."

"I live to serve, my lady." The next moment he plunged inside her.

Her inner muscles clenched around him as she gave in to wave after wave of glorious sensations.

Geoff collapsed next to Elizabeth, drawing her next to him. He'd never come like that before. He'd never dreamed he could. The minute he'd entered her she milked him dry.

He nuzzled her hair as he wound the thick mass of silken curls around his hand, watching as they tried to hold on to his fingers when he let go. Her hand splayed over his chest. And even though she was clearly asleep, a smile played on her lips. When she woke, he hoped he'd be able to mate with her again.

Pulling the covers over them—this time he'd had the forethought to have his valet turn down the bed—Geoff closed his eyes. They had all the time in the world to be together now.

* * *

For the rest of the day and the next, they coupled. Occasionally, they would wander into their dining room to find food had been set out. The first time she had licked chicken juice off her fingers, he had picked her up and taken her straight back to bed.

"I had no idea licking my fingers would have such an effect on you." Elizabeth grinned. "I shall take care not to do it in public."

Geoff was beginning to believe her mere existence was enough to make him hard. "Shall we see what else has the same effect?"

"I think we shall have to." She ran her tongue along his neck. "I am still hungry."

Before he could stop her, she was out of the bed. He rolled over onto his back and watched his wife's plump bottom as she left the bedchamber. This time she didn't even don her chemise. From the dining room he heard her giggle. "Someone brought us ices."

He swung his legs out of the bed. "There are many interesting uses for ices."

On the morning of the second day, he woke to the sound of Nettle banging around in the dressing room.

Elizabeth opened heavy-lidded eyes. "What is that noise?"

"I believe it is our notice to join my parents for breakfast."

She rolled into him, wincing a little. "I should bathe."

Considering their bedroom smelt like a brothel, he should probably bathe as well. "You may go first if you'd like. Soak for a while. It should ease your muscles."

"I shall." She kissed him before leaving the bed, donning her chemise as she walked stiffly out of his room into hers.

He should have exercised more caution with her. Even if she had instigated several of their couplings. After all, he was the one with the experience.

* * *

An hour later, they were dressed. Geoff took her hand in his.

"They all know what we were doing, do they not?" Elizabeth's voice was more than a little uneasy.

"We *are* married." The only problem was he was feeling a little nervous as well. This was most likely the reason couples went on wedding trips.

She straightened her shoulders. "Yes, we are, and I cannot imagine them saying anything."

"No." Still, he was relieved when they were the first ones to arrive in the breakfast room.

Father's under butler directed the placement of the dishes while Gibson looked on.

"I have a feeling Gibson will be happy to see Preston gone," Elizabeth whispered.

"I think you are correct," Geoff whispered back. "Come, you can show me what you like to eat, and I'll fix your plate."

"Thank you."

She declined the kippers, but took the baked eggs and ham. He pulled out a chair for her in the middle of the table, and a footman placed a pot of tea, sugar, and milk down next to the plate. "Thank you. I would like toast as well, please."

He liked the way she addressed the servants. Not everyone thanked them, but he had found he received better and more loyal service when he did.

A few minutes later, his parents arrived.

"Good morning, my dears," his mother said, taking her place at the foot of the small table. Preston placed a plate of eggs and kippers in front of her.

"Tea?" Elizabeth asked.

"Yes, please." More toast was set on the table. "One lump of sugar and milk."

Father spent more time selecting his food from the dishes on the sideboard, before joining them.

A fresh pot of tea was set on the table next to his mother, and she fixed Father's cup. After Mama had taken a sip of tea, she said, "Elizabeth, your mare arrived the day before yesterday. I also received a note from your aunt and brother saying they would visit you this afternoon." Mama's lips pressed together in an expression of displeasure. "Your father has returned to the country."

"Please do not feel bad for me," Elizabeth said, spearing another piece of ham. "It is nothing more than I expected. I will be glad to visit with Aunt and Gavin."

"Please feel free to invite them to luncheon if you wish."

"We could entertain them in our dining room, if you'd like," Geoffrey said. "You have not been able to show our apartment to anyone." He did not think Elizabeth had seen her bedchamber for more than the time it took to dress today since it had been finished.

Her face brightened. "That is an excellent idea." She turned toward his mother. "Would you like to join us?"

"No, dear. You will want to spend some time alone with them." His mother grinned. "I am afraid you will be with me most of the morning. I have a list that I received from my mother-in-law, oh, years ago, but I believe it is still pertinent, regarding items you might need that you have not already thought of." Geoff opened his mouth to protest that he'd had a list from his father, but Mama held up her hand. "It will not hurt anything or delay your journey."

Later that morning, he was surprised to see trunks filled with linens and other bedding. As well as a set of dishes, and who knew what else. And he had thought he had everything they required. Obviously, he was wrong. He'd not packed any household items.

His wife strolled by, staring at a list, a frown on her lovely face. "I am of two minds," Elizabeth said, looking up. "Your mother has offered to give us Preston if we would like to take our own butler. His mother is French, and he speaks the language. He would like to come with us. I know hiring a butler is in your purview. What do you think?"

"It would be helpful to have a servant who speaks French," Geoff tried to divine what she might want.

Her face cleared. "That is what I thought. I shall tell him we would like him to join us."

"Aside from bedding, what is in the trunks?"

"Everything we will need to immediately set up our household." Taking out a pencil, she made a mark on the paper and glanced at her pin watch. "I must finish this. Aunt and Gavin will be here shortly, and I have yet to speak with your grandmother."

Elizabeth crossed the final item off her list, and made her way to the dowager's apartment. Cousin Apollonia answered the door. "Come in. We have not had a chance to welcome you to the family properly. Her ladyship's parlor is this way."

They walked into a room off the small entryway. All the apartments must be set up in the same fashion as Elizabeth and Geoffrey's. The dowager's parlor was decorated in creams and large patterns with vines, birds, and flowers.

*"Welcome, welcome."* Squawk, squawk. A gray parrot flapped its wings in a large cage.

How delightful! She snoodled forward, not quite sure how to approach the animal. "Thank you. What is your name?"

The bird tilted its head first one way then the other, and blinked. *"Florian, Florian. Nice chit, nice chit."*

"Your name is Nelson, and cease using that word. She is a lady," the dowager said. "If I have told you once, I have told you a hundred times. Nice, lady."

*"Nice chit, nice chit."*

"He does not appear to be at all convinced." She grinned and curtseyed to her grandmother-in-law.

The dowager sighed. "Ever since he heard the name Florian, he has insisted it belongs to him."

Elizabeth stifled a giggle. "How are you doing, ma'am?"

"I'm better than I ought to be at my age." The older woman's sharp eyes focused on Elizabeth as if looking for something. "The question is how are you doing? Is my scapegrace grandson treating you as he should?"

Thinking about yesterday and last night, her cheeks began to warm. "I think he is." Elizabeth wished she had a fan. "At any rate, I have no complaints."

The dowager nodded. "I'm glad to hear it. Now, I assume you have the list I gave Catherine when she joined the family. Do you have any questions?"

"I am a little concerned about all the items I am taking with me. I'm afraid you won't have anything left."

"Piffle." The Dowager Lady Markham waved Elizabeth's concerns away. "You need all of it, and it just gives us an opportunity to buy new. Will you take Preston with you?"

"Yes, ma'am, as well as the second housekeeper, who is able to cook if need be, a maid, and a footman. I have a personal footman as well. That will give us two. We should be able to make do until we can hire local servants."

"Yes, that should be sufficient. I understand the government is putting its hands on every vessel it can to ferry the soldiers and equipment over. You might be in Harwich for the nonce."

"That is what we heard as well. With that in mind, Harrington made arrangements for a ship to meet us there. Naturally, we will take anyone else who needs passage onboard with us."

Again the dowager nodded. "It sounds as if you have everything well in hand. I only have one thing to say. The honeymoon doesn't last forever. Just keep in mind what brought you together, and tell him what you need. Men can be totally oblivious much of the time. Most of the time they can't see what's right in front of their noses. Now give me a kiss, and I shall let you finish your preparations."

Elizabeth dutifully bussed the dowager's cheek. "Thank you. I'll remember what you said."

Not long after her conversation with the dowager, Aunt and Gavin arrived. Before sitting down to eat, Elizabeth showed them around the apartment.

"I like what you've done with your bedchamber and the entry," her aunt murmured approvingly. "I agree that you should keep the rest as it is for the time being."

They took their places at the table, and Gavin raised his wineglass. "To you and Harrington. I'm glad I was able to bring you together."

Aunt glanced up at the ceiling and shook her head, but Elizabeth raised her glass as well. "Thank you for all you did. You are truly the best of brothers. Perhaps I can help you find a wife as well."

"Not in the near future," he said drily. "But someday."

Luncheon was served by Preston and Kenton, her personal footman she had chosen to accompany their little household overseas. Jacobs, the new footman, stood at the door in case he was needed.

"I'm sorry I am late." Geoffrey kissed Elizabeth's cheek before taking his place at the end of the table. She was glad when he joined them.

"Have you finished your preparations?" Aunt asked.

"Almost. I am so looking forward to the journey, and between Harrington and Gavin, I have met several people who will be in Brussels as well."

"I've half a mind to come with you," Gavin said. "Unfortunately, someone must be here to mind the estate."

As much as she loved her brother, he would have been very much in the way. "You can plan to visit us after we are settled in Paris."

They finished eating and lingered over cups of tea until

her aunt rose. "I imagine you still have a great deal to do before leaving in the morning." Aunt embraced Elizabeth. "We shall write, and perhaps I will be able to visit in the spring."

"I'll miss you." She hugged her aunt tightly. "Thank you so much for sponsoring me."

"I am glad I was able to."

An hour after her aunt and brother left, Elizabeth was concerned there would not be enough hours to finalize their plans, but she managed to ensure everything for their journey was completed so that they could leave the next morning as planned.

The last of her new gowns had arrived a few hours ago, and Vickers had the packing in hand. Elizabeth had accomplished the shopping for all the other bits and pieces she would need until she arrived in Paris. Although, who knew how long that would be with this dreadful war that was looming. She sent a quick prayer that it would be over quickly and successfully without too much loss of life. They knew so many men who would be fighting.

# Chapter Twenty-Five

Elizabeth entered Lord Markham's secretary's office with a copy of her maid's, footman's, and groom's employment contracts in hand as well as the list of servants she was hiring from her in-laws. "I hope I am not interrupting you, but Lady Markham said I should speak with you."

Mr. Grantham, an older man with silver hair, rose and bowed. "Not at all, my lady. How may I assist you?"

"Lord Harrington and I are hiring five of Lord and Lady Markham's servants and three of my father's servants. I require new employment contracts for them reflecting their change in status." Elizabeth handed the contracts for her servants to the secretary. "These are for my lady's maid, footman, and groom."

"Leave it with me, my lady. I shall ensure all is in order and have them signed."

"Thank you." That was one more thing to cross off her list.

Elizabeth headed to the kitchen to speak with the cook about a hamper for the coach. She should have sent the man a note or called him to her, but she was in a hurry to have the arrangements completed.

Once she had discussed the basket, there was one more

thing she wished to consult with Geoffrey about. Yet, they had been crossing paths most of the day, and she had no idea where he had got to.

As she crossed the hall, the butler bowed. "Gibson, have you seen Lord Harrington?"

"Several times, my lady." Poor Gibson was not used to all the activity in the house, and it showed. "You might look in the library. I believe he required a map."

"Thank you, Gibson." She would have liked to assure him his life would be back to normal soon, but Elizabeth did not think he would take her solicitude well.

As she approached the library she heard Geoffrey's voice and her father-in-law's in response. Not wanting to interrupt them, she turned to go back toward the hall, when Lord Markham said, "Well done, on bringing Elizabeth up to scratch. You almost lost the position with Sir Charles."

His lordship's words halted her steps. She should keep going, but her feet refused to move. She waited to hear her husband tell his father that they had married because he loved her.

"Thank you, sir," Geoffrey replied. "It took a bit of doing, but I pulled it off. She was the last choice left, and I wasn't about to let her get away."

*Pulled it off. Last choice?*

Elizabeth's throat closed painfully, making it hard to swallow.

"She seems like a nice girl," Lord Markham continued. "Your mother is of the opinion that she'll make you an excellent hostess."

"I have to say I agree with her." Elizabeth had never heard Geoffrey sound so smug. "She has all the qualifications we discussed and then some."

*Qualifications.*

That truly was all he wanted. A wife who would meet the needs of his position.

Hot tears blurred Elizabeth's eyes as she heard the clinking of glasses.

*Everything he had said, everything he had vowed . . . it was all a lie!*

Every time he touched her she could have been any other female.

Despite what she had thought was him showing his love for her, he was simply making sure she had to marry him. Making sure she could not get away.

Tears threatened to spill over. She was not going to cry. Not for him. After all his trickery, he wasn't worth it.

She turned toward the servants' stairs. They were steeper and narrower than the main staircase, but Elizabeth ran up them, gasping for air when she reached the second floor. Taking deep breaths, she tried to calm herself before going the rest of the way to her chamber.

If only she could escape to her father's home, but he would just tell her to return to her husband. Even Gavin and her aunt would tell her she must try to make her marriage work.

Straightening her shoulders, she stepped into the corridor and strode to the apartment she and Geoffrey shared. Once in the entry, she turned toward her room.

Since their wedding she had slept in his bedchamber. Beginning tonight she would sleep in hers.

Vickers was closing a trunk when Elizabeth entered. She hadn't thought of what she would say to her maid. Mayhap nothing yet.

"I'm not feeling well," she said, avoiding her maid's sharp eyes. "I shall take a tray in my room this evening."

"I knew all this hustle and bustle was going to wear you to a thread." Vickers hurried to Elizabeth. "Just give me a minute, and I'll have you in your nightgown."

Blinking her eyes to keep the tears at bay, she stood

while her maid unlaced the gown. Despite all her efforts, one tear, then two slid down her cheeks. She dashed them away, hoping Vickers would not notice.

But when Elizabeth sat at her toilet table, her maid met her eyes in the mirror. "What's this now?"

"I can't talk about it." She shook her head. "Not yet. Tell his lordship"—if he should ask—"that I am indisposed."

"Yes, my lady. A cool cloth dipped in lavender water might help, and some chamomile tea."

"I just want to rest for a while." Elizabeth could barely think.

She did not know what she was going to do next. All she knew was that she could not share a bed with him until she worked it out. The thought that she had given herself to him so willingly made her ill.

How could she have been so wrong? At least she wasn't the only one. He had deceived her friends as well, and they were watching him closely.

Her chest ached as if her heart was actually breaking in two. She felt as if she was sinking into a black pit and could not climb out. All she wanted to do was sleep until all the pain went away.

Tears pooled in her eyes again. She blinked them back.

*I will not weep, I will not weep, I will not weep.*

For a moment, she considered marching into the study and telling him what she thought. Unfortunately, his father would be present. And what would she do if he told her that of course he didn't love her and she had been a goose for believing he did? Well, she might have to travel with him, but that was all she was going to do. She would be his *qualified* wife.

*If that is all Geoffrey Harrington wants from me, that is all he shall get!*

If only she had known now deceitful he was. If only she could disappear.

Geoff finished his conversation with his father, and made his way to the main stairs.

"My lord," Gibson said. "Did Lady Harrington find you?"

"No, she did not. Do you know where she is?" The way she had been running around, she could be anywhere from the attics to the kitchen.

"I am sorry to say I do not, my lord."

"Very well. I'll find her." Elizabeth had talked about a basket for the journey. She might be with the cook.

When he got to the kitchen, he discovered she had already been and gone. He searched the main parts of the house and sent a footman to the attic.

After looking in at his grandmother's apartment he went to his own. She wasn't in his bedchamber or their parlor. Where the devil could she be?

Finally, he remembered she had a room of her own. Not that she had spent any time in it. When he knocked on the door her maid came out.

"Vickers, have you seen Lady Harrington?"

"She is indisposed, my lord." The woman's face was so stiff it might have been a mask.

This could not be happening. Nothing could happen to her. "Indisposed?" Geoff wanted to shout at his wife's dresser. "She was perfectly fine earlier."

"Well, she's not now, my lord." The maid stood in front of the door as if she would bar him from entering Elizabeth's bedchamber.

He raked his fingers through his hair. Damn. Had he been the cause? Was that the reason her maid looked as if she'd like to hit him?

Elizabeth had been walking stiffly this morning, but she seemed fine later on. "I shall just look in on her."

"She does not wish to be disturbed, my lord." The woman shifted, barring the way.

What would Vickers do if he moved her aside? But if Elizabeth wanted to be alone, would she be upset with him? "Will she be able to travel in the morning?"

"I believe so. At least she plans on it." He'd never before noticed how grim the woman was.

Plans on it? It suddenly occurred to him that she might be ill but was still intent on traveling tomorrow. Would it be like his wife to hide a serious condition? This seemed like that was something he should know. "Should I call for the doctor?"

"No, my lord." The maid's hands went to her hips. "A doctor isn't needed."

"Then what?" He had to do something.

Elizabeth could not simply have taken ill so rapidly. There had to be a reason. He was her husband. He would insist on seeing her. He'd order the maid to move out of his way. This was his wife they were talking about. He had a right to know what was wrong.

"Goodness, what in Heaven's name is going on here?" His mother entered the parlor. "Harrington, I could hear you bellowing from the corridor."

"Elizabeth is indisposed. Whatever that means," Geoff grumbled. All he wanted to do was have everyone go away so he could see for himself how his wife was doing.

"In that case, go away." His mother gave him a disgusted look. "You will not do her any good by stomping and roaring around. If I were her, I would insist on waiting to depart."

"I am going to send for the doctor." He started to walk out the door, but his mother's hand stayed him.

"You will not." Mama rolled her eyes. "He won't be able

to help her at all." Geoffrey stared at his mother. He had never seen her roll her eyes before. Not only that, but he distinctly recalled being punished for doing the same. "I cannot believe you are being so—so knotty-pated. Being indisposed is not an illness." She made a shooing motion with her hands. "Away with you."

This was not supposed to be happening. Everything had been going splendidly and now this. And no one would allow him near Elizabeth to ensure she would be able to travel in the morning.

How the devil was he supposed to care for her in sickness—he remembered that he had vowed to do so—if her maid and his mother wouldn't let him through the door?

Geoff went back to his bedchamber and paced.

He wanted to commiserate with someone, but the only two men left in Town that he might be able to talk to were Bentley, which would require too much effort, and Turley. Her brother, though, would be more concerned about Elizabeth than listening to Geoff. Father would only tell him to leave it to his mother.

He grabbed his hat and cane. There was one place he could go to that would help. Jackson's boxing saloon. If he wasn't going to be allowed to see his wife, at least he could hit something.

As luck would have it, he met up with Endicott crossing Bond Street and fell in with him. "Going to Jackson's?"

Elliott inclined his head in greeting. "Yes. You?"

"I need some exercise before the journey tomorrow." They reached the door and Geoff pulled it open.

"I take it your bride is being pulled in ten different ways." Endicott strode through the door after Geoff. "Devil of a thing about families. Don't want you around until they do. We had to pry my mother's hands off my brother and his wife when they left to go to Cumbria, and they were only going for a month. I can't imagine what the two of you are going through."

When they arrived there were two men in the ring, but no one seemed to be waiting. "We've already had to put off leaving for three days."

"Wouldn't be surprised if she took to her bed with a sick headache. I know my sister-in-law threatened to do just that."

Was that it? Had Elizabeth merely wanted time alone? God. Geoff prayed that was all it was. He wouldn't even blame her for it. She had taken on the logistical aspects of their journey like she was born to it. Still, it had to have taken its toll on her strength, especially after their coupling. "Care to spar with me?"

"Pleasure." Endicott grinned.

As they strolled into the changing room, Geoff's mood lightened. There was nothing like talking things over with a friend.

# Chapter Twenty-Six

"Now"—Elizabeth heard her mother-in-law say to her maid—"tell me if your mistress is having her courses, or if it is something else?"

"She . . . well . . . I . . . I'm not sure I should say anything, my lady." Elizabeth could practically hear Vickers's mind trying to come up with an excuse that would satisfy Lady Markham. Finally Vickers said, "It is not her courses. I don't know what's happened, my lady."

"Ask her if she will see me."

This was horrible. Elizabeth could not tell her mother-in-law of all people what she had heard. She was sure to take Geoffrey's side. He was her son, after all.

She was tempted to pull her covers over her head and pretend she wasn't awake.

"My lady?" Her maid was beside her bed. "If you don't let her talk to you, someone's going to call the doctor."

And then everyone in the house would know she was not physically ill. "Very well. Let her in."

A few seconds later, Lady Markham drew a chair up to Elizabeth's bed and peered at her face. "You have been weeping. I can only imagine it was something my beef-witted son said or did." Elizabeth nodded as her ladyship tapped her chin. "But not to you? If you'd had words, he would not be so at sea about why you refuse to see him." Not knowing where to begin, Elizabeth nodded again. "I can attempt to help you, my dear, but I am not a soothsayer. You will have to tell me what occurred."

Tears welled in her eyes again, and she dashed them away. "I—I thought he loved me. He never said it, but everything he did . . . and today I found out he does not. II-he just married me for his position and because I am qualified. I would not have wed him if I had known his feelings were not the same as mine. I wanted a love match. And I don't know what to do."

Another sob broke from her. Yet it was out.

Her ladyship sat back in the chair. "You do not strike me as a gullible woman. He must have been extremely convincing." Lady Markham started in the direction of the windows for a few moments. "In fact, if asked, I would have said that he is in love with you."

"Blast the boy." The dowager strode into the room frowning. "Someone get me a chair."

Vickers quickly found a chair and placed it next to the younger Lady Markham. "Here you are, my lady."

"Thank you," she said, looking over her shoulder at the maid, before turning back to Elizabeth. "I blame myself for this. Now then, tell us what happened and don't leave anything out. And you, Vickers, isn't it? We shall require tea."

"Yes, ma'am."

While Elizabeth's maid went to comply with the dowager's request, she scooted back in the bed against her pillows and sat up. "I suppose I should tell that he never *said* he loved me."

"Many men have trouble saying the words." Lady Markham's kind eyes had a soothing effect on Elizabeth. She was thankful she had someone in whom to confide. "It is wise to watch how they behave."

"That did not help." She rubbed her forehead in an attempt to ward off a headache. "Even my friends watched him and thought he was in love with me."

Lady Markham heaved a sigh. "What a pickle."

The dowager took a piece of foolscap from her reticule. "Did he do everything on this list?"

Elizabeth read it over three times. The only thing not on it was kissing her. He must have thought of that himself.

*Dance with her twice at every event.*

*Send her flowers.*

*Take her riding.*

*Remain by her side all evening even if she dances with others.*

*Ask her questions about what she likes. By the end of the conversation you should know her favorite color, which flowers she prefers, and her favorite piece of music.*

*Take her someplace she would like to go. Gunter's for an ice is always pleasant. A picnic in Richmond is nice as well, but you would have to get up a party.*

"All this and more. Why?"

"I knew we should have let him figure it out for himself," the older lady said, more to herself than to Elizabeth or her ladyship. "But he told me he liked you, and he wanted help courting you. So I gave him this list thinking that while he was doing all those things he would come to realize he loved you."

Lady Markham glanced at the paper and shook her head. "But how did you discover he does not love you?"

"I wanted to ask him a question. Gibson told me he was in the study. But when I approached the door I heard his lordship tell Geof—Harrington that he was proud of him for having brought me up to scratch." Elizabeth's throat started to close again, but she forced herself to go on. "His lordship said it looked like I would make a good hostess, and—and Harrington said I had all the qualifications."

"Skitter-brained boy." The dowager scowled.

"I must agree," Lady Markham said. "He is extraordinarily thick-headed. Much like Markham when I first wed him. Although, he was Harrington at the time."

"Just like my Henry at the beginning." The dowager glanced at Elizabeth. "Well, you can't stay in bed and cry your eyes out. Though, I understand why you are tempted to. What do you intend to do?"

"I—I suppose I shall tell him that I overheard his conversation with his father, and it . . . it . . ." Elizabeth tried to finish the sentence, but could not.

"I can almost assure you that will not work." Lady Markham patted Elizabeth's hand. "We shall attempt to think of some course of action for you to take."

"Do you really think he might love me?" Elizabeth's hopes had been raised by what her mother and grandmother-in-law had said. If these ladies thought so, he must have some feelings for her.

"It appeared that way to me, but Harrington has never looked for a love match," Lady Markham said. "He had two close friends who fell violently in love and married the ladies. Within a year both couples were at each other's throats."

"Was your marriage a love match?" Elizabeth asked.

"Well"—her ladyship smiled rather wickedly—"not on Markham's side at first, but he discovered being in love was not such a bad thing after all."

"Henry fought falling in love tooth and nail, but he finally came around." The dowager glanced at the door as Vickers entered with the tea tray. "Put that on the night table."

Lady Markham poured tea, handing it around. "What you do not want is Harrington simply telling you that he loves you."

"Would he do that?" For the first time Elizabeth was glad she had not confronted him.

"He would," the dowager said. "Men will always take the easy way out when it comes to feelings. And you are married, so for him there would be no difficulty in lying to you if it made you happy."

Taking her cup, Elizabeth sipped the tea. She could see it all now. She would tell him what she overheard and, fearing a scene or some other such thing, he'd take her in his arms and convince her she was wrong. Then she would never know how he felt. "No. I would never trust that his feelings matched his words."

"That young man needs to be made to see how much he needs you in order to admit he loves you." The dowager tapped her hand in a tattoo on the arm of the chair.

Lady Markham sipped her tea, and the bedchamber was silent for several moments. Then she said, "He was most distraught that your maid would not allow him into the room."

"Oh, I have no doubt he wants Elizabeth." The dowager frowned. "And that will help. When it comes to women, men lead with their nether parts."

Elizabeth glanced first at the dowager and then at her mother-in-law. "That still doesn't tell me what action I should take." She let out a breath. "What did you do?"

A slow smile formed on the older lady's lips. "I led Henry a merry dance. We were in Paris, and I flirted with every Frenchman around, including the king. That last part almost got me into a fix I couldn't get out of. Henry was so jealous, he finally forbade me from flirting. That's when I told him that if he didn't want me there were a lot of gentlemen, including the king, who did."

Elizabeth's jaw almost dropped. She could not imagine telling her husband that. Although, based on Geoffrey's reaction to Lord Littleton, it might work. The only problem was she had never flirted very much.

"That was when he realized I was right." The dowager smirked. "And it was either admit how he felt, or lose me."

"I was not quite as daring." Lady Markham cut a look at her mother-in-law. "I decided to show him what a marriage without love and passion would be like. I was cordial and much cooler to Markham than he wanted me to be. He wracked his brain trying to gain all of my attention. Yet, I was firm. It took him several months, but he finally realized that he loved me."

"I do not think I could be as bold as you, ma'am," Elizabeth said to the dowager. She also did not know how long she could be cold to Geoffrey. Yet, she had to do something, and being cold to him was the only option that might work. "What if I were to let him know I am angry"—*heartsick* was a better word—"with him, but only drop hints as to the reason?"

Both ladies stared at her for a few moments, then Lady Markham said in a doubtful tone, "It might work."

"It might at that," the dowager said. "Although men aren't quick to understand hints."

"That is true," Lady Markham agreed.

That settled that. Elizabeth would have to try being cool toward him. She would also see if he took her hints.

Both ladies rose. "I shall send Harrington to you when he returns," Lady Markham bent over and smoothed Elizabeth's hair back. "I believe Gibson said he was muttering something about Jackson's."

"Just like a man"—the dowager shook out her skirts—"instead of staying here and making you see him, he'd rather go punch someone." She kissed Elizabeth's cheek. "There are times I think the Amazons had the right idea about men."

"Mama!" Lady Markham's sound was somewhere between a gasp and a laugh. "You adored Henry!"

"That was after I got him sorted out," the dowager said loftily.

"Thank you both for your help." The weight that had been pressing on Elizabeth's breast began to lift. If they were correct, somehow, she would make Geoffrey realize he loved her.

She had to if the rest of her life was not to be ruined.

"It was our pleasure, my dear." Lady Markham had her hand on the latch. "That you call him by his first name is an extremely good sign."

Elizabeth slid out of bed and padded to the mirror. A woman with swollen, red eyes stared back. Even the cucumbers had not helped. There was nothing for it. She cringed. This would be the face she showed to Geoffrey and the rest of the household for she still had a few things to accomplish.

Mr. Grantham sent her a note that the contracts were ready for her signature, so that was Elizabeth's first stop.

On her way to speak with her new housekeeper, her mother-in-law found her. "I forgot to mention this before, but if Harrington wishes to ride in the coach with you, you must put him off. If he is anything like his father, he will be able to find several ways to make the ride more interesting."

It took two or three seconds for her to understand Lady Markham. "Oh." Elizabeth's cheeks grew warm.

"Indeed." Her ladyship nodded. "I suggest you make some excuse about your maid having to ride with you."

"That is good advice." In fact, she would not have even thought about what could occur in a carriage.

"There you are, my dear." Lord Markham strolled up. "Have you seen Harrington?"

Her mother-in-law shook her head, and Elizabeth said, "I believe he has gone out for a while."

"In that case, tell him I have already had your horses sent ahead. You'll be using mine. I've also posted horses along the road."

By the time Elizabeth dressed for dinner, she was confident all was ready for the departure in the morning.

After donning a muslin evening gown, she selected one of the new books she'd bought and sat on the chaise near a window. Unfortunately, she never seemed to get past the first page.

When her husband had not returned home by seven—indeed, he had not even bothered to send word when he would be home—Elizabeth ordered dinner to be served to her in her dining room.

That was just as well. If she could not be honest with Geoffrey, she had no idea what to say to him. Yet, his grandmother was correct. If she told him she was upset because he did not love her, he might just say it to make her feel better, and that was not what Elizabeth wanted. She wished for him to realize he was in love with her rather then just tell her he was.

Elizabeth used the rest of the evening considering and rejecting different ideas. She briefly considered continuing to share his bed, but did not think she could go through with it. Not when she didn't know if the act meant as much to him as it did to her. Although Elizabeth rarely had suffered from headaches, she supposed a series of the things were in her future if she was to avoid him.

Later, Vickers brought Elizabeth a cup of warm milk sweetened with honey, and when the clock struck ten, she went to bed, alone and with no good idea how to proceed. It was strange how quickly one became used to sharing a bed. Well, Geoffrey would be alone as well. That should give him a thing or two to think about.

Rolling over, Elizabeth hit her pillow. Blast it all. Being in love was not supposed to hurt this much.

After going a few rounds with Endicott at Jackson's, the two of them had taken themselves off to Boodle's. Not even returning home to change into evening kit. They dined and discussed the possibility that Wellington would not have a sufficient force to win against Napoleon.

"The question is, Who is the better general?" Endicott said.

"My money is on Wellington." Geoff signaled the servant to bring more wine.

"That is what we all hope." His friend drained his wine-glass. "I'd join you over there if it wasn't for the Peace Party making difficulties about the funding."

"There are a lot of peers still in Town for that reason. Even my father. Although he said it was because m'mother didn't want to miss my wedding."

"Wish your bride safe travels for me." Endicott glanced around. "How would you like to find some other fellows for a game of whist?"

"Only one or two hands. I have to be up early tomorrow."

It was after eleven o'clock that evening when Geoff opened the door to his bedchamber, praying Elizabeth was there. Instead, a large, empty bed greeted him. Damn. He knew he should have gone to her no matter what her maid and his mother had said.

Nettle appeared from the dressing room. "Her ladyship is in her own chamber."

"How is she doing?" Geoff sat on the bed while his valet removed his boots.

"Your mother and the dowager visited with her for a time. After that she finished the preparations for tomorrow, then she read. When you did not return to dine, she ate alone." He could hear the rebuke in Nettle's tone. "You did not send word that you would be dining out."

Devil take it! Geoff had forgotten to write a note and send it.

No matter how aggravated he'd been at being shut out of her chamber, he should have been here for her. His first challenge as a husband and he had failed. Now, in addition to being overwhelmed, she'd probably be angry with him for not dining with her. What other reason could there be for her not being in his bed?

He vowed to do whatever was necessary to find a way to make whatever it was up to her. Perhaps the journey to Harwich would give him an opportunity to get back in Elizabeth's good graces. Surely it couldn't be that hard. They had been getting along so well.

# Chapter Twenty-Seven

The following morning, Geoff woke before dawn. He hadn't slept well without Elizabeth next to him. Even the fact that they were finally leaving for Belgium didn't make him as happy as it should have.

He waited until Nettle had set out his shaving kit before rising. Once he was dressed he went into the apartment's dining room to find Elizabeth with an empty plate in front of her drinking a cup of tea.

"Good morning." He kissed her cheek, hoping it would turn into more than that.

"Good morning." The smile she gave him didn't touch her eyes. He really was in trouble with her. "Would you like a cup of tea? It is still hot."

"Please." Plates of ham and roast beef had been set on the table along with toast. "I take it you are ready to depart?"

"As soon as you are." Geoff suppressed a shiver. Her tone was so full of ice it rivaled Lady Mary's.

Her mood made the temperature in the room feel more like March than June. She poured him a cup of tea adding only one lump of sugar and too much milk. He kept his grimace to himself.

"Are you feeling better?" he asked, taking the cup.

"I shall survive." She broke a piece of toast in half and took a bite.

Not knowing what else to do or say, Geoff applied himself to his breakfast. He had intended to travel in the coach with her, but perhaps he'd be better off riding his horse instead. Maybe time without him would help her forgive him.

A few minutes later, she rose from the table. "I must see to the disposition of the servants."

Servants? When he'd left yesterday they were taking two personal servants, two grooms, two coachmen, and a butler. Were there more? When had that happened?

He glopped the rest of his food, and hurried after her. He arrived in the hall as she was bustled through the front door. Lengthening his stride, he followed.

Two traveling coaches piled high with trunks stood in the street. In addition to the servants he knew were joining them, two additional females were getting into the carriage assisted by two footmen. One footman climbed up to sit with William Coachman after the housekeeper and maid were settled. The other went to stand by Elizabeth's carriage.

She called to the coachman, "We'll see you at luncheon."

"Yes, my lady." The carriage took off at a smart pace down the street.

"My lady?" Geoff said.

Elizabeth turned to look at him, then, in an excruciating polite voice, replied, "Yes, my lord?"

A groom he didn't recognize and her dresser were standing by. Damn, he didn't want to talk to her in front of the servants. He held out his arm. "Will you come with me, please?"

"Of course." Placing her fingers lightly on his arm she allowed him to lead her a short way away from the carriages and servants. "Have you added to the number of staff?"

"Both your mother and grandmother suggested a footman in addition to my own, a maid and a housekeeper who can also cook were necessary. I agreed."

Geoff couldn't very well argue with her. After all, both women had more experience than he did in setting up a household in a foreign country. "Very well." He glanced back at the coaches just as Riddle, his groom, drove his phaeton up and was startled not to see his Roan Blues hooked up to the vehicle. "I take it there was not enough room in the second coach for all of the servants?"

"No, as a matter of fact, there was not." Elizabeth's tone was still slightly below freezing. He was beginning to detest being in her black book. "Vickers, my maid, will have to travel in our coach."

He had no idea if Elizabeth did not wish to spend time alone with him, or if the servants' coach really would have been too crowded. Not that it mattered. She'd already sent the other servants on their way. "You don't happen to know where my pair is, do you?"

"Yes." She gave him another too-polite smile. "All the horses we are taking with us have been sent ahead. Your father has posted some of his horses along the way. After keeping us here for so long, he wished to ensure we made good time to Harwich. This way we will not have to spare the horses."

That would not have been difficult for Father to do. Geoff just wished he'd been told about it. "Do you happen to know when he sent them?"

"The day before yesterday. Your father told me before dinner last evening." She raised a brow, and regarded him with eyes that seemed to be devoid of emotion. "I assume if you had bothered to come home, you would have known about it before this morning."

He thought about how his mother would have reacted to his father failing to appear for dinner and not sending word, and decided Elizabeth was not being nearly as hard on him as she could be. Then again, who knew what punishment she had in mind for later?

The option of riding his horse had been taken away from him. He cleared his throat. "Would you mind if I drove my phaeton?"

"You may do as you wish." She walked back to the coaches and then turned to face him. "We must depart."

Geoff knew it was an act of pure cowardice that had kept him from Elizabeth's side. She was upset and rightfully so. He simply did not know how to make it better.

Before he could assist her into her coach, his mother beckoned from the door. "I wanted to see you off." Mama hugged Elizabeth and whispered to her. Next she embraced him. "I wish you great joy in your marriage, but to have it you must come to care for Elizabeth as you should."

"I do," he whispered back.

"No, you do not." Mama stepped back from him. "You will have to figure it out on your own, but I have faith that you will. Your father and grandfather certainly did."

Geoff was more confused now than he had been before. Leaving the house yesterday had obviously not been one of his better ideas. Or should he have demanded to be let into Elizabeth's bedchamber? "I hope you'll visit when things settle down."

"Perhaps we will." She gave him a little push. "Go help your wife."

He got to his carriage just as a footman was getting ready to assist Elizabeth into the coach. "Please allow me, my dear." Again, she regarded him with an apathetic gaze, but placed her hand in his. After she had arranged her skirts, he helped her maid into the vehicle. "I shall see you at the first stop."

"Until then." Elizabeth did not even turn her head to look at him when she spoke.

Guilt warred with growing anger as Geoff closed the door, and went around to his phaeton. He did not enjoy being treated this way. Her mood can't last long, he told himself, praying he was correct. "I'll drive 'em."

The second groom jumped down. "I'll be happy to sit with the coachman, my lord."

Climbing onto his carriage, Geoff said, "I've never seen him before."

"No, my lord. That's Farley. He'd be her ladyship's groom."

Riddle climbed on the back, and Geoff started the pair. "Motion for her ladyship's coach to follow. That way we won't have to deal with their dust."

Although the residents of Mayfair were, for the most part, still in their beds, servants, drays, and other wagons were rapidly filling the streets. He worked his way through the morning traffic, keeping an eye out for Elizabeth's coach. By the time they reached the first toll on the other side of the metropolis, they had been on the road for almost two hours.

"I hope we'll make better time now." He also needed time to think about what had happened with Elizabeth and the meaning of what his mother had said.

He thought he had been treating his wife properly. Yet, obviously, neither his mother nor wife agreed. It was his going out so shortly after their marriage that was the problem. He would have been better off staying at home. Even Nettle had been miffed with Geoff. Still, all he could do was give her a few days to mend her temper and not make the same mistake twice.

At the first stop to change the horses, he was met with the news that they would have luncheon at the Queen's Head in Chelmsford.

Arriving just ahead of her, he strode to the vehicle carrying his wife, opened the door, and let the steps down.

"Do you wish to stretch your legs? We can walk around the yard until our refreshments arrive."

"Yes, thank you," Elizabeth said. She seemed to be in a better mood than earlier.

Fortunately, the area was neither too dusty or too damp. They were able to make one full circuit of the large yard before the inn's servants rushed out with cups of tea and plates of biscuits. As soon as they were able to consume the repast, and the new horses were harnessed, they left again. His wife had still not spoken more than was strictly necessary.

He climbed back in the phaeton, passing the coach before signaling they should follow. The day remained dry and fair, and the traffic was light. Shortly after noon, they sat down to an excellent luncheon.

"I know your father arranged rooms for us here," Elizabeth said. "But if you think we will arrive in Harwich before dark, I would prefer to press on."

"I'll inform the landlord, and Nettle." Geoff found himself wondering if it was him she was trying to avoid or if she simply wanted to reach Harwich.

*Considering her behavior it's probably me.*

Leaving the room, he called for his valet first, sending that worthy on his way. The innkeeper he dealt with himself. He was pleased to discover that his father, already perceiving Geoff's need to complete the journey in as short a time as possible, had notified the inn the rooms would not be required.

"Good luck to you, my lord," the innkeeper said. "We will hope to see you back on good English soil before too long."

"Thank you." Glancing out the door, he saw Elizabeth was almost to her coach, the footman standing by.

Rushing out, he made sure he was there to help her up the steps. Once she and her maid were settled, Geoff gave the coachman the office to depart. A few minutes later, he easily caught up to and passed the carriage.

Before the sun set that evening they pulled into the Three Cups in Harwich.

The hotel's landlord hurried to the door to greet them. "Welcome to the Three Cups, my lord, my lady. I'm Abraham Hinde, the owner. Everything is in readiness for you. Your man arrived not more than an hour ago and said you'd be with us this evening."

"It was a long day of travel, but we are very grateful to be here, Mr. Hinde." Elizabeth gave the man a gracious smile. One that Geoff would kill to receive at this point. "Thank you."

"Your maid is just inside to show you to your rooms, my lady. I've a private parlor for you overlooking the garden. Dinner will be served as soon as you're ready for it."

Geoffrey held out his arm to Elizabeth, and she could do nothing other than place her fingers on it, ignoring the tingling she always experienced when touching him. All day, he had been considerate and contrite. Obviously, he knew she was angry with him—heartbreakingly—was that even a word? It did not matter. That was how she felt—hurt was more like it, but she doubted he would comprehend that. All day she'd had to hide her despair and pretend she was irritated. Not telling him what he had done to hurt her grated on her nerves. She wanted it all out, but Geoffrey's mother and grandmother knew him best, and they had agreed that he would merely tell her what she wanted to hear. She did wonder what he would say when he discovered they were not sleeping together.

Vickers, who had traveled with the other servants after the last change of horses by the expedient of having the housemaid ride with the coachman, waited at the foot of the stairs. "I've got your wash water ready, my lady."

"Thank you." Elizabeth did not even consider having

dinner with Geoffrey. She could not keep up the pretense needed for that long. "I will take a tray in my room and retire after I have dined."

"As you wish, my lady. I'll send a message to the land-lord while you wash."

She was soon in a very comfortable bedchamber large enough to contain a massive bed, a round table with four chairs, a chaise, and two chintz-covered chairs next to the fireplace that had been lit. Once she was out of her carriage gown and in a day dress, she washed her face and hands. Not long afterward dinner was served.

"How was the last part of your trip?" she asked her maid.

Vickers grinned. "I don't think I ever traveled so fast. Mr. Nettle was determined he'd be here to make everything ready for you and his lordship."

A vase of fresh flowers stood on the table, and the scent of lavender was a nice surprise. Elizabeth's own pillows were on the bed. "I am glad he did, but I see your hand in this room. Thank you."

"You might as well be comfortable, my lady." Despite her maid's words, the woman flushed pink. "I'll ring to have these dishes collected."

"Tomorrow, we shall take a stroll around the town." Elizabeth tried to hide a yawn, but she could never fool her maid.

Vickers put the dishes outside the door. "Let's get you ready for bed, or you'll be fagged to death in the morning. I don't know why we even had you put on that gown." As quickly as she could make it happen, Elizabeth was nestled under the covers. "His lordship wished you a good sleep."

Wishing her maid had not told her, she didn't answer. Instead, she rolled onto her side, and longed for her hus-band's strong, lean body to be next to her. Could she keep this act up long enough for him to fall in love with her or figure out that he already was?

Once the candle had been extinguished, she pulled a pillow around to her back. It wasn't him, but it might help her sleep.

Elizabeth woke long after dawn the next day to the news that Geoffrey had left their hotel to leave a message for the ship's captain, and look around the medieval market town.

She did not see him until much later that morning when he came striding into their private parlor. "I spoke with the captain of our ship. If we can get everything loaded by tomorrow afternoon, we may depart on the evening tide and arrive in the morning."

Although she had spent a great deal of time on boats, she had never taken a journey on one. Never mind one large enough to carry their horses and coaches. She was a little worried that it would not all fit.

She was sure Geoffrey had told the skipper how many people, animals, and coaches they had with them, but still. . . . "Did you discuss where he would put everything?"

"It will be enough room for everybody and everything." His grin was so boyish, it almost melted her heart. Why could he not love her as she loved him? "If it had not, my groom would have stayed behind to bring what was left across."

"Where are the horses?"

"In the hotel's stables. They traveled by easy stages and arrived early yesterday. They all look to be in good condition."

"I hope they do well on the crossing." Thinking of that, she should speak with the landlady about remedies for *mal de mer*. Many people suffered from seasickness.

"The ship should be at the dock. I'll take a look at our quarters. Which trunks would you like to have taken on board first?"

Elizabeth was trying her best to be cool toward him, but she was so excited to be on their way, she almost forgot. Still, if she wanted him to want her, she had to keep up the pretense. "I shall coordinate that with Mrs. Robins, and meet you at the ship."

That afternoon, all the trunks with the household items had been placed in one of the holds. Elizabeth was amazed at how much the ship could carry. Accompanied by her housekeeper, she toured the area where the horses would be stabled. "How do you get them in hold? I cannot imagine they can climb down the ladder."

Mr. Havers, the *Sally Ann's* first officer, chuckled. "No, my lady, we'll have a sling rigged up and lift them from the pier into the boat. They'll come out the same way."

"That's clever, don't you think, my lady?" Vickers said, gazing at the ship.

Elizabeth nodded. "I do think it. Exceedingly clever."

He went on to tell them that the crew would load the carriages on the boat in the same fashion.

"What about the wind?" she asked. "My husband seems sure we will be able to depart tomorrow evening, yet I have heard one can wait for days waiting for it to be in the right quarter."

"We'll have a few days of good wind before she changes. Always happens like this, my lady. If the captain says we'll be in good skin, you can trust him to know."

"Thank you." With her questions answered, she and Mrs. Robins bid him adieu and headed down The Quay toward Church Street and the hotel. When they were almost at the hotel, Elizabeth asked, "Have you ever been on a ship?"

"Yes, my lady. I've been to Ireland and back. Don't worry for me. I never get seasick. I know those who do, and it's not fun to nurse them."

Elizabeth imagined it would be a great deal of work. But if any of their people fell ill, she would do her part. By the time she returned to the hotel, the landlady assured her that all the remedies she likely needed would be ready.

Luckily, she and Geoffrey had each been so busy they had not had time to exchange more than a few sentences all day. Elizabeth dressed for dinner, dreading the meal. It would be the first time they were alone since she discovered that he did not love her.

However, the Fates must have been with her. Just as she was about to go down to the parlor, Geoffrey came running up the stairs.

He eyed her warily. "There are a group of fellows with the 73rd Regiment staying at the Black Bull. They've been waiting a week to leave here, and they are out on the morning tide. If you do not mind, I'd like to find out what I can from them."

Elizabeth almost gave him a heartfelt smile, but remembered her role just in time. "Have a pleasant evening. I shall be fine by myself."

For a second his lips pinched together as if he was displeased. Would he finally mention her behavior? But all he said was, "Very well. I will. Do not wait up for me. I shall likely be late."

She took great gulps of air as he turned and walked down the stairs.

*I will not cry, I will not cry.*

# Chapter Twenty-Eight

Geoff's excitement at seeing two of his old school friends and meeting other members of their unit died under Elizabeth's frosty reception.

At some point he was going to have to address the problems they were having. Yet, he couldn't seem to bring himself to the point. Tomorrow, after they sailed, he would insist they work out what was upsetting her.

But tonight, he was going to discover what he could about the situation into which he was taking his wife and his household, such as it was.

The officers had a private room off the taproom of the Black Bull while their soldiers filled the common room.

"We're the last of us to arrive," Captain Lord Thomas Prendergast, one of Geoff's Eton friends said. "Thought we weren't going to make it in time."

"I don't mind telling you that I'm concerned about all the new recruits we've got." Another officer drained his wineglass and refilled it.

"I hear Uxbridge was sent to Wellington," Geoff said. "Have you heard what his reception was?"

Thomas barked a laugh. "My father got a letter from one of his friends. Someone asked Wellington about Uxbridge running off with Wellesley's wife, and our illustrious general said, 'Lord Uxbridge has the reputation of running away with everybody he can. I'll take good care he don't run away with me.'"

The others joined in the laughter.

"Damned good commander," another officer said. "My cousin served under Paget, as he was then, in Spain."

The talk turned to commanders they were glad to see back and those they would have been happy never to see again.

Then one of the younger lieutenants said, "I hear we're missing all the best entertainments. I hope there are some left to attend when we arrive."

"Unless we go immediately into battle, which is unlikely as Napoleon has yet to leave Paris, the last I heard, you can count on Wellington having a ball," Thomas said. "They have been doing more dancing than marching from what I've heard."

Elizabeth would like attending balls and other entertainments, Geoff thought. Yes, he definitely had to make things up with her. The passage to Ostend would be the perfect time. He had made sure they had a room to themselves. As long as she didn't become seasick, it would be the perfect time.

"Do you think Wellington will take the battle to Napoleon?" he asked.

"Not unless he has all his brigades in place," his friend replied. "Are you not concerned about bringing your bride with you?"

Interestingly enough, Geoff had never considered leaving Elizabeth behind. He wasn't a soldier, and if they had to flee, that's what they would do. "I shall watch the situation closely."

"You and Harry Smith. I heard he and his wife, Juana, are already in Belgium."

"Harry Smith?" Geoff shook his head.

Thomas spent the next several minutes telling Geoff about Major Smith and the young woman he had married after the battle of Badajoz. "She was only fourteen, but they took one look at each other and Harry said he was going to marry her, and she agreed. Best little campaigner you've ever seen."

It was after midnight when Geoff finally left the inn, telling Thomas and the others he'd see them in Belgium. Geoff wondered if Elizabeth would like to host a dinner for them and some of the other gentlemen she'd met that would be there. That reminded him that he must attempt to find Colonel Lord Hawksworth when he arrived.

The next day, Geoff, Elizabeth, their servants, horses, carriages, and luggage had no sooner been loaded on the boat than a man with the insignia of a colonel approached the captain. They chatted for a few minutes, after which Captain Higgins motioned toward Geoff.

"My lord," the colonel said. "I am Colonel Lord John Fitzhenry of the 73rd Regiment of Foot. I hear you're headed to Ostend. I must get my men across. The rest of my unit already landed but we were held up. We've been waiting for a week now, and have been unable to obtain transport. May we trouble you for a ride?"

"A ship left this morning," Geoff said, knowing the man would have been on it if he could have been, and it was too late now in any event. Selfishly, he did not want to give up his time to reunite with Elizabeth.

"Unfortunately, we arrived after the ship was already underway. I asked around and we were told we might be able cross on the *Sally Ann*."

Part of him wished to deny the request. Geoff had been in his wife's black book long enough, and he'd planned to use the passage to try to discover what he had done and make amends. Then again, he had a duty to offer assistance. He was damn lucky the ship hadn't been commandeered. It was possible the colonel could force him to take them. Still, if he could find a way out of it, he would. Perhaps he could find another vessel for the soldiers to take. He did have some influence after all.

Yet, before he could speak, the feminine voice that haunted his dreams said, "Of course you shall come with us, Colonel." She dipped a shallow curtsey. "I am sure there will be enough room for you and your men."

Hell and damnation! Geoff clamped his jaw shut and fought to keep the scowl off his face. Would he never have time to speak with her? Still, he couldn't very well object after she'd made the offer. She would be even more furious with him than she already was. "My wife is absolutely correct. You are more than welcome to join us. We sail on the evening tide."

"Thank you, my lord, my lady." The colonel bowed. "We will not hold you up."

"Think nothing of it," Elizabeth said. "We are happy to help in any way possible."

The man went off, Geoff supposed, to gather his troops. "It will be crowded on the ship," he mused, hoping Elizabeth was paying attention to him.

"Yes, but it is only for a matter of hours." She surveyed the vessel. "I am sure we will be comfortable. The *Sally Ann* has sufficient cabins that we need not give up ours. Although, I believe we must share the salon with Lord John and the officers he will have with him."

*Sufficient cabins that we need not give up ours.*

Geoff breathed a sigh of relief. Perhaps she wished to settle their difficulties as well. "I should speak with the captain about the new arrangements."

Elizabeth watched Geoffrey stride off in the direction of the captain who was, again, in conversation with the

colonel. She should have asked how many additional people
would be onboard. The hotel's landlady had provided her
with enough remedies for *mal de mer* for Elizabeth's party,
but with the soldiers accompanying them she should ask if
the hotel's cook should make up more. Even if the *Sally Ann's*
cook had remedies, he might not have enough for the new
passengers, and who knew how many of the soldiers would
become ill.

"Vickers, I must return to the Three Cups. Please find
one of the male servants to accompany me." Elizabeth mentally reviewed the arrangement of the cabins they had been
assigned.

Fortunately, there was enough room on the ship that the
captain had not felt it incumbent upon him to give up his
room for her and her husband. She and Geoffrey had, however, been assigned only one cabin. It was large enough to
accommodate the two of them—if she wished to share a bed
with him, which she did not. Trying to avoid him—which
was becoming more and more difficult—might present a
problem. "It is possible that I could become quite ill during
the crossing."

"My lady"—Vickers's eyes widened in shock—"you've
never in your life been sick on a boat."

"Be that as it may," Elizabeth said quietly, "I have never
been in such rough waters." She glanced at her maid who
was just staring at her and sighed. "You are most likely
right. I doubt if I could successfully manage to pretend to
be ill. In fact, if any of the colonel's men succumb, you and
I will be busy helping nurse them. In that case, I shall not
have time to do anything but that. It might be a very long
night for us."

"I don't know what he did, but avoiding him will not
solve the problem. That's what my mother always said."
Vickers looked as if she wanted to roll her eyes.

Under the circumstances, Elizabeth could not blame her

maid. Vickers had not been in Elizabeth's bedchamber for the whole conversation she'd had with Lady Markham and the dowager, therefore, did not know what Geoffrey had said. Elizabeth did not even know if her maid would agree that a love match was necessary for her happiness. "You must trust me that I am following my mother in-law's and my grandmother-in-law's advice concerning his lordship."

"In that case, I'll keep mum." Her maid went to do as she had been asked.

Fortunately, no matter how she decided to avoid him, Geoffrey would be none the wiser. He had never asked her about her experience with ships and would no doubt be surprised to learn she had sailed from a very young age with her maternal grandfather.

Several hours later, the *Sally Ann* was ready to sail. Elizabeth had obtained a quantity of ginger soup, ginger biscuits, and ginger tea if the worst occurred and most of the others became ill. All of which were guaranteed—according to the landlady of the Three Cups—to aid, if not cure, *mal de mer*. Something Elizabeth had no experience with since none of her family ever got seasick.

She had been told that even many experienced sailors suffered from *mal de mer*. Admiral Nelson being the most famous. She would take a nap that afternoon in the event she did not get much sleep that night.

Four hours later, Elizabeth stood at the rail wrapped in a thick wool cloak. The wind blew briskly out of the southwest, which would make for a quick passage to Ostend. Yet, it also meant the seas would be high.

The crew had raised the first of the *Sally Ann*'s sails, and she began to make her way out of the harbor. For a second, Elizabeth thought she could see Holland, but it was most likely the clouds on the horizon.

Her neck began to prickle and she knew Geoffrey was behind her. "Would you not be more comfortable inside?"

"No, thank you for asking though." Not that he actually cared about her. She was merely his means to an end. "It is not wet, and I like watching the other boats and the harbor."

"You must not call her a boat, my dear." He chuckled. "The proper word is *ship*. A boat is much smaller."

"I am sure you are correct." She looked toward the land, wondering how long it would be before they could no longer see it. At least an hour or more. "Have you ever made a long sea voyage?"

"No. My experience is limited to crewing on the Thames or a rowboat on a lake." He placed his hands on her shoulders, and she wanted to shrug them off before she began craving his touch more than she already did. She had enjoyed making love with him, and missed it. Still, she had to make herself remember that to him it was never more than marital relations. Love never played a part. "Nevertheless, I am certain I shall be able to take care of you should anything occur. Not that I expect it to. Higgins seems to be extremely competent."

"I'm sure we will be perfectly safe." The sound of the rest of the sails being set gave her a thrill. Elizabeth had not been on a ship since her mother died and had forgotten how free it made her feel.

"The captain has asked us to join him for dinner." Geoffrey slid his hands down her arms, and she repressed the shiver of delight she felt at his touch.

"So I was informed." The *Sally Ann* passed the mouth of the harbor, and Elizabeth turned to face her husband. "I shall go to the cabin and wash up."

"I'll join you shortly."

She grabbed the rail to steady herself as the ship heeled. The helmsman must have just set their course.

"Careful, my lady." Captain Higgins appeared next to her. "Would you like a hand getting to the cabin?"

Elizabeth thought about telling him she was perfectly

capable of doing it herself, but that would be churlish, and he had done nothing to displease her. "Thank you." Ignoring her husband's scowl, she placed her hand on the captain's arm. "When do you think we will make Ostend?"

"It is eighty nautical miles as the crow flies. With this wind, we should be there in the morning."

That is exactly what she had thought. They had reached the cabin she and Geoffrey had been assigned, and she inclined her head. "Thank you for your escort, sir."

"Thank you for not objecting to having the soldiers and their equipment onboard, my lady. I could not have denied them."

"No, I imagine they could have taken over the ship. But even if we could have refused to take the colonel and his men, we could not. Wellington needs all the soldiers he can get."

"That he does, my lady. That he does." The skipper bowed. "I shall see you at dinner."

"Until then."

She opened the door and found Vickers waiting. "I asked Mr. Nettle if he would dress his lordship in the cabin he's sharing with Mr. Preston, and he agreed." By the time she'd finished the sentence, Elizabeth was out of her traveling gown and washing. "What I want to know, my lady, is how you expect him to fall in love with you if you keep pushing him away?"

Elizabeth's jaw almost dropped. How did her maid know about that? She did not remember Vickers being in the room at the time.

Elizabeth dried her face and stood as her maid placed a pale pink gown over her head. "Not pushing him away did not work." She heaved a sighed. "I have to find something that will work. My only hope is to try this."

"If you ask me, he was acting like a man in love." Vickers rewound Elizabeth's hair into a knot high on her head.

"So I thought." So everyone had thought and they'd all

been wrong. She was about to ask her maid how much the woman had overheard, when the door opened, and Geoffrey, in a fresh cravat and jacket, entered the room.

Lord, he was handsome. His jacket molded his shoulders before skimming down to his slim waist. Elizabeth did not dare glance at his knee breeches. That would be her undoing.

Ruthlessly, she shoved her desire for him away. Or tried to. Even after his betrayal, her body and mind responded to him in the most wanton fashion. The sooner they were around others, the better.

God help her if she had to sleep in the same bed with him. She did not think she'd be able to ignore the temptation.

# Chapter Twenty-Nine

"You look particularly lovely, this evening." Geoffrey held out his arm. Trying not to touch him more than necessary, Elizabeth placed her fingers on his jacket. "Shall we join the captain?"

As they strolled down the passageway she made sure she kept her other hand on parts of the ship—one hand for the boat, her grandfather always used to say. The ship heeled sharply, and Elizabeth held Geoffrey's arm as he stumbled.

"Are you all right?" he asked after finding his feet again.

"Perfectly. You?"

"Yes, of course." His voice was firm, yet he seemed a little shaken. "I wasn't expecting the ship to move that way. Ah, here we are."

She was surprised to see that the captain had a separate dining room for himself and his officers. In all the ships she had been on, the captain's table was in his cabin.

"My lady, welcome." Captain Higgins bowed.

"Good evening, Captain." Elizabeth smiled. The long table was set for eight. It was affixed to the sole of the ship, and was so highly polished that it gleamed under the lamps attached to the wall, and one larger lamp hanging from the ceiling. Eight heavy wooden chairs were tucked along the sides and at either end. A sideboard with raised edges to keep the plates from sliding off was filled with covered dishes.

Lord John stood at another cabinet, holding a glass of wine.

"What a lovely cabin," Elizabeth said.

"Thank you, my lady. I hope you will enjoy the food as well." The captain bowed to Geoffrey. "My lord, good evening."

"Captain." Her husband inclined his head rather stiffly. Could Geoffrey be a little jealous that she had allowed the captain to escort her below earlier? She remembered what his grandmother had said.

*"I led him a merry dance. We were in Paris, and I flirted with every Frenchman, including the king. That last part almost got me into a fix I couldn't get out of. Henry was so jealous, he finally forbade me from flirting. That's when I told him that if he didn't want me there were a lot of gentlemen, including the king, who did."*

She could hope her husband would be jealous as well.

"My lord." Elizabeth dipped a curtsey to Lord John as he bowed.

"You have definitely got your sea legs, my lady," Lord John said. "I'm afraid it's going to take me a while."

Motioning to the cabinet, Lord John said, "I hope you will join us for a glass of wine."

As his lordship poured, Mr. Havers, his first officer, and Mr. Benchley, the ship's master, entered the room along with Major Dalton, Lord John's Brigade Major, and greeted those already assembled.

Rather than stand, they took their places at the table. After several minutes of stilted conversation about the weather and other innocuous subjects, she decided to encourage the gentlemen to discuss the coming war.

"It's a shame Wellington can't have his old Peninsular army back," Captain Higgins opined.

"Many of his old units were diverted, and some have returned, but others are still in America," Lord John said. "We still have too great a number of raw recruits as well. From what I understand, the duke plans to spread his experienced soldiers among the inexperienced ones. It's a good idea. We'll hold those recruits together. Isn't that right, Will?"

Major Dalton nodded. "Right you are, my lord."

"It is my understanding that the duke has never before met Napoleon in battle," Mr. Havers, the first officer, said.

"That may be the case." The major sipped his wine. "But neither has Boney met the Beau."

A few moments later, two sailors served a hearty oxtail broth. Elizabeth kept an eye on Geoffrey, Lord John, and the others not used to sailing, looking for signs of *mal de mer*. From what she had been told, the earlier one was treated, the better the person would fare.

The soup was removed and a savory fish dish made with a cream sauce had just been served when Major Dalton hastily covered his mouth with his hand. "Forgive me. I must leave."

Across from her Geoffrey turned an interesting shade of green. "I have some ginger tea and alike. If you will allow me, Captain, I shall take them to your cook."

"If you wish, my lady. Although, normally, he is prepared and has what's needed in his stores." Just then the ship's quartermaster entered the room and whispered to the captain. "Tell him to use what we have for the soldiers." He grimaced. "It appears whatever you have on hand will be welcome, my lady. Most of the soldiers have become ill."

The quartermaster held her chair out. "I'll be just a moment." Turning to hurry to the door, she stopped. "Harrington, I believe you should lie down before you become ill."

"Nonsense. I shall be fine. I am never sick." The next

second he clapped his hand over his mouth, and rushed past her into the passageway.

She fought the urge to roll her eyes. "If anyone else is feeling not quite the thing, I beg you will find your bunks. You will feel much better for it. Captain"—Elizabeth inclined her head—"I and any of my household who are able will stand by to assist you."

For the next several hours, Elizabeth, Vickers, Nettle, Mrs. Robins, and Lord John tended to ones who had fallen, including Lord John's batman.

While Elizabeth helped in dispensing medicines to the soldiers who had become ill, she'd left Geoffrey with Nettle who vowed he would see his master drink all of the ginger soup she had ordered for Geoffrey.

Despite the valet's reassurances, she was uneasy that she had not nursed him herself and decided she would see to him as soon as she ate something. Her stomach had been complaining for the past hour, and if she was to keep going, she required nourishment.

Elizabeth had just finished drinking a much-needed cup of tea and eating a slice of beef between two pieces of bread when Nettle rushed into the dining cabin. "My lady. Please come quickly. I'm afraid for his lordship. He can't keep anything down."

"I'll come now." The thought that he deserved part of his illness for being so smug vanished when she entered their cabin. His face was as white as chalk, and he was retching into a chamber pot, but his stomach was clearly empty. "What have you tried to feed him?"

"Some broth, my lady. He didn't like the ginger much."

Wasn't that just like men, not following a woman's orders? "Bring me warm ginger soup and some ginger biscuits."

"But, my lady, he won't—"

"Do as I say and do not argue with me." Really, she had

had a surfeit of recalcitrant men this evening, and she did not intend to listen to another one.

"Yes, my lady." Nettle opened the door.

"I also want some warm water and cloths. He doesn't have a fever, but it might make him feel better." She searched for the lavender her maid always kept at hand.

Geoffrey groaned, and Elizabeth held his hand while she stroked his forehead and his damp hair back from his face. He was cold and wet to the touch and her fear for him began to rise until she reminded herself that she had never actually heard of anyone dying of *mal de mer*. Although she'd met several men tonight who wished they would die while going through it.

She could not stop herself from kissing Geoffrey's forehead and brushing her lips across his.

"Elizabeth?" His voice was a dry croak. He really was suffering badly.

"I'm here now," she said softly. "You'll feel better soon."

"I'm glad you're here. I've missed you." He slipped into unconsciousness, and she could only hope it was a healing sleep.

It seemed like ages before Nettle opened the door carrying two small metal buckets, a cup, and a plate of biscuits.

After setting one bucket on the floor, Nettle said, "The cook said the soup is better given to his lordship in a cup than in a bowl."

Elizabeth nodded. "Set the food on this chest and you may go."

He opened his mouth as if to argue, but must have seen the look in her eyes. "Yes, my lady. I'll be just outside the door."

"You will help Vickers and otherwise make yourself useful."

Not waiting for a response, she sprinkled crumbled pieces of lavender in the can holding the water and swished it around. Picking up a large piece of linen, she dipped it into the water, wrung it out, and placed it on Geoffrey's head. Mrs. Robins had told her that trying to keep the patient warm helped.

After a few minutes, he mumbled, "That feels good."

God, how she loved him. "This will make you feel even better." She slipped her arm under him, raising him just enough to put the cup to his lips. "Drink a little of this."

He made a face and tried to shake his head, but he was as weak as a kitten, and could do no more than attempt to protest.

Still, it took the better part of an hour before she was able to get a whole cup of soup in him. If he could hold that down, she would give him a biscuit. For now, he was sleeping peacefully, and his color was beginning to get better.

Elizabeth rubbed her eyes as exhaustion washed over her. She glanced at Geoffrey. He lay all the way to the outside of the bed. As ill as he was, he would not even notice she was next to him.

Climbing onto the side of the bed next to the wall, she stretched out. Someone would fetch her if she was needed.

Geoff opened his eyes. The ship was still rocking, but his stomach wasn't rebelling. He'd never been so sick in his life. For that matter, it had been the longest night of his life. At one point he had just wanted to die.

Not wishing to move too much, he turned his head to glance out the porthole window. Next to him, a soft, warm bundle moved.

*Elizabeth.*

It was the first time in days she had consented to be in the same bed with him. Although, *consented* might not be the right word. As crowded as this ship was, she hadn't had much choice in the matter.

As if sensing he was awake, she opened her eyes. "How are you feeling?"

"Better." In fact, he wasn't feeling at all sick. "I think I can get up."

Scrambling out of the bed, she rushed around to his side. "No, you will not." She straightened her shoulders and placed her fists on her hips. Her hair tumbled down her back. She pushed back a curl that fell over her forehead. He wanted nothing more than to run his fingers through her mass of curls and kiss her until she agreed to mate with him again. "We won't be in to port for another hour or so," she said. "You will not rise until you can do so without being ill again." She looked at the door. "Stay where you are. I'll be right back."

A few minutes later she returned with a bowl and a spoon. "You may feed yourself this time, and if it goes well, you may have some beef broth and ginger biscuits."

He took a whiff and frowned. "I don't like it."

"You may not like it when you are awake, but you drank it readily enough when you were too unwell to care." Her eyes held a martial light as she approached with the cup.

A vague memory flitted across his mind of her soft hand stroking his head. "Did you nurse me all night?"

"Yes. Now drink this." She practically shoved the cup into his hands.

He took a sip. The stuff wasn't nearly as bad as he'd thought it would be. "Where was Nettle?"

"Helping the others as was Vickers and everyone else who wasn't ill. The only one of the soldiers who remained unaffected was the colonel." Geoffrey finished the cup and she handed him a biscuit. "Chew it slowly."

"Yes, ma'am." He did as she said, and then waited for his stomach to rebel. When it appeared he would be able to keep the soup down, he asked, "May I have the beef broth now?"

"I'll fetch you some." She picked up the bowl. "Do not rise."

"I'll stay right here." And fantasize about her naked next to him. If only he knew what to do to make things better between them.

As much as he wanted to try to get her to open her budget, now was not the time. He might have been ill, but she had to be exhausted if she took care of him all night. Not only that, but she was being bossy, and was unlikely to listen to him at present. He'd never seen that part of her before.

Several moments later, he was sitting up in bed, eating a broth so thick it was almost like stew. Elizabeth could have left nursing him to Nettle, but she had not. It was more than he expected after the past sennight. Did this mean she was no longer angry with him? "How did you know to bring the medicines?"

"Many people suffer from *mal de mer*. It made sense that someone would fall ill on this passage. Although, I truly did not think it would be almost everyone but the crew."

Dark circles bruised her eyes. He wondered how much sleep she'd had if she was nursing him and, possibly, others. "You didn't become sick."

"No. I felt confident I would not." She tidied the bedding and fluffed up his pillow as if she needed to do something other than talk with him. "I spent much of my childhood on boats and private yachts. I have never been ill while onboard."

"I didn't know."

She arched one blond brow. The ire was back. "Did you even care?"

"Of course I care." What the devil was she so livid about? It had to be something other than him going out and not sending word. "You are my wife. Why would I not wish to know?"

"Ah, yes." Sarcasm infused her tone. "I am your extremely qualified wife." Striding to the door she opened it. "I shall send Nettle to you."

"Elizabeth," he called out. If he could just keep her talking he might discover why she was so upset.

Halfway out the door she stopped. "Do you wish for something, husband?"

*Yes. Tell me why you are so furious with me.* Yet, he didn't say it. "No. I wanted to thank you for nursing me."

"You are welcome." She swept out of the cabin, and he was left alone again with his own thoughts.

Somehow he had to bring her around.

He wondered why she had mentioned how well qualified she was. He had always thought so. In fact, he'd made sure of it. His wife would have responsibilities and she should know how to handle them. Elizabeth was actually even more well suited to her position than he had known.

Still, there was something about the way she had said it. As if she was unhappy about her qualifications. Why would that be when he was delighted with her? Clearly, something else was wrong. If only he knew what it was, he would make it better, give her anything she wanted.

Before long, Nettle entered the room looking as well groomed as always—which for some reason irritated Geoff—carrying a large ewer. "The captain says we'll reach the port in about an hour." His valet poured water from the ewer into a bowl set in a wooden stand. "Her ladyship says that if you can sit up, wash, and be shaved, you may leave your bed. But if you are feeling like you are getting sick again you are to lie right back down."

Geoff wondered if he should pretend to be ill just so she would return to their cabin. He sat up. "I'll brush my teeth first."

An hour later, Geoff sat on the bed as he wound his cravat around his neck. So far, so good, and he'd be on dry land soon. One day in Ostend to recover from the crossing, and they would continue on their journey.

The last letter he'd received stated that Sir Charles wanted Geoff to come to him in Brussels. The question was if those instructions were still valid, or would Geoff be sent to The Hague, or Brussels, or some other place. It would behoove him to send a messenger and ask.

No matter where he was assigned, his father had arranged for houses in Ghent—because the French king was there, The Hague—which he did not understand at all—and Brussels where it seemed everything of import was taking place.

His only real concern was that he might be called upon to ride ahead. Thus far, Elizabeth had proven herself to be equal to anything, but he would not like leaving her alone to manage in a strange country.

Well, there was no point worrying about what might happen when he should be applying himself to what was happening, or rather not happening with his wife.

Who, it appeared, was once more avoiding him. Geoff stood slowly; fortunately, he still felt fine. He made his way along the corridor to the companionway and onto the deck. The crew was busy lowering some of the sails. When he glanced toward the bow, he could see the town of Ostend.

To the front and sides of him, sailing vessels crowded the harbor.

"We're getting ready to anchor," Mr. Benchley, the ship's master said.

"I didn't expect to see so many ships."

"More than usual. It will be the same in Antwerp. If it doesn't go well for us, there will be a lot of people trying to get back to England."

For the first time, a spike of fear for Elizabeth speared Geoff's chest. Sir Charles had not brought his wife, Lady Elizabeth, but Geoff had never even thought to leave his wife in England. Perhaps he was being selfish wanting

Elizabeth by his side. He could offer to send her back, but with matters so unsettled between them, the rift might grow. Was that selfish of him as well? If her life was at risk here . . . He should allow her to decide.

"Will you remain in Ostend for the nonce?"

"I expect we will." The master glanced at Geoff. "Lady Harrington is welcome to sail with us anytime she'd like. We wouldn't have been able to nurse everyone who got sick if it hadn't been for her." He wondered what exactly she had done, but did not want to betray their problems by asking. He needn't have worried. Benchley was happy to talk about it. "You were ill yourself, so you might not know. She not only had your servants, the ones who were not feeling poorly, help with the soldiers, but I don't think there is any ginger left in Harwich in any form, so much did she bring aboard. She even helped nurse the others herself until you needed her. We're grateful for her assistance."

"Thank you for telling me." Geoff was surprised she hadn't slept longer. Elizabeth must be exhausted. "When I awoke this morning she was more interested in making sure I had recovered, than relating to me what she had done."

"I had the feeling when I met her she was that type of lady. Doing for others and not bragging about herself. Women like that don't come around often."

"No, they don't." He thought back to all she had done to prepare for their journey, never once complaining about it. She'd simply taken on the task and done it. He was beginning to think there was nothing Elizabeth could not do. She was definitely more capable than he had thought even a week ago. What other talents did Elizabeth have that Geoff had no idea she possessed? "If we have need of you, where can we send a message?"

"At the Schip. The landlord there will get word to us." The master stood back and executed a short bow. "I'd better get back to my duties."

"Thank you," Geoff said. "Do you know when the captain expects to be able to dock?"

"They move them in and out at a pretty smart pace," Benchley said, eyeing the harbor. "Sometime tomorrow or even this afternoon, if we're lucky." The ship jerked, causing him to brace. "Ah, good, the anchor's set. The skipper will have orders now."

Geoff watched as the man moved toward where the captain was standing, next to his first officer. He scanned the deck expecting to see Elizabeth, but there was no sign of her. He hoped she had taken a nap, but, somehow he doubted it. It occurred to him that she gave the impression of being restful when in reality she was in constant movement. The only time he's seen her still was when she was asleep. It had been much too long since he'd held her against him.

Soon, he vowed to himself. Soon they would be back to the way they were right after their wedding.

# Chapter Thirty

By the time the ship had anchored in the Ostend harbor to await a berth, Elizabeth had washed and changed in her maid's cabin. She did not dare go into hers. Geoffrey in bed, now that he was feeling better, was simply too much temptation to bear. The only way she had found to rid herself of her need for him was to turn into a shrew. And she could not keep that type of behavior up for long.

Her mother-in-law had agreed she could drop hints, and Elizabeth had tried, but they had slid right by Geoffrey, just as the dowager said they would.

She rubbed her forehead, hoping she was not getting a headache. The best thing she could do was to continue to keep her distance and pray he would realize that he loved her. If only she could think of a better plan.

She climbed up the companionway, spying Lord John at the rail. With his soldiers recovering from *mal de mer,* the colonel decided to ferry his men to land rather than wait for the ship to dock.

Glancing her way he smiled at her and bowed. "I wanted to thank you for your help and that of your servants, my lady."

"I only did what was necessary, my lord." Honestly, she hadn't done anything anyone else would not have done.

He gave her a lopsided grin. "Be that as it may, I do not know many ladies, even soldiers' wives, who would have nursed common soldiers as you did. Your husband's a lucky man."

She could not stop the warmth that rose in her cheeks. "Thank you, my lord. I wish you a safe journey and good luck afterward."

"Thank you my lady. I think we'll need it." The lines etched in his face seemed harder.

"Perhaps we shall see you in Brussels." She smiled brightly, trying to lighten his mood.

"I hope we do." He smiled, and inclined his head before striding off and ordering his major and batman into the first boat with orders to find them places to stay until their provisions could be offloaded.

"Do you wish to go ashore as well?" Geoffrey appeared at her side, taking her hand and tucking it in the crook of his arm as he waved farewell to the colonel's men.

Normally, she would be happy to remain aboard, but then she'd be faced with having to sleep in the same bed as her husband. "Yes. We may as well leave the captain to deal with finding a berth and not have to bother with us. Nettle said we have a hotel arranged. We can send him and Vickers ahead to get everything ready."

Geoffrey tugged her a little closer, and she fought the urge to lean into him. "Very well. I'll let the captain know."

But just then Captain Higgins strolled up to them. "If you don't mind, I'll send you to shore as soon as I get the last of the soldiers off."

Trying and failing to ignore the tingling sensations caused by her husband, Elizabeth grinned at the captain. "We just now decided the same thing."

"Famous. If you tell me where you're staying, I'll send

a message when we're ready to offload your cattle and carriages."

"The Princess Henrietta," Geoff said promptly. "I understand it is inside the city walls. Have you any idea how long it will be?"

"Give me an hour or so to get your trunks out of the hold and these fellows"—he nodded to the soldiers—"into port, and I'll be ready for you."

"Thank you. We'll be ready." Geoffrey led Elizabeth back to the companionway. "You were awake most of the night. Do you wish to rest when we get to the hotel?"

The question took Elizabeth by surprise. She had honestly not expected him to notice. "I am tired, but I think I would like to see some of the town. And discuss where we go next." She took in the wan look in his face. "But if you would like to rest? You were quite ill."

"No. I'm happy to stroll around Ostend." She was about to mention their further travel when he said, "I sent a messenger to Sir Charles with the first boat that went in asking him for instructions."

"Will we wait here until they are received?" How long would that take? she wondered. It was already close to the middle of June. Lord Markham had assured Geoffrey that as long as they were on the Continent by the fifteenth, Sir Charles would be happy.

"It is over one hundred miles to Brussels, and we will not be able to travel quickly. I would like to start out as soon as the horses are rested."

"That sounds like a good idea." It also meant that he would be too busy to care about them sharing a bedchamber. Or so she hoped.

Later that afternoon they were settled into their hotel, and the next morning, Captain Higgins sent a note round that the horses and carriage would be offloaded within the next two hours.

Geoff and Elizabeth strolled down to the port to watch. One would have thought that the inhabitants of Ostend would be used to that type of thing, but despite that, a small crowd gathered in front of the pier. Even he had to admit that seeing the horses come out of the hold in a sling was impressive.

"They do not appear frightened at all," Elizabeth said in a tone of wonder. "I thought for sure my mare would be terrified."

"They've done well," Geoff agreed.

As soon as they were stabled, he'd inspect them himself.

In a very short time, their grooms had the horses harnessed and a small procession started off to the hotel's stables.

Now that they were in Holland, Geoff was eager to be on his way, but the horses needed to rest, and until he heard from Sir Charles, he had no idea in which direction to travel. Fortunately, Geoff did not have to wait long.

Early the following morning as they were breaking their fast, a message came for Geoffrey from Sir Charles. He shook open the missive and read it quickly. "We travel to Brussels."

"That is where I hoped we would go." Elizabeth called for their senior staff to attend them.

Reading the letter again, Geoffrey frowned. "Do you mind if I ride?"

"No. Is something wrong?" He glanced from the letter with a look of chagrin. "I may have underestimated the number of outriders we require."

She twitched the letter from his fingers.

*I become concerned about the state of the roads. Rumors abound about Napoleon, but we still do not know which way he is going. I am certain he is on his way here. Some of our countrymen have already*

*made arrangements to return home. Others are
waiting to see what the duke will do. It is clear that
many people have grown uneasy.*

"Elizabeth." Geoffrey took her hand, enfolding it in his.
"Do you wish to return to England? It might be safer."

"No. I will be fine." It was a shame Lord John had already left, but she and Geoffrey could never hope to match
their pace. How bad could it be? The battle had not begun
yet and, as far as anyone knew, Napoleon was still in Paris.
"Ask the landlord if he has any servants you can hire, and
ensure all the coach pistols are loaded with extra balls and
powder handy."

Once their servants were assembled, Elizabeth started issuing orders. "We depart within the hour. Mrs. Robins, Preston, Nettle, Molly, and Kenwood will ride in the baggage
coach and leave as soon as the trunks have been packed.
Vickers, you will accompany me. His lordship's curricle
will accompany the coach. His lordship will ride Hercules.
We are arranging for some of the inn's servants to act as
outriders, but I want all our pistols and muskets to be
loaded." The servants exchanged glances. "We shall meet
for luncheon. If, for any reason, you feel we should remain
together, I wish to hear it now."

Riddle folded his lips. "We'll see how it goes, my lady.
We'll stop at an inn if William Coachman and I feel we
should."

"Very well. I shall leave it to you." Elizabeth smiled at
them. "The sooner we depart, the sooner we will arrive at
our new home."

As their servants left the room, Geoff took her hand.
"Well done, my dear."

"That is the reason you married me, is it not?" She
quickly ate the last bites of bread and cheese. "I shall make
sure Vickers has our trunks down to be loaded onto the

coaches in short order. I do not wish to be too far behind the baggage coach."

He didn't know how to answer her. Her ability to manage was not the only reason he'd wed her. He wanted her in his bed as well. But before he could begin to explain himself, the door closed behind her with a snap.

*I've lost another chance to find out what is wrong with her.*

Still, he wasn't a stupid man. Obviously it had something to do with her abilities. Was he putting too much pressure on her?

By the time Elizabeth reached her bedchamber, she had her anger under control. She had wanted to rail at him. Tell him that if only he could look beyond her abilities he might be able to see the woman she was. One that needed her husband to love her the way she loved him.

If only she could figure out a way to tell him what she wanted without an immediate and false declaration of love from him. Something had to change because she did not know how long she could keep up her pretense of not wanting him.

She changed into a traveling gown and helped her maid pack what little they had removed from the trunks. "I think this is it."

"How dangerous will it be?" Vickers asked.

"To be honest, we don't know. That said, I plan on being prepared for anything."

A knock sounded on the door. Her maid opened it.

"We're here to take the trunks down, if you're ready," Kenton said.

Elizabeth strolled into the inn yard as the last trunks were being loaded.

A few moments later, Geoffrey joined her. "I can hire three men for a day."

She let out a frustrated breath. "That is better than nothing I suppose." Not much. Everyone would have to remain vigilant. "At least we will have an idea of what we are up against."

For the first time since she had heard his conversation with his father, he pulled her into his arms. It was all she could do to keep her own arms by her side when she wanted so much to hold him as well. If only she had not heard what she had.

But past was past and she could not change it.

After a few moments he released her, and Elizabeth wished his arms were still around her.

"It is time to depart." He tilted his head, a sly grin forming on his lips, making her want to throw her arms around him and kiss him. "Tell me you know how to shoot a pistol."

"Well, I will tell you that." She turned to walk away toward her coach, but looked back over her shoulder. "And I am accounted an excellent shot."

In three long strides, he was with her. She placed her hand on his arm, and stepped into the coach. "Be careful."

The one thing she did not want was for him to be murdered before he discovered he loved her.

"I will."

The coach started forward and, for a time, she gazed at the flat countryside. "It is very different here than in England."

"It is that, my lady," Vickers responded. "Reminds me of The Fens in a way, but clouds are higher here, and I can't see a marsh."

"I've never visited The Fens," Elizabeth said. "What are they like?"

"Flat like this, but with marsh everywhere. I always felt like the clouds were pushing on top of my head."

"That doesn't sound particularly pleasant." She was glad the clouds here weren't low.

"They're not my favorite part of England, but a great

many people love them." Vickers glanced out the window. "I like it better here."

"I'll like it immensely if we do not have any problems getting to Brussels."

Elizabeth placed her pistol in her lap and took out her book, but was unable to read it. The traffic was steady with farmers and a few carriages. Yet, nothing out of the ordinary appeared to be going on. Finally, she was lulled to sleep by the swaying of the coach.

She woke when it was time to rest the horses.

At luncheon, Riddle deemed the roads safe enough for the servants to go on ahead of Elizabeth and Geoffrey.

That evening they stayed in a small town about ten miles outside of Ghent. The day had been pleasant, but, due to the number of times they'd had to rest the horses, it would take another two days to arrive in Brussels.

And Elizabeth was no closer to knowing what she should do about Geoffrey, other than what she was already doing. If he continued to hold her, she would end up kissing him, and that would lead to other things, and before she knew it she'd be back in his bed without ever knowing if he could love her.

She was, therefore, relieved to find that Nettle had once again arranged for separate bedchambers with an adjoining parlor.

After they had washed and changed, she and Geoffrey took a walk in the town. Stores were still open, and no one seemed to be nervous about the coming battle. With luck, it would remain that way for the rest of their journey.

By the time they had dined, all she wanted was her bed. Tomorrow would be another long day.

# Chapter Thirty-One

Geoff, Elizabeth, and their small household started early the next morning.

He had hoped to get all the way to Ghent the previous day, but they were several miles short of their destination, and he'd decided not to push the horses any more than necessary even if it took them longer to arrive in Brussels.

Throughout the day, the traffic grew heavier with people both on foot, by horse, farm wagon, and carriage.

A few worried souls even tried to convince him to turn around, always with the same warning. "Napoleon will march north soon. They say his army is so large it will destroy Wellington's forces."

Geoff thanked them for their advice, but shortly after noon, he began to grow concerned. At one point he rode up to the coach and asked Elizabeth if she was sure she did not wish to turn back. As expected, she told him to press on.

Still he wavered back and forth between her immediate safety, and the possibility that they might become separated, putting her at more of a risk than she already was.

He finally put the question to her in a slightly different way. "Would you like to go back to Ghent?"

She narrowed her eyes at him and was silent for several moments before answering, "Why would I do that?"

"You might be safer." Even as he said the words he knew he could never let her go. No one would do as much to keep her from harm as he would.

Her countenance relaxed. "No, I would rather continue on. At this point, by the time I could return to Ghent, we shall be in Brussels. I would rather make the journey only once."

That was true enough. "Very well."

She had thought to have a basket packed, and he ate a sandwich while riding. By dark, they had only made it as far as Asse, and Geoff called a halt for the night.

Elizabeth climbed stiffly out of the coach. "Thank you for stopping, I know you wanted to reach Brussels this evening, but this way we will be able to send the servants to the house to make it ready before we arrive."

"It amazes me how you always find the good side of situations." He tucked her hand in his arm to steady her.

She shrugged. "There is no point in belaboring the bad points when there is nothing one can do to change them." They strolled around the garden in back of the hotel while Nettle and Vickers saw to their rooms. "I would like to know what is going on. All we have heard is that Napoleon is coming north. Yet we have heard nothing of what Wellington is planning."

"Mayhap someone at the inn will know," Geoff said to appease her. Although he doubted the innkeeper would know more than anyone else they'd come across today.

His military friends had told him cannons and other weapons could be heard many miles away from the actual fighting. How many miles away he didn't know. Thus far they had not heard anything indicating the armies were engaged. It would be a relief to reach Brussels where all their questions could be answered.

Following the routine they had fallen into, they rose early. The previous day, Nettle consulted the landlord's map of Brussels to find the address of the house Geoff's father had rented for them.

Unfortunately, the innkeeper was unable to tell Geoff where he might be able to find the English delegation in Brussels.

Most of their servants left just before dawn, leaving him with his wife, her lady's maid, a housemaid—no one had bothered to explain why the girl did not accompany the housekeeper—the grooms, and one footman.

Just as their party reached the outskirts of Brussels they were met by news that the Corsican had taken Wellington by surprise and that Napoleon was marching north.

Geoff galloped up to Elizabeth's coach. "If you do not mind, I'm going to ride into the city. If anyone will know where I can find Sir Charles, it will be the Duchess of Richmond who is a friend of my mother's. At least I know her address. It is not much farther. Do you feel comfortable traveling the rest of the way or would you like to find a place to wait until I return?"

"I shall be fine," Elizabeth replied with the aplomb he was coming to expect from her. "I am quite sure that if this fight was over, we would be seeing British troops coming this way."

"I'll see you later then." He wanted to hold her, and kiss her, and tell her she was the bravest woman he knew. Instead, he rode off, sticking to the sides of the roads to avoid the exodus of people now filling the road.

Once he arrived at the duchess's house, she had, indeed, been able to direct Geoff to Sir Charles's residence. Yet, when Geoff arrived there, he was directed to Wellington's headquarters on *rue Royale*. Luckily, Sir Charles was just coming down the steps as Geoff road up to the building.

"Good day, Sir Charles," Geoff said, holding out his hand.

"Lord Harrington, well met. I'm glad you've arrived."
The older man clasped his hand warmly. "Come walk with
me, and I shall tell you what has been going on. Do you
have a place to live?"

"Yes, sir. My father arranged it. I rode ahead of my wife
to see you, but our servants should have been there a few
hours ago. It's on *rue Zinner*."

"Yes, yes." Sir Charles nodded. "Good location. Across
the park from here and on a small street. How was your
crossing?"

"As well as could be expected. For the past two days
we've seen a steady stream of people headed for Ostend and
Antwerp."

"No matter that nothing has yet occurred there are
always those who will panic." The older man shook his
head. "I look forward to meeting Lady Harrington. In the
meantime, there is a great deal to be done. I congratulate
you on having the forethought to send your servants ahead."

Obviously, Geoff was not going to be able to spend a
great deal of time with Elizabeth or at his new home. "I
look forward to getting started."

He spent the next several hours making notes, copying
reports, and writing letters, all the time wondering if Elizabeth was safe. By five o'clock, he began to worry. He should
have heard something by now.

One of Sir Charles's servants was acting as a messenger.
If Geoff didn't hear something soon, he'd send a message to
the house.


Elizabeth watched as Geoffrey cantered toward Brussels.
At this point, she wished they could all ride the rest of the
way. It would be easier than picking their way through
the sea of people, carriages, carts, and wagons.

Some of the vehicles had been abandoned along the way

as if their owners took what they could carry and fled. An hour later, she ordered his phaeton to drive ahead. The carriage could get through the traffic more quickly than her large traveling coach.

Three hours later, after making very little distance, Elizabeth was tired of riding in the coach. There were some shops in the area, and her people needed to eat.

Banging on the roof she called, "Stop the coach." As it came to a halt, she glanced at her maid and the housemaid, Molly. The poor girl had been left with them because she had not been feeling well, and the baggage coach would be traveling as quickly as it could. "I am going to that bakery across the road. If I had imagined we would run into this type of traffic, I would have had the landlady make us a basket. Vickers, please go to the cheese store next to it and buy what you can to put in the rolls. Molly, come with me." Once Kenton, her footman, helped Elizabeth down from the coach, she shook out her skirts. "I am not quite sure what is going on, but keep a good watch on our coach and horses. If anyone gets too close, warn them off. Use a pistol if you have to."

Crossing the street, Elizabeth entered the bakery and greeted the shop girl. The aroma of freshly baked breads and rolls was heavenly. It also caused her stomach to protest its fairly empty status.

She was in the process of ordering enough rolls to keep her party fed until they reached the house when Molly screeched, "My lady, there's a man trying to take our horses!"

Elizabeth whirled around. Who in God's name would do something so evil?

The coachman had his pistol out waving it between a gentleman and a servant who kept attempting to touch the harness. Did the cur actually think he could take her cattle and get away with it?

Taking some coins from her reticule, she handed them to

the maid. "Get the bread. I'll take care of the horses." She marched out of the shop and up to her coach, pulling out her pistol as she went.

When she was on the opposite side of the team from the gentleman and his servant, she pointed the gun at a young man who was nervously trying to unhitch her horses from the coach. "Stop now or you will be extremely sorry." The servant jerked his head up in surprise, then glanced toward the coachman who had his gun out and was holding it on a gentleman she judged to be in his mid-thirties to early forties. Elizabeth raised one brow. "Is this your groom?"

"He is indeed." The man raised his chin, and in a haughty tone said, "I assure you I urgently require your horses."

"As it happens," she said, in what she hoped was a loftier tone than the gentleman's, "I also have an urgent need of them. Additionally, I believe I have the greater claim in that they belong to me, and I shall not part with them." She cocked her pistol. "Now, unless you wish to be responsible for your servant being injured, you will both step away from my team and my coach."

The man actually heaved a sigh. "I am afraid you will have to shoot one of us, ma'am, as I insist that my need takes precedence over yours. I must return to England immediately."

"William," Elizabeth said to the coachman, "sit back a bit and keep your pistol on the groom." Once her coachman had followed her command, and without saying another word, she aimed her gun at the gentleman and fired, blowing off the beaver hat on his head.

As one, the servant and gentleman screamed and jumped back. Next to her, Vickers took Elizabeth's smaller weapon and handed her one of the coach pistols. "You and Molly get in the carriage and pull down the shades."

A second later, the gentleman shouted, "What the devil do you think you're doing?"

"Protecting my property from being robbed." She pointed the heavy gun at him.

"Do you know who I am?" He sounded as if he was as well known as Prinny.

"That is a ridiculous question. We have not been introduced. Therefore I cannot possibly know who you are. For that matter I do not care to know you. As far as I am concerned you are nothing but a thief." She cocked the pistol, making it clear to the fool she would have no problems shooting him again. "Unless you wish me to injure something more valuable, I suggest you leave. Immediately." Elizabeth kept the gun pointed at him until he and his groom had walked down the road and were no longer a threat. "Let's go, but keep a watch for other people who think they can rob at will."

"Do you think he'll be back, my lady?" Molly asked.

"Not if he knows what's good for him," Vickers answered.

"That was a pretty piece of shooting, my lady." Farley, her groom, chuckled. "Ain't never heard a gentleman scream before."

"Like a little girl." William Coachman slapped a hand on his knee. "Wait 'til his lordship hears about this."

"That was well done, my lady," Kenton said, as he handed her into the carriage.

As soon as the door was shut, he scrambled up next to William and the horses started forward.

For the next hour or more, Elizabeth kept the coach pistol in her lap before she finally felt safe enough to return it to the holster. "I will be extremely grateful when this journey is over."

"Who would have thought that a gentleman would try to take horses from a lady?" Vickers mused.

"One who was desperate. But I was not about to allow him to place us in an untenable position." Elizabeth wondered what Geoffrey would think about the encounter. By the way he had been behaving recently, he might be upset about it. Then again, he had asked if she could shoot. Maybe he would think of it as part of her *qualifications*.

Vickers and Molly began to make sandwiches. Vickers offered Elizabeth the first one, but she shook her head. She would eat after the others had been fed.

Molly handed them through the window to the men before Elizabeth took the one that was offered to her. It was only after she had taken a bite, that Vickers and Molly ate their sandwiches.

Two hours later, they pulled up before a moderately sized house down a nice street on the back of a large park. The moment the horses stopped, Preston had the door open, and Nettle and Riddle, Geoffrey's groom, came out to help with the trunks and horses.

"You will have to guard the horses," Elizabeth said. "We almost had ours stolen today."

"There's a stable in the back with a lock, my lady. I'll move a cot down from the upstairs, and we'll take turns sleeping with them."

That should do it. "Keep the pistols loaded and do not hesitate to sound the alarm."

Naturally, it was not long before everyone knew how Elizabeth had driven off the would-be horse thief.

"Shot a hole right through his hat, an' never even blinked," William told the others.

"Your chamber is ready, my lady." Mrs. Robins led Elizabeth and Vickers up the stairs to a large room overlooking a garden.

The fireplace had been lit. Beyond a set of French windows, Elizabeth could see a small terrace with two chairs and a table.

"The house was in good condition," the housekeeper said. "There's a Belgium couple taking care of it full-time. She had some maid helping, but since the army and everyone has been here, she's been doing it mostly by herself."

As Elizabeth discussed the menu for this evening and tomorrow morning with her housekeeper, it dawned on her that she finally had her own household to run as she saw fit.

"Madam knows a very good cook, if you would like to hire him," Mrs. Robins said.

"Let us at least try him," Elizabeth replied. If he was local, the cook would know where to buy the freshest food.

"Very good, my lady. I'll tell Madam know."

A copper tub was carried into the room, and in a short time it was filled.

Elizabeth lowered herself into the hot water that her maid had scented with lavender and lemon balm and allowed herself to relax after the day she and her servants had experienced.

Her mind wandered to her husband. Had he found Sir Charles? Most likely Geoffrey had. None of the staff had seen him, and she wondered if he had been put to work or if he had run into old friends of his.

There was only one way to find out. "Vickers, send one of the men to look for his lordship. I would like to know that he arrived safely, and I wish him to know that we are here."

"Yes, my lady."

Elizabeth decided that she would enjoy what little time she would have in the city. If the battle with Napoleon went well, they would be moving to Paris shortly. If not, they'd be fleeing back to England.

# Chapter Thirty-Two

Elizabeth must have fallen asleep. The water had cooled significantly, and Vickers was shaking her shoulder.

She blinked. "What time is it?"

"Right around five o'clock. Stand up, and I'll hand you a towel."

She did as she was told and was surprised that the towel was warm. "You put it near the fire."

"There is a rack there for it. Or I suppose that's what it's for."

"Has his lordship been heard from?" She did not even know if she was to plan on him joining her for dinner.

"A note just came." Vickers handed Elizabeth a robe. "That's the reason I woke you. That, and you'd be chilled to death if you stayed in there much longer." Her maid reached into her pocket. "Here it is."

*My dearest Elizabeth,*

   *Kenton found me. I trust your travel the rest of the way to Brussels went well, and I am relieved that you arrived safely. I wish I would have been at the house to greet you. Unfortunately, I will not*

*be home until late this evening. Shortly after I saw
Sir Charles, I was put to work.*

*We have been invited to dine with the Duchess of
Richmond tomorrow before the duchess's ball to
which we have been invited.*

*Wellington is waiting to hear from someone in
Mons before he takes any action.*

> *Yr devoted husband,*
> *G*

She blinked back the tears that pricked her eyes. If only
they had the type of marriage she wanted, everything would
be perfect. Still, she had to have faith. The dowager said it
had taken time for Geoffrey's grandfather to come around.
It must be something to do with the men in his family.

Someday, she hoped, he would love her.

In the meantime, she would play the role of his qualified
wife. "He will not dine at home this evening, but I want
soup, meats, cheese, and bread ready for when he returns in
the event he is hungry."

Vickers nodded. "I'll tell Mrs. Robins."

Once Vickers shut the door, Elizabeth went out to the terrace and sat on one of the chairs. The tower of a church rose
in the distance, and the roofs of other houses could be seen.
The garden was a riot of colors intersected by paths.

Tomorrow, after she had the house set up the way she
wanted it, she would explore the garden and mayhap ven-
ture out into the city. It really was beautiful here.

Still, she must find more to occupy her time than running
the household. Perhaps she would meet some other ladies
who would have some ideas on how Elizabeth could be
helpful. She did not think she already knew anyone here,
but there was always a possibility she did.

Elizabeth picked up the note from Geoffrey again and gasped.

*The Duchess of Richmond's ball. How did I come to overlook that?*

His friends had not been joking when they said everyone was hosting entertainments.

A few minutes later, her maid came back into the room. "Are you ready to dress, my lady?"

"Yes. Just a day gown. But"—she grinned—"you might want to make sure one of my new ball gowns is pressed for tomorrow evening. We have been invited to the Duchess of Richmond's ball."

A broad smile appeared on her maid's face. "So all we've heard has been true."

After a quiet dinner alone, it was still light enough to take a look at the gardens, and Elizabeth decided not to wait until morning.

The privet borders were fronted by a mix of lamb's ears, Sweet William, and cat mint. The middle of the squares featured hollyhocks, delphiniums, phlox, and daisies. Other squares had smaller boxwood edges framing in roses. Under the roses lavender bloomed.

Nestled in the middle of the garden was a fountain with a few tables and chairs on a cobblestone surround. She sank onto one of the chairs and listened to the water, the soft sound of hooves somewhere nearby, and people chatting.

As the sun began to set Elizabeth went inside, poured a glass of wine, and found a cozy chair in which to read her book, hoping to see Geoffrey when he came home. Yet when the clock struck ten, she went to bed.

Later that evening or early the next morning, she heard the front door open and the low sound of voices. Geoffrey must be home. Elizabeth hoped he appreciated the food she had ordered for him.

When next she opened her eyes, the sun was shining

through the lace curtains. A bird sat on the edge of an open window, chirping. It was time for her to be up as well. She tugged the bell-pull. There was a great deal to be done today.

Geoff cursed the damned bird. Even his valet wouldn't wake him up this early. He hadn't arrived home until after midnight.

Although he had eaten dinner with Sir Charles, it was a hurried affair. He had been surprised and appreciative that Elizabeth had left orders he was to be fed whenever he returned home.

Before retiring, he made a hearty meal of a bowl of onion soup followed by ham, some sort of creamy cheese, bread, and wine.

Her thoughtfulness reminded him that she had nursed him though his seasickness after he had been so pompous about *not* suffering from *mal de mer*. And never once complained.

It wasn't until Nettle was assisting Geoff to undress that he discovered how Elizabeth had managed to stop the theft of their horses.

Damn, she was turning out to be a remarkable woman.

"According to Kenton she marched right up with her pistol and pointed it at the servant trying to unhitch the horses and ordered him to cease."

"What do you mean, *servant*?" He could not imagine that any master would order his servant to steal anything, much less a team of horses from a carriage.

"There was an English gentleman who said he needed the horses to get back home."

"Do we know who he is?" If he found the cur, he'd write his father and have whoever it was arrested.

Nettle gave a rare chuckle. "The gentleman asked her

ladyship if she knew who he was and she just stared at him like he was mad and said something about how could she know him when they had not been introduced, and she didn't care who he was. She shot his hat off his head."

Shot? For a moment Geoff couldn't speak. "She did what?"

"Shot the gentleman's hat off. Then told him if he didn't want to lose anything more valuable, he'd leave." His valet pulled off one of his boots. "By then she had one of the coaching pistols."

Geoff was glad he was sitting down. Otherwise the news of his wife actually shooting at a thief would have had him falling down. Dear God. If anything had happened to her . . . He never should have left her alone, and the moment he saw her he would beg her forgiveness for having done so.

Devil it all. He was damned lucky she was all right.

When Elizabeth had said she knew her way around a pistol, he had no idea she would be forced to confront such a bounder. Most ladies he knew would have been in a panic. But she—his wife—had remained calm and in control of the situation.

She had also protected their servants from a possible arrest by shooting at the gentleman herself. If the man had been a peer, and based on his attitude, he might very well have been, Geoff's coachman could have been in a precarious situation by threatening the man.

He didn't know how he had been so lucky to have found and married her. In fact, his life would be perfect if he knew how to get her back into his bed, short of going to her room and carrying her to his.

Geoff had missed waking up to her and mating with her. His dreams had revolved around her and the two days they'd had together after their wedding. By the time the blasted bird had woken him, he'd had the hardest erection he'd ever experienced.

There had to be a way to get her to soften toward him. Including her in all his decisions hadn't worked. Or only marginally. She *was* speaking to him. If his next course of action—being more affectionate with her—didn't produce results, he might have to try pure seduction.

Striding into the breakfast room, he was glad enough to find Elizabeth just sitting down to the table.

Bending, he kissed her cheek. "Good morning. I heard you had an interesting journey yesterday."

He lowered himself into a seat next to her as a fresh pot of tea seemed to magically appear at her hand. She poured him a cup adding two lumps of sugar and milk. He took a sip, savoring the malty quality of her blend.

"More than I would have liked," Elizabeth responded drily. "However, I believe I acquitted myself rather well."

"From what I heard, you were superb." Her cheeks became pink, and he was glad he'd pleased her with the accolade.

"Thank you." She took a roll from the basket on the table. "How did you find Sir Charles?"

For the first time, it occurred to him that apologizing to her for not being there might insult her in some fashion. Still, he had to say something. "I will tell you in a moment, but first I wish to ask if you are angry about having to deal with the attempted theft by yourself."

She drew her brows down, considering his question for several moments before saying, "The situation would not have occurred if you had been there. The man saw a coach with no gentleman to contest his right to take the horses. I assume he believed there was nothing *I* could do about it." A small smile played around her lips. "In that, he was mistaken. He actually dared me to shoot him."

That was when Geoff understood how she felt about the incident. "It was a challenge. You enjoyed it."

Her smile became full-fledged. "I did, rather. My brother taught me how to shoot, and I have always been good at hitting targets. To be able to hit what I wanted to in a real situation was thrilling. Being able to foil the thief's plans was an exhilarating experience." She waved her hand. "It made me feel . . . powerful." She took a piece of toast from the rack that had been set on the table. "Now, how was your day?"

This was the most animated he had seen her in too long. Was she beginning to forgive him? "Unexpectedly busy." He grinned. "I found Sir Charles easily enough. But there seems to be a great deal of chaos and uncertainty. The fact of the matter is that we are all waiting to see what happens when Napoleon arrives. I did discover why so many people were on the road yesterday. There was a rumor going around that the French were marching north and some of the civilians are fleeing."

"Do we know when he is expected to arrive?" She took a bite and munched.

Preston placed a plate of meat and eggs in front of Geoff. "I take it there were no kippers to be had?"

"Not this morning." She raised one dark blond brow. "Napoleon?"

"That's just it. We don't know anything. There has been no word confirming that he has even left Paris. King Louis is still in Ghent." Geoff pressed his lips together. She had done so well setting the house up in a short time. He did not like to tell her they may be moving soon. Yet, there was no way out of it. "We may be asked to move to Ghent to keep an eye on him."

Elizabeth nodded as she dug into a soft-boiled egg that had been placed next to the toast. "Do we still have a house there?"

His jaw dropped, but he recovered almost immediately.

Elizabeth was taking this extremely well. "I believe so. At least, it has not been given up."

"If you are ordered to go to Ghent, we shall pack the trunks and move." The faint sound of artillery floated on the air, and she pulled her lower lip between her teeth. "I believe one of my questions may have an answer."

He quickly ate the rest of his food and gulped his tea. "I should go."

On his way out, he kissed her again. This time on her mouth. "Do not forget the ball."

Elizabeth turned in surprise. "Do you think it will still be held?"

"Deuce if I know. If it isn't, I'll send word. Otherwise be ready by seven. We dine with the duke and duchess."

Elizabeth placed two fingers on her lips as she watched Geoffrey stride out of the breakfast parlor. Both kisses had surprised her. The first because she had not been expecting it.

He had not attempted any intimacies since she had heard the conversation with his father. She had not been at all prepared for his kiss on her lips. She missed his kisses and caresses. Still, she must keep the long game in mind.

What, exactly, did his kissing her mean? Did they mean that her pose of being cool to him was working? She could think of no other reason for him to suddenly be so affectionate. That must be the reason. Geoffrey was finally beginning to truly care about her.

Elizabeth smiled to herself. It will not be long now.

She finished her breakfast and called for her bonnet, cloak, and gloves, and said to Preston, "I shall need Kenton as well."

Vickers hurried down the stairs. "Do you want me to go with you, my lady?"

"Not this time. I wish to see what is going on, and I do

not know how safe it will be." After Vickers placed Elizabeth's bonnet on her head, she drew on her gloves. "Which gown did you take out for the ball this evening?"

"The new pale pink gown with the silver netting," Vickers said.

"Perfect."

"You'll be careful?" Her maid's brow wrinkled and her lips were pursed.

"If there is any danger at all, I'll come right back," Elizabeth promised. "I will carry my pistol as well."

Elizabeth and her footman strolled through the park. When they reached the other side, she was shocked at the number of carriages in the street. "And I thought yesterday was bad. Is everyone in Brussels evacuating?"

"Does seem like it, my lady," her footman said.

"I've seen enough." In a few minutes they were back at the house, and she called for Mrs. Robins to attend her in the back parlor.

"Yes, my lady." The woman bobbed a curtsey.

"Please tell the cook that his lordship and I will be dining out this evening." Elizabeth tapped her finger on the writing table deciding what she should tell her staff. "There is a good chance we will be departing soon. I want you to tell Preston. I shall notify Vickers. How much is unpacked?"

"Just what we required for a few days, my lady. It won't be a problem to get everything ready again."

Elizabeth did not know what the circumstances would be when they did leave, but it was better to keep their business to themselves. "Not a word to anyone else."

"No, my lady."

Once her housekeeper left, she decided to act as if nothing out of the ordinary was happening. That, however, was easier said than done.

Fortunately, the day went more swiftly than she'd thought

it would. She wrote letters to her aunt and brother, and then to her father. Then she wrote Geoffrey's mother and grand-mother, telling them the same thing she had told her family. They had arrived safely and he was busy with Sir Charles.

Before long it was time for Elizabeth to dress for her first ball as a married lady.

# Chapter Thirty-Three

Geoffrey appeared only just in time to change before they were to depart.

As soon as Elizabeth had finished dressing, she went to his bedchamber and engaged in some very wifely behavior by watching while he tied his cravat.

Mayhap being a little nicer would help him along.

It only took three attempts before she could applaud his results. "That's very elegant. What is it called?"

"The Throne d'Amour." Nettle helped Geoffrey don a dark blue jacket of Bath suiting and handed him his watch and quizzing glass. The only fobs he wore. Offering her his arm, he said, "Shall we, my dear?"

The endearment took her aback for a moment. He was not in the habit of using sweet nothings, except "sweetheart," and that was only when they were in bed.

She had been correct this morning. He was definitely improving. She hoped it would not be long before he could tell her he loved her.

Once they arrived at the Duchess of Richmond's house on *rue des Cendres,* she and Geoffrey were announced and shown into a drawing room.

"Harrington." The duchess came forward to greet them.

"I am so pleased you were able to join us." The lady then glanced at Elizabeth. "You must introduce me to your bride."

Geoffrey released his hold on her arm so that she could curtsey. "Your grace, I am proud to introduce my wife, Elizabeth, the daughter of Lord Turley."

"How lovely and so graceful." The duchess smiled at her. "Harrington is lucky to have found you, my dear. Welcome to our home."

"Thank you, your grace." Elizabeth returned the smile. "I am glad we arrived in time to attend."

Geoffrey had already claimed Elizabeth's arm again, but her grace placed her hand on his other arm. "I shall introduce you to the others. But first, Harrington, you must tell me how your mother is doing. I know how she says she is going on, but one never knows."

"She is very well, ma'am," he replied. "When the conflict is successfully resolved, we have invited my parents to visit Paris next spring."

"Excellent. Spring is the perfect time to enjoy Paris." Her grace led them into the drawing room, making introductions as they went.

There were several foreign princes, including the Prince of Orange, and other foreign aristocrats as well. All of whom were either counts or barons, a smattering of other peers, but Elizabeth was disappointed that the Duke of Wellington was not present.

Geoffrey handed her a glass of wine. "These are the types of people we shall be associating with in Paris. What do you think?"

The question surprised her. She had expected him to praise her on her deportment—that is what he had done previously. "Naturally, they are all polite. I would have to get to know them better before I could tell you what I think of them."

He saluted her with his wineglass. "Just so, my dear. An astute observation."

Elizabeth tried not to smirk as a gentleman in a foreign uniform ogled her, and Geoffrey drew her a little closer. Definitely better.

A lady a little older than Elizabeth came up to them. "Harrington, Mama said you had arrived. I have not seen you since we were children."

Geoffrey stared at the lady for a moment. "Georgy! I'm glad to see you here." He released Elizabeth's arm enough so that she could make a shallow curtsey. "My wife, Elizabeth."

"My dear, Lady Georgiana Lennox, the third daughter of the Duke and Duchess of Richmond."

"It is a pleasure to meet you." The lady smiled warmly. "Congratulations on your marriage. I hope we will become good friends."

"It is very nice to meet you as well, my lady." Elizabeth hoped they would be friends as well. "How do you like Brussels?"

"We have been extremely gay here. I hope it will continue. But please, call me Georgy."

"In that case, you must call me Elizabeth."

They joined a group of Prussians, and the conversation turned to German.

Shortly after that dinner was announced. To Elizabeth's delight, Geoffrey claimed the right of a newlywed to sit next to his bride. She had never heard of such a thing, but the duchess laughingly agreed.

The dinner was everything one would expect it to be before a grand ball and made even more special by the attention her husband paid to her, selecting the choicest cuts of meat and fish. Always asking what Elizabeth preferred and if she would like wine or another libation.

Talk of the coming war was discouraged, and everyone acted as if nothing unusual was going on. It was too unreal.

Once they were in one of the series of rooms decorated for the ball, she whispered to Geoffrey, "I know that we should not be discussing the likelihood of a battle with Napoleon at dinner, but do you not think it strange that no one has mentioned it at all?"

"Perhaps they are purposely avoiding thinking about it." He glanced around. "Many of the men here might not return."

He was right. Elizabeth should have thought of that herself. And right now, she was exceedingly thankful her husband was not in the army. If there was time, she'd have his friends to dinner.

Soon the other guests began to arrive, and the rooms were filled with colorful silks, playing off the reds, greens, and blues of the officer's uniforms.

She danced the first set with Geoffrey, and the second with Captain Lord Thomas Prendergast, and the third with Captain Lord William Toole, a friend of Geoffrey's who had sought them out.

After that set, Geoffrey asked that she remain with him for the next set. As they partook of glasses of champagne, a tall dark gentleman in the uniform of the 95th Rifles strode up to them. "Lord Harrington?" Geoffrey nodded. "I'm Hawksworth. I've been told you've been looking for me."

"I have indeed." Geoffrey grinned. "I have a message from your brother Lord Septimius to write more often." He looked at the man's uniform. "I was told you were in the Life Guards."

"When I had an opportunity to change units, I did," Lord Hawksworth said.

Geoffrey glanced at her. "I've been remiss. My dear, may I present Colonel the Marquis of Hawksworth? My lord, my wife, Lady Harrington."

"A pleasure, my lady." His bow was almost courtly. "Would you do me the honor of standing up with me?"

"I would be delighted, my lord." He led her out to dance as Lord John strode up to Geoffrey. Elizabeth wondered if her brother's friend Captain Sutton was at the ball or her husband's friend Major Cotton.

As she and Lord Hawksworth twirled by Georgy she was arguing with the young Lord Hay. Elizabeth wondered what had upset her husband's old friend.

Later in the evening, Lord John requested a set. "We have been ordered to be ready to march at three in the morning."

Elizabeth almost stumbled. "So soon?"

"Old Boney caught us out." He grimaced. "Never fear, the duke will see us through." His lordship immediately changed the conversation, and Elizabeth finally appreciated why no one was discussing the war. A gentleman who had become a friend might not survive. "Will you remain in Brussels?"

"Until we are ordered elsewhere," she replied, but her mind was already thinking of how many soldiers here would not make it home.

The duchess had arranged entertainment in the form of some of the enlisted members of the Royal Highlanders and the 92nd Foot to dance reels and play their bagpipes. Geoffrey joined her to watch the performance.

When it ended he asked, "Have you heard anything?"

"Lord John said they were to be ready by three in the morning."

Geoffrey looked at her with a troubled gaze. "That soon. Wellington hasn't arrived yet."

They had not long to wait as the duke arrived shortly before supper. He appeared to be in a mood to be pleased until the Prince of Orange strode up to him and began whispering in the duke's ear.

Some of the older officers appeared worried, but the younger ones were full of energy.

"I cannot understand why young men wish to go to war," Elizabeth whispered to Geoffrey.

"Generally, it's only the ones who have never been." He wrapped his arm around her waist, and she was thankful for the comfort.

As they went to supper, Lord John came up to them. "I'll take my leave of you. It was good to see you again."

Elizabeth held out her hand and he bowed over it. "You will be careful."

"As much as I can be." He gave a rueful smile. "Farewell."

Geoffrey shook Lord John's hand. "Good luck, and may God be with you and your men."

Silent tears escaped from Elizabeth's eyes. "I'd like to go home."

"I should as well." Geoffrey handed her his handkerchief and she accepted it gratefully.

On their way back to the house, they were surprised by the number of Belgians pouring out of their houses, embracing soldiers and wishing them well.

He stopped their carriage and they watched. The park was filled with men and equipment. The sound of drums filled the air. And wagons of all sorts passed by, heading south.

The next day dawned and silence had taken the place of the noise that accompanied the army's march out of Brussels.

Geoffrey was on the heels of Vickers who brought Elizabeth's tea. He was dressed and smelled of fresh air. "Have you already been out?"

"Yes." Her bed dipped as he sat on it. "May I have a sip?"

She handed him the cup. "You may have a whole pot, if you wish. What were you doing?"

"I shall when we break our fast. Then I plan to get some

sleep until someone tells me I'm needed." He took a sip of tea and handed the cup back to her. "I changed and went back out to watch the troops leave."

There would be a battle today, and she could do nothing. "I feel so useless. There must be something I can do."

He pulled her into his arms. "If anyone can find a way to be of use, you will do it."

She sank into him and for the first time in ages, put her arms around him and they remained that way for several long moments. "I'll see you in the breakfast room."

Geoffrey nuzzled her hair, and kissed her. Not a ravenous kiss, but one that was sweet and gentle. Maybe it was time to end her pretense, and tell him she loved him. Since arriving in Brussels he had changed. Surely he must return her affections. "I'll see you downstairs."

An hour or so later, as luck would have it, just as Elizabeth had finished giving her staff their instructions for the day and was searching for something to do, a message came for her from Georgy Lennox, one of the Duchess of Richmond's daughters.

*Dear Elizabeth,*

*I realize you do not know many people here, and I thought you might be interested joining a group of ladies who are making bandages for the wounded. We are meeting at the home of the Comtesse de Beaufort on rue de la Blanchisserie at ten this morning.*

*Your friend,*
*G. Lennox*

Thank God. "The very thing I need at the moment," she said to an empty room.

Before summoning Vickers, she wrote Geoffrey a note telling him where she was going and what she was doing. "Would you like to accompany me, or shall I have Kenton escort me to the countess's home?"

"I'll go, my lady," Vickers said firmly. "I'd like to help as well."

"I suppose they will need supplies." They did not have much, but . . . "We can bring some of our sheets."

"I'll get them now." Her maid went off.

By the time they arrived at the comtesse's house, a group of ladies were already present, including Georgy, who greeted Elizabeth with a warm smile. "I'm so glad you came."

"Thank you for your missive. I was wracking my brain for a way to assist." She glanced around. "Where do you want these sheets?"

"Lady Harrington?" The comtesse came up to Elizabeth. "Yes."

"I am happy you are here. We met briefly last night. But you are new to our little community and it is impossible to meet many people for the first time and remember them all."

"Thank you for understanding." Elizabeth had a faint recollection of the woman and her husband. "We were, indeed, introduced last evening."

She was introduced to the other ladies present. Some of them had brought their maids as well and Vickers joined them. Soon Elizabeth was cutting strips of linen while others were scraping lint to ensure that no fabric could get into a wound and cause an infection.

Sometime post-noon, there was a faint rumble in the distance. Elizabeth stopped what she was doing. "Artillery."

"Already?" a lady said in a trembling voice. "My husband told me the battle would not be until tomorrow."

They worked mostly in silence for the next hour or so

before breaking up to go home. Georgy walked with her to the *rue Royale*. "I shall most likely see you tomorrow."

"I only pray that the bandages we made today are not needed." A useless prayer, but the only one Elizabeth could think of.

"I as well."

Geoffrey had still not returned to the house when she and Vickers arrived.

With her walking gown covered in lint, Elizabeth changed into a day dress and waited for him to come home. Fortunately, he arrived a few minutes later.

Striding into the parlor at the back of the house Elizabeth had claimed as a morning room, he kissed her. "Let me wash off my dirt, and I'll be right down. When do we dine? I'm famished."

For the first time that day, she laughed. "There is time for you to wash and have a glass of wine. Do you have news?"

"Yes. I'll tell you what I know after I've washed and changed."

Several minutes later, he was back, and she handed him a glass of claret. "We heard the guns today."

"So did we all." He drew her to the sofa and sat down beside her. "Napoleon surprised Wellington by attacking Charleroi. We had heard that, but today there was a battle at a place called Quatre Bras. There has been some pretty heavy fighting there." He swallowed half his glass. "The king is in Alost. We will be leaving in the next few days. As soon as Napoleon is defeated, Sir Charles wants to get him to Paris as soon as possible."

Elizabeth took a sip of her wine wishing she could gulp it down like her husband did. "Will we move to Alost?"

"I'm not sure yet, but I think we will. Unless the king comes to Brussels, that is." Setting down his wine, he took her hands in his. "Do you mind all this uncertainty?"

"Not at all." Or only a little, but not enough to matter.

"I have informed our senior staff that they must be ready to depart at any time."

For the second time that day, he pulled her into his arms, and she forgot she was supposed to be cold to him. "You are the best wife a man could have."

Elizabeth's heart swelled with joy, but her head was less sanguine. What did that mean to him? She had been so sure he'd begun to love her before she was afraid to trust herself now.

Unable to stop herself, she put her arms around him.

Drat the man.

# Chapter Thirty-Four

Geoff dressed quickly and opened the door to Elizabeth's room. The curtains were still drawn and she was sleeping soundly. He considered waking her, but satisfied himself with kissing her lightly on her lips. She stirred for a moment, and he waited, but it came to nothing when she rolled over.

Soon she'd be back in his bed where she belonged.

Last evening, he was certain she had almost forgiven him. Unfortunately, he couldn't pursue the matter now.

He left the house, and as he turned onto *rue Royal* he was met by the sight of bloodied soldiers straggling back from the battlefield. He did what he could to help a few of the men, but he had to get to Sir Charles.

Dragging a hand down his face, Geoffrey's mind slipped to Elizabeth; she was never far from his thoughts. He had no doubt once his wife was up and about, she would be aiding wherever she could. Mayhap he should send a note telling her to remain in the house.

From the corner of his eye, he saw a lady kneeling to give water to one of the soldiers and knew he'd not be able to stop his wife from giving succor to those who needed it.

When he arrived at work he was informed that Wellington

had sent a dispatch to Sir Charles that had arrived shortly after seven that morning providing an account of the battle and stating that the allies still held their ground.

"The next few days will tell," Sir Charles said ominously. "Stand ready to remove from Brussels at a moment's notice."

"My wife has already given our servants that exact same order." Geoff was more than grateful that Elizabeth had their household firmly in hand.

"Remarkable young lady you married, Harrington. I congratulate you for having such good sense."

"Thank you, sir. I agree she is extraordinary." He glanced around for something to keep him occupied, but he wasn't sure what he should be doing. Since Geoff arrived, everything had been in such turmoil. "I await your instructions, sir."

Sir Charles's remarks about Elizabeth reminded Geoff of what his father had said just before he and she left to come here. He hadn't thought to tell his father that he had come to care for her deeply. He cared for her even more now but had no words to define what he felt for her. All he knew was that he wanted to follow the path they were on to see where it would lead.

"Instructions?" Sir Charles gave a gruff snort. "I am instructed to keep the English calm. Wellington doesn't want everyone panicking."

"From what I've seen," Geoff retorted, "our ladies have been damn phlegmatic. Yesterday my wife was cutting linen for bandages, and I'd wager that as soon as she sees the carnage in the streets, she'll be out there doing her bit in any way she is able."

"I did not want my lady wife here, but I understand what it's like not to want to be separated." Sir Charles stared out the window for several seconds. "Harrington, if the impossible occurs and the French start marching this way, send her to Antwerp straightaway. Don't even think of doing

anything else. In any war, the women always get the worst
of it."

A feeling of dread rose in Geoff and for several moments
he couldn't breathe. Nothing could happen to Elizabeth.

He still refused to believe Wellington would lose, but if
it did happen, the only thing on his mind would be to safe-
guard his wife. Geoff would not and could not allow her to
be harmed. "She will be ready, sir."

"Good man. Take care of your own. That's all we can do."

The rest of the day was spent waiting for dispatches and
assuring their anxious fellow countrymen that all was proceeding as planned. They received a report about a group of
Flemish cavalry riding through Brussels creating havoc and
shouting that the French were on their heels.

It turned out to be no such thing, but once again, English
gentlemen besieged their office wanting to know if they
should take their families and flee.

By the time Geoff left for the day and was trudging up
the *rue Royale,* he'd had his fill of comforting panicked
gentlemen.

Up ahead his wife was kneeling in the road giving a
wounded soldier a drink of something from a flask. The
man had a fresh bandage around his head, and his arm was
in a sling.

Elizabeth's gown was dirty with streaks of blood on her
skirts and bodice. Her face was drawn, her hair escaped
every way it could from under her bonnet, but her chin had
a mulish cast, and she was scowling at a gentleman standing
on the pavement.

He had no doubt she was arguing with the man, refusing
to leave until the soldier was taken somewhere he could be
cared for. Vickers, looking worse for wear herself, strode
toward Elizabeth, leading a local woman to the soldier.
When the woman saw the soldier she kneeled down and
motioned to a young man following behind.

By this time Geoff was close enough to make out what the woman was saying.

"He lives with us." To the young man she said, "Go quickly and fetch the cart. The sergeant must be put in bed and the doctor sent for."

"I can walk, madam," the soldier insisted. "Just need some help."

"Thank you, milady," the Belgian woman curtseyed. "We will take care of him."

The English gentleman shrugged and walked away.

Geoff helped Elizabeth to her feet, and put his arm around her waist. "Are you all right? When was the last time you ate?"

He started walking with her the rest of the way to their house. "Yes," she replied rather distractedly. "I knew it would be horrible, I just did not realize how dreadful the reality would be." Attempting to tuck her hair back under her hat, she laughed rather distractedly. "Did that make any sense at all?"

By Jove's beard, she humbled him. All he had been doing that day was reassuring people, and he'd been bloody tired of that. She had been bandaging gaping wounds and finding the Bruxellois who had housed the injured.

A sudden need to tend to her himself came over him. He didn't understand the compulsion, but there it was. "You could not have been other than shocked at such carnage and waste of life."

By the time they had walked the few blocks to their house her head lay against his shoulder.

When they entered the hall, Vickers began giving orders for a bath to be filled for Elizabeth. Geoff made sure the maid ordered one for herself as well.

It would be ironic if this war brought them back to each other. Yet strangely, that was exactly what seemed to be occurring. At least from his point of view.

Geoff had never really looked beyond her qualifications as his wife and having a comfortable marriage. It never occurred to him that he would worry about her.

Later that evening as he held her in his arms, Elizabeth lifted her head up and kissed him. Geoff was so shocked, he almost forgot to return the gesture. The kiss was warm and sweet, and full of a longing stronger than he had ever experienced before.

"Take me to bed." She kissed him again.

"Yours or mine?" he asked, wanting to be absolutely positive about what she wished.

"Your bed." Her voice was firm.

"Are you sure?" He still had no idea what had happened between them and was afraid she would regret their coupling.

She stared up at him, her blue eyes searching his. "Absolutely sure."

Geoff carried her up to his bedchamber. They undressed each other slowly, kissing and tasting as each piece of clothing was removed. This had none of the frantic mating they'd engaged in before, but was all the more poignant for not being rushed and so filled with lust they couldn't keep their hands off each other.

Elizabeth cried out as she came, bringing him with her. Afterward, she lay in his arms not speaking. Then again, she never needed conversation after they had coupled.

Yet, for some reason he refused to study, he did. "Why now when you have put us off for so long?"

She rolled over, propping herself on his chest and meeting his gaze. "I heard what your father said to you the day before we left Town. Congratulating you on getting me to the altar. About how qualified I was to be your wife." She shook her head as if to clear it. "And I heard your answers. They cut me to the quick. I realized then that, although I had fallen in love with you, you didn't love me." Her eyes darkened. "I was resolved not to share your bed until you loved me, too. Yet, after what I have seen in the past day . . . The anguish of the injured and dying, the women who lost their husbands and sons"—tears shone in her eyes and he didn't know what to do to comfort her—"I—I could not remain apart from you any longer. It doesn't matter that you do not love me. What matters is that I love you. And if anything was to happen to you, and I had not told you how I feel, I would always regret it."

She patted his chest, rolled over, and dropped off into a deep sleep. Leaving him with more questions than he had ever had in his life.

All this time he had thought she was angry with him because he'd gone out without telling her where he was or when he'd return. He'd had no idea she was in love with him. If what she felt was love—and he had no reason to doubt her—this was not the type of love he'd seen his friends go through. Full of jealousy, and arguments, and then passionate making up in a repetitive cycle until the passion and joy were no longer there.

Had they been wrong about what love was? Had he? And if so, if what Elizabeth felt for him, a steady companionship, filled with small joys, and earnest discussion on how to make their lives together a home, was real love, then what *was* he feeling?

If she had made love to him, did that not mean he'd made love to her as well?

Geoff had been so careful not to use the word *love* in anything they did. But, perhaps he had been wrong. Had he purposefully ignored the vow of love he'd made during their wedding?

The question was how would he know if he was in love?

\* \* \*

The next afternoon it rained.

Geoff reported to Sir Charles that morning to discover the allies had held their ground through the night. He continued to meet and attempt to calm his fellow countrymen. And every time he wanted to tell them to stop acting like children, he reminded himself of what his wife was likely to be up to. He'd rather be with her.

That afternoon when a great crack of lightning followed by thunder rent the air, and the heavens opened up to pour down buckets of water on the city, everyone around him started to laugh.

"I feel like a fool, but what is so bloody funny about rain?"

Sir Charles slapped Geoff's back. "This, my boy, is Wellington weather. Almost every one of his successes has been in pouring rain."

That was good news. Geoff's thoughts immediately turned to Elizabeth. "I'll be back straightaway." Sir Charles raised a brow. "My wife, sir. She is helping tend the wounded. I want to make sure she gets out of this downpour."

"Come back as soon as you can. We should be receiving more news."

Geoff rushed out into the street, and just as he'd expected, down the street, Elizabeth, her muslin gown clinging to her, was helping a soldier at least a foot taller than she was. "Here, let me." He relieved her of her burden. "Where is your maid?"

She pushed her bedraggled bonnet out of her eyes. "Finding the house. This soldier's house."

They walked a few more blocks before Vickers appeared with a middle-aged Bruxelles couple hurrying toward them. "I have 'im now, *monsieur*," the man said as he supported the soldier. "Thank you. He has become like a son."

"Geoffrey," Elizabeth said when the man left. "What are you doing out here? You are going to be soaked."

"I think I already am. But what am I doing? Making sure you don't become ill from being in the rain. Come, sweetheart. I'm taking you home."

Elizabeth's heart soared when Geoffrey called her "sweetheart." Was it because of what she had said the night before? It really didn't matter. She had become tired of the game and could not bring herself to play it any longer. Not when there were so many people who would never see their loved ones alive again.

"Very well." She slipped her arm around his waist. "You must change as well. I do not believe Sir Charles will appreciate you making puddles on his floors."

Geoffrey's chuckle warmed her from the inside out. "No, I don't suppose he will." They had already reached the door of their house when he said, "Did you know they call this rain Wellington weather?"

"Pouring down rain?" Unless the general had turned into a duck, that made no sense at all. "Why would they call it Wellington weather?"

Geoffrey grinned. "According to Sir Charles, the duke always wins when it's raining."

It still did not make sense, but people had to grab on to whatever hope they could. "I suppose that has made everyone feel better."

"That, and the news that the allies held their ground last night." He gave her a swift kiss.

"Now that is good to hear." And something solid to hold on to.

Vickers helped Elizabeth strip off her wet clothing. "Looks like you and his lordship made up."

"Yes." After a fashion, and only because she had been forced to see how fragile and precious life was. Yet, despite what his mother and grandmother thought, it was clear that he did not return her love. She gave herself a shake. There would be plenty of time after the war was over to think about her marriage. "Thank you for helping me."

"I wanted to do it," Vickers said gruffly. "They're our soldiers fighting for us. Seems like we should return the favor when we can."

"That's how I feel as well." Elizabeth wiped a drop of rain off her face. "I'm not happy about this war, but I am glad that we are here to give whatever assistance we are able to."

Her maid nodded. "Let's get you out of that gown before you take a chill."

Elizabeth went into the hall as Geoffrey was departing to make sure he had his waterproof cloak.

"I don't know when I'll be home tonight." He hugged her gently.

Cupping his cheek, she kissed him. "Send word if you will be too late. I'll hold dinner until seven. Even if you miss that, there will be something for you to eat."

"I can't tell you how grateful I am that you make sure I'm fed no matter what time I get home."

Yesterday, she would have made an angry comment about her qualifications, but today, she could simply accept his appreciation. "I want to ensure you are properly fed. I know you have dined with Sir Charles, but your lack of enthusiasm about his table makes me think it must not be very good."

Geoffrey barked a laugh. "I'm glad you keep a much better table than he does."

That night, he held her close to him. He might not love her, but he did care for her and took care of her. She wished she could be satisfied with that. Unfortunately, she knew herself too well. Something would have to change or this marriage was doomed.

# Chapter Thirty-Five

The next several days were a blur. What Elizabeth had prayed, hoped for, and believed would happen did. Napoleon was routed, but at such a cost. She could not imagine there was a family in England, or at least in the *ton,* who had not been touched by a deceased or wounded family member. The total number of dead was horrendous.

Yet, Geoffrey's and her part was, in a fashion, just beginning. Sir Charles was tasked with returning the French king to his throne, and for that, they must travel to Paris.

It pained her to leave her friends, some of whom still did not know if their loved ones were dead or alive. Before she departed, though, she made arrangements for the house to be made into a sort of hospital. Colonel Hawksworth promised he would see it happen.

Of the friends she and Geoffrey had before they arrived, Lord John and Major Cotton had been wounded. As long as an infection did not set in, they would live. Lord John's Brigade Major had died. Neither Geoffrey nor Elizabeth had discovered what happened to the rest of them before they had to leave, but the others said they would send word if they were able.

As she had done before they'd left England, Elizabeth supervised the packing. Fortunately, the cook, who was extremely good, agreed to remain in their employ. They tearfully bid farewell to the Belgian caretakers who had allowed her staff to take over the house while they were in residence, and agreed to the injured staying at the house.

Wellington and the soldiers he had that could travel accompanied King Louis, his retinue, and Sir Charles's staff as they left Brussels.

It soon became clear that many of the French cities considered the allied army the enemy and, much to Wellington's ire, would only open their gates to King Louis XVIII.

When they arrived in Cambrai, the king issued a proclamation that only the instigators of the war would be punished. He was also forced to admit that his government had made some mistakes, but promised to correct them.

Geoffrey didn't think much of that. "He will be surrounded by the same fawning sycophants and other ministers, so tell me how he is to change?"

She had to agree with her husband that unless someone took the king in hand, change was unlikely to occur.

At the end of June, a delegation of five from the Chamber of Deputies and the Chamber of Peers requested that Wellington replace Louis with a foreign prince, but he refused, saying that Louis was the best way to preserve the integrity of France.

Elizabeth, Geoffrey, and the rest of the procession were preparing to finally arrive in Paris when one of their horses threw a shoe outside of a small village that had only one inn and a blacksmith.

Although it was early in the day, Preston and Farley, Elizabeth's groom, took the horse to the blacksmith only to discover that the man would not be able to get to it until tomorrow.

"I swear, my lord," Farley said, "it's because we're English."

Elizabeth frowned. "But Preston's French is excellent."

"Oh, aye, he gabbered at him in French, and that Frenchie smith understood every word, but the minute he says his lordship's name, the man said he couldn't do it today."

She glanced at Geoffrey. "You go on. I can wait until the horse has been re-shoed."

"After what happened the last time I left you?" He raised a brow. "No. I shall wait with you. The countryside is not safe. If we are not to have the protection of the troops, I would rather we stayed together." Leaning over, he kissed her. "I am certain Sir Charles would say the same. What I will do is send Farley with a message to him."

Truth be told, she was glad Geoffrey had decided to remain with them. "If you wish."

The butler made arrangements at the only inn in the village. For some reason she could not understand, the landlady was no more happy than the blacksmith to have their custom. And they looked at Preston and her cook with disdain.

The rooms were small, with dingy walls and curtains that could use a wash. Mrs. Robins, Vickers, and Molly were doing what they could to make their chambers more comfortable when Preston came up to her.

"My lady," he said in a low voice, "I am loath to tell you this, but they are supporters of Napoleon and do not want us here."

That raised all sorts of interesting possibilities. "Just how badly does she wish us gone? Will she, for example, try to poison us?"

"I do not think she will go that far, but I plan to be in the kitchen to watch her when she prepares your dinner. She refuses to allow our cook to use the kitchen."

Unfortunately, the basket of food she had wouldn't feed

all of her household until tomorrow. "Take Kenton with you. He might not speak French, but he has sharp eyes."

"Cook will be enough, and he knows the herbs and spices here better than we do."

"Very well." It had never before occurred to her that someone might want to murder them because they were English.

Geoffrey came up to her as their butler was heading to the kitchens. "Trouble?"

"Nothing we cannot handle." She grimaced. "They do not want us here, and Preston expects there might be trouble."

"In that case," Geoffrey said in a grim tone, "perhaps they will hurry the smithy just to be rid of us."

"One can only hope." The corridor seemed colder than it had before. "I am going to see if our rooms are ready. Vickers insisted on using our sheets. She said the other ones smelt of mildew."

"I'll be in shortly. I want to make sure our horses are settled." He pressed his lips together for a moment. "I think Riddle and Farley, when he returns, will sleep in the stable. Such as it is. I'm glad we brought our own feed for the horses."

After looking at their rooms, Elizabeth found them much improved. She was glad they had their own sheets. When she sat on the bed, it sagged and the ropes creaked. "Well, this will be an uncomfortable night."

The food was neither plentiful nor particularly appetizing. The bed ended up being so bad that Geoffrey turned the frame over and tightened the ropes.

"I had no idea you were so handy," Elizabeth said after he'd righted the bed and she was remaking it.

"Even we peers-to-be can acquire skills. I frequently restrung my bed at Oxford." He watched her tuck in the sheets. "I see you have acquired skills as well."

"My mother insisted I know how everything was done."

When she was finished, she perched on the edge of the bed, propped her chin on her fist, and smiled. "It is truly fascinating the things I learn about you."

"Minx." He grinned, jumped on the bed, and rolled her over with him. "I'll show you fascinating."


Only an hour after they'd left the inn the next day, Geoff began getting a bad feeling. It started with a tingling on the back of his neck as if he was being watched. That put him in mind of the conversation he'd had with parts of his staff.

It wasn't only the innkeeper and blacksmith who had not liked having them there. His male servants reported that the villagers hadn't wanted them there either.

He tried to shake off his foreboding when a gunshot rent the air. "Take cover."

"They're coming from the left," Farley bellowed.

Geoff rode his horse to the right side of the coach. He wasn't at all surprised to find his wife had her pistol out, and Vickers had the coaching pistol in her lap. He didn't know how many of the bounders there were, but he'd wager he knew where they came from.

He rode up to his coachman. "Do not stop unless you have to."

"Right, my lord."

A man ordered them to halt and William Coachman kept going.

A ball hit the side of the coach, but bounced off the metal trim. Then Geoff saw the large tree branch lying across the road. Damn, the blackguards had set up an ambush. There was no way his coach could go over the branch.

Riddle, who had been riding with William Coachman, climbed up onto the carriage roof. Farley, his Brown Bess across the front of his saddle, rode up to Geoff. "I saw five. Two on each side and one on horseback."

"Tell Kenton to get up on the roof and face the opposite direction of Riddle. You take the left and I'll take the right."

"Aye, my lord."

At least the coach carrying their other servants was ahead of the trap. It still terrified him that Elizabeth was in the carriage.

As the coach slowed, men carrying muskets and wearing ragged French uniforms ran out from the woods on either side of the road. More than they'd expected.

Another cur rode up on a fine-looking horse. "You must be carrying much of value." A man on a horse leered into the window on Elizabeth's side. "I like pretty things. How much will you pay to keep her?"

Before Geoff could answer, a shot rang out from his coach, and the blackguard on the horse screamed, grabbing his crotch near the thigh as blood poured from a wound. Four more shots were fired as his grooms picked off two of the curs one on each side of the carriage. Geoff killed one of the scoundrels, but not before he got a shot off, hitting the coach.

"I got the last one," Kenton said.

"My lord, come quick," Vickers shouted from the coach. "Her ladyship's been hit."

Geoff didn't even remember jumping off his horse, as he wrenched open the carriage door. Elizabeth was slumped over onto her side, bleeding profusely from the head.

*No! No, this could not happen!* He began to pray.

"Riddle, Farley, one of you ride ahead. We have to get a doctor." Farley took off before Geoff had finished speaking. "Vickers, get a pad and put it on the wound. Keep it pressed down to stop the bleeding." He glanced around. "Everyone else, we need to get that tree out of the road."

In a very short time, they were careering down the road. Sometime later, they met Farley cantering toward them. "We have a doctor waiting at a hotel. Follow me."

Time seemed to slow for Geoff as he carried Elizabeth into the bedchamber where a doctor was waiting.

"I am Dr. Benoit." He bowed.

"Harrington." Geoff put her down on the bed. "My wife was shot in the head."

"I am aware." The doctor moved to her head and searched through her hair. Finally he stood. "There was no shattering of the skull, which is good. However, the wound is deep, and there is swelling. At the moment, I cannot tell you how serious it is. You will need cold compresses. Ice, if you can find it, would be better."

Geoff looked down on her pale face and his stomach clenched. Her breath seemed shallower than it ought to be. He couldn't lose her. Not now. Elizabeth was too important to him. "Will she live?"

The doctor packed his bag. "It is in God's hands now, *monsieur*. *Madam* is in a coma. If she does not sleep for too long she may live."

That was not the answer he wanted. What good was the damn doctor if he couldn't make Elizabeth well? For the love of God, she was still breathing. Other than the lump on her head, there was no internal injury as far as they could see. She had to live.

Geoff raked his fingers through his hair. "There must be something I could do to help make her better. You must know of a remedy, medicine that will help her."

"Try to make her take nourishment to keep her strength." The doctor's lips formed a moue. "Talk to her. I have heard it can help."

He turned to find his staff only to run into Nettle. "Broth for her ladyship. It has to be nourishing."

"Mrs. Robins has already gone to have some made, my lord."

Geoff nodded because he couldn't think of anything else to do. His mind was blank. The fear he felt for her threatened to overwhelm him. But she would not react this way. Elizabeth would figure out what to do and not allow herself to be paralyzed with inaction.

Talk to her. He had to think of something to talk to Elizabeth about. That shouldn't be hard. They always had a great deal to say. Surely he could find a topic that did not require her response. Or, mayhap he should ask what she thought. Perhaps she would need to tell him so badly she would wake up.

"My lord?"

"What is it, Nettle?"

"You should eat as well. I can bring you a tray here."

"Yes, yes, anything you like." Geoff began to pace the small room. Books. It seemed like she was always reading. "Find out from Vickers what her ladyship is reading."

"Right away, my lord."

He hadn't even noticed his valet had left when Vickers came and handed him a book. "She's been reading *Guy Mannering,* my lord."

"Thank you, Vickers."

"If I might make a suggestion." The question seemed to hang in the air. Like a tangible thing.

He didn't know if he would like it or not, but the servant had been with Elizabeth much longer than he had. "You may."

"The book is a fine idea, but she does like it when you talk to her." When he couldn't think of anything to say, her maid continued. "I understand you will eat in here today, but you will need to rest at some point or you'll fall ill yourself. Mrs. Robins and I shall help watch over her."

Geoff's first reaction was to tell the woman that he

would remain with his wife until she woke. He would not even entertain the prospect that she would not recover. But Vickers was right. He could not stay awake all day and all night for what could be several days. The bed was large enough for both of them, but until the swelling in Elizabeth's head went down, he did not want to chance hurting her by moving the wrong way in his sleep.

"Very well."

"Thank you, my lord." The maid dipped a curtsey and left him alone with his wife.

Book in hand, he pulled a chair up to the bed, and began to talk. "I'm so sorry. I wish I could have prevented you being hurt. If only I'd known how dangerous it was to be separated from the group. You must come back to me. To all of us . . ."

He didn't know how long he talked, all the while rubbing her arm or touching her face, praying she could hear him and would wake up.

His voice became scratchy and he called for tea. Food came and he ate it. But he couldn't remember even tasting what he'd consumed. He held Elizabeth up and tried to feed her the broth, but ended up having to call Vickers to help him.

"If you will hold her up, I can get it into her mouth," the woman said.

It was a slow process, but they managed to empty the bowl.

"If you will help me, my lord, I'll get her out of this gown and into her nightclothes."

He thought surely she would awaken, but the only sound she made was a moan when he forgot to hold her head and it bounced against the pillow.

The next day, he wrote a letter to Sir Charles telling him about the attack, and Elizabeth's injury, and sent Riddle off to find him.

And every day he prayed. Geoff didn't think he had ever prayed as much in his life, but he had never cared as much about anyone else before.

And that was when he knew he was in love with her. As soon as she woke, he would tell her.

# Chapter Thirty-Six

The next day, even though the swelling had gone down, Elizabeth remained in the coma.

"You have to wake up, sweetheart. I am praying for you. Everyone is. The landlady went to the church and lit candles for you to get better." He took a sip of the now ever-present tea. "You have to awaken so that I can tell you that I love you. I was so bird-witted I didn't see it for what it was. But I've never been in love before." His voice ended on a sob as he held back tears. "Please don't let it be too late. I can't lose you. We can't lose each other."

Elizabeth had drifted through a cloud. Everything was so white. She thought she was going to heaven. She could even see the tree she and her mother used to sit under and Mama was there, waiting for her.

"Elizabeth, go back. You cannot come here yet." Her mother made the shooing gesture she remembered so well. "Everything you want, your husband and your child, are back there. Go to him. Hear what he has to say."

She looked down, and Geoffrey was there, holding her hand, and telling her he loved her. And then he was crying.

She had never seen a man weep before. She tried to move her hand to hold his, but nothing happened.

Well, how could it when she was above him? That must be what her mother meant by telling her she had to go back.

"Elizabeth, you must return now. Before it's too late." Mama's voice was almost frantic.

"Yes, Mama. I'm going."

There was a dull ache in Elizabeth's head, but Geoffrey was there holding her. "Don't leave me now, sweetheart. Not when I love you so much."

She turned her hand in his. "I know you do."

"You're awake!" He grabbed her up, holding her tightly against him.

"Geoffrey, my head!"

"Forgive me." He laid her down as if she was made of fine porcelain and would break. "I was so afraid. I've never been this afraid in my entire life, but you've come back to me."

"To us." She cupped his cheek.

"You heard me?" He stared at her as if he couldn't believe what she had said. "The doctor said you might, but after so many days . . ." Geoffrey brushed his lips across hers. "I love you."

"I love you, too." Elizabeth slid her arms up around his neck. She had so many questions, but all she wanted to do right now was hold him. "I had begun to fear you would never love me."

Geoffrey winced. "All I had seen of love between a man and a woman was with friends who were either happily in the clouds or sunk down as if they were drowning." He tightened his grip, kissing her again. "I didn't know that love could be like this, steady and comforting." He grunted. "Until you got shot. Then I thought I'd die if you did. There wouldn't be any reason for me to go on."

It really was true that men didn't see what was in front

of their noses. How had he not seen the type of love his parents had?

Still, none of that was important now. "I do not understand it, but I heard my mother's voice telling me to go back."

"Thank God she did." He nuzzled her neck before lowering her back down onto her pillows. "I'll call for the doctor."

Shortly after he left the bedchamber, Vickers burst into the room. "My lady! Thank God you've come back to us." She stood there for a second staring at Elizabeth. "Are you hungry? Do you want a bath?"

"Both." She laughed. "You would not believe how famished I am. And you must help me to the chamber pot. One would think that after going without sustenance and liquids for so long, I would have nothing in me."

"His lordship and I fed you broth several times a day. As much as we could get down you. He rubbed your limbs, too. His groom told him to do that. Said he knew a man who couldn't walk for a long time, but they massaged his legs, and he finally walked."

She had never heard of such a thing. "Did his lordship spend much time with me?"

"Every waking hour, my lady. Mrs. Robins and I had to practically drag him away from you. We kept reminding him that it wouldn't do you any good if he got ill from not resting. He even took his dinner on a tray here. And he talked to you so much he almost lost his voice. And that's not all . . ."

As the tale continued, Elizabeth was amazed, but proud, of how their little household pulled together to help Geoffrey take care of her. His valet insisted he dress properly every day. Her groom pressed him to take exercise of some sort, riding or walking. Even the landlady did what she could by making sure the food was fresh and tasty to tempt Geoffrey's appetite.

But most surprising of all was the way he took care of

her. She would never have expected to receive nursing from him. If she had given it any thought, she would have supposed that he'd have ridden ahead and left her with the servants. Obviously, she had misjudged how much he truly loved her.

Mayhap, he had even been in love with her for a much longer time than he thought.

Her maid had a tub carried in for Elizabeth's bath. Her only regret was that she could not wash her hair. The rest of her felt better clean.

By the time she was bathed and in a fresh nightgown, Mrs. Robins carried in a tray with roasted chicken, a fresh green salad, and bread. Geoffrey had a tray brought to him as well, and they were able to talk while they ate.

The remains of their meal had no sooner been removed than Dr. Benoit was announced.

"I am pleased to see you have awoken," he said. "If I may, my lady?"

Geoffrey stood back from the bed, giving the doctor access. Dr. Benoit examined her head. "The wound is healed sufficiently for you to wash your hair, if you wish. You may take light exercise. A stroll in the garden and around the hotel, but do not overdo it. When you feel fatigued, rest. You are on no account to travel. Injuries such as you received must be treated with caution." He bowed. "I will see you again in two days." Turning to her husband he said, "Call for me immediately if she faints, or becomes weaker."

Each day she felt stronger, but Geoffrey refused to make love to her until the doctor proclaimed her well enough to travel. "I am not going to risk injuring you, my love."

He called her "my love" a great deal and she never tired of hearing it. "Have it your way, but do not be surprised at the results."

Giving her a wicked grin, he didn't even pretend not to understand her. "I shan't."

The next day, Riddle returned accompanied by four soldiers and a message from Sir Charles instructing Geoffrey to remain with his wife until she was well enough to travel. The older man also apologized for not having the forethought of providing them with an escort when their horse threw a shoe.

A week later, the doctor said she was well enough to travel. Which was a very good thing. She was tired of being treated like an invalid.

Geoff was determined that he and Elizabeth would have a romantic evening after which he'd do his damnedest to keep their lovemaking slow. The thought struck him that this was the first time he had used that term for mating. Yet it was apt, and he should have recognized it before.

He arranged for them to dine in the garden. He had wanted candles, but the sun was still high and wouldn't set until nine o'clock or so.

Going to her bedchamber, he knocked on the door before opening it. Elizabeth was as exquisite as usual in a pale pink evening gown trimmed with blond lace showing her bosom to perfection. Yet, what surprised him was that instead of her pale golden curls being styled in an elaborate design, they tumbled down her back, controlled only by a thin ribbon. "Do not think I am complaining, but is your head still hurting?"

"No." She grinned. "I merely thought you might like it this way."

Strolling forward he reached out, running his hand over the silken mass. "You were right. I love your hair almost as much as I love you."

Elizabeth chuckled and slid her hands over his chest and shoulders, until her fingers tangled with his hair. "I love you."

"I love you. I am never going to get tired of saying that."

He'd thought it, love, would never happen to him. Pulling her against him, he sought her mouth. "I love your kisses and the way your body fits to mine."

"I love the way you touch me." Her eyes twinkled alluringly. "Perhaps we could dine in here again."

"That is a tempting offer, but I think you will enjoy what I have planned." He placed her hand on his arm. "Come, my love."

Geoff led her to the garden where the table was set and waited.

Her face lit with joy. "It is beautiful! Oh, Geoffrey, what a wonderful idea."

"I hoped you would think so." He motioned and their butler carried out a tray with two glasses and a bottle of champagne. Handing one to her, he said, "To your recovery."

"To our life together," she said, taking a sip of wine.

"To our very long life together." Once they arrived in Paris, he'd make sure she was never in danger again.

After dining, they strolled the rest of the gardens, and kissed, not caring who saw them. Elizabeth was finally his in every way. To think it took almost losing her . . . How stupid he had been.

Later, it seemed they both held back, wanting their lovemaking to last, and when they finally came, it was together and better than it had ever been.


Their assemblage reached Sir Charles's party the day before it rode into Paris with King Louis XVIII. Much to their relief, the crowds, though huge, were cheering the return of their monarch. Immediately, plans were made for grand dinners and balls to celebrate the occasion.

Geoff and Elizabeth wasted no time finding their house, a grand old building, not far from the British embassy. In an amazingly short period, Elizabeth made the house seem like home, and they planned their own entertainment. It was not until several days later that he discovered, after speaking with the agent, that his father actually owned the house.

"It has been in your family for three generations, my lord," the agent said. "Your great-grandfather wished to have a Paris residence. Your grandparents and parents also resided here."

"I'm surprised it wasn't requisitioned." So many people had lost their houses.

"The servants protected it, and it was rented to a merchant who did business with Napoleon. Once he lost, the man had no reason to remain in the house."

"Were you responsible for that?"

The man bowed. "Your mother was very sad to leave. I hope you and your lady will be as happy here as she was."

Later that evening, when he and Elizabeth were having tea, he remembered to tell her about the house.

"And that would be the reason for the green bedchamber." She pressed her lips together and she shook her head. "As much as I care for your mother, I wonder about her taste in decoration."

"What, on earth, does her leaving Paris have to do with the bedchamber in London?"

"Has no one told you?" she asked.

"Told me what?" He gazed at her, waiting to be educated.

"Your mother told me that once a boy is born, they had to move back to England. It's a tradition in your family that the heir may not remain overseas with his first son. She loved Paris and was extremely upset to have to leave after you were born."

Geoff shook his head. "You mean to say that I was born here?"

Elizabeth nodded. "Did no one tell you? Apparently, your father was born here as well."

"No one said a word." To think Father and Geoff were both born in Paris, and no one thought to tell him. "So you mean to tell me that if we have a male child, we'll be made to return to England, but if we have girls we remain here?"

"Precisely." She set her cup down.

"Please promise me you will not redecorate your bedchamber in dismal colors when we go back to London."

She laughed lightly. "I promise." Rising Elizabeth slid him a glance. "You must promise as well."

"Naturally, I—wait. I'm not in charge of decorating anything."

"You might help with the nursery."

"You're with child?" Geoff hadn't thought he could be any happier than to be with the woman who was the love of his life, but this?

"I think so." She pulled her plump bottom lip between her teeth. "I have not had my courses since we wed. That has never happened before."

Grabbing her, he lifted her up and swung her around. "We're going to be parents!"

# Epilogue

*Eight months later*

"Mother, what the deuce is that thing?" Geoff raised his quizzer as a particularly ugly piece of furniture, at least he thought it was furniture, was carried through the door.

Less than two weeks after he had notified his parents that Elizabeth was in a delicate condition, his mother and grand-mother made plans to arrive for the birth, along with Eliza-beth's aunt.

"A birthing chair," his grandmother said. "It will make Elizabeth's time much easier. I wish I'd had one."

This wasn't making any sense. "If it's not yours, where did you get it?"

"Lady Kenilworth sent it." His grandmother watched Kenton maneuver the chair up the stairs. "Elizabeth told her we were coming to Paris. She recommended it."

"I hope you've been praying for a boy," Mama said.

Geoff had almost rolled his eyes when his wife had told him about his mother's way of ensuring a girl. It hadn't worked the third time for her.

Fortunately, he was saved from answering by Elizabeth waddling into the hall.

"I heard the commotion and knew it had to be you." She embraced his mother. "No matter what I say, the prevailing belief in our house at the moment is that I should not be disturbed." She raised a brow at Geoff. "I wonder where that came from, hmm?"

Perhaps he was being a little overcautious. But when she'd told him she was expecting their first child, he counted back and realized she had been pregnant when she'd been shot. It was a miracle Elizabeth had not lost the child.

His mother peered at her. "You look as if you are about to deliver."

"Any day now." She smiled. "I am so ready to have this baby."

"I remember those days," Mama said. "It's as if it has worn out its welcome."

"I just want to hold her in my arms." Elizabeth rubbed her stomach.

Geoff was tempted to roll his eyes again. From the beginning Elizabeth had referred to the baby as a girl—exactly opposite from what his mother did.

He didn't care if the child was a boy or a girl. Yes, he liked Paris and his position, but he would be happy wherever Elizabeth and his child were.

"If you'll take my advice," his father murmured. "You'll pray for her to be happy. Your mother might not remember when she decorated her bedchambers those dismal shades of green, but I do. It was after she had you. Not that she loved you any less; she simply wished to remain in Paris."

Late that night, or early the next morning, depending on one's point of view, Elizabeth's eyes popped open. No light slipped through their east-facing window, and between her legs the bed was wet. As she debated waking Geoffrey, her first contraction came. It wasn't bad, but she doubted she would get much more sleep. Not only that, but the linens had to be changed.

She almost left him where he was, but he had been hovering over her for months, and she did not want to scare him by simply disappearing. "Geoffrey, love. We should move into my room. Even if we do not sleep, we can rest. I don't want to wake the whole house when it will be hours before anything of import occurs."

Still asleep, he rolled over, pulling her next to him. Then, as if he sensed there was something amiss, he opened his eyes. "It's begun, hasn't it?"

"I am afraid so. My water broke, and I had my first contraction. It is going to be a long day. I suggest we move into my room and try to rest."

A few hours later, the sun began its slow ascent above the horizon. After they'd climbed into her bed, Geoffrey held her back against his chest, his hand over her swollen stomach. Elizabeth had just experienced another contraction.

"They are getting closer. I've been watching the clock." He rubbed her belly again. "What can I do to help you?"

She had received letters from Dotty, Louisa, and Charlotte, all of whom had recently given birth and were full of advice. Some of it contradictory. Elizabeth had yet to understand how one could remain on her feet and have a foot rub at the same time.

When she had mentioned it to Geoffrey, he'd chuckled. "I think you can sit down long enough for me to rub your feet."

The most embarrassing piece of advice though came from Dotty—she must spend a great deal of time talking to her tenants because no lady would give that type of counsel. Elizabeth blushed just thinking about it. "I have heard that making love can hurry the process along."

For a moment, Geoffrey looked at her as if she had gone mad. Then he barked a laugh. "In that case, my lady, there is no time like the present. Never let it be said I did not do all within my power to bring our daughter into the world."

Three hours later, Geoff perched on a chair next to Elizabeth and watched in awe as the tiny person they had made was cradled in his wife's arms, nursing. Downy wisps of pale blond curls covered their daughter's head, and one small hand gripped Elizabeth's nightgown, pressing down on her breast. The midwife had arrived just as Elizabeth began to push.

He thanked the deities for Mrs. Robins—who was the eldest of a large family and had attended her mother more than once—for her knowledge and Vickers for her placid, good sense. Much to his surprise, the birthing chair actually seemed to help.

For the first two hours after the birth, it seemed as if every servant in the house found a reason for entering the room to see the baby. He was almost surprised their grooms and coachmen hadn't come up.

According to Nettle, who had gone to the stables with the news, Riddle and Farley were arguing about which one would be the first to put the baby on her pony when she was old enough.

Geoff sighed. He should have taken his daughter downstairs, but he did not want her to take a chill.

"Have you decided on a name?" They had been debating several names and combinations and he finally told Elizabeth to choose.

Brushing her hand over the baby's head, she smiled. "I have. Theodosia Unity Jane."

"I know where Jane comes from, my mother. I assume Theodosia is your mother." Elizabeth nodded. "But Unity?"

Elizabeth covered his hand with hers. "To remind us how fortunate we are to have achieved our unity together."

Raising her hand he pressed his lips to her fingers. "Perfect."

# Author Note

Those of you who have studied Waterloo and the events leading up to it, and I hope some of you have, will have noticed that I condensed the timeline. I did that because this is not a book about Waterloo. Instead, the events became a secondary character in the book. For readers who were frustrated that I didn't go deeper into the Battle of Waterloo, please remember that Harrington was not a soldier, and he could only know what he read in Wellington's dispatches to Sir Charles. There weren't nearly enough of them as far as I'm concerned. As in the story, Sir Charles and Wellington left within a day or so—from what I've been able to discover—to rush King Louis XVIII to Paris.

Because of my son and husband's involvement in contemporary wars, writing anything about a battle is not something I wished to dwell upon. Quite frankly, I cried my way through the parts placed in Brussels and upset the flight attendants because I was on my way to a conference when I was writing it.

I can't tell you how happy I was when Geoffrey and Elizabeth were on their way to Paris.

For those of you who have read my series, *The Marriage Game*, you might have noticed the character Colonel Lord Hawksworth as being the hero of *Miss Featherton's Christmas Prince*. His brother, Lord Septimius Trevor, first appeared in *Lady Beresford's Lover*.